The
Midnight
House

'An intriguing story with wonderful characters in a beautiful setting
I loved it'
Rachael English

'Intriguing, moving and I loved the way the stories moved back
and forth in time. A lovely book'
Sinéad Moriarty

'Amanda Geard is a warm and lively new voice and has a
wonderful storytelling talent. I loved *The Midnight House*'
Rachel Hore

'A wonderful debut. I loved it! Three timelines deftly handled, layers
of mysteries unfolding cleverly and beautiful writing. Most excellent!'
Tracy Rees

'I was pulled in from page one. It's beautiful and I love it'
Liz Fenwick

'With its gorgeous setting, wonderful characters and secrets
that kept me glued to the pages, it's a beauty!'
Jenny Ashcroft

'Compelling and brimming with lush historical detail,
The Midnight House weaves a wonderful tale of family secrets and
female friendship, told over eight decades. Amanda Geard is
an exciting new voice in fiction'
Hazel Gaynor

'I really, really loved it. It was so refreshing but also written
in that old-school, descriptively beautiful way I adore.
Totally atmospheric and wonderfully escapist'
Lorna Cook

'A gorgeous book. I loved it'
Emma Curtis

Born in Australia, **Amanda Geard** has lived all over the world, from a houseboat in London to a Norwegian Island, before settling in County Kerry in Ireland. Her writing has appeared in *The Irish Times*, *The Journal*, writing.ie, *Nordic Reach* and *Vertical Magazine*. Her short story *Not Yet Recycled* won the New Irish Writing Award in October 2019.
The Midnight House is Amanda's debut novel.

The
Midnight
House

AMANDA GEARD

REVIEW

First published in 2022 by Headline Review
An imprint of HEADLINE PUBLISHING GROUP

1

Cataloguing in Publication Data is available from the British Library

Hardback ISBN 978 1 4722 8370 2
Trade Paperback ISBN 978 1 4722 8371 9

Typeset in Bembo by CC Book Production

Printed and bound in Great Britain by Clays Ltd, Elcograf S.p.A.

Headline's policy is to use papers that are natural, renewable and
recyclable products and made from wood grown in well-managed forests and
other controlled sources. The logging and manufacturing processes are expected
to conform to the environmental regulations of the country of origin.

HEADLINE PUBLISHING GROUP
An Hachette UK Company
Carmelite House
50 Victoria Embankment
London EC4Y 0DZ

www.headline.co.uk
www.hachette.co.uk

To Mum, with love

The truth, however ugly in itself, is always curious and beautiful to the seeker after it.

Agatha Christie, *The Murder of Roger Ackroyd*

Have the hindsight to know
Where you did go,
And the foresight to look where you're going.
Have the insight to see
Where you will be,
And if you're too far along, stop rowing.

Tabby Ryan, 'The Hundred-Year-Old Poet'

The Rathmores (1790 – Present)

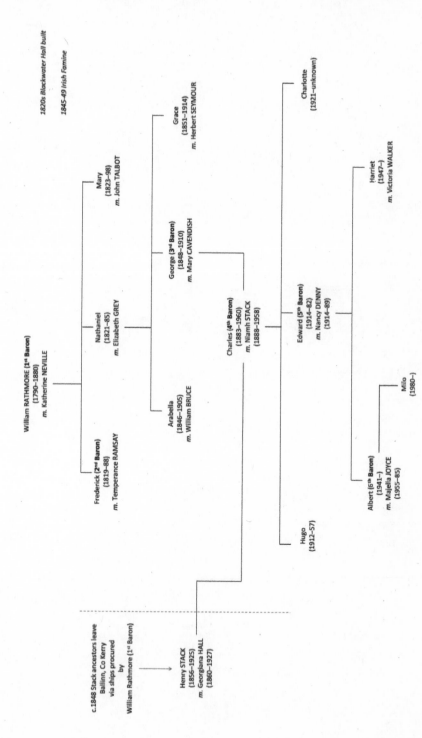

1820s Blackwater Hall built

1845–49 Irish Famine

William RATHMORE (1st Baron)
(1790–1880)
m. Katherine NEVILLE

Frederick (2nd Baron)
(1819–88)
m. Temperance RAMSAY

Nathaniel
(1821–85)
m. Elizabeth GREY

Mary
(1823–98)
m. John TALBOT

Arabella
(1846–1905)
m. William BRUCE

George (3rd Baron)
(1848–1910)
m. Mary CAVENDISH

Grace
(1851–1914)
m. Herbert SEYMOUR

Charles (4th Baron)
(1883–1960)
m. Niamh STACK
(1888–1958)

Hugo
(1912–57)

Edward (5th Baron)
(1914–82)
m. Nancy DENNY
(1914–89)

Charlotte
(1921–unknown)

Albert (6th Baron)
(1941–)
m. Majella JOYCE
(1955–85)

Harriet
(1947–)
m. Victoria WALKER

Milo
(1980–)

c.1848 Stack ancestors leave
Ballinn, Co Kerry
via ships procured
by
William Rathmore (1st Baron)

Henry STACK
(1856–1925)
m. Georgiana HALL
(1860–1927)

Prologue

The house, it's said, was once a great ringfort, piled purple stones placed with such precision that its smooth wall – a perfect circle – rose from the earth without a sliver of mortar to hold it together. It saw the arrival of the Bronze Age. The passing of the Iron Age. The coming of Christianity to this emerald isle on the edge of the tumbling Atlantic Ocean.

Its stones – they say – were moved, one by one, by rough tenant hands, into a new shape, a rectangle, all evidence of curving geometry lost. More stones were added, taken from the base of the mountain that towers behind. And cool blue slate – at dawn it turns to warm magenta – was brought from Valentia Island, where it was cleft in neat regular slivers, its smooth scales forming a weatherproof skin, the veins lined with lead.

To delay decay, local timber was shunned. Even beams made from the slow-grown oaks of Ireland's woodlands could not compete with rich resinous pitch pine shipped across the ocean. The walls – held together with mortar, unlike the fort from which they are said to have been pulled – were given a sheath: alkaline powder mixed with the inky waters of the lough.

Even back then, ivy crept from the wooded surrounds,

reaching eagerly towards the new walls with curious fingers. The gardeners would cut it back, year after year, but still it came.

Once the house was watertight, work on the inside began: green Connemara marble fashioned into fireplaces, quarry tiles imported from a thousand miles east, hand-painted silks unfurled from the Orient. Countless sash windows peered from the elevation like sentinels. They were eyes on the world, and when they blinked, they let in fresh Kerry air rolling damp from the ocean below.

Over the years, the house was added to, extended piece by piece: a wing here, a boiler room there, a hall for the servants at the back. Each postscript tied in by new layers of that blue-then-magenta slate. There were times when the chimneys puffed white peaty smoke. There were times when they didn't. Generations came and went. Malevolent landlords. Benevolent landlords. Absent landlords. And their children too.

Ireland fought for freedom; the old order tumbled.

And Blackwater Hall survived. But it could yet disappear.

Because ringforts disappear.

Houses disappear.

People disappear.

Chapter One

Ballinn, County Kerry

September 2019

It was the contents of her mum's bookshelf that finally drove Ellie out of hiding; Moira Fitzgerald's taste in literature was chalk and cheese to her daughter's. Heaving bosoms versus timeless classics. And two weeks of plot lines where the guy gets the girl and everything turns out hunky-dory was just too much.

In a desperate bid to fill her days, Ellie had devoured a dozen old editions of *The Kerryman* scattered here and there about the house, read the crumpled ageing news of local sporting victories and items lost and found. When she'd asked Moira to pick up the *Guardian* from the village shop, her mum had loyally obliged, bringing the paper back each day between two fingers as though it might be contagious. Ellie knew she would have made some excuse to Deidre O'Brien, the proprietor – and purveyor of gossip – about why she was ordering it (*sure, Ellie's career is flying in Dublin – a freelance article in the* Guardian*!*).

A little white lie.

Now, browsing the shelves in Ballinn's only charity shop, Ellie admitted to herself it had been a mistake to come out of exile, to wind her way down from the safety of her mum's farm to the village, where prying eyes and flapping ears were sure to be lying in wait. Her large sunglasses, meant as a disguise, had attracted more attention than they'd diverted, and her mum's green Nissan Micra, which made a wince-inducing crunch in second gear, drew a friendly wave from every local on Main Street, their hands poised in mid-air as they realised it wasn't Moira Fitzgerald behind the wheel but someone altogether different.

But still, she'd snuck into Threadbare undetected, and with any luck she could leave a few coins on the counter, tuck some books under her arm and slip out unseen.

'Eleanor?'

Oh dear.

'Is that you?'

Ellie looked and saw . . . nothing. No one. The shop was as dead as she felt inside. She added *going stir crazy* to the long list of things that were wrong with her.

The disembodied voice called again. 'Ellie?'

She squinted into the gloom. 'Hello?'

A head appeared. It floated above a shelf of women's clothing then emerged atop a large body covered shoulders to toes in an amorphous collection of fabrics, a hundred jagged colours stitched together as though they'd been thrown in a blender and pulsed.

'Bernie?' Ellie's shoulders dropped with relief. Bernie was her mum's best friend and relatively discreet confidante; a rare commodity in Ballinn. 'Bernie, I . . . if I'd known you were working here, I'd not have crept in . . .'

'In disguise?'

Ellie removed her huge sunglasses. It had been a ridiculous notion: hiding in plain sight in a rural Irish village.

Bernie stepped forward, a grin on her wide face, and pulled Ellie into a technicolour bear hug. 'You poor, poor *cratúir.* Your mammy said you'd be at the homeplace for a bit.'

'It's great to see you,' Ellie said truthfully. 'It's good to be back.' *Another little white lie.*

She *did* love Ballinn – it was charming in its way, sandwiched neatly between the heather-flecked foothills of the MacGillycuddy Reeks and the wild Atlantic. It had a church, two pubs, a café whose ownership changed with the seasons, a well-worn charity shop selling well-worn things and a garda station open every second Tuesday. And, of course, a corner shop where gossip was dished out gratis to the few dozen locals – and few hundred holiday-home owners – with every carton of milk. In winter, the village smelled of peat, its earthy smoke mingling with the fog that rolled off Kenmare Bay. In summer, it could be glorious or sodden; some days it cowered under incessant rain thrown from the Gulf Stream, other times it was bathed in sunshine, the square packed with gaggles of delighted tourists buying Irish-wool sweaters and overpriced ice cream. It was beautiful. Quaint. *Grand.* But it was still *coming back.* Still *the homeplace.* Not home, as such. But a safe house. Comfort, familiar surrounds and her mum's butter-laden cooking.

'There's a bit of Dublin in you now,' said Bernie, holding her at arm's length. 'They've been starving you up there?'

'I haven't been looking after myself.'

'No. Course you haven't.'

Ellie wasn't sure how much Berne knew, but no doubt Moira had given her an overview, titbits of Ellie's broken life. Or, at least, the titbits her mum knew about. She sighed and stepped back, looked past Bernie to the sheets of rain washing the window pane. But by avoiding Bernie's gaze, she caught her own, there in the glass, staring back. Her usually neat fringe messy. Her hair an Ozzy Osbourne wig. She wore a black leather jacket and pale jeans: her uniform. And a smear of red lipstick: her armour.

'. . . and my Sean always said you were top of the class.'

She turned back to Bernie. 'Sorry?'

'He considered you his best pupil.'

'Out of twelve students?'

'Wilful but bright.' Bernie nodded. 'Or . . . not so much bright as *curious*.'

'Didn't curiosity kill the cat?'

Bernie touched her lightly on the shoulder. 'You're not dead yet, pet. Far from it.'

But Ellie *felt* dead. Inside. Outside. She ached with the desire to turn back the clock. Her old job. Her old love. Her old life.

The older woman reached forward and squeezed her hand in a way that said *feck 'em*, and it took her by surprise. Ellie dropped her eyes, felt a familiar prickle behind them. Pushed it away as she took back her hand. She despised this new weakness inside her, and yet it was there.

Bernie frowned, then turned on her heel. 'As vice chief volunteer at Threadbare, Ellie, I'm offering you VIP shopping.' She went to the door, flicked the lock, then waved an arm around the room as though somewhere among the jumble lay the answer to all Ellie's problems.

Despite herself, Ellie smiled. 'Vice chief? I thought you'd be the boss.'

'The chief'd never give up the top spot. Anyway, I can't think of anything worse.' Bernie leaned forward conspiratorially. 'Last week we started block colouring. In a charity shop!'

It was true, a feeble effort had been made. Reds on one rack graduating to pink then off-white. Blues gathered in the back corner. And yellows piled high by the doorway as though attempting an escape.

Bernie took a scarlet shirt and moved it across to the greys with a nod of satisfaction. 'Now, El, I know you don't need any fancy clothes. Tell me . . . what *are* you looking for?'

My old life, Ellie wanted to say, but instead she ran her hand along the line of tattered spines. 'Reading material. Anything to pass the time.'

Bernie took her intimation – that she had nothing else to do – in her stride and removed a paperback from the shelf, held it up.

'Well, not *anything* . . .' said Ellie.

Bernie sifted, pushing books along the shelf. 'No. No. No. Penny dreadful. Too violent. Horrible cover. Ah . . .' she held up Frank McCourt's Irish classic, 'there's always a few copies of *Angela's Ashes* about.'

Ellie had enough misery in her life and Frank McCourt was the last thing she needed. She shook her head and ran her hand along the books. It was an odd assortment of fiction and non-fiction flung together – a seventies cookbook sandwiched between *Hen Keeping for Beginners* and a chunky Ken Follett.

Bernie held up a sausagey finger – 'Hold on a minute' – and disappeared through a door at the back of the shop. The sound of dragging boxes spilled from the room and Ellie turned her gaze to her own ring finger, ran her hand over its smooth surface, felt for something that was no longer there.

'Any of these take your fancy?' Bernie returned carrying a large cardboard box. 'No one buys them, so we keep them out back.' She held it out: *Twenty Thousand Leagues Under the Sea*, a Conan Doyle, several Austens.

'You keep these out back?'

'Sure.' Bernie scratched at an invisible stain on her dress.

'Really?'

'I know what you're implying, but it's strictly against Threadbare policy to save items for friends and family. The chief would eat the face off of me. She's always hated me, you know . . .'

'Bernie!'

'Look, someone dropped them off from Blackwater Hall . . . the old place on the plateau,' she added, as though it was something Ellie should know. 'I haven't had time to sort them. So when I heard you were coming, I just . . . put them aside.'

A lump formed in Ellie's throat. 'Thank you.' There was nothing like returning to Kerry to soften the hard edges of the city.

Bernie grinned and put the box in Ellie's arms, pushing away the money that came in the other direction. Then she took a paperback from the shelf, held it up. On its cover, a woman stared with longing into the dark eyes of a man who had evidently misplaced his shirt. She laid it on top of Jane Austen and winked.

'There,' she said, 'that one's for your mammy.'

୧ଈ

Outside, the rain fell in fat drops and Ellie ran the last few steps to the car. She fiddled with her keys and dropped them once, twice, before wrenching open the passenger-side door and flinging the box into the car's dry interior. By the time she slid herself into the driver's seat, her fringe dripped with rain.

The gloom of the afternoon looked like dusk, but sunset was hours away. That was Ballinn in September; it could be summer or winter or anything in between. Next to her sat the box of books, its top flap half open as if inviting a quick peep. Reaching past the damp cardboard, she retrieved Moira's bodice-ripper. *Look away*, she wanted to say to the woman on the cover, *save yourself*. She put it aside, leaned over the remaining titles. At the very bottom was a mottled slipcase with a book lodged inside, spine first. She picked it up and slid it out.

The ABC Murders by Agatha Christie.

Its cloth-bound spine creaked in protest as she eased it open. As she did with all old books, she brought it to her nose, sniffed.

Any scent of its owner was long gone, its pages infused with damp and time.

The book was still attached to her nose when her phone rang, bringing her back to the car, back to the village. Back to now. It had been so long since she'd answered a call that she tensed in fear. But when she looked at the screen, her shoulders dropped. *Mum landline.*

'I'm on my way,' she said. 'Fifteen minutes max.'

'There's no need of rushing, Ellie,' came Moira's reply, 'but dinner'll be ready at five.'

Ellie smiled to herself. Dinner was always at five. 'I'm just leaving the village.' She wedged the phone under her ear and placed the open book in her lap. The text was neat and slightly raised; gentle Braille beneath her fingers. 'I bumped into Bernie. She knew I was back . . .'

'I can't be keeping a thing like that from Bernie! You know what she's like. Knows what you're going to say before you even think it.'

'A mind reader, is she?'

Moira blustered, and Ellie experienced equal measures of guilt and pleasure. 'Had some books for me, as it turns out.'

'Oh?' Moira's voice rose a notch.

Ellie paused. 'You *knew* about the books?'

The line became muffled. 'Oh . . . I have to go . . . The spuds, they're . . . boiling over. The divils.'

'Right.'

'See you soon, love.' Love? Oh yes, thought Ellie, wincing as a tractor raced past on the empty street, Moira knew about the books. Another of her ploys to get Ellie out and about. Back into the fray. Because Moira was of the generation who worked through grief and sadness and the horrors of life with action, and Ellie was from the generation who tackled it with Netflix. But as the farm didn't have broadband – or mobile reception, for that matter – Ellie's only escape had been books. And now she had the box. She patted it fondly as she snapped *The ABC Murders* shut, returning it to the top of the pile.

'See you soon,' she said.

She hung up and appraised the phone. It had come to life that very afternoon as she'd wound her way down the hill into Ballinn, pinging and chiming so that she'd arrived at Threadbare with a full email inbox and countless messages waiting to be read. Another time, she thought. She put the phone deep in her pocket, then turned the Micra's key, and the car spluttered reluctantly to life, the windscreen wipers clearing a path before her.

Reminding herself to skip second gear, she pulled out on to Ballinn's main street and away.

Chapter Two

Blackwater Hall, County Kerry

July 1939

It was early evening when the car finally turned up the wooded avenue and drove the last slow mile to Blackwater Hall. July was running to its close and the chauffeur said that the locals were already predicting an Indian summer. But the oppressive heat wasn't the only reason for Nancy's slick palms.

Teddy reached across the back seat and took her hand. 'You're intolerably hot,' he said. 'Are you all right?' It wasn't the first time he'd asked the question since they'd left the station.

'It's sweltering.'

'A southern English lass shouldn't have trouble in heat like this.'

She loosened the collar of her dress. 'It's just so . . . muggy.'

'This is dry, trust me!' He laughed, an easy sound that she knew belied his nerves.

She smiled and took back her hand, using it to twirl the ring on her finger, to count the five tiny diamonds on its now-familiar contour. This was their first visit to the estate since the wedding. And she hoped it might be their last.

'It'll be fine,' he said in the voice he reserved for times when it certainly didn't feel that way. He looked beyond her and she followed his gaze, a tightness growing in her chest.

Across the dark, slick surface of Lough Atoon, Blackwater Hall hove into view. It was less grand than she remembered, but handsome enough – not quite a pile; more sprawling than imposing. Thick ivy covered the walls, and its blue slate roof was scattered with a dozen chimney pots. Three rows of white sash windows – some of them open against the warm evening – peppered the front elevation. French doors led directly on to a sloping lawn that ran a hundred yards to the reedy edge of the lough.

And now out of those French doors came a slender figure in white.

'Ah, Mother's here,' Teddy said. 'I'm *so* pleased.'

'Me too.' Nancy smoothed the Gibson bun she'd risen especially early to attempt. She had packed numerous hats under which to hide her unruly hair; Teddy's mother was fastidious about neatness. In her compact mirror, she checked her make-up. Despite the heat, her foundation remained matte, her dark brows and lashes still neatly set with a touch of mascara. An English rose in the Irish countryside. 'I bet she's spent all day . . .'

'Cleaning?'

'Or cooking?' she said, and Teddy laughed. 'A cake. To welcome me warmly into the family.' Two comrades, thought Nancy, making light of the approaching domestic war.

'The weeks will fly.' But even he sounded unsure. Now that they were married, there was his inheritance to consider, documents to sign. In person. They'd put it off for long enough.

Nancy turned to the lough, partly to hide her apprehension, partly to take in the view of Cottah Mountain. It towered over Blackwater Hall, an eight-hundred-foot fell of rock and wild vegetation, dazzling with the rich purple of flowering heather. In winter, the south-facing slope heated up during the day, and the family maintained that when the evening breeze rolled over the summit, the mountain's warm breath kept the frost at bay.

But as they pulled up to the house, Lady Rathmore's expression was icy in the heat. She stood watching. Waiting.

Teddy turned Nancy's face gently towards him. 'You're beautiful, I love you.' He brushed her cheek. 'Those eyes, Nancy. You've incredible eyes. So rich, so blue.'

Unlike my blood, she thought, but she simply said: 'I love you too.'

ᐞ

They walked through the French doors into a bright room; duck-egg-blue walls and a pale carpet so immaculate it might have been laid the night before. Nancy kept to the centre of an oriental runner that led through the space and spread left and right towards two dark timber doors. On the far wall an enormous sideboard groaned with polished silverware. Half of a twelve-seater table was set for dinner, and at the other end of the room, two oxblood wingbacks huddled around a green marble fireplace, peat and kindling piled but unlit in the warm afternoon.

The smell of roasting meat hung in the air. 'I thought we'd eat informally tonight,' said Lady Rathmore. She talked at Nancy but not to her. 'That will, I'm sure, make you more comfortable.'

Nancy bit her tongue and smiled. 'How thoughtful.' She spoke with ease but clasped her hands behind her back, fingernails pressed painfully into her palms. It was, she hoped, the only outward sign of her irritation.

Lady Rathmore nodded. 'Very well.' She was an elegant woman with a soft East Coast American accent. Tall, pale, and wearing a floor-length white dress so pristine and impractical that only a lady could get away with it. 'I had thought six thirty, but as you were *late*, shall we say seven?' Not waiting for an answer, she followed the runner and disappeared through a door to the left, leaving Teddy and Nancy alone in the room.

Somewhere in the house, a clock struck six, and Nancy leaned forward, whispered to Teddy: 'So, no cake?'

'I'm *so* sorry.'

But she laughed. Everything was different now. *She* was different. This time she had a ring on her finger; she felt safe, secure. Now she and Teddy were one and nothing could come between them.

She slipped off her shoes and stepped onto the cream carpet. It was cool and luxurious between her toes. 'At least I didn't babble.' She leaned down and stroked it. Wool. It must have cost a fortune. 'Last time I waffled about Edward's abdication . . . I went on and on. And then – *after*, mind you – you tell me your mother is friends with Wallis Simpson's cousin . . .'

That, though, was three years ago. She'd been a twenty-two-year-old overawed by the grandeur, the pomp. And taken in by the beauty of Kerry – the only true thing, she thought, about Blackwater Hall. That, and Charlotte. She had been newly in love with Teddy and they shared everything. Their life in London was just taking shape, their independence slowly annealing into partnership.

She picked up her shoes and crossed the carpet. 'This time I'm determined to keep my opinions to myself.' She paused at the window. Outside, the lough threw back a crisp reflection of the mountain, and inside, the walls were covered with Rathmore portraits, Rathmore blood. Four barons, their wives, and a handful of children.

The family walked a strange line – a heritage split between Irish, English and American. Between Protestant and Catholic. Between past and present. And although Teddy was the second son – the spare – they'd had high hopes for him. *Higher* hopes. Nancy's arrival on the scene had shaken up an already shaky relationship.

She turned to Teddy, who had joined her at the window. 'I'd hoped Charlotte might meet us when we arrived.' He stepped behind her, a hand on her waist. Warmth ran through her body but, checking for observers, she peeled his fingers away.

In her handbag, Nancy carried the last letter she'd written to Charlotte – she hadn't posted it; they'd only have chased it across the Irish Sea. In their correspondence the women exchanged hopes, dreams; they sent them back and forth like trinkets, sharing the details of their lives.

Not all the details, Nancy thought, and felt a pang of guilt at the secrets she kept. At the grief she wasn't yet ready to put into words. Charlotte had always been candid, however; she was a prolific letter writer, to Nancy, to Teddy; she had a dozen pen pals scattered here and there. It was, Nancy knew, her way of escaping the confines of her life.

'She'll be here,' Teddy said. Now they stood side by side at the window, barely touching. 'I wish my only sister idolised me as much as she does you.'

'I'm quite sure that's not true . . .' But she turned and gave him a wink, suggesting she knew it was *absolutely* the truth. His dimples gave him away; he was smiling as he looked to her.

But as his eyes hovered over her shoulder, his expression fell away. Nancy paused, frowned. And from behind her, the silence was filled. 'Ah.' A loud voice. Confident. Self-important. 'You've arrived.'

She turned, her face set in a practised smile. The man who crossed the room ignored the runner, his shoes leaving momentary imprints on the carpet.

'Hugo,' Teddy said, placing his hand gently on the small of Nancy's back.

'Little brother.'

It was fascinating for Nancy, seeing these two men together. When she'd last met Hugo, they'd looked remarkably similar, but the few intervening years had added pounds to the older man, etched fine lines around his eyes. She wondered where the crow's feet had come from – she had never seen him laugh. It was as though a likeness of Teddy had been expanded upwards and a little outwards. Each feature accentuated, and occasionally, as with the nose, slightly too much. They were both fair, but while Hugo's hair shone with Brylcreem, Teddy's parted naturally at the side. It flopped to his temple and he was forever pushing it out of the way.

After a beat too long, Hugo turned to Nancy. He didn't move to take her hand. 'Ah, your lovely wife.' He glanced at her stockinged feet. 'My dear, I do hope Mother has made you feel at home,' he said in a way that suggested he didn't hope anything of the sort.

'Yes, of course.'

'And the trip?' This to Teddy.

'Long.'

Hugo took his brother by the arm and led him towards the wingback chairs. 'Not looking forward to it myself.'

'What do you mean?' Teddy glanced back at Nancy. A shared look: *here we go.*

'I'm coming to London shortly. An opportunity has presented itself; imminent war tends to have that effect. We'll discuss it . . . later.' This last was said after a pause, with the slightest nod towards Nancy.

She almost laughed. The patriarchy taking care of business while the little woman kept her place. Hugo would blanch to know that their relationship transcended such old-fashioned constraints. Nonetheless, Nancy didn't expect Teddy to protest – Hugo was the sort of man, he'd always said, one must just endure.

'Let's get settled from the journey before we talk shop.'

Hugo clapped his back, his younger brother wincing at the force of it. 'Absolutely, old man.'

Nancy crossed the room and took Teddy's hand. 'Where's Charlotte?' she said. 'I was hoping to see her before dinner.'

'Off on one of her mercy dashes, one presumes.' Hugo took a cigarette from a holder. Tapped it irritably against the silver surface. 'Silly girl.'

Nancy's smile slipped. She coaxed it back into place, but the look on Hugo's face suggested he'd seen her lapse, noted her stumble. And, she suspected, had locked it away for later use. She gently let go of Teddy's hand, put her own to her forehead with exaggerated calmness. 'I need to lie down before supper.' She nodded to the room, made for the door. Stepped through and paused on the other side.

Hugo laughed. 'A very difficult pupil to teach decorum, I dare say. But do try. For Mother's sake.'

Teddy took an audible breath. Pulled his temper into check. They'd discussed it before they'd arrived, she and Teddy: *we must just get through this. No drama. No argument. Sign the documents and get out.* She felt no betrayal at his lack of retort. Instead, he said, 'Mercy dashes?'

'Our little Charlotte has been visiting Ballinn. Teaching the savages to write or some such. Ghastly. But you know her, she has a soft heart. And a soft head . . .'

A muffled protest from Teddy. Nancy gripped the door handle, straining to hear as Hugo lowered his voice. Then a sharp rejoinder from her husband: 'You mustn't speak of her like that.'

'Nonsense, Edward. It's all quite tame.' Hugo's voice had moved across the room. A box opened, snapped shut. Then the click of a lighter. 'Besides, this charity work puts her in rather a good light. She'll make a fine match.' Heavy footsteps crossed the room. 'After all,' Hugo paused, 'isn't that what we were brought up to do? To make a fine match?'

Nancy stepped back from the door. She was strong. She could handle this. And after this visit, she would never return to Blackwater Hall.

Never, ever again.

Chapter Three

Cahercillin Farm, County Kerry
September 2019

Ellie had always loved that boreen, the one winding up out of Ballinn and inland; it led past the patchwork of stone-edged fields that lay below her mum's farm and climbed through the valley until it became just a desolate track crossing the scrubby heather commons. And there at the end was the Fitzgerald homeplace: a white bungalow perched on the edge of the mountain and surrounded by a wind-tattered laurel hedge that appeared to be holding on for dear life.

As she turned up the driveway, the rain eased and a riot of colour lit the heather-capped mountain, its valleys and ravines flowing with white water. It'd be gone in a few hours, that water, rushing off down the hill and away to the brackish bay. Things to do, places to be. In the space of fifteen minutes, Ellie had driven from wintery Ballinn back into autumn at Cahercillín Farm. Ironic really, because coming home *was* like travelling back in time, in more ways than one.

As she pushed open the front door, a wave of starchy humidity hit her, mingled with the smell of something over cooked − pork chops? − and the soupy scent of a long-boiled vegetable. She dropped the box of books to the floor before stripping off her jacket and hanging it on the laden coat stand.

'Hello?' she called.

A head, wild with curls, popped into the hallway then disappeared. 'Just in time,' came Moira's muffled voice, a Limerick lilt licking at its edges. Even after forty-five years, Moira was still a blow-in. She'd arrived in the seventies when the only things that brought people to Kerry were blood or love. She had found the latter in Ellie's father, a Kerryman through and through. The farm had been his. He was born there. *Literally* born there, in what was now the kitchen, weeks after his parents inherited the scattered hundred acres. Ellie's grandparents named the farm for him: Cahercillín. Birthplace of Cillian.

As a teenager, Ellie had found that embarrassing, such an intimate name for the farm, but nowadays she appreciated it: when she drove through those gates, her father's name was always there to greet her, even though he was not.

She picked up Moira's gift and stepped into the kitchen. 'From Bernie,' she said, 'for you.'

Moira's face crumpled in surprise, then cleared in delight. 'For me? Well I never . . .' She flicked through the book and turned it over, reciting the blurb with the same rapid execution she applied to her catechisms at church each week. Then she looked up. 'The trip wasn't too much? Was it good to be out?'

Ellie narrowed her eyes and considered her next words carefully. Because if it *had* been too much, it would have been Moira's fault, scheming as she clearly had been with Bernie. 'It was fine. Fine,' was all she said.

A copy of the *Guardian* sat on the cluttered windowsill, and Ellie glanced at a headline about the latest UK cabinet reshuffle. Moira followed her gaze. 'Picked that up from O'Brien's today. Deidre knows you're here . . . she outright asked, the divil. I had to tell her my arthritis was playing up just to change the subject.'

'You don't have arthritis.'

Yet another little white lie.

Moira cleared her throat. 'Did you . . . hear anything?' She gestured to Ellie's hand.

There in her palm was her phone. So connected to it had she been for all these years that even without reception it stuck to her like glue. She put it aside. 'I didn't check.'

'Nothing from Dylan? Moira said his name as though it was contraband.

'No.'

'Ellie . . .'

'Mum.'

Moira turned back to the potatoes, muttered something.

'What was that?' Ellie suppressed a smile; she knew what this was about. Moira had been at it for years.

'I'm your mammy, not some Dublin mum.'

Ellie poured a glass of water, wishing it were wine. 'No one calls their mum Mammy any more.'

'They do,' said Moira, lobbing a hefty slice of butter on the potatoes and holding up the blunt knife in an intimidating manner. 'You did once!'

Ellie filled a second glass, set it down. The tiny table was wedged under the window of the shoebox kitchen – room enough for two, an option for three if you knew each other well. It was already set: chipped bone china, a Pyrex butter dish, faded place mats of Irish tourist attractions.

She let the silence settle. Then broke it. 'Can I help at all?' But looking at the stovetop, she saw that dinner was done. *Well* done.

'No, no. You just sit yourself down there . . .' Moira was bustling around the kitchen, taking Ellie's shoulders, steering her to a chair, 'and have a hearty meal. That's all you need.' It *wasn't* all Ellie needed, but she did as directed, and without delay, two charred and shrunken chops were deposited on her

plate. They were swiftly followed by a large portion of floppy broccoli and a pile of floury potatoes. She added a pat of butter and watched it melt into the vegetables. Calories be damned. 'This looks lovely, Mum,' she said.

Moira squeezed herself into the opposite seat, her left elbow wedged beneath the low window that looked across the valley.

Ellie raised her glass, tried to raise her spirits. '*Sláinte*. Thank you.'

'Thank you, *Mammy*,' Moira mumbled, holding her drink forward. '*Sláinte*, Ellie. God be with you.'

'And you,' Ellie replied. She sipped the water; it was heavy with tannin from the farm's peaty well. If God was really with me, she thought, would He not give me one small break and turn this water into wine?

ᔥ

After dinner, Moira and Ellie sat before the crackling fire nursing bowls of cream-drenched apple crumble and watching RTÉ news, something that, until a couple of weeks before, Ellie hadn't done for years. She'd become so used to curating the information she consumed that the variety and structure of the six o'clock news came as something of a shock.

In recent months her own bubble of news interest had shrunk to just that: a bubble. The housing bubble. *Dublin*'s housing bubble. It was growing every day, expanding to gobble up new areas, pushing people out of them as though they were a piece of fluff and it a broom. Everyone in Ireland, even the young, carried the scars of the Celtic Tiger. And now it was happening again: buyers priced out of the market, renters left to rot.

In the first week she'd returned to Kerry, housing was all over the news. But of course it was; that was down to her. But now the six o'clock bulletin was back to its old self: politics, far-flung conflicts, a dog on a skateboard in Sligo. And who wouldn't mind the odd feel-good story, because, well, life needed both darkness *and* light, didn't it?

When the news finished, Moira stood and turned off the television. 'Cuppa tea?' she said, bringing Ellie back.

'A *strong* one would be grand.' Ellie said it firmly.

'A strong tea? At this hour?'

'Please.'

Moira muttered a warning, 'You won't sleep,' patting Ellie's shoulder as she passed.

The fire had died to embers, and Ellie got up to stoke it, added a piece of turf, its liquorice scent overpowering in the small room. She went to the door, opened it. And her eyes dropped to the hallway floor.

The box.

Something into which she could escape.

She reached down and picked up the book from the top of the pile. *The ABC Murders* by Agatha Christie.

Turning it over in her hands, she walked back into the sitting room. She hadn't even taken her spot on the sofa when a paper tucked into the back of the book dropped out. It fluttered gently to the ground and nestled at her feet.

As though finding its place.

She frowned and picked it up. Unfolded the single crease and scanned the faded blue handwriting.

A letter.

She raised her eyebrows in surprise.

An *old* letter.

The date – 3rd August 1940 – was neatly hand printed in its top-left corner below a header half covered with a smudge of brown. *Wynn's* something. She frowned at the familiar word, pushed aside the connotations. Ran her hand down the page. Then turned her back to the fire and began to read.

❧

Moira returned with two mugs in one hand and Bernie's gift in the other. She set the drinks down and sat in the armchair that matched the faded tartan sofa. The chair had been Ellie's father's, and she remembered him fitting into it perfectly. Sometimes she swore she could see the large indent made from years of evenings by the fire, dad jokes delivered to rolled eyes, proud pats on her back for school projects well done.

But when Moira sat in it, she looked tiny.

'What's that?' she said, pointing to Ellie's lap.

Ellie handed her the letter and picked up her mug. 'A clue straight from Agatha Christie,' she said with a wink, sipping her pale tea, wondering if Moira had used a thimble to add the leaves to the pot.

Her mum took the page, her eyebrows raised in delight, and the crow's feet that worried her temples deepened as she read it. 'How mysterious . . .' She handed it back to her daughter.

Ellie thumbed the indentation the pen had left on the paper eighty years before.

3rd August 1940

My dearest T,

Whatever you hear, do not believe it for a moment. Life twists and turns, as you well know, and my situation is this – I can no longer remain at Ink House. The place is as dark as midnight.

I am quite sure this will come as less of a shock to you, of all people. You knew my feelings. On what I wanted for my future. You encouraged me to seek out my own destiny, and so I will.

But I must ask for your help. I am coming on the next boat – I am so excited, but so apprehensive. What an adventure, really. I have it all planned. I've been rather

clever and will tell you all about it when we are together.
I won't be a burden as I am well prepared!

I don't need to tell you to keep the existence of this
letter secret from the family, but please, please, I beg of
you, for the sake of more than you know – do. Keep it
a secret and guard my intentions with your life.

All will be revealed when I arrive.

Yours,

Charlotte

The words overflowed with youthful passion. Ellie tried to
imagine the girl – for she must have been young. Yet not so
young that she couldn't travel to wherever she was going alone.
And Ink House? The only clue on the letter, along with the
smudged header with that familiar word, *Wynn's.* The castle?
Surely not. Ellie's heart tugged at the possibility.

Aware of Moira watching her, she cast the letter aside. She'd
had quite enough of prying into other people's business. She
gave her mum a raised eyebrow – *means nothing to me* – and
picked up *The ABC Murders*, but no sooner had she turned
the first page than she looked up to see Moira disappearing
through the sitting-room door.

There was a creak, accompanied by a cascade of thumps and
the inevitable huff that followed the opening of the hallway
cupboard. It was always over stuffed, packed with memories of
the past that Ellie could never bring herself to look at: documents, books and trinkets once treasured. One whole shelf
was crammed with locally penned histories and novels; it was
obligatory to buy a copy from O'Brien's each time a new one
was released into the community.

Moira returned bearing one such book.

'Oh, Mum.' Ellie raised her hands in surrender.

But Moira wasn't listening. She ran her eyes down the index

as she sat, then passed the open book to Ellie. 'Ink House,' she
said, with no little triumph.

On the page was a blurred and faded photo of a country
house covered from base to roof with ivy, a dozen sash windows peeping through. Behind it, a craggy mountain towered.
A large lawn led to the rough edge of a lough so black that it
appeared to reject the surrounding daylight. The name of the
house was written in the caption.

'Blackwater Hall?'

What had Bernie said as she'd presented the box of books?
*Someone dropped them off from Blackwater Hall. I haven't had time
to sort them.*

She turned to the book's title page. *Manor Survivors: A
Catalogue.* Page after page of Ireland's remaining old houses.
It was a slim book – the 1920s had wiped out much of its
subject matter – and most entries contained only a handful of
lines, whole histories encapsulated in a few disparate words.
Blackwater Hall's record was no exception:

> Blackwater Hall is one of the few remaining significant
> Georgian residences in southern Kerry. It was built on
> the shores of Lough Atoon by Lord William Rathmore,
> *c.*1820s, on the large Rathmore estate that spanned areas
> of Munster and Connaught. Mortgaged in 1845 to pay for
> grains and oatmeal and provide assisted emigration for ten-
> ants to America. The demesne and house remain. Extant.

Extant. Still surviving. Still in existence. Ellie took the word,
turned it, applied it to herself.

Moira was speaking. '. . . shadow of its former glory now,
o'course. Tucked away on the plateau, well off the road, halfway
to Kenmare. A wonder we don't hear more about it, but then
the state of the place . . .'

As always, Moira's gossip came in a torrent, and Ellie held up a hand. 'How do you know all this?'

'The box of books,' Moira said, shrugging. She sipped her tea and leaned back in her chair. 'Bernie told me a fine set of books was dropped down from somewhere she called Ink House. *Perfect for Ellie*, she said . . .' She stopped short. Mother and daughter eyed each other.

Moira cleared her throat. In a tiptoe voice, she continued, 'So we passed the time about Ink House. Real name: Blackwater Hall. And I assumed it would be there in one of Dad's books.' At the mention of Dad, Ellie, as always, dropped her eyes to her hands. Nodded. 'Bernie said the owner's struggling. And his son's back for a bit. Sent away when his mother died, poor child.'

'Oh?' Ellie opened the letter again. It was written with a stiff upper lip in a country that didn't stiffen upper lips. Charlotte sounded decidedly un-Irish. A woman fleeing her lot, just like Ellie. But unlike Ellie, she wanted to leave and never come back. And she seemed to relish the uncertainty.

Whereas Ellie – nowadays – despised it.

Moira said, 'I wonder who this Charlotte was.'

Someone with fewer problems than me, Ellie thought, but she said, 'A daughter? An unhappy wife? A ward of Blackwater Hall?'

'Perhaps,' said Moira, opening her book and looking beyond the pages in that way that people do when their minds are elsewhere.

Ellie put the letter on the coffee table and slid it as far away from her as she could. She knew what was coming, and she didn't like it. Once, finding a letter, an old letter, one that said *Keep it a secret and guard my intentions with your life*, would have been nectar to her. But no longer. Her world was in tatters, and this girl, this Charlotte, was just a collection of words on a page, a shadow of the past. Not another investigation to take over Ellie's life only to ruin it again.

It's all your fault, Ellie.

Dylan had said that, as she'd returned the engagement ring. As she'd left the apartment. All her fault. Lives destroyed. Because she couldn't leave other people's business alone.

'Of course . . .' Moira was looking at her again, her book now closed on the armrest beside her, 'the letter really belongs to Blackwater Hall, doesn't it?'

'Yes, I suppose it does.'

'Might be important to them. To Lord Rathmore.'

'Lord, is it?'

'So Bernie says.'

So Bernie says. Ellie felt she might be having words with Bernie. 'Yes, you're right, Mum,' she said, opening her book and staring at a page, one word blending into another. 'You should take it back.'

'Me?' Moira said. 'No. This is *your* letter.'

'I don't think so.'

'It's only a half-hour spin.' She'd already calculated, then.

Ellie took the page from the table. She wasn't totally without heart, and part of her was intrigued to see this Ink House, this Blackwater Hall. But only to return the letter. Nothing more. No enquiries, no questions, no trying to find answers to mysteries, to scandals, that she had no right to be investigating. No more *other people's business.* 'Fine, tomorrow morning. I'll drop it there. But I don't know where—'

Before she could finish, Moira was up out of her chair, saying, 'I'll get directions from Bernie,' and digging noisily through a drawer in the bureau at the back of the room. She tried half a dozen pens before finding one with ink, then she disappeared into the hallway and picked up the phone.

Chapter Four

Blackwater Hall, County Kerry

July 1939

Charlotte wasn't at dinner, and Lady Rathmore's fury filled the too-hot room. Her anger was not, thought Nancy, for the fact that her brother and sister-in-law were newly arrived and anxious to see Charlotte, but rather that her absence interfered with her ladyship's already disrupted timetable. Cook had insisted the lamb could be kept warm, but Lord Rathmore clapped his hands and dinner was served.

Over the consommé there was discussion about Charlotte's new charitable enterprise, an evening school in Ballinn where local girls took lessons in literature one night a week. Despite his air of distaste, Lord Rathmore seemed resigned to allowing his daughter this freedom for the time being.

'Her community-minded spirit will be a distinct advantage for her marriage,' he said to no one in particular, 'for organising events and so forth.'

Lady Rathmore refolded her immaculate napkin. 'It's hardly a fundraising do, Charles.'

'I daresay Charlotte will need to impress with the quality of her personality, my dear.' This term of affection he used with cool emphasis. 'The money she comes with will not be wholly sufficient and I'm afraid her blood is not as pure as it could be.'

Lady Rathmore pushed aside her soup. She half turned to the footman. 'Tell Cook I need to see her after dinner. And send for the chauffeur; he was to collect Charlotte an hour ago.'

Nancy had bitten her lip. She knew from their correspondence that her sister-in-law's enterprise wasn't the genteel charity her family thought it to be. Charlotte's great passion wasn't the classics.

It was the stage.

As the conversation moved on around her, Nancy wondered how the Ballinn Dramatics Secret Society was coming along. At the start of the year, Charlotte had written begging for a script from London, and Nancy had complied, feeling both guilty for encouraging the deception and satisfied at being implicit in it. She had wrapped *Three Wise Fools* in a silk scarf and sent the package to coincide with Charlotte's birthday, thereby avoiding Lady Rathmore's scrutiny. According to her sister-in-law, there had been no end of problems, as everyone wanted to play Sidney Fairchild and no one wanted to be the lawyer, the banker or the judge. After this, Charlotte had decided the society had gone as far as it could with girls only and had opened it up to boys. Or rather – as became apparent from the changing tone of her letters – young men.

❧

Neither Lord nor Lady Rathmore took breakfast at the table, and Hugo was not yet up, so when Charlotte joined Nancy and Teddy the following morning over boiled eggs and tea, there was free and eager conversation.

'I've been simply *dying* for you to return,' Charlotte said, taking Nancy's hand. She looked at Teddy. 'Both of you. How was the boat? Is it a menace to be on deck? I've heard the Irish Sea is beastly!'

Teddy laughed. 'Questions . . . always questions.'

Charlotte waved her hand. 'Please, give me something to dream about on the long winter nights.'

Nancy said, 'Charlotte, you look beautiful.' It was true. In three years, Charlotte had grown tall and slim like her mother. Still a teenager, but a woman already.

'Oh.' She flopped down at the table. Grinned. Her deep dimples were intensely attractive. 'I look dastardly. Such a late night!' She looked behind her as the footman left the room, then leaned in. 'It's fabulous. We'll make *Three Wise Fools* into our first production.'

Teddy's gaze jumped between the two women over his cup of tea. He cleared his throat. 'Charlotte,' he said, 'whatever you're up to, be careful.'

She laughed lightly, a strand of blond hair falling loose. 'I always am.'

Nancy marvelled at her sister-in-law's new-found confidence. The years had eaten away at her shy giggle. She no longer talked with her hands; her movements were purposeful, deliberate. Instead of a girl with dreams, she seemed altogether like a woman with plans.

'I'm nineteen next year and quite old enough to be making my own decisions.' Charlotte reached across the table to pick up a still-steaming egg, juggling it in her fingers. 'Besides, if Nancy can do it, so can I.'

Nancy put down her toast. 'Do what?'

'Pave your own way.'

'Charlotte, that's very different . . .'

'How so?'

'You know perfectly well how so,' said Teddy.

'Times have changed, Teddy. The *world* has changed. How many estates like this do you think are left in this country? I was born during the war—'

'I hate to contradict you, but the war finished in 1918.'

'The War of Independence. *Irish* independence.'

'Ah.'

'Ah? *Ah?* Just like Father – pretending that Ireland is an outpost of England,' said Charlotte. Teddy's face hardened. She tapped at the side of her egg, lifting off its cap to reveal a gooey yolk. 'Well, it isn't.'

Teddy's reply was bitten back as the footman returned. His nose was turned to the side and he held a pot at arm's length, balancing it on his fingertips as though it might explode. 'Coffee,' he announced with distaste.

On her previous visit, Nancy's request for coffee had been met with Irel – a flavoured syrup that tasted almost exactly the way a person who had never drunk coffee might imagine it should. Fearing a repeat performance, she'd snuck down to the kitchen the night before and left a bag of beans on the table.

'Mother will have a fit,' said Charlotte, leaning over to pick up a cup. She held it out and watched the dark liquid fill it to the brim.

She took a sip. Nodded politely. Then, after a beat too long, said, 'Delicious.'

Nancy laughed. 'You get used to it. *Too* used to it.'

Charlotte pushed the cup aside. 'Teddy, do you want this?'

'No thank you, Charlotte. I had better be *just like Father* and leave the women to their gossip.' He got to his feet, his gaze anywhere but on his sister. In a swift movement he pushed his chair beneath the table and left.

Nancy steadied Charlotte with a soft hand. 'Let him be.'

Charlotte stared at the door, as though willing him to return. 'I don't know why I said that.' Teddy and Charles Rathmore were night and day.

'You didn't mean it.' Nancy ran a finger around the rim of her glass. It was half full of reconstituted orange juice and smelled like sherbet lemons.

Charlotte said, 'This family doesn't understand what life is like outside these four walls. The Rathmores are a dying breed.'

'Charlotte . . . I can't help but feel these words aren't your own.'

'They are. Quite my own. The world is changing and my life should change with it.' She leaned towards Nancy. '*Dress suitably in short skirts and strong boots, leave your jewels and gold wands in the bank, and buy a revolver.*'

'Well,' said Nancy, '*those* words can't possibly be your own.'

'Countess Markievicz said them in 1915.'

Nancy looked blank.

'She was sentenced to death. For the Easter Rising.' Charlotte took a gulp of the cooling coffee and winced.

'Yes, of course.' Nancy had read something of Markievicz. The daughter of a baronet, sentenced but eventually released. Her story, her passion appealed to both high- and low-born. But for Charlotte, she might be more than aspirational; she could be a blueprint.

'These are dangerous times, Charlotte. Not just here but across the continent. Take a care.'

Charlotte shook her head. 'I want more in life, Nancy. Like you have.'

'Me?' Nancy looked over her shoulder. The room was empty. She said flatly, 'I'm a secretary at a newspaper.'

'You're an orphan. Everything you are you did yourself!' Charlotte was becoming animated. 'You have *ambition*. And before you know it, you'll be a journalist.'

'Hardly *before I know it*.' Nancy had sent off a dozen articles. None had been published. Her most recent – a piece proposing more prominent female involvement in the military – she had given directly to her boss. He didn't print it. The next week King George approved the formation of the Women's Auxiliary Air Force. Nancy thought she ought to have been smug, but

the warm feeling of being right was chilled by the absence
of anyone knowing it. 'The grass is always greener,' she said.

'*Bíonn adharca fada ar na ba i gcéin.*'

'You'll have to enlighten me . . .'

'It's Irish. It means *horns are always longer on the cow abroad*,
or some such thing. The gardener taught it to me.'

Nancy raised her eyebrows. 'So this is where you're learning
all your revolutionary talk?'

Charlotte blushed a little, continued: 'I *am* rather interested
in my culture.'

Nancy peered over her cup. 'Whose culture?' *English or
Irish? Or American?*

Charlotte took a deep breath, as though it would give her
the courage to stop dancing around questions and find answers.
'You know . . . I'm from the type of family that isn't wanted
here. People stare at me when I go to Ballinn. I live only ten
miles away, but you'd think I was from another planet. It's
because I'm half Protestant . . .'

Nancy laughed. 'I rather think it's your blond hair.'

'. . . and from the big house.'

'Houses like Blackwater Hall were burned to the ground
in the 1920s – yours escaped that fate. Your family *is* wanted
here.' Nancy didn't add: *or at least tolerated.*

Charlotte said, 'Only because of Grandpapa William.'

Nancy paused. 'Ah yes, the one who broke the bread. Fed
the masses.' Teddy had told her of the first baron, Lord William
Rathmore. He had arrived, newly ennobled, in Kerry in the
1820s and begun construction of Blackwater Hall, selling off
his lands in Connaught to pay for it. The rumour in the village
was that a great ringfort had been demolished to make way
for his vision. 'That's all nonsense,' Teddy had said in a rare
dismissal of Kerry's rich oral history, 'made up because of our
name.' When Nancy had frowned at this explanation, he'd said,

'Rathmore. It *could* be translated to An Ráth Mhór in Irish. It means *big ringfort.*' But, he'd argued, the Rathmores were Rathmores long before they arrived in Ireland. 'You can't go around Irishising everything for the benefit of the rambling house.' The story, true or otherwise, had lingered, but there was no ill-feeling towards William. Twenty years after his arrival, he mortgaged his estate to buy food for his tenants during the Great Famine. And in 1848, he hired ships to assist villagers to emigrate to America.

'It was his generosity,' said Charlotte, 'that saved the house. That and Mother's grandfather.'

Nancy nodded. Niamh's grandfather had been one of the tenants who'd taken up William's offer; he'd moved his family from a famine-ravaged Ireland to the United States. Within two generations, the Stacks had become a firm fixture in new-money America. Niamh's father, Henry Stack, had grown up with stories of the old country. In 1910, he'd visited Ballinn for the first time. His daughter came with him. And she'd never left.

'He was born in Ballinn, wasn't he? Your mother's grand-father?'

Charlotte nodded. 'Not that she cares to acknowledge it.'

Niamh Rathmore was a fish out of water on Irish soil. Not a dent had been made in her American drawl in the three decades she'd lived at Blackwater Hall. For the briefest flicker, Nancy wondered what it had been like to be sold off to a lord, as so many American heiresses had been; to leave your home one day and never return. But the way Niamh had looked at her the day before stopped her short of feeling any sympathy for the woman.

'But things are different now,' Charlotte was saying, pulling Nancy from her reverie. 'We can no longer pretend Blackwater is a piece of England. A piece of America. The Irish rule their own country. Thanks to the IRA.'

Nancy had hoped to avoid being dragged into politics on her first day at the house. 'Of course. Ireland's independent. But . . .' she sniffed her toast; the butter was rancid, 'the Irish Republican Army are outlawed.'

'Yes, I know plenty about the IRA.' At Nancy's raised eyebrow, Charlotte added, 'I read *The Irish Press*.'

'Éamon de Valera's rag?'

At the mention of the Taoiseach's name, Charlotte visibly brightened. 'Outlawing the IRA, it's just appeasement. A simple nod to the English.' Then, as quickly as she'd ignited, her flame waned. She put a hand to her mouth. 'Sorry,' she whispered.

Just as Nancy reached out to reassure her she'd taken no offence, Hugo entered the room. Charlotte quickly dropped her hand, sat up straighter. Let a veil slide over her face.

He breezed past the table, picking up bain-marie lids. 'Talking about me?'

Charlotte laughed. 'Does the world revolve around you, Hugo?' She rounded her vowels with aplomb. It was camouflage not flattery, and the realisation gave Nancy a jolt of pleasure.

Over his shoulder, he asked: 'Another late night?'

Charlotte's voice became soft, soothing. 'I know. I know. But the girls show so much promise. One of them has written the most magnificent tragedy . . .'

'I don't know why you bother. None of them has any hope.' His back was turned, his plate piling high. 'You should be concentrating on Lord Hawley's visit.'

Charlotte reddened.

'Lord Hawley?' Nancy drank the last of her coffee, gritty but prized.

Hugo took a place at the head of the table. 'Mother and Father have invited him to stay next month. He has a particular interest in acquiring a wife.'

'I see,' said Nancy. *'Acquiring* a wife?' She bit her tongue. *No drama. No argument. Sign the documents and get out.*

But if Hugo heard her intimation, he didn't flinch. He merely opened the newspaper. Its week-old headlines were familiar to her; she'd read them in London before they'd left.

Charlotte got to her feet. 'I don't care what you say, I won't—'

'Charlotte,' Nancy cut her off, 'you mentioned that the sweet peas were blooming. Would you show me?' She stood and moved towards the French doors, then opened them towards the inky lake, letting the outside in, changing the room's stale air. Looking over her shoulder, she gave Charlotte a steely look. 'I'd like some for our bedroom.' She spoke slowly, enunciating every word as she watched the younger woman smooth the tablecloth beneath her palm. Deep creases remained where she'd clutched it.

After a moment's hesitation, Charlotte replied: 'Of course.' She turned her head to the side, away from Hugo, to wipe a single tear from her cheek. Nancy glanced to see if he'd noticed.

But Hugo's eyes were fixed on the paper, hand hovering over his breakfast, crumbs already scattered on his jacket. Behind him, a new painting by an artist called O'Conor had been hung on the wall: some jugs and apples, a rich red cloth lying under them like a pool of blood. It matched the cravat that clung to his neck. Watching him from the door as Charlotte stepped out into an overcast Kerry day, Nancy remembered that it was at Hugo's insistence that a morning buffet was served. The same content each and every day. 'Tradition,' he always said, 'is what sets us apart.'

From what, or whom, she had not dared ask.

Chapter Five

Approaching Blackwater Hall, County Kerry

September 2019

The day was crisp and cloudless; not a breath of breeze licked off the Atlantic. Ellie rolled along a narrow boreen, following Bernie's instructions, looking for a set of looming iron gates.

After several wrong turns, she'd returned to the village – and 3G – and used the map on her phone to find Lough Atoon. She'd zoomed in on Blackwater Hall, its shape distinctive among the surrounding trees. It looked intimidating. Dark and uninviting, nestled there amongst the woods.

At the gates, she paused, flicking on the Micra's hazard lights out of habit, then immediately turning them off – there was no one else for miles. She swung the car door open, listening. The only sounds were the scuffle of some small creature and the far-off pip of a bird. Wild fuchsia edged the lane, the blush and bloody flowers a riot of colour. She traced snippets of the boreen she'd followed up to the plateau through the farmland below; emerald green in the sunshine, a patchwork of fields. Beyond lay Kenmare Bay, shimmering and glistening in the fresh morning light.

She got back in the car. The house wasn't far.

One minute Ellie was navigating the narrow lane, the next thick woodland opened up to reveal a large lough, black as night. Lough Atoon. She slowed the car to a stop, let her eyes slip across its smooth surface to the far shore. And there it was, as she'd imagined, in the faded colours she'd conjured from the grainy photo of the night before when Moira had placed the house right there in her hand.

Blackwater Hall.

It sat, as it had for two centuries, on the furze-rimmed water's edge, its walls hidden behind a thick curtain of ivy, its windows and doors shut to the world. Russet and yellow leaves, discarded from the surrounding woodland, littered the hummocky lawn. A weak puff of smoke rose from one of a dozen chimneys, spires against the mountainside. Ellie tried to imagine the opulence the house must once have represented, tried to summon it from the photo she'd seen, tried to imagine a lord, or his agent, riding down from the plateau to collect money and goods from tenants who could ill afford them. She'd read last night that the first baron had been benevolent during the famine, buying grain and hiring ships to give people a new start in the New World. Perhaps the house had been a beacon of hope as so many weren't. But it certainly didn't look hopeful, nor was it a beacon, all its brightness had been snuffed out long ago. And what of Charlotte? *I can no longer remain at Ink House.* What horrors had she encountered there?

Ellie put the car into gear and carried on; she was here to return the letter to its rightful home. That was all. Nothing more.

❧

Ellie couldn't decide where to knock. There was such a collection of doors and windows that it was difficult to impose any conventional architectural norms on Blackwater Hall. She saw no sign of a welcome mat, but to the side of the house, near where she'd parked the Micra, there was a small doorway where the ivy had been recently trimmed. It was this door she decided to approach, but before she did, she paused, reached into her pocket for a comb, found it empty. She ran a hand through her tangled fringe. It would have to do.

She knocked.

The man who answered barely looked at her as he let the door swing on its hinges, his stooped figure shuffling back into the gloom of the house. 'The O'Conor's in the front room,' he said with only the faintest trace of an Irish accent.

Ellie hovered on the step. 'I . . .' But the man was gone. Tentatively she stepped over the threshold, not knowing whether to follow. 'Er . . .?' She made her way slowly down the dim hallway, her boots crunching on gritty tiles. The house was cold and smelled of damp – not the overpowering scent of mould but the mustiness of an unheated building in a humid place. The smell of neglect rather than decay.

She stopped, alone in the dark. 'Hello?'

'In here.' The voice came from her left, where a crack of light shone around the edge of a pulled-to door. She opened it and walked, blinking, into a bright room. Its duck-egg-blue walls were covered floor to ceiling in gilt-framed paintings and a huge dining table sat at its centre, heaving under piles of books. It was cluttered but not unclean. The view from its wide French doors encompassed the lough beyond.

She looked for the man who had opened the door. 'I'm Ellie Fitzgerald,' she said to the room, feeling more like an intruder every passing second.

She saw him then, folded into a wingback at one end of the room, his feet propped on a matching oxblood footstool. He was glaring at his hands – they were clasped in front of his face – as though he thought they'd done something wrong. An open fire crackled at his feet.

'Well,' he said, 'what do you think?'

'I'm sorry?'

He twisted in his chair and pointed past her. His complexion was alarmingly pale. 'The painting? You'll take it?'

On the floor, resting against the longest sideboard she'd ever seen, was a small painting. Still life; some jugs, a few apples. The strokes were thick and rich, the canvas built with texture. Ellie didn't know much about paintings but she knew she didn't want this one.

'I'm sorry,' she repeated, spreading her hands in apology. 'I'm not here about the painting.'

The man looked confused. He muttered, more to himself than her, 'He said you'd call today. Or was it tomorrow?'

Ellie chanced a step towards him. 'Are you Lord Rathmore?'

His brow crumpled, as though she'd asked him the way to the shops and he was considering the most direct route. 'Do I know you?'

'No.' She inched forward. 'I was hoping I could ask Lord Rathmore a question about his family . . .' She stopped herself. She wasn't here to ask questions; she was here to return something that wasn't hers.

Abruptly he said: 'But *I'm* Lord Rathmore.'

She felt very hot, her leather jacket too warm in the room. 'May I sit down?'

Lord Rathmore nodded and returned his gaze to his hands. He was elsewhere. Ellie said conversationally: 'My family live in the valley over the way . . .' she indicated in a vague direction, not sure if it was the right one, 'and I'm staying for a while. Back from Dublin.'

'And what work do you do?' he asked.

'I'm a journalist.'

He unclasped his hands slowly, carefully laying them aside. He turned his head away from her. 'I'm not discussing it with you.'

Ellie leaned back. She was used to this. The admission of her profession generally provoked one of two reactions – hostile silence or extreme verbal diarrhoea. 'I'm not here to ask—'

'It was 1958! I knew,' he shook his head sadly, 'your lot would find out eventually.'

'No, I—'

'Sixty years ago!' He'd pulled away from her as though she might strike him.

She said quickly: 'No . . . no, I'm not working. I'm home for . . . for my mum's health.'

Silently she apologised to Moira. But her words seemed to relax him; he pursed his mouth and nodded. Then, seemingly forgetting his anger as suddenly as it had arrived, he lifted his eyebrows. 'Would you like tea?' he asked.

'No thank you . . .' she said, faltering. But when his face fell, she added the universal acceptance: 'I wouldn't want you to go to any trouble.'

'How terribly rude of me,' said Lord Rathmore, his voice now formal and full of welcoming pomp. At any moment he would call her *old sport*. He pushed his tall frame out of the chair. 'Lemon all right? We're out of milk. I must ask Mama to get some.'

Ellie stood. 'Please, let me . . .'

'No, no.' He waved her back down. 'You wait right here. Make yourself at home.'

Once he'd disappeared into the hallway, Ellie sank into the chair. What was she doing here? Lord Rathmore was clearly unwell. He needed help. Assistance. There were community programmes, she knew. Home visits. Hot meals delivered a few times a week.

Pulling out her phone, she was surprised to see two bars of reception. She sent a message to Bernie – *Is Lord Rathmore getting any help up here?* – then flicked to the home screen; the little red number on her mailbox read *1,003*. There were several new missed calls. She put the phone back in her pocket. Real life could wait.

She stood and paced the room. The removal of the O'Conor painting (surely not *that* O'Conor?) had left a dark gap on the wall, showing the rich hue of the original colour. The floor was covered with an oriental rug of faded reds, blues and yellows. It was at least twenty-five feet long and almost as wide – at one time it must have cost a small fortune. At its edges, she could see the patchy beige of the underlying carpet. She realised it was probably once white. A colour, she thought, unlikely to have been chosen by someone who grew up in the muddy surrounds of County Kerry.

In the far corner of the room, a small glass-topped cabinet sat in shadow. She went to it and peered inside. A single object lay at its centre, nestled in a spill of deep blue velvet. It was the shape of a butterfly, a dozen prongs reaching from its base like so many claws. A comb. Smaller than the palm of Ellie's hand and so tarnished the silver of its setting was almost as black as the obsidian jewels that rimmed its edge. Each prong held a sapphire, their hue matching the velvet beneath. At the base of the lower wings, two scarlet rubies peered out like bloodshot eyes. The glass was covered with a thick layer of dust, and she wiped her hand across it, but when she took it away, her palm was clean.

The dirt, it seemed, was on the other side.

'Don't touch that!' Lord Rathmore's voice came loud across the room. He had appeared in the doorway holding a silver tray.

She took her hand away from the glass. 'I'm sorry, I . . .'

'For your own protection,' he said matter-of-factly. 'It's cursed.'

Despite herself, she took a half-step back. 'Cursed?'

'Yes. We mustn't touch it.' A flicker of something passed across his eyes. A memory? Doubt? Fear? The tray wobbled in his hands and Ellie took a rapid step towards him. It broke his reverie, brought him back from wherever he had gone.

He righted the tray. 'Come. Take a seat.'

Ellie did as she was bid.

'Now, tell me,' he said when she was settled, legs crossed, a nervous placating smile plastered on her face, 'you look so like Mama. Are you a cousin?'

Ellie shook her head. 'No, I—'

'But a friend?'

'No. No. I don't know your mama.'

'Don't *know* her?' He laughed heartily. 'You're in for a treat!' He smiled as he set out the cups. Three of them. 'Nancy. That's her name,' he said, looking up. Waiting for her reaction.

'I . . . I look forward to meeting her.' She frowned; Nancy Rathmore must be elderly indeed.

'You'll love her.'

She'd seen it before, the way he spoke of his mother – filled with awe and wonder. Dylan was the same. No matter what she did, no matter how she made Ellie feel, no matter the interference, his mother could do no wrong. As though, through the very act of giving birth, they were joined by an unbreakable chain.

Glancing at the extra cup and checking over her shoulder, she said, 'Lord Rathmore, I came by because—'

'Call me Albert.'

She nodded. 'Albert. I came by because I found a letter.' She pulled a new white envelope from the pocket of her jacket and held it out to him. 'It was in a book I picked up in the charity shop in Ballinn. I thought . . . I felt I should return it to you.'

With steady hands he took the envelope and withdrew the aged paper. Glanced at the handwriting. Then he folded it, returned it to the envelope and laid it on the coffee table at his side. 'This letter couldn't belong to me, young lady. It was written before I was born.' He picked up the blackened silver pot and poured tea into the three grubby cups. It was as thick as tar, and Ellie thought that somewhere between her mum and Albert, there would surely be the perfect brew.

'Maybe it's not your letter,' she said, 'but I think it belongs to the house. To Ink House? That's another name for Blackwater Hall, isn't it?'

'A terrible name,' he said.

She took a sip of her tea and quickly put her cup aside. 'The letter seems to have been written by someone called Charlotte . . .' She closed her eyes. Shook her head. No questions, no enquiries.

When she opened her eyes, Albert's hands were empty. His cup lay on the floor, the dark liquid a pool on the oriental rug, already merging into decades of faded stains.

'Oh!' Ellie took a paper napkin from the tea tray and fell to her knees, dabbing at the ground. She righted the cup, set it on the table, then looked up and gave Albert a smile to reassure him that everything was okay. But his eyes were locked on the fire, his hands gripped together like a vice. His lips moved silently, as if to mutter an incantation. He was long gone, and she wondered for a moment if she would be able to bring him back.

'Albert?' She laid a gentle hand on his. 'Are you all right?'

He turned his green eyes to her. 'Charlotte?' he said. 'She's gone.'

'I'm so sorry.' This had been a mistake.

'And it's all her fault,' he added.

Ellie frowned. Those words, that apportioning of blame; both were familiar to her. *So* familiar.

It's all your fault, Ellie.

She blinked. Once. Twice. But her feelings came flooding in a great rush: the grief, the sorrow. The guilt. Rising, rising, so she felt she had . . .

'Drowned,' said Albert, as though reading her mind.

Ellie started. 'Pardon?'

'Charlotte. She drowned in the lake.'

There it was, through the French doors, down the hummocky leaf-strewn grass. That mercury surface, slick with reflection. Lough Atoon.

Albert continued, though his gaze was now on the fire. 'But she's still here.'

Ellie looked around the room, alarmed. Glanced at the third cup. 'She's *alive*?' The letter had been written nearly eighty years before.

'Who?' Albert was smiling at her now.

'Charlotte.'

He shook his head slowly, looking at her as though it might be her that was confused. 'I don't know any Charlottes.' In a soothing voice he added, 'Would you like more tea?'

Ellie nodded and let go of his hand. He busied himself with refilling his empty cup and topping up her near-full one. The third cup sat to the side. As she stood, Ellie glanced down at her leg; in her haste, she'd kneeled on the sodden napkin and the tea was cooling on her shin. She picked it up, the napkin, and went to the fire, dropping it there, where it hissed. The chimney sucked the steam up and away. By the time she looked back to Albert, he was sipping his tea, a gentle smile on his face.

'Where were we?' he said, as though they'd merely been interrupted by some minor distraction.

Ellie grappled for familiar territory. 'The painting . . .'

'Yes?'

She crossed her fingers. 'Do you have any . . . details about it? Perhaps in the archives?' As she'd driven up the lane, she'd imagined the house was perched atop of basement full of records. Two hundred years of receipts, deeds and photos of generations long past.

He laughed. 'My *dear*, the Rathmore records would disappoint you! Daddy's old study has some correspondence and reports. About the extent of it, I'm afraid. There was a historian asking questions when we first moved here. She planned to put some of the family history in a book. Brigid someone? A handsome woman.' His eyes shifted back to the fire, his face impassive again. 'She left disappointed; almost everything was thrown out when Grandmother renovated. She had a hard heart, Grandmother Niamh. She always said that if people didn't hang on to history, her life would've been entirely different.' He paused, then turned to Ellie, his expression eager. 'A fine sentiment, don't you think?'

'Yes,' she heard herself say. And she realised she believed it. *It's all your fault, Ellie.* She uncrossed her fingers, held her hand to her stomach.

Behind her, a clock chimed.

Albert leaned forward. 'Grandmother Niamh bought the O'Conor. Been in this house for more than eighty years. And as you can see . . .' he paused, indicating the space on the wall, 'it's always been well stored.'

She made a non-committal noise. Then smiled and said, 'Thank you, I'll think about it. I'm sorry to have disturbed you, Albert.' And she was.

'Not at all.'

She leaned in and put her hand on his arm. 'Listen, do you have someone I can contact about the painting?' The thought of leaving him on his own in this big house made her uneasy.

He shook his head sadly.

'You mentioned that someone said I'd be visiting today? Or tomorrow?'

'Milo?' The name was like a wonderful surprise. 'My son! My son!' he said, as though the boy had just been born.

He got to his feet and went to the sideboard, a new spring in his step.

While his back was turned, Ellie looked around the room with a fresh eye. It wasn't neglected, this room. It was comfortable, clean – a stark contrast to the musty hallway and the house's ivy-choked exterior. The hearth was piled with split timber. Flowers adorned the sideboard. The shortbread on the tray was fresh. Someone was calling to Albert, looking after the old man. His son?

And what about the mother, Nancy? Albert had laid out three cups; was she here somewhere?

A phone call to check would do no harm.

Albert returned and handed her a piece of paper. 'Here you go.'

'Thank you,' she said, taking it. There were two numbers written in scrawled handwriting. And two names.

Milo and Hattie.

Ellie frowned. 'Hattie?'

'Hattie, yes,' Albert said, agreeing with her question.

'Who is she?'

'You know Hattie! Harriet. My sister. Yes, yes. You're good friends. Mama always said so.' His gaze was far off again, lost.

She slipped the paper in her pocket. Stood. 'I'll see you again, Albert.' As soon as she said it, she didn't know why she had. She reached out and squeezed his hand. 'You'll be okay?'

At her touch, he smiled. Bright again. 'Of course, of course,' he said. He dropped her hand and held up a finger. 'But . . . hang on . . .'

'Yes?'

He picked up an envelope from the coffee table. 'Don't forget your receipt.'

The letter.

'But I . . .'

He placed it in her hand. It was heavy, full of something she didn't yet understand. She wanted to give it back, to let it be, and yet . . . Charlotte's words were safe with her, weren't they? Until she could pass them on. She slipped the letter back into her pocket. When it was out of sight, his face exploded in a smile. 'Excellent, excellent. A done deal!'

And before Ellie could protest, she was walked to the door, out of the house, and waved off as she drove down the lane. As she passed the rusted gates, she promised herself she'd call Milo. Call Hattie. Check that Albert was okay. And give one of them the letter.

But for now it was once again back in her possession.

Chapter Six

Ambleside, Lake District

November 1957

Hattie came in from the rain. She wiped her eyes with her sleeve and hoped yet another day's tears would blend into the water that dripped from her fringe. It wasn't an unusual occurrence, the crying. She hated school. And school hated her.

She peeled off her soaked shoes and silently pulled the door to, shutting out the cold air that rolled off Lake Windermere and threatened to chill the house to its bones. Already Ambleside's streets had heaved that soft sigh that signalled the beginning of winter, and she shivered as she removed her coat and ran a hand through her wet hair. Frowned. Something hard was stuck in her ropy auburn plait. She pulled it out – a Pontefract cake, sticky with someone else's saliva. The tears threatened to reappear, and she pushed them back with an angry swipe of her little fists.

She set her satchel next to Papa's briefcase; it was as sodden as her own. Mama's papers were there on a footstool, scraggly piles of scrawled notes that seemed to grow of their own accord and follow her around the house.

But Albert's bag was nowhere to be seen; her big brother was late home from school again. And Hattie knew why. The reason – to which her parents remained oblivious – was blonde and beautiful, two years older than him, with eyes as blue as the summer sky.

She stopped. Listened. Heard the clock ticking in the kitchen, the gentle bubble of a pot on the range. The pitter-patter of rain as it washed down the window. The house was quiet. Too quiet. No music, no garbled conversation, no cooking sounds spilling from the kitchen with the promise of the evening ahead.

Something was wrong. She held her breath.

There. A murmur. Just a whisper. Bleeding through the keyhole of the living-room door. The *closed* door. She heard Papa's voice in her head: *Open doors, open minds, Hattie.* The Rathmores' living room was porous, as a rule.

She approached tentatively, her sodden socks leaving shiny footprints on the oak floor, and pressed an ear to the timber.

'. . . never really recovered from Bergen-Belsen, that's my best guess . . . I had no idea he couldn't cope. How would I?' That was Papa.

'I know, Teddy.' This was Mama; a comforting, breathy statement, the type said with eyes closed, hands gripped.

Papa's voice was staccato. 'That isn't the official line . . . the papers will say it was an aneurysm.' He stopped. The four bells of the mantel clock drew out the silence. Distractedly, he said, 'What if it runs in the family, Nancy?'

The gentle creak of the sofa – Mama leaning forward? 'What do you mean?'

'Suicide.' Hattie took a quick breath; she'd heard – *overheard* – that word before and knew what it was. What it meant. 'He drowned himself in the lake. Drowned right where Charlotte disappeared.'

Silence.

As Hattie leaned against the door frame, she began to shiver, but she couldn't turn away, couldn't leave. The door silently opened a crack and she pulled back her hand.

The sofa sighed as Papa stood. 'I've heard these things can run in the family. This type of . . . malaise.' His quick footsteps went to the sideboard, crossed Hattie's view. She rolled back from the door, caught her reflection in the hallway mirror. *Hair-iet Rash-more*; that was what the girls at school called her, on account of her red hair and freckles.

When Mama spoke again, her voice was softer. 'I don't think that's true, Teddy. It was the war. Before that, well, you know what he was like. It's been nearly twenty years since you've seen him. Since *we* saw him at Blackwater Hall in 1939. Nobody parted on the best of terms.'

'No,' said Papa. 'But we did write. His letters . . . there weren't many.' He cursed. 'Always so chipper . . . full of bravado. God help him.'

In the silence that followed, Hattie brushed aside her fringe, appraised herself. Then looked away. Mama said that beauty lived within, which Hattie had come to learn was something only beautiful people said.

'And your father?'

'He could barely speak . . . distraught.' The clink of ice, the splash of liquid. Papa was closer to her now. She could hear the gulp as he drained his glass. Then more ice, more liquid. 'We may have our differences, but . . . his son gone . . . how does it feel to lose a son? What if I lost Albert? I can't imagine. I can't.'

'Your mother . . . how is she?' Mama's voice was full of distaste.

'Confined to her bed.' He moved to the door, inches from Hattie.

'Funeral?'

'Next week.'

A murmur from Mama she couldn't make out.

'Yes, perhaps it's best you stay here. I'll go alone. It's a long trip. But then . . .'

'Yes?'

'But then in the new year, we must return.' *To where?*

'Yes, of course. The children can meet their grandparents.' Hattie's scalp prickled at the prospect. *Grandparents*. She could barely imagine it. 'We'll go for the summer.'

Papa paused as though gathering his thoughts. Or his courage. 'No, not just for the summer.'

'I won't.' This was Mama's *I've made up my mind* voice.

'It's my duty now.'

'Oh, *tradition*, is it?'

'Don't say it like that.' Hattie was lost. *What duty? What tradition?* If Albert were here he could translate; he always knew what things were and what they meant.

'Times have changed . . . we don't have to go back to Ireland.'

Papa said, 'But it has to go to me. Then it has to go to Albert. We're the last of the line.'

Mama scoffed. Began to say something. Paused.

'It's a peerage, not a raffle prize.' Papa drained his glass, the final chink of ice signifying the end of the conversation.

But Mama didn't stop there. 'Teddy, I won't go back to that house. After what happened . . . after what happened to Charlotte.'

'I'm sorry, Nancy. I'm so sorry.'

There was a gentle brush of linen, a slow released sigh; the sound of a warm embrace. Mama's voice was muffled. 'I won't go back, Teddy, I won't.' But her resolve had melted away, her fire put out, and although she didn't understand exactly how or why, in that instant Hattie Rathmore knew her life was about to change for ever.

Chapter Seven

Blackwater Hall, County Kerry

July 1939

Charlotte was waiting by the sweet peas.

'You didn't tell me about Lord Hawley,' Nancy called across the empty walled garden. She'd seen the gardeners down by the pier, noticed them because of the noise they were making, hammering timber boards onto the boathouse walls as the morning sun licked vapour from the still lake. But people aside, the garden brimmed with life. And colour. A magnificent assortment of vegetables and flowers, and birds hopping on recently turned soil.

'Why didn't you mention anything? In your letters?' Nancy said as she picked her way along a gravel path half hidden under squash leaves. The smell of damp earth reminded her of her final foster family, Rod and Barbara. They'd loved to garden; Rod was obsessed with his prize-winning pumpkins and Barbara her roses. They were very elderly when she'd been placed with them, and she wished they'd been younger. So they could see her now.

'What was there to say?' Charlotte had amassed a collection of pastel flowers. Even from where Nancy stood, the scent was heady.

There was a great deal to say. 'Does Teddy know?'

Charlotte shook her head. Nancy had supposed, or rather expected he didn't.

At the far end of the garden, built over a cast-iron bench, was a living arbour, its green leaves entwined with drooping blue clematis. It was surrounded with white and yellow lilies. 'Let's sit under the willow over there,' Nancy said.

Charlotte followed her sister-in-law's gaze, her eyes swinging past the seat. 'The what?'

'Willow.'

'You mean the sally?' She led Nancy to the seat, still damp from the night's sprinkle. 'The farmers curse this tree, it grows so quickly. This one was only planted a few years ago.'

Nancy couldn't believe it; the tree was bedded in, heavy with foliage. It blended into the wild walled garden.

They sat in silence. The air was pleasantly heavy with some far-off rain, the scent of lilies almost overwhelming. Nancy reached out to touch one, its orange pollen staining her fingers.

'So, what does it mean?'

Charlotte picked a flower from above her. A sprinkle of dew rained down on them. 'It means my life is mapped out.'

'It's just a visit. It can hardly—'

'I heard Father discussing figures with Mother.'

'Perhaps we'll still be here, Teddy and I.' Nancy didn't think it would help.

As if reading her mind, Charlotte said, 'I'm grateful. But it won't help.' She plucked a petal from the blue clematis. 'I've written to him, Lord Hawley. Thads, what a funny name.'

'Thads?'

'Thaddeus. His father was a classicist. He's actually rather pleasant. A bit eccentric. He lives in some sort of castle, and is obsessed with the concept of destiny and inevitability. A big fan of Conan Doyle, and I mean more the spiritualism nonsense,

not the detective.' Nancy smiled, but her expression slipped
when Charlotte added: 'But he's old.'

'How old?'

'Forty-five.'

She bit her bottom lip. 'Perhaps when you get to know
him . . .'

'No.' Charlotte shook her head. 'I want to break away.'

Nancy paused. 'You should talk to Teddy. He'll understand.'

'Yes, he found his own path,' said Charlotte, 'and it changed
our family.'

Nancy was quiet.

'Don't . . . don't misunderstand my meaning. In a *good*
way.' Charlotte grinned, a little of her humour returning. 'But
still, maybe I should call you Trouble from now on. Trouble
Rathmore.' At Nancy's raised eyebrows she continued, 'I want
my own life.'

Nancy felt she was being drawn into something dangerous.
'Charlotte, I don't know how to put this.' She rubbed pollen
into little circles on her palms, its stain satisfyingly rich. 'Teddy's
a man. It's different. I wish it weren't.'

'But I have skills. I could come to London. I could be a
secretary too. Or I can work with my hands. Needlework?'

Nancy looked at this creature from another era. 'When was
the last time you went to a city?'

'Dublin, two years ago.'

'And?'

Charlotte turned over her sister-in-law's hands, tracing the
orange stigmata. Then she let go, suddenly self-conscious.
'It was busy . . . so busy. I simply couldn't understand how
everyone knew where to be. And cars, everywhere. Bicycles.
Trams, of course. They reminded me of Mother because they
would never have stopped if you stood in their way. We stayed
at the Gresham. And the Abbey Theatre was wonderful. *Juno*

and the Paycock. I insisted on going, but Father only made it to Act Two. I'm afraid I never saw the end.'

Nancy shifted. 'It *is* lovely to see that side of the city. The hustle, the finery. The entertainment. But city *living* is quite something else. Particularly on a budget. Everything costs something. And at the end of each month when the rent is paid and the cupboards are bare, you simply start again.'

'I know what you think of me. Spoiled girl. Can't get her hands dirty.'

'I don't think anything of the sort.'

'You're probably right.'

Nancy didn't want to let it hang. She changed the subject. 'So, can I come to the next society meeting?'

Charlotte coloured. 'Well, I . . . I'd be embarrassed. We're only playing at it really.'

'Good, that's settled. Thursday, is it?'

She laughed. 'I see your plan, Nancy. I can change subjects too. Let me see . . .' She scratched her chin, a theatrical move. Nancy noticed the translucent skin on her hands; so fine, so delicate. She folded her own away in shame. 'You've been married . . . how long?'

Nancy smiled. 'Two and a half years.'

'What's it like?'

'Well . . . what can I say?' An Englishness overcame her. 'It's nice. We have a good time.' She laughed, a cork releasing pressure. 'I'd feel odd discussing it . . . Teddy's your brother.'

Charlotte made a face.

'I feel very lucky. I've never made that a secret in my letters, have I?' said Nancy.

'You seem happy together.'

'I won't lie to you – we are. But some people find a happy marriage highly suspicious, so we won't spread the news too far.'

A tiny robin dropped from the garden wall to peck at the base of the rosemary. He stopped to look at them, the rouge on his scrawny breast scruffy.

'This little boy has a big year ahead of him,' said Charlotte and Nancy felt a fondness flood her heart. For a girl with silken hands, she didn't miss the nuances of nature.

'So, what's the secret?'

'Secret?' said Nancy.

'To a happy marriage.'

She thought. 'Respect, mostly. And an even footing.'

Charlotte looked confused.

'Not socially, you understand. When you marry – no, before that – you must know your partner wants you for yourself, not for something you should be or could be.'

The robin sang, jumping staccato over an invisible skipping rope.

'I see . . .'

Nancy closed her eyes. 'Charlotte, I didn't mean . . .'

'Of course not.'

'I'm sorry.' How many times would either of them say that today? Nancy felt the conversation was spiralling down and away, out of her control.

Charlotte took her hand. 'I'm happy for you and Teddy. Goodness, if you hadn't met, I wouldn't know you.' She smiled. 'And where would I be then? Who would I write all my secrets to?'

Charlotte *had* been very candid with her during their correspondence – her admission about the Ballinn Dramatics Secret Society, her feelings about her mother, her dissatisfaction with her lot. Nancy felt a pang of guilt. Why could she herself not be so frank? She had nothing to be ashamed of.

As if reading her mind, Charlotte asked: 'And children? When will you start?'

Nancy looked away. 'Not for a few years, I'd imagine. Twenty-five feels too young for a family these days.' She wondered if she was blushing.

Teddy appeared through the archway, his hand held high to shield a sliver of sun cutting through the clouds. 'There you are. Thick as thieves.'

Charlotte jumped up and ran to him. 'I'm sorry, Teddy.'

'Hush now.' He put his arms around her, winking over her shoulder at his wife, seated amongst the sapphire clematis.

Nancy felt a tug deep in her chest. For a lesser woman, it would be jealousy. The worry that her husband might love his sister more than his wife. That their shared memories would be richer than those she and Teddy had forged together. But for Nancy it was something else. In that simple hug, Teddy had showed a different kind of love. A love of family.

She felt, not for the first time, inadequate. She only wished her body would stop failing and that she could provide him with another reason to feel that way. Another person to love. His own flesh and blood.

Chapter Eight

Ballinn, County Kerry
September 2019

Ellie stopped the Micra across from the new place on the edge of the village, a little green-fronted shop with a sign advertising *Great Coffee.*

Her need for real coffee was desperate, as was her desire to gather her morning's thoughts, scattered as they were like fallen leaves. She longed to rake them up, put them together in a pile, or let the wind blow them away. Her phone and its thousand emails were weighing down one pocket and Charlotte's letter was beginning to burn a hole in the other. She had to tackle them both. And to do that, she needed caffeine. Real, bitter caffeine, from real, bitter beans.

She eyed the café suspiciously. Two people sat inside drinking coffee out of double-walled glass mugs. Ellie watched the woman bring her mug to her lips and close her eyes in pleasure.

It was too much. Her veins tingled in anticipation. She stepped out of the car and crossed the empty street.

❧

The other customers nodded an acknowledgement as Ellie entered the café, the sound of a milk steamer piping her aboard. Twin scents of coffee and baking infused the warm room, and her shoulders instantly dropped. She could almost taste caffeine in the air.

The barista turned from his place at the coffee machine and gave her a hundred-watt smile. He looked like a Roman soldier. 'You might have to wait,' he said in a soft voice. 'I am running off my feet, *non*?' A continental accent ran his words together.

'Of course, I'm not in a rush.' She chose a table next to the wall and took out her phone. Then stopped and looked at his waiting face. 'You were joking . . .'

He raised an eyebrow. 'Not highly amusing, perhaps?'

Ellie put a hand over her eyes. 'It's been one of those mornings . . .'

'*Désolé*. Coffee?'

'Yes, black, please.' She walked to the cabinet and perused its contents. 'Does that say beetroot chocolate cake?'

'*Oui*.' He laughed at the look she gave him. 'No one wants the beetroot cake in Ballinn?'

'You never know . . .' She looked uncertain, but if it bothered him, he didn't show it. 'I'd better have a slice.' She wanted to add, *so it doesn't go to waste*, but instead she said, 'It looks delicious.'

He nodded as he packed grounds into the portafilter, his long fingers nimble. Glancing back over his shoulder he said, 'You sound . . . how can I say? A little local?'

She wondered if it was a compliment. 'A *little* local?'

'*Mais oui*. You're no tourist. But your jacket, those boots and that hair – *non*, I don't think you are living here.'

'No?'

'I would have noticed you before,' he said lightly, before turning back to the coffee machine.

She let it hang. Three years and she'd forgotten how to flirt. But making eyes at a man was the last thing she needed right now. 'My mum has a farm up the hill.'

He plated up a huge slice of the chocolate beetroot cake. Slid it across to her. 'You look nothing like a farmer.'

'No, I'm a journalist. Although I'm . . . between jobs at the moment.'

Mock fear crossed his face. 'You're not a food critic, are you?'

'No. But I look forward to criticising this.' She winced.

He laughed lightly. 'Nils,' he said, holding out his hand.

She reached across the cake display. 'Ellie.'

Three young tourists entered the café, their eyes lighting up at the timber-clad interior. They peeled off plump Puffa jackets, and as they approached the counter, Ellie retreated to her table and listened to their orders. Beetroot cake, vegan pumpkin slice and three soy lattes. Over their shoulders, Nils gave her a look. She shook her head. Perhaps the guy was onto something.

She took a bite of the chocolate cake. *Not bad, not bad at all.* She chewed slowly, savouring it. What a morning she'd had. After two weeks holed up at the house, she felt exhausted but somewhat invigorated to be out. And relieved that no one seemed to care. The contrary, actually. The people of the village – several walked past the window now, looking in with suspicion – were quietly getting on with their lives; it was she who'd been standing still.

She unlocked her phone, then withdrew the slip of paper from her pocket. The two phone numbers were written in a shaky sloping hand. She tapped Milo's into the keypad.

The number you have dialled is incorrect.

She tried the second number, Hattie's.

The number you have dialled is incorrect.

Poor Albert. All alone and several relatives who may or may not exist. She called Bernie's number – no answer – and reminded herself to try again in an hour.

Then she took a deep breath. Opened her email and scrolled

through the messages, looking for one sender in particular.

Nothing. She typed his name into the search bar. The most recent email was the last message she'd sent him. It made her mouth dry rereading it. She hadn't thought for a moment he would agree to let her go. Let it hang. Allow everything they had, everything they'd been through, wash away.

It's all your fault, Ellie.

She felt a familiar swell of anxiety and tried to bring herself back to the present. The fine autumn day, the smell of coffee in the air, the anticipation of its bitter taste on her tongue. She let the sounds from the warm café wash over her as she closed her eyes. Counted backwards from ten. When she opened them again, Nils was standing there.

He held out two mugs.

'Both for me?' she said.

'Yes.'

One of the drinks looked delicious, the other rather unusual. 'That one's a funny colour.'

'Turmeric latte.'

She made a face.

'Good for the stress. It's . . . how do you say? On the house.'

Had her distress been that obvious? She blustered, trying to think of a clever rejoinder, but her head was too jumbled and instead she replied simply, 'Thank you.' He gave her a nod, and left almost as quickly and quietly as he'd arrived.

She looked back to her emails, scrolled aimlessly through them, concentrated on keeping her face natural. But the silence from Dylan had cut a hole in her. She'd played at being okay, brushed aside her mum's concerns. More than once. More than twice. Even to Bernie she'd almost said, 'The wedding's only delayed, sure it is.' And maybe it was, she couldn't be sure. Could she? Everything had been left . . . hanging.

She touched her hand to her stomach as she sipped her coffee. It was good. It tasted like the city, like the life she'd left behind. Like the long morning walk from home to office, coffee mug in hand. Her very own time to think. To breathe. Before the day stole her away.

Get a grip, Ellie. She turned back to her phone and performed inbox triage, selecting all the spam, junk and subscriptions and deleting them. Then she quickly read emails from friends: *Where are you? I heard you were away. Haven't seen you for ages. Why can I never get through to you?* She opened WhatsApp and sent a group message: *Sorry about the radio silence. Down at Mum's – no reception. Having a slice of beetroot chocolate cake in an actual café in Ballinn, can you believe it? Anyway, I'm alive. Love, Els x*

Amongst the remaining emails, there was one from Jeremy, her editor at *The Irish Times*. Or rather, her ex-editor. *Reluctant* ex-editor, she liked to think. A man who had been overruled and outmanoeuvred by the powers that be. 'I'll make this up to you, Ellie,' he'd promised, as he delivered the blow. As he'd fired her.

She opened his email:

Ellie,
Not much to report from this end. I'm still fighting to have you reinstated but I fear all in vain. Vincent from that rag you said you would never work for has been asking after you; I've attached his email below. I've given you a glowing reference, of course.
Jez

PS I assume you haven't been online down there in the bog, so . . . you've got to see this.

She frowned at the postscript link, then clicked it and was taken to a Twitter page. She stared at it, confused. Blinked once, twice. Then realised what she was seeing.

Oh God.

This wasn't good.

There she was, her face Photoshopped onto a red-and-white-striped Where's Wally sweater. *Where's Ellie*, the account was named. The profile had over ten thousand followers and thousands of mentions. All were unconfirmed sightings. Printed cut-outs of her at the pub, in the park, on the beach. They were all posted under the hashtag #StanleyStreetScandal.

This was the last thing she wanted, the tattered remnants of her career ripped apart by a meme. As she scrolled down the page, her long-gripped dream of property editor for *The Irish Times* evaporated before her eyes. She returned to the profile; there, in blue text, was a link to *Dubble*.

She clicked on it.

Error 404.

At least she'd had the foresight to do something right during the whole debacle.

Dubble – a portmanteau of Dublin and bubble – had been her blog, started on a whim. Just a few disparate articles about the property market squeeze. Over time, the site gained a handful of loyal followers; millennials who insisted they weren't buying avocado toast, boomers who didn't *want* to downsize, renters who'd long abandoned the dream of owning their own home. She had given voice to them all, blending their thoughts with hers. It was a hobby, a record she felt might come in handy when the bubble burst.

That was all.

Until the email arrived. A tip-off from a disgruntled employee of the property developer Maxwell Cray. God, how she despised that man. Him and his pal Davy McCarthy. She couldn't bear to think of them. Of how they'd won in the end. How she, and Dublin, had lost.

She tasted the turmeric latte, hoping Nils was right about it being good for stress.

Cray's Abu Dhabi-based construction company, Maxibuild, had purchased a disused council depot in Stanley Street, a central Dublin location previously earmarked for social housing. One hundred and twenty flats.

Despite the Dublin Agreement, which forbade the sale of public land, the development arm of the council, headed by Davy McCarthy, sold the site to Maxibuild on the proviso the company deliver affordable housing. It was hailed as a great step forward for public–private collaboration, and Ellie herself wrote a couple of articles about it, praising the council's foresight.

That was when the secretary in Cray's Dublin office, tired of his sexual advances – and herself unable to get on the housing ladder – had emailed Ellie with the allegation that Maxibuild planned to delay development at Stanley Street until the building permit lapsed. A new planning application was in progress for thirty three-bedroom luxury apartments. The three penthouses alone would be valued at four million euros. Each.

Public housing, it seemed, was off the agenda.

Ellie got to work. She obtained a copy of the purchase agreement and found it contained an unusual clause: that Maxibuild would work *to the best of its ability to provide social housing if economically viable*. It was clever. With the growing property bubble, she was sure social housing was no longer economically viable in central Dublin. She was also sure it had *never* been economically viable. She befriended a Maxibuild architect, got hold of the new building plans. They were untitled, undated and unlocated.

That had told her all she needed to know.

Jeremy had salivated at the story when she'd laid the copy before him. He'd been sitting, she remembered, at his desk, a cup of coffee halfway to his lips, his trademark Hawaiian shirt as jarring as ever.

'Ellie, this is gold.' He'd looked up. 'Your sources are good?'

Were they watertight? At the time she'd thought there might be a few leaky seams, but with the scale of the revelation, the story was thick enough to plug the holes on its own.

Jeremy went straight upstairs to get the go-ahead.

And ten minutes later, he was back.

He'd been overruled.

Maxibuild were key advertisers in the property section and editorial pushed the story aside with a wave of a hand. *A bitter secretary isn't a reliable source. An untitled schematic isn't evidence. A contractual clause is just that, a clause.*

And then Ellie made her mistake.

She'd put so much time and energy into the exposé that she couldn't let it go. She had always considered her stubbornness a virtue. But now it became a curse. With the push of a button, she published the article on *Dubble*. Because people should know. But she didn't expect anyone to care.

How wrong she was.

By the time she woke up the next morning, the post had gone viral. *She'd* gone viral. *Dubble, Dubble, Toil and Trouble* screamed a tabloid newspaper. People were angry. Outraged. They demanded the council revoke the sale. #StanleyStreetScandal trended on Twitter for a week.

But Councillor Davy McCarthy vehemently, and very publicly, denied the accusations. Claimed there was no proof of any wrongdoing. And in a way, he was right. All Ellie had was a legal clause in a contract and the word of an employee. No evidence of money changing hands. No tangible confirmation of collusion, no whiff of corruption.

McCarthy called on *The Irish Times* to answer for their staff member. Ellie was given a dressing-down and the paper published a letter saying it took no responsibility for the personal opinions of its staff.

The end.

Or so it seemed.

But Davy McCarthy was like a dog with a bone. His lawyer demanded Ellie's dismissal. And to her horror, with his fingers crossed behind his back and cowering under pressure from upstairs, Jeremy complied.

Ellie had been thrown to the lions, and within six weeks she had gone from a respected, soon-to-be married journalist to an unemployed singleton sleeping in her mum's spare room.

She sighed and closed her emails. The inbox had updated accordingly, its angry red numbers now filed away. But it had done nothing to put her thoughts in order. Nothing to calm her. In fact, the revelation that she had been made a meme sank her even lower than she'd been before.

She had several missed calls and she scrolled through them now: Jeremy, a couple of friends, some unknown Dublin numbers that were at best telemarketing, at worst lawyers. And one other, an hour ago.

Mum landline.

Moira answered on the third ring. 'Ellie, where are you?'

'At Procaffination. The new café.'

'Bernie heard they serve coffee in *glasses*.' Moira paused. Pregnantly. Then continued: 'Listen, as you're in the village . . .'

'Yes?' Ellie said with suspicion.

'Would you stop by the village hall?'

'It depends what—'

'Good, because I said you would.'

'Mum . . .'

'There's a fellow there who's interested in your letter.'

The letter. Still in her pocket. 'I did try to give it to Albert, but—'

'Jules Bristole. *English*,' Moira continued. 'He's started the Ballinn Historical Society.'

'Good for him,' said Ellie.

'He's a nice man.'

Was this a set-up? A bit soon even for her mum. 'And how did he find out about the letter?'

'Bernie told him.' So the village telegraph had been at work. Moira rushed on. 'Grand. Thanks, Ellie.' There was a pause, then: 'Now, speaking of Bernie, I was just . . .'

Ellie drained the last of her turmeric latte and grimaced at the cold grit at the bottom of the glass. She gave Nils a thumbs-up. *Good*, she mouthed.

She took a pen from her pocket – the occasional 'mmm' murmured to the gossip coming down the line – and jotted a message on her clean napkin.

Fantastic coffee, great atmosphere and cake. Rating? 9/10 :)
PS Get some mugs for the locals.

She left it on the table, waved towards the counter on her way out.

As she started down the street, her mum's chatter still attached to her ear, she turned back to the café, saw Nils go to her table and pick up the note.

And smile.

Chapter Nine

Blackwater Hall, County Kerry
February 1958

Hattie quelled her excitement. The family's mood during the journey from Ambleside had been subdued, to say the least, and she felt now wasn't the time to ask – once again – if they were there yet.

Instead, she leaned forward and tapped the broad shoulder in front of her. 'Are those the gates, Papa? The ones you mentioned?'

Two purple sandstone pillars loomed either side of the road ahead. On them hung a black pair of iron gates, their curved profile swung open to the lane beyond.

'That's them,' said Papa. He turned to the driver. 'Would you stop a moment?'

The car pulled to the side of the lane and Hattie looked expectantly at Mama, who opened one shadow-rimmed eye and said, 'Go on,' before closing it again.

Hattie poked at Albert, who was snoring next to her. He awoke with a snort. His voice was thick with fatigue, and sparse stubble shadowed his skin. 'What is it, squirt?'

'We're here,' she said.

Albert looked out of the window. A derelict cottage sat in the green expanse of a nearby field, leafless wintry saplings holding on to cracks in the roof. He raised his eyebrows with exaggerated surprise. 'It's not *quite* what I expected.' He grinned, his dimples cheeky.

She looked at the abandoned farmhouse and giggled. 'Albert!'

He opened the door and swung his legs out as Hattie squeezed past. Then he flopped back, his head in Mama's lap. Without opening her eyes, she laid a gentle hand on his head. Papa always said they were like peas in a pod.

'Aren't you coming?' Hattie asked.

'No,' Albert said, pretending to snore with a strangled final note to each breath. 'I'll stay here and dream of home.'

By this, Hattie knew he was thinking of his girl. He'd met her under the leafless sycamore tree the weekend they'd left for Ireland. Her skirt had waved sadly in the breeze as though it knew what was coming. In her hands she held a small posy of yellow primroses. And when they'd embraced, Albert's shoulders shook in a way that made Hattie melt away, so he'd never know she'd been there.

The truth was that she – and it seemed she alone – was thrilled with this turn of events; this adventure they were embarking on, this new life. When her teacher announced to the class after New Year that Hattie would be leaving, there was sniggering from the back row and she'd turned to see one of the girls pretending to cry, her hands balled in fat fists, wringing at her eyes. For the first time she could remember, her classmates' taunts didn't bother her. Freedom was only weeks away, and by February Ambleside School would be just a memory.

Papa was striding ahead down the lane ahead of her. 'Smell that?'

Hattie sniffed the air. It was certainly fresher outside than in the car, where the sticky heat of five people had steamed up the interior as they drove through the steady drizzle. But now the grey sky had lifted, leaving only a white haze that topped the inland peaks. 'I can't smell anything,' she said. 'Not after Albert's cologne.'

Papa looked over his shoulder, laughing. They could just see Albert's long legs sticking out of the car, one unlaced shoe dangling precariously from his foot.

'It's the smell of the ocean,' he said.

'I can't *see* anything.'

Papa knelt down and patted his back. 'Hop on.' She looked at him warily. 'Hop on,' he insisted.

She clambered up, and when Papa stood, a magnificent view spread before her, the crisp greys and blues of the ocean backed by cloud-shrouded mountains. Three seagulls hung in the air, observing them, then swung low into the valley below.

'The sea?'

'Kenmare Bay,' said Papa. It shimmered and shifted in the afternoon light. 'A great place for oysters, all that brackish water.'

'Disgusting,' said Hattie.

'If you're going to be a chef, Hattie . . .'

'But they're so . . . slimy.'

Papa laughed. 'And what else?'

There was a sweetness in the still air. Flowery? No, she thought. Something else. The smell was familiar. Like coconut.

'Furze,' said Papa, pointing to the sea of yellow below them; it rolled down the valley to stop at a patchwork of fields where a dozen houses scattered, smoke puffing from their chimneys. 'It'll flower for a few months now.' He lowered Hattie to the ground. 'But usually you can find a few flowers at any time of year. *When gorse is out of bloom, kissing's out of fashion.*'

'It's gorse? Like home?'

'Yes,' said Papa. 'Like home.' A lick of hair fell across his eye and he pushed it away. 'Come on, time to meet Nana and Gramps.'

These were also new words for Hattie – actual grandparents she could see and touch. She felt a jolt of excitement as she hopped back into the car.

ॐ

As they passed the gates and drove the last mile to Blackwater Hall, Hattie clambered onto Mama's knee and peered through the window, opening it to howls of protest at the chilled air. But her family quietened when she stuck her head outside and hooted, letting her have her moment of joy before the house hove into view across the inky lake.

Hattie took a breath. There it was. More ivy than roof, nestled beneath a mountain with cloud spilling over its summit. Smoke puffed from several chimneys and a neat lawn ran to the shore. Dusk was falling, and as Hattie watched, a dim light flickered behind two central double doors. 'Is the power connected yet?' Mama had asked a few weeks before they left Ambleside. Papa shook his head. 'Kenmare was connected last year and Ballinn's on track for 1959. I'm afraid Blackwater Hall will be some way behind that . . .' Rural electrification in Ireland, he'd said with a laugh, was destined to be completed by the turn of the millennium. Mama had barely raised a smile. No power? Hattie couldn't imagine it. Her eyes were drawn back to the warm weak light – a candle, a lantern? – that shone from those French doors; she envisaged opening them, stepping out onto the manicured lawn, then rolling across the grass, somersaulting down to the furze that lined the water's edge.

ॐ

Dinner at Blackwater Hall wasn't at all what Hattie had expected. They ate in a large blue room, a small fire smouldering weakly at one end: a full table setting and three courses. Storm lanterns filled the room with plenty of fumes but very little light, and the candelabra in the table's centre bathed the family in an eerie glow. The conversation was stilted, and Hattie's eyes drooped as the days of travel began to catch up with her and her pall of excitement dissipated.

'Sit up straight' was the first thing Grandmother said to her, other than 'hello'. Her American drawl was far less romantic than Hattie had expected. She was very slim and tall, if a little stooped, and she walked with a cane that clicked on the hallway tiles, foreshadowing her imminent arrival.

Hattie pulled back her shoulders and set aside her spoon. 'Sorry.' When she picked it up again, there was a smear of brown on the otherwise pristine tablecloth.

Grandmother's eyes slid from the stain to Hattie's face and back again. She was incredibly pale, and the deep lines above her mouth turned to valleys as she shook her head. 'Good manners are required in this house; you would do well to remember that.' She looked to Papa.

'Father,' he said, rather too loudly, 'how was the pheasant season last year?'

Grandfather – who hadn't yet acknowledged Hattie at all – chewed loudly. 'I haven't shot a pheasant for a decade, Edward.' He picked up his glass, the wine sloshing on the tablecloth. Hattie looked at Grandmother, but her face was impassive. 'Take your brother out with guns? I hardly think so.'

'Hugo always mentioned the shoot in his Christmas letter . . .'

At the mention of Hugo's name, Grandmother gave a whimper, put a palm to her chest. 'I have an astonishing headache.' She said *astonishing* so theatrically that Hattie wanted to applaud. As she left the table, she neglected to push in her chair, and an eddy of cold air raced into the room as she closed the door behind her. Mama shivered.

Hattie glanced at Albert, trying to catch his eye as they often did across the dinner table in Ambleside. As they had often *done*. But he only stared at his food as though it was somebody else's problem. She had never seen her brother refuse a roast dinner before.

'May I have some wine, please?' he said, mostly to his plate.

Before Papa could reply, Mama passed the carafe of Beaujolais. Albert gulped the last of the water from his cut-crystal glass and replaced it with wine. A small flicker crossed his face, as though he'd just remembered Hattie was at the table. He gave her an unenthusiastic wink. Tiredness pinched at the corners of his bloodshot eyes.

'He's too young,' said Papa, his eyes flicking to Grandmother's empty seat, as though he was afraid she lingered still.

'For heaven's sake,' Mama said. 'He's touched nothing on his plate. He can have something to settle his stomach.' Only Hattie, who sat on Mama's left, heard her mumble, 'And his nerves,' as she refilled her own glass.

Grandfather frowned, his wiry eyebrows dropping low over his blue eyes.

'Nancy,' he said, 'how's the . . . erm . . . writing coming along?'

Mama put down her near-empty glass, caressing it gently before turning towards Grandfather. 'Well, Charles, as you can imagine, I've had to give up my job at the paper.'

'Surely you can write from here? Opinion pieces?'

Mama laughed, then took a large gulp of wine. '*A woman's place may be something, but it's not to give her opinion.* Isn't that what you once told me? Back before. Before Charlo—'

Papa patted his belly theatrically and cut across Mama. 'I haven't had a jot of exercise today. Perhaps we should forgo dessert and move to coffee.' Hattie was the only one who returned his smile.

'Nothing to say, Charles?' Mama refilled her glass. 'Nothing at all?'

Grandfather took a bite of meat. No one else was eating. 'It was nearly twenty years ago. Let it rest. Let *her* rest. This conversation is not for the table.' Only then did he swallow.

Mama pushed her plate aside. 'Not for the table? Like the last time I sat here . . . I remember I said, *You cannot make a girl marry an old man.*' She turned to Hattie. 'I told him that your aunt – *Charlotte*, there I've said her name, seeing as no one else will, Charlotte, Charlotte, Charlotte . . .' Mama's eyes swam, 'I said Charlotte wasn't for barter, and *he* said,' she pointed to the head of the table, '*A woman's place may be something, but it's not to give her opinion.*'

Hattie became hot all over and looked to Papa.

'Nancy, please,' said Papa.

'She was frightened. She wanted to get away.'

'She could never handle the concept of responsibility. Of duty.' Grandfather used a heel of bread to mop up the juices on his plate.

'Duty killed her!' A sob caught in Mama's throat. 'She was just a child.'

Grandfather brought his fist down and the flames on the centrepiece flickered. Hattie's heart pounded. She wanted to cover her ears, yet wanted to hear more. He cleared his throat, composed himself, then said quietly: 'A *child* could never take her own life.'

Mama's hands went to her mouth and she stood. Her gasp left a gap in the argument that required no filling. Then Papa was at her side, his arm around her shoulder. 'Father, I think that's quite enough. We are all exhausted. It's been a difficult journey.'

'It's a filthy lie,' Mama cried. 'The telegram said *Drowned in an accident in the lake*. An accident. It specifically said an accident . . .' She trailed off, looking around the table as though grappling for someone to back her up. When her eyes rested on Papa, he avoided them.

She pulled back. 'Teddy, you think Charlotte *drowned herself?*'

Silence hung over the table. Albert looked back and forth between his parents, his glass poised in mid-air. He drew breath as though to join in the conversation, then stopped.

Papa hesitated. 'I understand that's what the telegram said – an accident – but Hugo wrote to me after the war. It was too staged, Nancy.' He paused. 'I wanted to tell you, but what good would it have done?' Grandfather moved across the room, threw a log on the fire. Papa lowered his voice. 'The marriage to Lord Hawley, she couldn't do it. Hugo believed Charlotte faked the abduction so her . . . suicide wouldn't reflect badly on the family.'

Mama's voice was as sharp and quick as the slap of a hand. '*This* family?' She laughed, a bitter sound. Grandfather stood with his back to the table, his hands held over the crackling flames. She announced to the room: 'What you say can't be true. Because if there was anything that would have given Charlotte the will to live, it would have been to *bring* shame on this family.'

Grandfather didn't turn.

Mama shook her head, 'You're wrong, you're very wrong.' She touched Albert on the shoulder and kissed Hattie's forehead, whispered goodnight. At the threshold, she turned back. 'Charlotte – beautiful Charlotte – cherished life above all else.' As the gentle tread of her footsteps ascended the stairs, a cool breath of winter licked through the open door from the house beyond.

Chapter Ten

Ballinn, County Kerry
September 2019

The village hall was a large building sandwiched between Ballinn's two pubs. Its entrance – a squeezed space grandly called 'the Lobby' – was covered wall-to-wall in notices: yoga practice, a bed for sale, diggers for hire. Forgotten coats hung on hooks and a retro fixed-gear bike sat propped up against a shoe rack. A pile of books for swap or loan sat on a bench as though huddled together for warmth.

The last time Ellie had been to the village hall was as a teenager, when her parents had taken her to a Dramatics Secret Society production. Why the society was secret, she had never found out. The plays were always written by the pharmacist and the starring cast comprised local characters: the doctor, Bernie and several farmers who said their lines with such gusto that the entire audience giggled throughout.

The Lobby opened up into a spacious hall, chairs stacked against its walls, scarlet curtains gathered either side of a stage. A small trestle table and a large box sat in the middle of the room. Aside from the door Ellie had stepped through, the only other one was halfway down the left of the hall, and it swung outwards now as a tray topped with a pot, two cups and a pile of biscuits appeared. It tottered left, then right, before emerging from the doorway to reveal a man who looked like a retiree who'd been playing a nice round of golf in 1975 and been teleported to the future.

Ellie took in his appearance with no small measure of relief. Not a set-up, then.

'Ellie!' he said. 'Delighted you could make it.' He deposited the tray on the trestle table. His peach-and-cream argyle sweater was even more alarming without the cover of morning tea. Or was it lunch? Ellie checked her watch: nearly one o'clock.

'Jules Bristole?' She followed him to the table.

His handshake was firm. 'The very one.' He had a mop of white hair and eyebrows that could do with a trim. Ellie couldn't help but look down at his trousers; they were a shade of seventies brown. 'Your mother tells me you've found a very interesting letter.' He poured, then raised his eyebrows and the two cups in unison. His cheeks were speckled with very fine freckles. Or was that . . . *mud*?

She sat, and he eagerly took a place opposite, leaning forward with an expectant expression. 'Actually,' she said, 'I've just returned from Blackwater Hall, but Albert – Lord Rathmore – he . . . isn't well. He wouldn't accept the letter.'

'You have it here?' She could almost see his fingers tingling.

'Yes.' But she made no move to take it out. She peered suspiciously into her drink, but took a sip anyway, to fill the gap. 'This is good,' she said. Part surprise, part relief.

'Yorkshire Tea,' said Jules. 'Don't tell the locals.'

Ellie laughed. So, she thought, this particular blow-in was well versed in tea politics at least. She appraised him. 'You're from Sussex?'

His cup, lifted halfway to his mouth, teetered dangerously from horizontal. 'Born and bred. Your mother told you that?'

She shook her head. 'I had a colleague from Brighton. You sound just like him.' She leaned back. 'Trust me, Jules, if Mum knew *any* juicy details about you, I'd have heard them already. In long form. And several times.'

He began to say something, then smiled. Two dimples formed on his cheeks. They sat in companionable silence.

'So . . .' She dipped into her pocket and produced the envelope, spread the paper in front of him.

Jules took out a case containing a pair of round glasses. He perched them on the end of his nose and read the letter with a look of such anticipation Ellie wondered if he expected it to leap to life and spill its secrets. 'Poor Charlotte,' he murmured when he reached the end. 'Poor, poor Charlotte. When I heard about the letter . . .'

She frowned. 'Yes, when *did* you hear about the letter?'

'Your mum called this morning.' Moira had pointedly said Bernie had told him. Ellie narrowed her eyes. He continued. 'When I heard about the letter, I remembered something about that name.'

'Oh?'

'Charlotte was Lord Albert's aunt.'

'What?' This was a surprise.

'Yes, it's in here.' He leaned over and hefted a box onto the table. From it he took a slip of a book: *Ballinn: A History, A Legacy.* 'So I went back to check the details.'

Details. That was what Jeremy had said to her, back when he'd been overruled. *We'd have a chance of publication if there were more details. Places, times, witnesses. When and where did Cray and McCarthy meet?* She'd asked Cray's secretary, who said whole sections of his calendar were often blocked out. 'For one of his mistresses, I assumed,' she'd said bitterly. 'I don't have the *details.*'

Jules opened the book to a dog-eared page. 'Lady Charlotte Rathmore; she grew up at Blackwater Hall. Then . . .' He turned the page to face her.

In August 1940, tragedy struck the Rathmore family. Charlotte Rathmore was reported missing and staff gathered to search the estate. At 3 p.m. the gardaí were called. A string of pearls, reportedly Charlotte's eighteenth birthday present, was found broken and scattered by the lough and a wooden rowboat was missing from the boathouse. The search continued into the night, assisted by volunteers from Ballinn, where Charlotte was well known for her charitable endeavours. In the early hours of the morning the boat was found on the Atoon river, containing an oar caked in blood. The lough was dragged but Charlotte's body was never found. Two known IRA collaborators were arrested and questioned, later released without charge. The case remains open. She was nineteen years old.

Ellie blinked once, twice. Charlotte had disappeared the same month she wrote the letter, August 1940. She turned back a page, scanning it for details of Blackwater Hall and the Rathmore family, but there was little more than the paragraph she'd read the evening before, the house's two hundred years of history swept aside in a few disparate sentences.

'It's a great investigation for a journalist,' said Jules.

She looked up. 'What?'

'A wonderful mystery to get your teeth into. A letter from someone who disappeared.' This last said with wide eyes.

'Jules,' she said, 'cold cases aren't really my cup of tea.' She put aside her drink.

'Charlotte's words . . . they must interest you?'

Interest me? If she'd found this letter two months ago, the pull would have been irresistible. But that was *before*. 'The last time I investigated a scandal I lost my job and my . . .' She stopped short and pushed the letter towards him, felt grief tug at her heart, in her belly. 'Please, take it. Give it to Albert's son. Put it in your files. Do whatever you think is best.'

'These aren't *my* files, Ellie. They're Brigid Sullivan's. Took loan of them last month. What a find!'

Despite herself, Ellie said, 'Brigid who?'

Jules closed the book and tapped its cover. There was the name, Brigid Sullivan, author of *Ballinn: A History, A Legacy.* 'She was once the last word on local history. Her daughter didn't inherit her passion, but she did inherit her belongings.'

What was it Albert had said . . . *She planned to put some of the family history in a book. Brigid someone? A handsome woman.* Ellie turned to the back cover. There she was, Brigid; green eyes, dark hair. Handsome? Yes, in a permed, austere kind of way. She flicked to the title page: published 1958.

Jules withdraw a photo from the box and placed it before Ellie.

She couldn't help but look.

It was a soft-focus black-and-white portrait of a beautiful girl. Doe eyes that looked to the upper right of the frame, thick dark lashes. Though she wasn't smiling, faint ghosts of dimples brushed her cheeks. She had unlined, translucent skin and the top of her blonde hair was swept into two rolls, one pinned with a comb that stood proud of her head.

Ellie turned the photo over. *Lady Charlotte Rathmore, July 1940.*

Jules said, 'She was born in 1921. Daughter to Charles and Niamh Rathmore. Sister to Hugo and Edward.' He turned his notebook towards her. 'I've been putting together a family tree.'

Looking anywhere but at the photo, Ellie said, 'That's great.' Daughter to Charles and Niamh. *Grandma Niamh?* Albert had remembered *her* well enough.

Jules continued, 'Brigid wrote that the gardaí thought the

IRA was involved, which seems plausible. A wealthy girl. Probably Protestant. Potential for ransom.'

Ellie raised an eyebrow. 'But considering that the letter and the disappearance were in the same month . . .'

'They must be connected?'

'Given Charlotte's words, I can't think otherwise.' Because she *had* thought about them. Turned the letter over in her mind as she went to sleep. Conjured it as she woke. But it was one thing to think about Charlotte Rathmore and quite another to investigate her.

Jules nodded, lost in his notebook. 'They were, I suppose, difficult times.' He looked up. 'When did de Valera outlaw the IRA?'

'Just before the war, I think.'

He opened a second notebook. Two dozen Post-it notes marked the pages. 'June 1939. And three months later Ireland declared neutrality.' He spread his hands. 'Appease the IRA on one hand, keep the Germans at bay on the other. And dance a tango with Chamberlain, who was furious about the ports.'

Ellie bristled. 'Sweden and Norway declared neutrality too . . .'

'But in this country it was all so complicated.' Jules said this as though he relished the complexity rather than resented it. 'There was still rationing. Seventy thousand Irish fought for the British. And thousands more went to work in Britain, chasing wages.'

'And adventure,' said Ellie, thinking of Charlotte's words: *What an adventure, really. I have it all planned.* She leaned forward and frowned. 'She says, *You knew my feelings.* She must have been intimate with the person she was writing to. This *T.* But the letter seems both last-minute *and* calculated. I think . . . I think she couldn't wait to get where she was going.' She picked up Charlotte's portrait; that far-away gaze looking off camera, out of frame, into another place . . .

The thud of the Lobby door made her jump. She turned and saw a large, bright shape crossing the hall. Multicoloured fabrics, a huge grin. 'Bernie!' she said, feeling that same sense of relief she had the day before.

Bernie dragged a chair across the hall with a screech. 'Your mammy said you were here.' She nodded to each of them. 'I was up with Tabby Ryan. I tell you, Ellie, if I could be half as lively as her, I'd be delighted with myself.' Tabby Ryan was a former school teacher and fixture of the community. 'She was on mighty form.' Bernie sat herself next to Ellie, rather close. Then she leaned over and read the letter.

'So yer wan ran off?'

'Planned to at least,' said Ellie. 'Was she ever found?'

'Not that I know of.' Bernie picked up Charlotte's portrait. 'Ink House is on the border of the parish; hard to know if its gossip belongs to us or Kenmare. Don't want to be treading on any toes.'

Ellie looked down at Bernie's feet. They were huge. 'No,' she said.

'And you've been up to Albert?'

'Yes, he wasn't . . . well.'

'No.' Bernie was less concerned than Ellie had expected. 'I dropped up to the hall a couple of months ago. Thought he might want Meals on Wheels.' She paused. 'I was also a bit curious about the house. Went there once as a child, wanted to see it again. He agreed to take a meal a week.'

'Good, I was worried.'

'And now that the son's here, the old place has spruced up a bit.'

Ellie wondered how it had looked before. 'The son? He exists?'

Bernie gave her a look. 'As real as you or me.' She turned back to the letter. 'Still, Charlotte probably disappeared before Lord Albert was born. But hard to say. I only know about it because of the poem.'

Ellie frowned. 'What poem?'

'That ditty,' said Bernie, 'the one you kids used to run around chanting. Haven't heard it for a decade.' She looked to the ceiling, nodded her head:

> *'Grab your boots and leave your drink,*
> *Take your torches to the Ink,*
> *Search high and low among the reeds,*
> *Find a string of pearly beads,*
> *Tell me ye, what will it take . . .'*

She paused, gestured to Ellie, who nodded her head in time: 'To find the Lady of the Lake?'

'You remember?' said Bernie.

'I remember something of it. I thought it was about a mermaid.'

'Oh, Ellie!'

Jules scribbled in his notebook.

'And this . . .' Bernie touched the letter's header. It was smeared with a deep brown smudge. '*Wynn's* something . . . well, that could be Wynn's Castle.'

'Where?' said Jules frantically, as though his exams were coming up and he'd forgotten to study a module.

'It's in Glenbeigh,' said Ellie quietly. She'd been there once, as a child. And she'd never returned. Couldn't bring herself to. The trip had been with her father.

'Owned by Lord Heaney, I think,' said Bernie.

'Heaney?' said Jules.

Bernie frowned. 'Yes, I think so. Or was it Healy? Something like that.'

Jules laid out another photo. 'I also found this, taken at Blackwater Hall.'

It was a formal shot of a group of people arranged in two lines; one seated, one standing. There was a distinct difference in the dress style and poise of the two rows. Jules ran his finger along the seated figures. 'This is the family.' He traced the standing row behind them. 'And staff.'

Ellie turned the photo over. *Summer Party, 12th August 1939.* A list of names was written across the bottom. She returned to the image, searching for Charlotte.

'Here she is.' Jules pointed to a girl seated at the far left of the photo.

'And,' said Bernie, frowning, 'this is Edward – or Teddy, as he was known – Charlotte's brother.' He was fair and had the same dark oval eyes as his sister. His hand was raised near his face, as though he had been about to push a flop of hair from his eyes. 'I met him that time I visited the house as a child.'

Ellie raised her eyebrows. 'Teddy?' She turned the letter to face her. *My dearest T.*

Jules followed her gaze and nodded, scribbled down Teddy's name. Then he moved his finger along the line of seated aristocrats. 'This is Lord Charles Rathmore, and Lady Niamh Rathmore . . . and their elder son, and heir, Hugo.'

Between Charlotte and Teddy sat a woman, her long legs tucked neatly under her. Her face was beautifully framed with arched eyebrows and wavy hair. The masculine Pied Piper hat she wore dropped low over her right eye, one hand up to steady it, and her head tipped towards Charlotte. Ellie looked closer. 'Who's this?'

Jules said, 'That's Teddy's wife, Nancy.'

Ellie frowned, thinking of the third cup Albert had poured,

the one she had thought was for his mother. 'Charlotte looks worried,' she said, then regretted reading so much into an expression captured eighty years before.

Jules surprised her by saying: 'Yes, I agree.'

'Well, none of them really look all that delighted,' said Bernie, her attention beginning to wane.

Ellie studied the two women, Charlotte and Nancy. Nancy's hand rested on Charlotte's and they were looking halfway between each other and the photographer, as though they had been interrupted sharing a secret. The formality of Charlotte's long dress looked dated compared to the below-the-knee pencil skirt that Nancy wore.

'Are they the same age?' she asked.

'According to Ms Sullivan' – Jules consulted his notebook – 'Nancy was born in 1914. Seven years before Charlotte.'

'It doesn't say any more about her?'

'No,' said Jules. 'The Rathmore story is a tiny part of the book; just those few paragraphs.'

Ellie thought back to her visit to the house that morning. 'Lord Albert said that when his grandmother – Niamh – renovated Blackwater Hall, she . . . decluttered. So perhaps Brigid didn't have much to work with.' She paused. 'And anyway, people round here are probably not so interested in reading about landed gentry.'

Bernie added, 'It's a bit of a sore point.'

'I see what you mean . . .' Jules looked down at his notebook, deflated.

'Doesn't mean the Rathmores' history isn't important,' Ellie said quickly. She looked between them. 'How old is this historical society anyway?'

Jules rallied. 'This is our first meeting.'

'I see.'

'It's just us three so far,' he added.

Ellie was alarmed. 'Thank you, Jules, but I—' she said at the very same time Bernie offered, 'Ah, listen, I'm not dilly-dallying, I only dropped in because Moira called me—'

Both of them stopped at the man's crestfallen face. Then Bernie stood and muttered, 'I'll get some fresh tea,' while Ellie busied herself with studying the hall's high windows.

After a moment, she said, 'How long have you lived in Ballinn, Jules?'

He flushed. 'A year. I visited last summer, took up a friend's offer of a cottage near Derrynane Beach. I stayed for three weeks, and when I returned to London, well, it felt . . .' he paused, 'empty. I tried to keep up with my old life, even though I'd retired.' He took off his glasses, set them on the table. 'I was a lawyer for forty years. My whole world was work. And when that finished, I really had nothing. I never married. Never had children. Everything I did was for my own benefit.'

'I'm sorry.'

He rubbed his eyes and replaced his glasses. 'Kerry stuck in my mind. The peace. The space. The lack of trying to be someone I wasn't any more. So I just came back.'

'You'd be surprised how many stories like that there are around here,' said Ellie. From Killarney to Kenmare, Kerry's hills were littered with blow-ins, running to – or escaping from – another life. She thought of Bernie's kindness in putting aside the books, the comfort of her mum's home, the feeling of rolling back into the village after Dublin spat her out the other side.

He smiled with satisfaction. 'My old colleagues wouldn't recognise me. And a good thing too. I feel renewed. I want to do something that isn't on the clock. Something interesting. Something that matters.'

'Why do you think *this*' – Ellie touched the portrait in front of her – 'matters?'

He rotated the summer party shot so it faced her. 'Look at Charlotte again.'

Warily she leaned in. Charlotte's face *was* marred with worry. Or was it sadness? Perhaps Nancy had reached across to comfort her . . .

Ellie gasped. 'Jules, look at her hand!' A white bandage, half obscured under Nancy's grip, was wrapped from her wrist to her fingertips.

He nodded. 'At first I thought it was a glove, but it's not, is it?'

'No.'

'I don't think Charlotte looks worried . . . I think she looks *afraid*.'

'You're reading too much into this.' But she knew Jules was right. Charlotte Rathmore had been afraid.

When Bernie returned, she said, 'I've checked the whole kitchen . . . nothing but this muck.' She plonked the Yorkshire Tea down with a huff. 'I take it this is yours?' The Englishman grimaced.

Ellie glanced at her watch. It was twenty to two. 'Look,' she said, getting to her feet, 'I have to go. I need to drop into the doctor's surgery. Here . . .' She pushed Charlotte's letter towards Jules, towards Bernie, towards anyone but herself. 'I think it's best if one of you takes this.'

Jules looked up. 'What about this son of Albert's . . . Milo, is it?'

Ellie's hand lingered on the back of the chair. 'Did I mention his name?'

'Of course!' said Bernie, butting in; she and Jules once again aligned. 'You could drop the letter off while you're there.'

'And,' Jules said, riding the wave of Bernie's enthusiasm, 'while you're at it, you can ask him to look into the surgery records. See if the local doctor attended Charlotte in the summer of 1939.'

Ellie narrowed her eyes. 'While I'm where? Why would Albert's son have access to the surgery records?'

Jules closed his notebook. 'Milo Rathmore is the new locum.'

'Please tell me you're joking.'

A satisfied smile was plastered on Bernie's face.

Ellie shook her head and snatched the letter from the table. 'You two,' she pointed at each of them, 'you're both as bad as my mother.'

'I'll take that as a compliment,' said Jules as he put the boxes away in a trunk beside the stage, the meeting evidently over. His hand hovered over Charlotte's photo. 'Here,' he said, placing it in her hand. 'Look after that for now.' She began to argue. He cut her short. 'Just for now.'

Bernie was off, out the door. 'Places to be,' she shouted back over her shoulder. 'I'll see you Saturday.'

Ellie called, 'Saturday?'

Bernie paused, her hand resting on the door frame. 'It's Tabby Ryan's one hundredth birthday. Here in the hall. Open invite.' She looked at Jules. 'Even blow-ins are welcome.'

Ellie paused. Moira *had* mentioned something about a hooley; a whole village-worth of people chatting, asking questions. 'I hadn't planned on going.'

'Really?' said Bernie. 'Is that so?'

'It is.'

'Because,' she continued, 'you should know that Tabby worked up at the big house, at Blackwater Hall, before the war. I imagine she knew Charlotte. Before she . . . disappeared.' And then, with a speed that belied her size, Bernie was gone.

Jules followed Ellie out. He went to the shoe rack in the Lobby and lifted the fixed-gear bike she had thought long abandoned.

'You ride that thing?' she said.

'My new toy,' said Jules as they spilled onto the street. 'As I said, my old colleagues wouldn't recognise me.' He swung his leg over the saddle and pushed away from the kerb, calling over his shoulder: 'Don't forget to ask Milo about your girl.'

Your girl, she wanted to shout after him, but he was already halfway down the street.

Chapter Eleven

Ballinn, County Kerry
September 2019

'Hi,' Ellie said. Then, again, 'Hello?'

'Ah.' Dr Milo Rathmore looked up from his computer and Ellie paused, one hand on the door. *This* was Albert's son? She had expected a frump. Someone much older. Excessive amounts of tweed.

'Eleanor Fitzgerald? Please, take a seat.'

'Thank you. And call me Ellie, please.' She smiled, but his eyes had already swung back to the screen, his hand on the mouse. All business. 'You haven't been into this clinic for' – he raised an eyebrow – 'seventeen years?'

'I'm back from Dublin. For a bit.' She clasped her hands in her lap. 'Just visiting.'

'I see.' He had that manner of speaking that forced rather than invited the other party to fill the silence.

'It's been a tough few months. Work isn't going well and . . .' She wanted to add *and other things*, but Dr Rathmore began to type, irritating her immensely. 'And I'd like a bit of help with . . .'

Tap, tap, tap. His hair was dusky blond.

She paused. 'Are you listening to me?'

'I am.' His face softened a little. He pushed the keyboard

aside and placed his palms flat on the table; the gesture, she supposed, was meant to be reassuring.

She hesitated. The room was hot – stifling – and she unzipped her jacket.

He waited. 'You were saying?'

But her conviction was gone. She had come to the medical centre with the vague notion of finding a temporary solution to her troubles in pill form. Now she was here, she wanted nothing more than to leave. Was it Dr Rathmore's bedside manner? Or perhaps the image of Albert's shaking hands . . . did she blame the man sitting in front of her for not being there to steady them? She cleared her throat, sat a little straighter. 'I'm having trouble sleeping,' she said. It was true. But not the whole truth.

'Okay.' He leaned back. 'This is a recent concern?'

'The last couple of months.'

He nodded. 'Has anything changed for you in that time?'

Everything, she wanted to say. 'I . . .' She paused. 'I've had a lot on my mind.' *Grief. Such grief.* She bit her lower lip.

He appraised her, let the silence linger. Then said, 'Professional problems?'

Grateful for the way out, she said, 'I've lost my job.'

'What do you do?'

'Journalist.'

He tapped something into her notes. 'Have you lost weight?'

'Hardly.' The word came out as *hoardly*, as she reverted to Dublin's rounded vowels. 'Mum's cooking is quite . . . whole-some.'

Tap, tap, tap.

Ellie's fingers prickled with annoyance. This was not what she'd envisaged when she'd finally plucked up the courage to make an appointment. 'I just want a few nights of uninter-rupted sleep.' She spread her hands in a manner that said, *Is that so much to ask?* There were shadows under her eyes; slugs crawling beneath her skin.

He nodded. 'And exercise?'

'Yoga, a few times a week,' she lied, trying to remember the last time she'd touched her toes.

'Have you been prescribed sleeping tablets before?'

'No.' She looked at her fingernails; they were down to the quick.

If he had been wearing glasses, this would be the point he removed them. 'How's life at home?'

'It's fine. If I avoid Mum's bookshelf.' She laughed, but he only gave her a small smile.

'I meant your *other* home. In Dublin?'

Ellie became acutely aware of the door behind her and how desperately she wanted to be on the other side of it. 'Nothing to report.'

'You seem a little hesitant . . .'

'I don't know what you mean.'

'Ellie, is something worrying you? Something you haven't mentioned?'

She bit her bottom lip in contemplation. 'Not that I can think of.' She appraised him; his eyes were a vivid green, crinkled at the edges, the suggestion of a sense of humour she couldn't imagine.

He dug in a drawer and pulled out a brochure. 'There's a great mental health support group here in Ballinn . . .'

She recoiled in horror. 'I don't need to talk to anyone . . .' News of her life would spread like wildfire.

He appeared to understand her concern. 'There's also a weekly clinic in Kenmare.'

The forty-five-minute drive between Ballinn and Kenmare was nowhere near enough. 'No,' she said firmly. They stared at each other across the table.

He looked away. 'Okay, Ellie. I'm going to give you some-thing mild to help you sleep, but I'd like to check in with you again, maybe this time next week?' Before she could argue, he continued, 'In the meantime, returning home to live with a parent—'

'For a bit.'

'For a bit,' he conceded, 'can also be . . . difficult.' He paused. 'Make sure you're getting enough space. Enough exercise. And stay off the caffeine, if you can.'

'Okay,' was all she said.

Across the room, the printer whirred. Dr Rathmore stood to collect the prescription. He was taller than she'd expected, and the fit of his dark blue chinos distracted her for a moment.

She cleared her throat. 'Actually, I have something else I wanted to mention . . .'

'Yes?' He turned back to her.

She cursed Jules inwardly. 'Or rather, not so much mention as give . . .'

He folded the prescription into an envelope and took his seat once again. 'Go on.'

She pulled the letter from her pocket. 'This is a bit awkward, but seeing as I'd already planned to drop in today . . .'

He raised his brows; under them his eyes looked tired.

'I met your father this morning. Albert.'

Dr Rathmore blinked once, twice. A flicker of something crossed his face. Annoyance? More than annoyance? Anger?

'It seems to me he needs . . . help.'

'Yes.'

She paused. 'You agree?'

'I do, and I'm working on it.'

'Only he did seem very . . . confused,' she pushed.

Dr Rathmore took a deep breath. 'My father is in the early stages of dementia . . .'

'I'm sorry.'

'. . . as I'm sure you've surmised. He refuses to have anyone stay in the house but family. Hence' – he spread his hands wide – 'me. Here. Now.' He looked at his watch. 'In fact, I need to be getting back.'

'You're *staying* at Blackwater Hall?' She felt a pang of guilt at how quickly she had judged him.

He barely managed a smile. 'Like you, Ellie, I'm back. For a bit.' He let the end of his sentence hang. Then he said, 'I'd rather you didn't call to the house.'

Her guilt melted in an instant, and in one movement she took the envelope from him and replaced the space between his fingers with Charlotte's letter. 'I wanted to give him this.'

He unfolded the paper, ran his eyes over the contents, his expression changing from a frown to surprise and then . . . yes, then, right at the end, when he read the last words . . . fear? The letter fluttered to the table as he stood. 'Your prescription.' He went to the printer, paused by the empty tray.

She held it up. 'I already have it, thank you.'

His back still turned, he said, 'Where did you get that letter?'

'From the books you dropped at the charity shop.'

'I see.' He straightened a few papers, then returned to the desk. 'Thank you. I'm sure we can find somewhere to file it. I'll talk to Harriet.'

'Your aunt?' *Albert's sister.*

The look of surprise on his face was quickly wiped away. 'Yes.'

She continued, 'You know your *great*-aunt, Charlotte, disappeared in 1940?'

'I'm vaguely aware of that, yes.'

'Well,' said Ellie, 'this letter was written that same month.' He glanced at the paper again. Was that the tiniest flicker of interest? 'There's a local man, Jules Bristole, he's intrigued by the contents.'

'Why?'

Ellie frowned. 'He's starting a historical society.' *Is that a crime now?*

'Well, I'm afraid I don't know anything about Charlotte.' Case closed. He started for the door.

Ellie turned in her seat. 'I've seen a photo of her from 1939, and in it her hand is bandaged. I was . . .' she corrected herself, '*Jules* was wondering . . . is there a possibility Charlotte was being mistreated?'

He half laughed. It wasn't full of warmth, but his relief was evident. 'That's a bit of a leap.'

She began to laugh along with him – *silly Jules* – but as soon as she started, he stopped. Clearing her throat, she said, 'Dr Rathmore, according to the plaque outside, this surgery was set up in 1889.'

'If you say so.'

'So you could always – for the benefit of this historical society – look into the records for August 1939, see if the local doctor attended Charlotte.'

'I absolutely won't be doing that.'

'Why not?'

'Patient confidentiality.'

'It was eighty years ago!'

'Look,' said Dr Rathmore, now waiting by the open door, 'I appreciate the society's interest. I'm sure you're all fascinated, but I can't see any reason to hang so much on a photo and a dubious letter that may or may not be from my great-aunt.' He turned towards the hallway.

Ellie flushed. Charlotte was his relation, she'd lived at Blackwater Hall, she'd disappeared from the house under the very noses of his great-grandparents. Her own reluctance to investigate was understandable, she reasoned, but his was inexcusable.

She hesitated for only a second. While his back was turned, she carefully took Charlotte's letter from the table and slipped it into her pocket. *For Jules.* 'Thank you, Dr Rathmore.' She breezed past him with an air of nonchalance. 'You've been incredibly helpful.' The thought of never seeing him again gave her a jolt of pleasure.

As though he'd read her mind, he said, 'I'll follow up with you next week.'

She faltered, paused in the doorway. They were standing close. 'You'll look into the records?'

'Not quite.' He held out his hand. 'Same day, same time suit you?'

Ellie glared at him, and any shame she felt for stealing the letter dissolved. 'I'll check my diary,' she said as she spun on her heel, out of the stifling medical centre and onto Ballinn's main street.

Chapter Twelve

Ballinn, County Kerry

July 1939

They stood on Ballinn's main street.

'You want to go where?' Nancy looked at Charlotte. Was she obliged to return the girl to Blackwater Hall before the sun went down? Her relationship with her parents-in-law was already fractured almost beyond repair.

'To the rambling house.'

For a week, Nancy had tiptoed around the Rathmore household, tucked herself away in the library, or out in the gardens when the sun shone. Charlotte's situation with Lord Hawley was bringing out the worst in her, and for six days she'd bitten back remarks she knew she would later regret. If she voiced her true feelings about the proposed marriage, the schism between her and the Rathmore family would rupture. Still, she thought, at least that would solve a problem; she would never have to return to Blackwater Hall.

But there was Charlotte to consider, and being absent was no support at all. 'It's time to go back,' she said, hating that she sounded like an overbearing friend. Or a high-handed mother.

'Nonsense. You'll absolutely adore it.' Charlotte flashed a cheeky smile. 'I promise.' She placed her hand on her heart.

Nancy knew the key to Charlotte's promises lay in the fine

print. She always had an ulterior motive hidden up her silken sleeves and Nancy was beginning to understand just how cunning her sister-in-law had become.

Charlotte produced a pout that could soften steel. 'A *seanchaí* is coming tonight . . .'

Nancy gave her a look of fear. '*Seanchaí*? Is that something revolutionary?'

'A storyteller.' Charlotte waved a pale hand. 'It'll only be a few tales and maybe a dash of *poitín*.'

Nancy put her hand to her forehead. It felt warm.

Charlotte winked. 'I'll only have a wee dropeen.'

Nancy didn't know where to begin. 'Charlotte . . . if your mother heard you . . .' She shook her head.

They had paused outside the village hall. The Lobby – as it was grandly called in Ballinn – had spat them out and the Dramatics Secret Society was dispersing. The evening had been full of surprises. Nancy had never been one for the stage; she preferred to build stories in her head, scooped up from the pages of the novels in which she was usually lost. She rarely went anywhere without a book – she'd brought *Death on the Nile* to the hall – and Teddy complained that Agatha Christie would have been present at their wedding if it hadn't been such a small affair. She'd expected to sit, discreetly reading, while Charlotte herded a gaggle of giggling girls into order. But she had underestimated the talent of the locals.

As they'd arrived, she'd recalled the society was no longer made up solely of girls, and those who had joined the artistic ranks were not just boys, but *men*. She had never had a wandering eye, but the broad-shouldered lads with their dark Celtic hair that made Charlotte's fairness so stand out were hardly going to make the evening difficult to bear. Their accents were thick and delicious and they had a natural talent for entertaining. They could read a verse, crack a joke or create a character without a script or a note to be seen. It was all in their heads, a part of their culture, a rich upbringing in homes without wealth. And when one young man took to the stage to sing all alone, the magical rhythm of his voice sent a shiver down Nancy's spine. As though someone had walked over her grave.

She looked down the road. 'Well, if your mother is quite so reclusive . . .'

'Frightfully people-shy . . .'

What was the harm? A few stories. A chat. A break from the house was just what she needed. She placed a hand on her stomach. Protected the secret inside her.

She could always forgo the *poitín*.

❧

The two women followed a rough track to the house. It was edged with fuchsias, red-purple flowers dripping from the foliage like blood from a pinprick. The soft light of the summer evening had faded fast and Cottah Mountain was bathed in shadow. Nancy was pleased that Blackwater Hall sat somewhere behind that summit.

Gentle puffs of smoke rose from the chimney ahead and the scent of peat hung in the air. A single magpie sat on the roof looking down at them. As the cottage door opened, the faint smell of cooking was chased out of the house by laughter. Nancy followed Charlotte over the threshold, her vision adjusting as she stepped inside.

The conversation stopped when they entered and a dozen pairs of eyes turned to them. Those assembled were scattered, squeezed, into the tiny cottage's lower floor. A stairway led to a sleeping level above. Four kerosene lamps lit the space and Nancy was shocked to see that the floor was made of neatly swept packed earth. There wasn't a soft furnishing to be seen.

Everything in the house was at a slight angle, as though, over time, the wicked Kerry winds had played a trick and nudged the house little by little so the occupants had never noticed.

A young woman stepped forward and waved her hand at the gathered group in a way that said *mind your manners*. Nancy recognised her as the maid from Blackwater Hall. They'd spoken briefly; she was a bright girl who responded eagerly to questions, words tumbling out of her until – abruptly – she would stop, then excuse herself to continue her work, demure as a mouse. As though she had suddenly remembered where she was, who she worked for, and quickly packed away her personality to get back to the task at hand.

'Tabby,' said Charlotte, taking the girl in a hug. Nancy had never seen them interact at the house, and it highlighted the double life that Charlotte now led.

'*Céad míle fáilte.* Welcome.' Tabby took Nancy's hands in her own – it was an unexpected intimacy, and Nancy blushed. 'We didn't think you'd come.' She wore a bright red blouse, at odds with the dimness of the room.

Charlotte said, 'It was her idea, wasn't it, Trouble?' Nancy bit back a protest. Charlotte had let slip her new name to Teddy, who had taken to it with gusto. *A cup of coffee, Trouble? A walk by the lough, Trouble? Come to bed for some trouble, Trouble.* 'She came to tonight's Dramatics Secret Society and—'

'And now half of the Dramatics Secret Society is here.' Tabby turned her head. A long birthmark ran down the left side of her neck. 'They're getting notions about the Abbey Theatre.' She said *notions* with one raised eyebrow and more than half a smile.

Several familiar faces sat huddled around a lamp, heads together, a picture of collusion. A boy lifted his gaze, grinned. It was Charlotte's turn to flush. She tucked a loose strand of hair behind her ear, then winked at Tabby, and when the young woman laughed, the room fell back into chatter. A little of Nancy's apprehension melted away, but something remained, a wayward thought, a niggling doubt that she'd just become complicit in something she didn't want to know about.

꒰ꙮ꒱

The group that sat around the table were fascinated with Nancy's tales of London, a world apart from their own. Suddenly she'd become the entertainer and they the audience. The talk soon turned to theatre.

'Ye've been to the Adelphi?'

Once. The view from her seat was half obscured. Teddy's was worse. 'It was wonderful. *Bobby Get Your Gun.*'

'Isn't there a Gaiety Theatre in London too? Like Dublin?'

'There is.'

One of the girls laughed. 'Can the English not think of their own names?'

Someone else: 'How'd I go at getting a job there?'

'At the Gaiety?' Nancy shifted.

'In London.'

'You need to be smart,' laughed one lad. 'Speak proper.'

'Broken Irish is better than clever English,' quipped another, downing the last of his *poitín*. He stopped short, tipped his glass at Nancy, coloured.

She fell into the moment, said with a certain Kerry self-deprecation: 'If I can get a job, *sure*, anyone can.'

Her inflection was appreciated and she felt a shift around the table, a relaxation. 'What kind of a job?' It was the young man with the singing voice that had, only an hour before, sent shivers down her spine. He sat on the other side of Charlotte.

'I'm just a secretary.'

'Soon she'll be a journalist. And write a novel.'

Nancy waved Charlotte's words away. There was a raucous

laugh at the other end of the house; some private storytelling, it seemed, had already begun. It broke the group's concentration, conversations spilling off to either side.

He prompted: 'A novel?'

'Maybe.' Nancy blushed. 'I tried once, but . . .' She let it hang.

'The next time,' he said, 'will be better. And then better again after that.' Something in the pit of Nancy's stomach flipped at this unexpected encouragement. 'Here, we say *hindsight is the best insight to foresight.*'

'Stealing more of my words of wisdom, Tomas?' Tabby was there, grinning. She put two cups on the table. '*Poitín.* And tea.' When Charlotte proffered her cup – *a taste?* – Nancy shook her head and took her own drink, wrapping her hands around it, though they were perfectly warm.

Charlotte nodded to Tabby. 'These two are brother and sister. Can you tell?' Nancy could. Tomas and Tabby. They had the same eyes; as green as the emerald fields that surrounded the village and rolled to the sea. 'And both work at the house.'

Nancy had never seen Tomas there. She was embarrassed at her ignorance.

As if sensing her discomfort, he said, 'I've been working in the copse since you arrived, helping my father. He's the gardener.' She *had* seen him, repairing the boathouse the day she'd met Charlotte by the sweet peas. She sipped her drink, nodded, tried to think of a question about the copse, to turn the conversation towards him. The fire behind them puffed smoke mostly up the chimney and the smell of peat was heavy in the air. On the griddle, flatbreads browned, and a steaming kettle hung from a fire arm.

Charlotte said, 'Tomas can tell you everything you ever wanted to know about coppicing.' Nancy raised an eyebrow, waited. 'And history.'

'He'll talk the ear off you,' said Tabby. Tomas raised his hands in surrender; his smile was cheeky, handsome.

'But it's so important,' Charlotte sipped her *poitín*, 'to understand how shackled Ireland once was. Still is.'

Sensing an impending lecture on the evils of aristocracy, Nancy said, 'We do need to know where we come from' – she recognised the irony in what she'd said – 'but we shouldn't let it hinder us.' She paused. *'Hindsight is the best insight to foresight.'*

Tomas flushed at the pleasure of being quoted, and Tabby gave her brother a playful shove before taking a seat beside him. 'We've got a treat in store for you tonight, Nancy.'

'Oh?'

She took a crumpled piece of paper from her pocket. 'I've been asked to recite some poetry.'

Tomas peered at the words she held in her hands. 'What's that?'

'Poetry,' she said with impatience.

'It doesn't rhyme.'

'No, it doesn't.' This conversation had clearly been had before.

'What's the point of that?'

'You eejit,' said Tabby. 'Poetry is a painting in words. It needn't rhyme. It *shouldn't* rhyme.'

'Airs and graces.' Tomas took a drag of his drink, then almost lost it as Tabby elbowed him with a laugh. He wiped his mouth with his sleeve. 'Go on, write a rhyme.'

'No.'

'Go on.'

'I'll tell you what, Tomas, I'll write you a verse on my hundredth birthday, how's that for you? A promise . . . to Tomas.'

He raised an eyebrow and Charlotte giggled, a flush creeping up her neck. Warmth from the drink, warmth from the room. Warmth from the company. Tomas said, 'It's a deal. You can enlighten everyone with your favourite proverbs.' He put out his hand and they shook on it. 'Only eighty years to wait,' he said with glee.

Around them, a hush descended and all eyes turned to the door. A small, wiry man stood there. He had unruly eyebrows that threatened to escape his face.

'The *seanchaí*,' whispered Charlotte unnecessarily.

He observed his audience, clearly revelling in the rapt attention, then broke the silence with a word: 'Splendid.' Then he stepped before the fire and began to speak. 'My brother fell in love with a German. I suppose it's happened before and it will happen again. They married, see. In the end. But in the beginning, things weren't so rosy . . .'

Nancy took a sip of her tea and stole a glance at Charlotte. She was leaning forward, the glow of the fire playing on her face, her mouth slightly parted. Her hair was flyaway; it had been ruffled by someone – one of the boys? – at the village hall, and strands had escaped her half-up do. She wore, as always, her butterfly comb, its jewels flickering in the muted amber light. And when she turned to Nancy, raised her half-empty glass of *poitín*, the smile she gave was as soft and warm as the first throes of love.

Chapter Thirteen

Blackwater Hall, County Kerry

February 1958

'But I *want* to learn.'

'You're too young.'

Hattie stomped her feet as she walked, a tree root catching her toe. 'It's because I'm a *girl*.'

'No.' Mama stopped on the rough track that led around the lough. The grey of the morning had stolen the blue from her eyes. She softened. 'When you're Albert's age, Papa will teach you too.'

'That's six years away . . .'

That morning, the family had walked to the heath that hung on the edge of the plateau, overlooking the mist-shrouded farmland below. Papa carried a shotgun and a bag of ammunition. *Not bullets*, he'd said to Hattie, who'd stood at the door of the gunroom the night before watching him clean the weapon with slow and steady hands, *shells*.

'The most important thing about using a gun,' he'd lectured Albert as they walked, the wet heather leaving dark marks on his legs, 'is to pay attention to what's around your target, not just the target itself. What's happening beside you, and in the distance. Where your companions are. What they're doing.' Albert had nodded seriously at the staccato of Papa's instructions, then turned and grinned at his little sister, tipping his tweed cap. He'd found a pair of old breeks in a trunk in the attic; they looked comical on him. 'The shotgun is a very different weapon to a rifle – hitting the mark is mostly instinctive,' Papa continued. 'We'll practise your mount, then' – he held up a jangling collection of tin cans tied with string – 'find a spot to set up.'

Albert looked two parts apprehensive, one part thrilled. 'And pigeon?'

'When you're good and ready.'

'Then deer?'

'We'll learn about rifles when you've mastered the shotgun.'

Hattie had stopped, her boots sinking into the marshy ground. 'I'll never speak to you again,' she said, 'if you kill a deer.'

'Venison is *delicious.*' Albert rubbed his tummy theatrically and Hattie looked away. 'More for me then,' he shrugged.

Papa had taken Mama in an embrace. 'See you soon, Trouble,' he said. It was the first time Hattie had heard him use Mama's nickname since they'd arrived in Ireland. Away from the house, they seemed at ease. Papa kissed Hattie on the head and waved goodbye. Beckoned that Albert should follow him.

Mama turned to Hattie. 'Come on,' she'd said, as the two men put ground between them, 'let's go home a different way.'

'I'll *never* eat venison,' Hattie had muttered as she followed Mama back across the heath to take the long path around the edge of the lough.

୬ଈ

They emerged from a clearing to find a lone figure standing at the water's edge. He held a sprig of gorse, his fingers rolling over the proud petals, a millimetre from the spines that waited beneath. A green and yellow rosary. Before him, the blackened remains of a pier stretched out into the glassy water, reflections like pinpricks.

Mama started to say *wait*, but Hattie had already skipped ahead. 'Hello.'

Her voice was loud in the heavy air and the man jumped, a reverie broken. His hands tightened around the gorse stem as he twisted violently away from her.

She'd surprised him, that was all. 'Hello,' she said again, more gently.

The man took a breath and his shoulders lowered. He half turned his face towards her, and when he saw her, something like relief flickered there. 'Hello.' The word came out half formed. But he smiled, just a little. His teeth were pearly white. 'Where'd you come from then?'

In the cushioned light of the morning, Hattie thought she recognised him. Had she seen him before, around the estate? She didn't think so. He looked just like a green-eyed Marlon Brando. But scruffier. Handsome under his weathered face.

She felt Mama appear beside her, and the man's expression changed.

'Nancy . . .' he said, once again unsure of himself. The smell of the gorse was sweet in the cool air, and beneath its spikes small orbs of blood formed on the fingers that held it.

Mama took Hattie's hand, gripped it too tightly. 'I'm sorry we . . . disturbed you.' She looked out across the lough.

'I haven't seen you for near on twenty years.' His voice was friendly, Mama's face was not.

'Yes,' Mama said.

'I'm the head gardener now. The *only* gardener.' He grinned lightly, but when it wasn't returned, he looked to his hands. 'You'd think I could find her something better. But February's been brutal, the primroses're late.'

Mama started to say something, then stopped. She shook

her head. Hattie wiggled her fingers; they were hurting. As if only just noticing her daughter was still there, Mama let go.

'This is where Char—'

'Yes,' said Mama, 'I know.'

He paused, gathered his thoughts. 'And you've heard the rumour?'

'What rumour?'

'About the suici—'

'Who told you that?'

'It's no secret.'

'I thought it was.'

Hattie felt she was watching a game, tennis perhaps, back-and-forth.

'Tabby told me when I returned.' He shuddered, as though remembering some long-forgotten chill. 'But Charlotte would never have done that.'

For the first time, Mama looked at him. Nodded almost imperceptibly. Then she said, 'Come on, poppet, we should . . .'

The man continued as if she hadn't spoken. 'This is where the pearls were found. Right here.' He scuffed the ground, as though something might be hiding in the dewy grass. 'The boys that did it . . . I tried to find them . . .'

Mama frowned. Made to say something, then stopped.

To fill the silence, the man turned from her. 'And who's this?'

'Harriet,' Mama answered, putting a hand on each of Hattie's shoulders. Once again, too tight. 'This is Harriet.'

'Hello, Harriet. You gave me something of a fright.'

'I'm sorry,' she said, suddenly shy.

He bent down to place the gorse on a large flat stone, brushing aside the sprig that was already there, its flowers now a withered brown. ''Tis no bother. I'm easily spooked these days.' He wiped his hands on the grass, wincing at the red trail they left behind.

Mama nodded in the way adults did when a conversation was over; once, twice, quickly. Her smile was a thin line.

Ignoring her intimation, or perhaps not noticing it, he stood and said, 'I should ask, did you ever write that book?'

A moment. Then: 'Pardon?'

'Your novel?' His voice was light, conversational.

Mama grappled for a reply. She took her hands from Hattie's shoulders. 'No, it seems I didn't learn from my mistakes with the first one.'

'*Hindsight is the best insight to foresight.*' He said the words knowingly, and Hattie saw this was a phrase only adults could understand. The small grin on his face was wiped away by the look on Mama's.

She stumbled over her next words. 'I didn't . . .' Clearing her throat, she took Hattie's hand once more. 'Life got in the way, Tomas.'

'It has a habit of doing that,' he said sadly.

Behind him, there was an outline in the overgrowth. It rested against the foreshore, its straight lines in contrast to the surrounding woodland. Young ash saplings grew there, but Hattie could now see it must have once been a building.

Tomas began to talk to his hands. 'I don't know why they'd target her. Why her?'

And at its centre, a pile of decaying foliage.

'She understood their plight . . .'

Mama seemed lost for words, grappling at the edges of something and missing.

Faded colours. Blues, reds, yellows. And something else. A ribbon that must once have been white.

Hattie suddenly understood. They were posies. Hundreds of them. Years and years of flowers, all piled there together.

She went to tug on Mama's hand, to point them out, to let her know the man might be sad and maybe she shouldn't be so mean. So cold. She squeezed her fingers—

Without warning, the still air split with a crack. Through their joined hands she felt Mama jump as the sharp sound raced across the lake and returned to them a second time as a muted echo. On the far shore, a single bird rose from the trees in a clatter of wingbeats. For a moment she fought down instinctive panic, then Mama's hand relaxed and she gave a nervous titter. 'Just Albert and Papa,' she said, flashing Hattie a weak smile.

But her expression slipped as she turned back to Tomas. He had fallen to his knees, hands over his head as though waiting for debris. As Hattie reached out to touch his shoulder, to tell him it was all right, that it was just Albert with a gun, Mama quickly pulled her hand away. 'Can we do anything, Tomas?' There was the smallest touch of tenderness on the edge of her voice.

The man made no move to answer.

She stepped forward, her own hand now hovering over his head, then thought better of it and said, 'We'll leave you be.' She nodded to Hattie, who began to follow her back to the path that skirted the lough. Past the pinpricks of the pier, past the long-forgotten building, past the thousand flowers that lay decaying into the earth beneath.

'What's wrong with him?' Hattie whispered as she stumbled after Mama.

'He's seen terrible things,' she said, puffing now in her haste to get away, 'in the war.'

'Like Uncle Hugo?' As soon as Hattie said the words, she regretted them.

But if Mama was mad her daughter knew things she shouldn't, she didn't show it. Her footsteps were quick and soft as they led the way. Her mind, Hattie thought, was already elsewhere.

Before the leafless woodland closed around them, Hattie turned to catch a final glimpse of Tomas, who had lifted his head heavenward.

As though he was waiting for the sky to tumble.

Chapter Fourteen

Ballinn, County Kerry
September 2019

'Back so soon?'

Nils stood behind the counter at Procaffination. He was armed with a relaxed smile and a whisk and he threw one at Ellie while using the other to churn a mixture that was two shades away from the Micra. It struck her that it was less than forty-eight hours since she'd made her first tentative foray into Ballinn, and here she was once again braving the village that had only days before filled her with dread.

'It was the turmeric latte,' she said, putting her bag on a table and approaching him. The café was empty. 'I couldn't stay away.'

He smiled and pointed to the bowl's mossy contents. 'In forty-five minutes you can try my new recipe. Matcha pound cake.'

'Great,' she said as enthusiastically as she could. Matcha, she'd read, encouraged weight loss.

He observed her. 'You look . . . a little different. Lighter, perhaps?'

She pulled her leather jacket down so it smoothed over her hips. Wondered if the cake Nils was concocting was meant for her. 'Well, I . . . haven't taken up exercise, if that's what you're—'

'Non, non.' He cupped his face. 'Here. More relaxed is what I mean.'

Relaxed was *not* how she felt. She'd been too annoyed with Dr Rathmore to contemplate a trip to the pharmacy to fill her prescription, and last night's sleep had been more broken than ever. In the early hours, she'd padded downstairs, seeking coffee and distraction. As the kettle boiled, she'd watched the rain pitter-patter on the window. Dublin would have been well awake by then, heaving into another day, no opportunity for pause, no *need* to pause. Just an onward march that filled life with action and purpose. She'd wiggled her toes – tender from the morning chill – and dredged up memories of under-floor heating, comfort at the touch of a button. In their apartment – *his* apartment really; she wasn't even on the lease – life was constant. Only summer's encroaching daylight and the shortening winter evenings signalled the changing of the seasons. She had been taken by such melancholy then she'd left the window, left the coffee, left her memories and gone to the sitting room. Set a fire. Let the methodical arranging of kindling calm her, and when the timber began to crackle, she'd lain on the sofa and finally fallen asleep.

So she felt rested, perhaps, but relaxed? She wasn't sure she'd ever feel that way again.

As though he could read her thoughts, Nils pointed to the wall behind him; it was painted black and covered in neatly scrawled handwriting. Quotes. He traced some text with his finger.

Vous n'êtes pas encore arrivés mais vous êtes plus proche qu'hier.

She frowned. 'Sorry,' she said, 'my French, it's . . .'

'It means *You have not arrived yet . . .*' he paused, thinking, '*but you are closer than yesterday.*'

Ellie frowned. 'Oh, I . . .' But he already had his back to her, filling the portafilter with those long, nimble fingers. Something inside her tugged. Just a little.

Because she did feel *closer* than yesterday, but to what? She wasn't sure.

She turned away from the counter, from Nils, from his well-intended kindness. He didn't mean anything by it, didn't mean anything by saying she looked . . . lighter. Because, although a small part of her felt it, the greater part of her had been left behind, heavier than ever, sinking to the depths of somewhere she couldn't reach.

≈

'Back to working?' Nils hovered beside Ellie with a black coffee. She'd laid out her remote desk – laptop, notebook, pen – and was waiting for her long-neglected computer to finishing updating. Outside, the day had brightened since the morning's deluge, blue sky blinking through rolling clouds.

'Thank you,' she said, taking the coffee. 'Perhaps . . . a *little* work?'

'Ah yes,' said Nils, 'my tic. A *little* this, a *little* that. John tells me I do this.'

'John?'

'My . . .' He paused. 'My partner.'

She looked around. 'He's not here?'

'*Non*. He's in Cork. Packing our apartment. But he'll be here soon. In a week or two.'

Outside, two farmers peered warily through the window. Nils crossed the room, opened the door, and after a murmured conversation – she caught the phrase *on the house* – he led them to a table at the back of the café, well away from prying eyes.

Ellie turned back to her laptop and made herself a deal. Before she began replying to unanswered emails, she would check one thing. Just one.

Did Charlotte Rathmore disappear from Blackwater Hall after she wrote her letter? Or before?

When she found the answer, she would pass on the information to Jules, or this Hattie, or the disagreeable Dr Rathmore if she had to. Wipe her hands of the matter and be done with it.

Nothing more.

She typed a name into her internet browser.

Rathmore.

There was no lack of hits. Page after page she sifted. But everything she found referred to towns, places.

She added *Lord* before *Rathmore* and was rewarded with a Wikipedia page.

Baron Rathmore, in County Kerry, is a title in the Peerage of Ireland. It was created in 1821 for William Rathmore, 1st Baron, who had earlier represented County Kerry in the House of Commons. The Rathmores arrived in Ireland *c.*1680, having been granted a total of 8,500 acres in Munster and Connaught.

William Rathmore mortgaged his estate in 1846 during the Great Famine (1845–49) to purchase food for distribution and hire ships to assist his tenants to emigrate. He died in 1880 at the age of 90.

The title was passed via his son to his great-nephew; both were absentee landlords, as was common in Ireland. Much of the family estate was sold during the intervening years to service the mortgage.

In 1910, the title passed to the engineer Charles Rathmore (4th Baron) who moved to the family seat from London. He married Niamh Stack, the daughter of American property tycoon Henry Stack, in 1911.

Charles Rathmore's second son, Edward Rathmore (5th Baron), a former journalist and distinguished WW2 veteran, inherited the barony in 1960, and his son, Albert Rathmore (6th Baron Rathmore), is the sitting lord. The heir apparent is Miles Rathmore (b.1980).

The family seat is Blackwater Hall, near Ballinn, County Kerry.

Ellie frowned. The page made no mention of Charlotte Rathmore. In fact, aside from the reference to Niamh and Charles's marriage, no women featured in the potted history at all. And Ellie suspected that if Niamh hadn't been the daughter of a tycoon, she might also have been just another unwritten female sentence.

She drained her coffee, logged into the *Irish News* archives and repeated her search. The first result was a short article from *The Kerryman* noting the arrival of Lord Charles Rathmore, Charlotte's father, to Kerry in 1910, with a quote: 'I am honoured to return Blackwater Hall to its former glory.' She flicked back to the Wikipedia page. If both the 2nd and 3rd barons had been absentee landlords, then Blackwater Hall had likely been empty for thirty years or so. It would have been in some state of disrepair by 1910.

In February 1936, the announcements column of the *Kerry News* contained a note of congratulation from the people of Ballinn for the recently married Mr and Mrs Edward Rathmore of Holborn, London. Mrs Edward Rathmore, of course, was Nancy, her name all but erased by marriage.

The next entries were snippets. A death notice for Hugo Rathmore, elder son of Charles and Niamh, from November 1957. Three years later, Charles himself died. And then there she was. Charlotte Rathmore. Right there on the page, 10th April 1940.

Lord and Lady Charles Rathmore of Blackwater Hall announce the engagement of their daughter, Miss Charlotte Niamh Rathmore, to Lord Thaddeus Hawley, major of the British Army and son of the late Lord Hawley. Details to follow.

An engagement! And only a few months before Charlotte disappeared. *Hawley.* Surely that was the name Bernie was trying to remember when she'd said the letter must have been written on paper from Wynn's Castle. Not Heaney or Healy. *Hawley.* Thaddeus Hawley. Ellie bookmarked the page. Felt a piece click into place.

She flicked through the half-dozen other hits. They were mostly photos of Charles and Niamh Rathmore at various community events, all published before 1920. Occasionally Niamh's name was anglicised: *Neve.* She was an uncommonly attractive woman. Tall and slim, her dark hair set in fashionable waves. In each photo she wore a pale colour that was probably white, as though she were an ageless debutante. Ellie searched her features for traces of her daughter. For a sense of Charlotte.

'You could always . . . zoom it.' Nils was there beside her.

She leaned back. He was right, of course. She'd had her face only inches from the computer screen. Lost.

He held a coffee towards her. 'Another?'

She nodded gratefully. 'It's like looking for a needle in a haystack.'

Nils appraised her. 'When looking for the needles, we burn the haystack, *oui*?'

She laughed. 'The problem is, I've already searched the haystack and it's not there. The needle.'

'What *is* the needle?'

'A woman. Charlotte.'

'Beautiful,' he said. 'My mother's name.'

'Really?' Ellie sipped her coffee.

'*Mais oui.* It *is* French.' He looked over his shoulder to see one of the farmers waiting at the display. He turned back to her, said, 'But every language has a Charlotte, *non*?' then started for the counter. 'Ah, Monsieur Moriarty . . .'

The farmer made a nondescript noise of embarrassment and

pointed at the beetroot cake. 'Couple of pieces of this lad for us, Nils.'

Ellie sipped her coffee. Thought. Then dropped her pen. *Of course!* Charlotte disappeared during the Emergency, during censorship, when Irish identity was everything. In a place where *Niamh* and *Neve* were used interchangeably. At a time when political statements were woven into the very fabric of everyday life.

But every language has a Charlotte, non?

Séarlait.

Charlotte. In Irish.

Frantically she typed *Séarlait Rathmore* into the search bar.

Thousands of results.

Nils passed carrying two plates. 'Of course, you could always blow away the haystack.'

'What?' But he was gone. She stared at the screen. A missing aristocrat surely couldn't have gone unreported in such a small place. It would have been on everyone's lips. They would have rushed to publish the news as it happened.

It was obvious.

Blow away the hay. Blow away the dates that didn't matter. And search for what did.

The needle: *Séarlait.* The hay: every date except August 1940.

Ellie pressed enter and leaned back.

And there she was, in the *Kerry Champion*, 1st August 1940.

A large party has been dispatched in the search for Séarlait An Ráth Mhór, 19, youngest child of Cathal and Niamh An Ráth Mhór of Ballinn. This reporter was able to extract a comment from one of the volunteers: 'We found a broken pearl necklace on the shoreline [of Lough Atoon] and a rowboat downriver. There were signs of a struggle.' Gardaí are allegedly treating the disappearance as suspicious. Three former IRA operatives were in custody at the time of going to press.

Even Charles' name had been written in Irish. But then Ellie knew that the *Kerry Champion* had been a staunchly republican newspaper. She tapped the end of her pen on the table. The Charlotte Rathmore who had written the letter did not sound like a girl who'd been abducted. But 'signs of a struggle' wouldn't have been the worst way to create a diversion in an Ireland on edge, the IRA dancing in the shadows, a continent at war.

Because Charlotte Rathmore disappeared on or before 1st August 1940. And two days later, she resurfaced.

Chapter Fifteen

Thirty kilometres west of Ballinn, County Kerry

September 2019

Ellie suppressed a groan. Before her, a reedy expanse stretched towards the distant sea, where whispers of mist rolled over the horizon. She looked at her watch. 'Is it far?'

'Not far.' Moira carried a set of binoculars that looked like they belonged on the deck of a destroyer.

'Not far across that . . . that *bog*?' said Ellie.

'The marsh, yes.'

She narrowed her eyes. 'Since when have you been interested in birdwatching?'

But Moira was already clambering over the fence. 'We'll follow the old rail,' she said over her shoulder. 'Then we'll hunker down.'

Ellie closed the gap between them, skipping to catch up. 'When *did* you become interested in ornithology?'

'Just something I've taken up this last year. You know. The third age and all that.'

Ellie had noticed a worn copy of *The Birds of Kerry* lying on the hall table. She wondered whether today's foray was her own first step into middle age.

'Keep a low profile,' Moira was saying as she crouch-walked ahead, the reeds now towering above her small frame. *Keep a low profile?* If only Ellie had done that, she wouldn't be back in Ballinn, traipsing across a bog. Her legs felt heavy, and she realised she'd barely used them today. Or her arms. Or any other part of herself. Just a few steps from the house to the Micra, from the Micra to Procaffination, then the whole process in reverse. If only she'd been able to linger at the café, she might have looked into Lord Hawley, traced Charlotte's steps.

I am coming on the next boat.

She pushed the girl from her mind. Leave her alone, she thought, let things be.

It's all your fault, Ellie.

Moira stopped ahead of her and parted the reeds. 'Here,' she whispered. And sure enough, only steps ahead, there was a small wooden seat hidden in the vegetation. It was overgrown and wonky, a long-forgotten treasure, deep in the reedy jungle.

'How on earth did you know this was here?'

'A friend showed me. Isn't it brilliant?'

A swarm of midges eyed them off from their vantage point a metre or so above. 'What friend?' Ellie couldn't picture Bernie in camouflage.

Moira lifted the binoculars, hissed, 'An egret! Look!'

Ellie followed her gaze. Nothing.

Shrugging, her mum said, 'Just missed him, so you did.' She patted the seat next to her. From a pocket in her vest – a new and very manly addition to her wardrobe Ellie hadn't failed to notice – she produced a small Thermos. 'Tea?'

On a normal work day, Ellie mused, she'd be arriving home about now, cracking a bottle of Shiraz. Preparing dinner. Chewing the fat with Dylan.

She huffed as she sat. 'What happens now?'

'Now,' said Moira, pouring steaming liquid into two tiny cups, 'we wait.'

Ellie wrapped one hand around her tea, then, as the warmth seeped into it, added the second. She looked down; her thumbs were draped over the cup's rim, forming a heart. The shape bothered her and she adjusted her fingers so they interlocked. A circle. How appropriate, she thought. Here I am, back in Kerry, back in Ballinn, with my tail between my legs. Oh yes, she'd completed the circle all right; all the way back to where she'd started.

'Ellie . . .' Moira began. It was *that* voice. The one that probed gently, seeking answers to questions she didn't want asked. 'El . . .'

Ellie stiffened. She knew what was coming, knew where this was going, felt ambushed sitting here in the reeds wearing the musty waxed jacket Moira had handed her as they left the house ('You'll stick out like a sore thumb,' she'd said, eyeing Ellie's blue waterproof). She sipped her tea in lieu of reply.

Moira changed tack. 'Hear that?' she said. The evening was still, heavy almost, in the way that Kerry's air was; cool but humid, the threat of rain even when none was to be found. 'The quiet chatter of a thousand ghosts.' She winked. 'That's what I call it.'

'Call what?'

And then Ellie felt something. A lick of wind lifted the free strands of her hair and brought with it the fresh tang of salt and sea. Around them, the reeds began to hiss and whisper, a million seed heads rubbing together.

'The onshore breeze,' said Moira, 'just before dusk. Like clockwork.' A dark shape rose from the far edge of the marsh. 'Here we go.' She handed the binoculars to her daughter.

Ellie lifted them and set them to her eyes.

'Mallard,' said Moira, her gaze following the birds' gentle arc as they sprayed across the sky and wheeled left, skimming the reeds. 'Searching for a place to spend the night.'

Despite herself, Ellie felt her heart beat faster. The birds poured overhead like water across rock, smooth and silky, silent but for the breath of wind that followed them. She scrambled from her seat to climb up and over the mound of the old rail line to lie on her stomach and peer over the leeward side. The flock descended ahead of her, gliding to a halt in a small pool. Behind them a pair of slow, blocky birds – 'Lapwings,' Moira whispered – hefted their iridescent wings in rhythmic clapping beats. They hung in the sky like contented lovers. Ellie turned to watch their flight; so unharnessed, so at ease. How would it be to soar like that, safe in the knowledge that your partner was beside you, that wherever your journey ended, you would be together?

'In decline, you know?' Moira lay beside her daughter on the damp rotted reeds of the sloping bank. 'Those two are lucky to find a mate. It's the first pair I've seen.' They were already just a speck in the sky, headed for some oasis in the far dunes. 'So many birds never find a mate. More and more common, unfortunately.' She stopped quickly, turned back to the empty golden sky. 'Beautiful, isn't it?' she said.

It was. For that moment when the lapwings had stolen her attention, when she'd forgotten to breathe as she watched them hang in the air, when the only sound was the quiet chatter of a thousand ghosts, Ellie had been simply . . . *there*. Simply existing. 'Yes,' she said, 'it's beautiful.'

Moira sat up. In the warm glow of the dying day, the skin on her face had turned to porcelain, the creases around her eyes deep and beautiful. She had a healthy flush to her cheeks and Ellie was gripped by the desire to capture the moment. She patted her pocket for her phone.

Empty.

Beside her, Moira gave a secret smile. And Ellie realised that the change of coat had been more than just a birdwatching practicality. No updating of emails, no distracted scrolling, no new-found phone reception.

Moira reached into her own pocket and withdrew something Ellie didn't expect. 'A wee dropeen?'

Ellie's shoulders relaxed. She shook her head, but then took the hip flask, wondering at this unfamiliar woman who sat beside her.

Moira said, 'It's Bernie's blackberry port, so don't be taking a gulp now.'

Ellie sipped the sweet liquid and a fire spread in her belly. She coughed, wiped her mouth. 'Jaysus,' she said, making to hand it back. Then, changing her mind, she took another sip.

Moira watched the empty sky. 'It's nice to have you home, El.'

Ellie turned away, afraid of that prickle behind her eyes. 'I'm not great company at the moment, Mum.' She took another sip of port. 'I'm sorry.' And she was. For the mess she'd made of her own life. For the upheaval she'd put Moira through when she landed at the train station bearing a large bag and a tiny explanation. 'The wedding's off,' she'd said, as though that covered it.

'Oh, El . . . 'Tisn't unexpected you'd be down. With the wedding and work . . .' Moira paused, waiting for the brush-off.

But to Ellie's own surprise, it didn't come. Instead she heard herself say, 'I just didn't think it would turn out this way.'

'No, love, o'course you didn't.'

'It's not what you think. I didn't get cold feet.'

'No.' And with that single word, Ellie knew that Moira had suspected all along. That Dylan had called off the wedding.

'It was him. Dylan. He . . .' That familiar tightness in her chest. She pressed her fingers together, closed her eyes, listened to the gentle wash of the incoming tide. Then Moira's hand was there. Her skin impossibly soft and smooth, warm in the cool air, and her fingers curled around Ellie's, holding them tight. Ellie held her breath, something welling painfully inside her. 'It was my fault, Mum.'

Moira frowned. 'No, El. No. I'm sure it wasn't.'

In the weeks Ellie had been home, Moira had been overly bright with her, and it had hurt Ellie's head and filled her with guilt. She'd tried to fill her daughter's pain with *things* – with tasks and ideas and distractions – and Ellie had bristled. Unfairly. Because Moira didn't know the truth of it, and the only way Ellie could protect herself from grief was to bury it beneath apathy and aloofness. She realised with a jolt that she'd been silently willing Moira to give up on her, to hate her as much as Ellie hated herself.

Moira took her daughter's face in her hands and said firmly, 'What happened?'

'I was pregnant, Mum.' Ellie felt a rush of tide and looked to her feet, expecting water, but they were dry and she realised the flood was inside of her. Before she could stop herself, she said, 'The heartbeat . . . gone.'

Moira spoke then, but the words were muffled because . . . well, the grip of her hands, the warmth of Bernie's blackberry port, the riot of pink that burnt the sky . . . it took Ellie's breath away, all of it, and she couldn't hear Moira's voice, couldn't understand her meaning because she had begun to cry. It was there before she even knew it. Those eyes that had prickled now overflowed, spilled tears down her cheeks, hot and full of pent-up rage and sorrow and everything else she'd denied herself. Her mouth hung open, gasping, but words wouldn't come amongst the sobs that rocked her shoulders, shoulders upon which Moira's hands were now pressing, pulling her daughter into an embrace that was warmth and safety, and they melted into one another, camouflaged against the marshy surrounds so that from above, they were just another part of that sinuous, winding river system.

When Ellie's cries began to ease, she emptied her lungs, pushing out air that she felt must have sat there for weeks. She slowed her breathing and, on cue, Moira held her at arm's length. Ellie felt a sharp sting of embarrassment and looked down at her palms, shiny from tears she didn't know she'd wiped.

Moira said, 'Els, I'm so—'

'I was pregnant,' Ellie whispered again. She picked up a piece of dead grey reed from beside her boot, began to break it into pieces. 'I was . . .' She stopped. Her throat felt tight. 'I was waiting until week eight to tell you. But . . . I had an early scan, so I could know before I told anyone . . . before we told you . . .'

'Oh, El.'

She tipped the slivers of reed from her palm, let them fall to the ground. They were so light and papery that the wind gobbled them up with ease, lifting them overhead and away. And now she'd started, she couldn't stop. It was like the breeze was coaxing her, like it had gently nudged the door inside of her that wasn't locked after all. 'It was something I'd never considered. Motherhood. I'd kept waiting, all these years, for the maternal instinct to kick in.' Moira stroked her long hair, as she'd done when Ellie was a child. 'When I found out, it was a surprise. But it was like a switch flicked and I just couldn't wait . . . to be a mother.' She squeezed her eyes shut, felt the tears come again. 'And Dylan asked me to marry him a few days later. I was happy. *We* were happy.'

'I know, I know.'

'And . . . oh God.' Ellie looked skyward. 'Mum, it was my fault.'

'No.' Moira frowned at her daughter. 'No, Ellie. These things happen to so many of us.'

Ellie leaned forward and wiped her eyes angrily. Wiped away the kindness and pity. 'You don't understand. It was the article. My *investigation*.' She spat the word. 'The stress of it . . . Two days after I published . . .' She couldn't finish the sentence, couldn't say it out loud. Could barely admit it to herself. Her tears came again, fire on her cheeks, and she pushed the heels of her hands against her eyes, shutting out the words. Shutting out the truth.

You did this.

She'd forgotten to look after herself.

You did this.

And the baby.

You did this.

Her baby. Their baby. Gone. All because she couldn't put her life before her work. Put another's life before her work.

You did this.

Moira took her daughter's shoulders again. 'Ellie, look at me.'

Ellie dropped her hands from her face and opened her eyes. But her gaze lingered on the sky.

'I never told you this,' Moira said, 'but before you were born, I had three miscarriages. *Three*. And two after.' She smiled at her daughter, dropping her hands from her shoulders. 'You were our miracle.'

Ellie sobbed.

'I know you feel like you should blame yourself. I did. For a time. But it wasn't my fault. That's just how life goes.' Moira turned the hip flask over in her hands. Traced the etching on its surface.

CF. Cillian Fitzgerald.

'That's just how life goes,' she repeated.

Ellie's gaze followed a skein of geese; they hung in the sky like a mobile above a crib. 'I would have called him Cillian. If he'd been a boy.' She said this before she'd even thought it. Then realised it was true. Moira's arm was around her then, across her shoulders. And when she turned, she saw her mum was silently weeping.

Moira said, 'I wish you'd told me.' It wasn't an accusation. 'I wish you'd said.'

'I wanted to, but . . .' Words failed Ellie. She tried again. 'But I was so stressed; I didn't eat properly, didn't sleep properly.' Moira frowned, not understanding. 'I was so worried about my job that I forgot about what was important. That's what Dylan said, and he was right.'

'What?'

'He said *you did this*.' Ellie's voice caught in her throat. 'He just wanted some time to come to terms with it, because I'd been so selfish.'

Moira's hand gripped tight onto Ellie's fingers, stopping her in her tracks. In the dying light she saw a flush creep along her mum's cheeks. 'No,' said Moira. She opened the flask and took three gulps. Wiped her lips. Her hands shook.

'Had I left the investigation alone—'

'Ellie, miscarriage is a fact of life. It's the roll of the dice. I would know. As would half of the women out there.' She indicated across the ocean, as if a silent army waited beyond the dunes. 'That Dylan would blame you . . .' She gulped more port. 'Well, I'm not able for expressing how angry that makes me.'

'He was in shock.'

She turned to her daughter. 'Feck him, Ellie.'

And Ellie stopped, too surprised to speak. It was the first time she had *ever* heard Moira use that word – that minced oath nestled somewhere between expletive and exclamation – and it brought her back to the moment. Back to the marsh, the sunset. The quiet chatter of a thousand ghosts. She sob-laughed, her voice thick with tears. 'What *did* Bernie put in that blackberry port?' Conscious now that the contents of her nose had run down her chin, she wiped at it with her sleeve.

'You listen to me, Ellie.' Moira's voice was fire. 'It's *not* your fault. If it was, then I am also to blame for things that I did or didn't do before you were born, and after. If Cillian had said a word against me, I'd have . . .'

Ellie licked her lips, tasted salt – salt from the breeze, salt from her tears. 'But he wouldn't have.'

'No.'

She nodded. In the valley beyond, pinpricks of light began to shine from scattered houses.

Moira said, 'You didn't tell anyone, did you? About your miscarriage?'

'No.'

Moira's face was pained. Her silence spoke. Because now that Ellie *had* told, it dawned on her the difference it would have made at the time. How it would have eroded the sharp edges of her loneliness. 'Looking back . . . maybe it would have been easier if I'd had someone to talk to. Someone to tell.'

'Yes.'

Ellie leaned her head gently on her mum's shoulder, turned her eyes to the horizon. Watched the last of the light leave. It was time for them to go. Time for them to return to their own pinprick of light somewhere in a distant valley.

Time to go home.

Chapter Sixteen

Blackwater Hall, County Kerry
August 1939

The bleeding that began the afternoon before the summer party was heavy enough that Nancy knew another miscarriage was imminent. When Charlotte came looking for her, she saw the raw red of Nancy's eyes and took her in an embrace. And when she asked what the matter was, Nancy hesitated.

'Nothing,' she said. She attempted a small grimace. *Not to worry.*

Charlotte took a chair next to her at the small card table at which she sat, and grasped her sister-in-law's hand, turned it over in her own. She traced her palm as she had done under the clematis, then looked up, her eyes hazel in the golden light that streamed through the open window. 'I can see it isn't nothing, Nancy.' Breeze licked the room, lifting a wisp of her fair hair; it danced and spun on some invisible thread.

Nancy's burden was so heavy she couldn't bear to share it. 'A headache, that's all.' She pulled her hand away and then felt guilty for doing so. Her mouth was heavy from crying. 'I get them sometimes.'

They were silent for a time and the lie sat between them. Charlotte rolled forward off her chair, knelt in front of Nancy like a mother would a child, rested her hands on her knees.

'Do you know,' she said lightly, '*when* I started the Dramatics Secret Society?'

Nancy frowned then half laughed, pleased with the distraction. She raised an eyebrow; a question mark.

'Three years ago,' Charlotte said. 'It's been a part of me for more than a sixth of my life.'

Nancy considered her own life. A sixth of it. Four years. Four years she'd been a secretary, four years she'd been trying to write. Four years was the longest she'd stayed with any foster family. Four years was her age when her parents died. She'd met Teddy *more* than four years before, although it felt – in a good way – like longer. And, of course, this pregnancy was also number four. She turned her eyes back to Charlotte. 'And?'

'In that time I've learned to be an actress. And recognise one.'

'Is that so?'

'And acting's just lying really.'

Nancy had read West End reviews that would contradict that. 'Your point?' Although she knew it already.

Charlotte narrowed her eyes theatrically. 'What *have* you done, Trouble Rathmore?' she said, squeezing Nancy's knees. Playing at interrogation. But if she'd hoped for a laugh, it wasn't forthcoming.

Nancy's brow crumpled and her lips pressed together in defiance of what she held inside. Guilt that she might be responsible for her body's inability to provide. Grief at her loss. Fear that she would never be pregnant again. She dropped her head and sobbed into her hands, great fat tears dripping through her fingers to the floor.

'Oh, Nancy. I'm sorry, I'm sorry. I was only playing. Only thinking you'd picked a fight with Mother . . .' Charlotte drew her once again into an embrace, and this time Nancy held it, let her forehead sink into her friend's neck, wrapped her arms around the girl's thin shoulders until her own ceased to tremble. Then, with her cheek pressed into that soft blonde hair, she whispered her secret.

Charlotte pulled back with a gasp. 'You're pregnant?'

Nancy unwrapped her arms, wiped her eyes. 'I was. This was my fourth. *Our* fourth. I had hoped it would be the one.'

'My God.'

'You mustn't tell Teddy.'

Charlotte frowned, then her expression was replaced by concern. 'He doesn't know?'

A shake of the head. Nancy couldn't tell him. Not this time. *This* time, she had decided to wait until she was sure. And then, when she was sure, she wanted to be surer. Surer that she wouldn't fail him.

But she had.

'He . . . he doesn't blame you?'

'No.' She thought of the last time, at their flat in London eight months before. She'd woken in the night, the sheets soaked sticky beneath her. It was Christmas Eve. He'd pulled her tight, held her head to his chest, whispered into her hair: 'Miscarriages are a fact of life, Nancy. It's the roll of the dice.' They would try again. 'No, it's nothing like that.' She stood and smoothed her skirt, then went to the window, breathed in the fresh scent of the mountain. It towered behind them, clouds kissing its summit.

'Because,' Charlotte said, 'you haven't done anything to cause this. I'm certain of it.'

Nancy sat on the oxblood leather chaise longue beneath the window, and took a deep breath. The air was sticky: hot and – strangely – cold all at once. She felt a trickle and wondered absent-mindedly how one would go about cleaning blood from leather. But her briefs were lined with one of the sanitary napkins she'd packed without intention, but with apprehension, in London. From her previous experience, she knew the flow started slowly. 'The doctors don't know what's wrong with me.'

'I'm sure there's nothing wrong with you.'

'Each time they say I need to rest more or exercise more, or eat less or eat more. They give me vitamins and pills. I take them. I think of every little one as it enters my body and I wonder if they are all down there, a tiny army working at my womb.' Her words tumbled over each other.

Charlotte's brow creased as the soft footsteps of a maid approached the closed bedroom door, then passed on.

'I'm being hysterical,' said Nancy.

'No.' When Charlotte took her hand, Nancy felt their positions were reversed, that she was the younger one and Charlotte was older, wiser. She began to weep again. A gentle sob, wholly in contrast to the soul-draining tears she'd already shed.

'I'm so sorry,' said Charlotte.

As she wiped her eyes, Nancy said, 'No, it's just . . . I feel relief. To tell someone.' She'd only known for four weeks, but a month holding a secret made time stretch.

'You can tell me anything.'

There had been times in Nancy's life when she'd felt a special flush of friendly connection, moments when someone said just the right thing at just the right time. But something – her happy marriage? The bustle of London? – had stolen those relationships and they'd faded, running their course until they spilled into memory. Now, as she sat in a bedroom that wasn't her own, in a house whose grand proportions had shrunk into a familiar maze, she felt such a warm fondness for the steady hand that held hers, for the kind words that appeared entirely unforced, and for the compassion Charlotte was able to show for something she couldn't possibly understand. There was a permanence about it. More than a pseudo-sisterly bond forged through marriage. It was, she thought, true friendship.

'We'll call for the doctor. From Ballinn. Or further, if you like. Sneem?' Charlotte smeared the *S* in Sneem, as a local might have done.

Nancy shook her head at the theatrics, and at Charlotte's cheeky grin. 'If your mother hears you talking like that, she'll have a fit. No. No doctor, thank you.'

'Mother's in a state of perpetual fit,' Charlotte said. 'And you *need* a doctor.'

Nancy's jaw set as the wringing inside her grew. She knew a warm bath would help, but the en suite didn't have a lock and the pink tinge of the bathwater would give her away. 'Don't worry. I'm an old hand at this.'

Charlotte stood. Outside, the light was fading fast, rushing off over the mountain and away. 'Dr Mortimer from Ballinn. I've met him. He's English, discreet.'

'And the Irish aren't?'

Charlotte laughed. 'God, no! My friends in the village have many virtues, but discretion definitely isn't one of them.'

❧

Charlotte didn't join the family for dinner, and when Nancy enquired as to her whereabouts, Lady Rathmore told her she was indisposed.

'An injury,' she said. 'I'll have one of the maids check on her after dinner.'

Teddy said, 'An injury?'

'Apparently she went down to the garden and slipped. A sprained wrist.' From the hallway there was a clatter, a dropped tray or pot. Lady Rathmore winced.

Hugo said, 'The quicker she's married off to Hawley, the better.' He turned to his father, who was diligently ignoring the conversation, his mouth full of food. 'What about this new terrorism Act?'

'Animals, the lot of them,' said Lord Rathmore. Though the carafe was within arm's reach, he snapped his fingers, indicating the footman should top up his glass.

A copy of last week's *Times* had been delivered to Blackwater Hall and Nancy had read with growing unease a bold-print list of last month's IRA attacks: seven bombs in England's midlands, two in London – at King's Cross and Victoria stations – and three more in Liverpool. A new law had been passed – The Prevention of Violence Act – and Irish deportations had already begun.

Hugo swilled his wine. 'I say round them all up and shoot them.' The declaration was made with gusto.

'I think,' said Teddy, 'the point is that they're rather difficult to find.'

Hugo scoffed. 'The Irish? Don't be absurd. Count their teeth.'

A twist rocked Nancy's abdomen and she suppressed a cry. The cramps were coming faster and closer now. Two miscarriages had passed in blood only, but her third had been different. More traumatic. *Much* more traumatic. Under the table she sank her fingernails into her thighs, pain and fear competing with the requirement to perform. And as Charlotte had already pointed out, she wasn't a natural actress.

Teddy was watching her out of the corner of his eye, his expression full of concern. He put his hand down to grip hers, leaned in, asked if she was unwell.

'Nausea,' she whispered.

At this, he visibly brightened.

'Just something I ate,' Nancy clarified. 'I walked in the garden this afternoon; under-ripe apples. Disaster.' Her lips were pale under a smear of rouge.

He squeezed her hand and his kindness gave her a jolt of guilt. 'Disaster,' he whispered. Around them, the conversation faltered.

'Speaking of children . . .' said Hugo.

'Were we?' A ripple crossed Teddy's face. Anger? Frustration? Sadness?

'I rather thought you two would have produced by now.'

Produced. Nancy held her fork a little tighter.

'Europe is headed for war,' Teddy said quickly. 'Not the best time to start a family.'

'I hardly think so, Edward,' said Lady Rathmore, as though he'd merely suggested they delay dessert. 'War. What an outdated concept.'

'Mother prefers not to think about such things,' said Hugo.

On another evening Nancy might have laughed. Niamh Rathmore was Irish only in first name. In everything else she was new-money American. Haughty, arrogant. Isolationist. Only last week Germany and the Soviet Union had signed a non-aggression pact. War in Europe was inevitable. But America would not be drawn. And neither would Lady Rathmore.

'I prefer,' she said, 'to be optimistic.' The notion was so ridiculous, even Lord Rathmore's mask slipped for a moment.

'I'm not sure that's going to help the situation, my dear.'

She continued: 'If there is to be war, I hardly think Ireland will be involved.'

Nancy, surprised at her insight, leaned forward. 'I agree. Neutrality may be the only option for de Valera.'

'The country, quite simply, has no capability. What are they going to fight them with? Pitchforks?'

'If a European war is imminent,' said Nancy, flicking a crumb off the white tablecloth, 'perhaps you should consider returning to the United States?' She knew full well that Lady Rathmore hadn't been back to the country of her birth since her first and only journey across the Atlantic in 1910.

'Perhaps, Nancy. Perhaps.' It was the first time Lady Rathmore had used Nancy's name. It surprised the younger woman. Instead of touching a nerve, as she'd hoped, she had found something else. A weakness.

Changing the subject, Lord Rathmore said, 'Tell me about this summer party, my dear. Are we to have proper food this year?'

Nancy's mind wandered to Charlotte. The younger woman had spent the early evening with her, only leaving once Nancy had stepped out of the cooling bath. She'd stood sentry, reading *Death on the Nile* from the other side of the door in an animated voice.

'We could make this one into a play,' she'd said, as one character after another succumbed to the plot.

'But you'd never agree as to who would be Poirot. Can anyone in your secret society do a Belgian accent?'

At this Charlotte had gone quiet.

'Well?'

'I'm thinking.'

'Thinking of that boy . . . what was his name?' Nancy played at being forgetful. 'Tomas Deenihan? Yes, thinking of Tomas with a continental accent, you mean?'

'Nancy!'

'It's merely a formality,' Lady Rathmore was saying. 'Only immediate relations will be allowed through the gates.'

The summer party was a day for the families of Blackwater Hall's staff to see the estate. Nancy had remarked to Teddy that it was an uncharacteristically generous gesture on the part of the lord and lady, to which he'd replied that the tradition had been established by his grandfather, Henry Stack, who'd ensured it coincided with his annual visits. After Henry's death, Teddy had managed to convince his mother that cancelling the annual event would cause consternation in the village.

'Mother's correct; limit the numbers at the gates,' Hugo was saying. Dessert was served as he talked: early raspberries plucked from the walled garden by Nancy that morning. 'Last year there were more than ever. You do understand the whole village is related?'

When, finally, dinner ended, Nancy made her excuses, and Teddy followed soon after. He lay beside her. Held her hand.

'You're not well.'

'Just those apples.' She watched shadows dance on the ceiling. Somewhere outside, the moon was a waxing crescent.

'You'd tell me if it was anything else?'

'Of course.'

'I'm sorry about my family.'

'Your family?' she said. 'I'm quite used to them by now.'

'I know. But still. It's not easy.'

'You didn't choose them.'

'No. I chose you.'

In the darkness, she smiled. His body felt warm beside her. She wished she could turn towards him, rest her head on his shoulder, her arm across his waist. But if she did, and he wanted her, she'd have to refuse.

Chapter Seventeen

Ballinn, County Kerry
September 2019

On the way to Tabby Ryan's one hundredth birthday party, Dylan called. Ellie was driving the Micra, Moira tucked into the passenger seat, the village of Ballinn in the distance and getting closer.

'Leave it,' she said when her mum picked up the vibrating phone. 'It'll be a McCarthy lawyer.'

'It's Dylan.' Moira held the phone flat on her palm: a frog rescued from a plughole. 'How do I hang up?'

Ellie put the brakes on. 'No, I'll—'

'Is it this red button?'

'No, Mum, don't . . .'

Moira cut off the buzzing.

'Mum!'

They sat in silence, paused on the empty lane. Between them the air thickened.

'I should at least have found out what he wanted.'

'No.'

'Mum, please. It's *my* life.' Ellie's voice was harsher than she intended. She reached across and squeezed her mum's hand. 'I'm sorry. I know you care.'

'I do, love, I do.' Moira had the good grace to look sheepish. 'I'm sorry, it's just . . .' She trailed off.

Ellie understood. Were the roles reversed, she would have done the same, or worse. Answered the phone, told the man on the other end exactly what she thought of him. But as it was, the roles *weren't* reversed. Ellie wanted to know what Dylan had to say. He had been in shock too, hadn't he? Had his own grief to deal with. Didn't he hold her hand after the bleeding started, tell her everything was okay? Or did he? Ellie could no longer recall that moment clearly. As though she might only have wished for it to happen.

As though it had never happened at all.

She put the car back into gear and rolled on. She would call him back. Tomorrow perhaps. Alone.

As they passed the garda station, Moira broke the silence. 'The squad car's there. On a Saturday. Beddy must be coming to Tabby's party. Bless him.'

Ellie, pulled back from her reverie, paused. 'Beddy?'

'Beddy Cullen.'

Ellie raised her eyebrows. Beddy Cullen. The school clown. In his final yearbook, Ellie had written, *Good luck with life! Try not to get arrested . . . immediately*, followed by a very small smiley face to show she was (half) joking.

'Beddy's not the local garda, sure he's not?'

'Well, he's our man on duty every second Tuesday.'

In fifth year, Ellie had seen Beddy dip his hand into the church collection basket, pull out a fistful of notes and stuff them in his pocket. They'd made eye contact at that moment, and Ellie was sure it was that which had saved her from ever being the butt of one of his numerous practical jokes.

On the outskirts of the village, they hit a traffic jam. A real traffic jam in Ballinn. Tabby, it seemed, was popular. 'Well, that's one for the books,' Moira said, and Ellie wondered if she was talking about the traffic, about Beddy or about the man with an argyle jumper who was swinging his leg, with surprising agility, over his fixed-gear bicycle.

इ&

Jules came to the window, brought his eyes level with Moira's. The mud that speckled his face today was less subtle than it had been on Friday.

'Jules!'

Ellie frowned. This was a new voice from Moira. It was somewhat breathy. She worried what it meant.

'Moira,' he said. 'Ellie.' He fussed with his poorly fitting helmet.

Ellie was concerned that her behaviour at Jules's historical society meeting had been so dismissive that he'd already decided she was a lost cause, but to her relief he looked up and gave her a broad smile. 'You came?'

'I couldn't stay away,' she said, and realised she'd used the same excuse to Nils in Procaffination only twenty-four hours before. She added, 'I wanted to see Tabby again.' The former teacher had been a regular visitor at Ballinn National School, a guest of honour, always given the VIP treatment at sports matches and Christmas concerts. The last time Ellie had seen her was more than seventeen years ago; she must have been eighty-three years old and as lively as a spring chicken. So she did want to see Tabby. That was the truth. But what if Tabby *had* known Charlotte? Would she not be the perfect person to ask about her?

Because the night before, as she'd sat in the marsh with Moira, Ellie had realised something. In returning to Kerry, she'd been fleeing not just the scandal. Not just the loss of her job. Not just her guilt. But also herself.

She was trying to run away from something that was always with her. That she couldn't shake off.

Curiosity.

She was curious about Charlotte Rathmore and the letter she'd written after her disappearance. And now she had time, didn't she? To just ... well ... not investigate exactly, but make enquiries.

That morning, for the first time in weeks, she'd felt *awake*. She'd slipped out of bed and down the stairs to the kitchen, relishing the cold wooden floor as she'd wiggled her toes and pushed aside images of Dublin. She'd made tea and toast for Moira, taken it up on a tray, as she'd done on weekends as a child. And her mum had been awake, a book open in her lap, her face bathed in light from the sun that streamed through the window into the small, tidy bedroom. The morning had disappeared like that, whiled away on inconsequential chat, mother and daughter sitting in the bed. And it dawned on Ellie that it had been years since she'd spent a morning just letting herself *be*, letting whatever happened happen. Since she'd sat sipping tea in bed and chewing the fat with someone she loved.

She looked across at Moira and Jules, who were discussing the weather with vigour. What was it Jules had said? *I want to do something that isn't on the clock. Something interesting. Something that matters.* Did a woman who'd gone missing eighty years previously *matter*? She did, thought Ellie, if her own family cowered at her memory. If she was due to be wed. If she'd written a letter full of hope and energy two whole days after she'd disappeared.

Because Ellie knew full well that to disappear from your life wasn't enough. She had tried it. The past had to be faced. Confronted.

It was possible to step out of a life, but not to leave it behind.

Because she'd tried running away.

And so had Charlotte Rathmore.

❦

The hall was full when they arrived. Bunting formed a spider's web across the ceiling and a huge banner hung over the stage: *Happy Birthday Great-Great-Granny.* The savoury smell of party food filled the room and the air was thick with the mass of mingling people. A hundred at least, with more filing through the door behind them. Ballinn had changed, morphed, in the years Ellie had been away. It was full of unfamiliar faces – blow-ins, growing families – and old friends whose names had slipped away from her. And hers, presumably, from them. She felt a pang of guilt; she'd let go of where she'd grown up. Left it behind like it didn't matter.

She weaved through the crowd to a table and deposited the two bottles of reasonable Shiraz she'd found at O'Brien's. Deidre had feigned surprise when she'd seen her, asked when she'd arrived back in Kerry. They'd completed the polite proprietor-customer discussions (weather, the ever-extending tourist season, weather again) and Ellie managed to extract herself before she was subjected to, or implicated in, any village gossip.

She opened the wine and poured three glasses, leaving the bottles among a rapidly amassing collection.

'To Tabby,' Jules said when she returned. They drank a toast as the buzz in the room grew. Something old and jolly played through the hall's tinny speakers.

Bernie, draped in what perhaps had once been a quilt, appeared through a gap in the crowd. She spread her arms and wrapped Moira and Ellie in a single hug, then took Jules by the arm. 'How's things? How's your history group coming along? Any members yet?'

'Well,' said Jules, clearing his throat, 'it's more of a *society* really.'

'Ah, spoken like a true politician.'

Moira leaned in. 'Speaking of historical societies . . .'

Jules sounded cautious. 'Yes?'

'Well?' She indicated her head towards Ellie. 'Any progress?' This last she hissed as though Ellie were out of earshot.

Jules paused. 'No,' he said. 'I think we'll leave the letter with the family. Post it, perhaps. That's what we decided, didn't we, Ellie?'

Her heart leapt at his support. He'd accepted her unwillingness with a grace that Bernie and Moira had not. And yet the two women had known her so well that even as her indifference turned to objection, they'd pushed on. Known that eventually the letter would draw her out from the place where she'd locked herself away.

She turned to Bernie, who was glaring at Jules, disappointment written across her face. 'Bernie,' she said, 'when you put aside that box of books, you knew about the letter, didn't you?'

Bernie looked sideways at Moira. A pair of rabbits in headlights. 'I *may* have flicked through the pages of a few titles . . .' She took a gulp from her glass. 'But I put everything back where I found it.'

'I see.'

Jules looked between the three women, clearly trying to work out the game being played. Clearly wondering if *he* had been played. But before he could say anything, Ellie took the letter from her pocket. 'This was written two days after Charlotte disappeared.' Around her the atmosphere changed, softened. 'Did you know that?'

Evidently they didn't.

'The *cratúir*,' said Moira, and Ellie wondered, not for the first time, who she was talking about: her or Charlotte. Charlotte because, well, what *had* happened to her? And Ellie because she'd been drawn in and Moira knew she wouldn't let go now until she had answers.

And nothing would stand in her way.

৽৲

'Tabby was a maid at Blackwater House, back when she was a Deenihan.' Since Ellie had revealed her willingness to engage on Charlotte Rathmore, Bernie had not stopped talking. 'Until 1939. Or was it '40? Because that would make a difference, wouldn't it?' Before Ellie could answer, she carried on. 'She was Mammy's first teacher. And *she* must have started school in . . .' she looked to the ceiling, '1942?' She shook her head, began to recall second-hand memories of her mother's childhood: dance halls, the mart and the Rose of Tralee.

Ellie whispered to Jules, 'This could go on a bit.'

A child raced past, knocking her glass, which was – thankfully – empty. It surprised her: both the impact and the fact she'd finished her wine. She felt relaxed. She smiled at this; something to tell Nils. And she knew it wasn't just the wine that had allowed her shoulders to drop. It was the acceptance that her life must carry on, step by tentative step.

'Another?' she said to Jules. He looked around at the sea of unknown faces, a sheen of perspiration on his brow. 'I think I'd better.' He downed the remainder of his glass. 'Dutch courage.'

She patted him on the shoulder. 'You'll fit in,' she said. 'One day.'

'Reassuring. Thank you, Ellie.'

She tilted her head towards Moira and Bernie. 'Make a note if they come up with anything concrete.' The two women were in full swing, their arms flapping, their mouths motoring. Their glasses were full, the wine playing second fiddle to chatter. Jules nodded and took a small black notebook from his top pocket. She wanted to laugh at his keenness, but she actually kind of admired it.

At the table, someone passed her a Cabernet Sauvignon.

'Oh, thank you,' she said, taking the bottle and inspecting it. 'New world, notes of oak, comical label containing a cat and a frog. Delicious! Just my taste.' Laughing, she set down both glasses and the bottle in an awkward juggle. When she looked up, her mouth froze mid-smile.

'Dr Rathmore.' Her intonation lifted at the end of his name, as though she were questioning the audacity of him standing directly in front of her. Or his audacity full stop.

'Ellie,' he said. On his face, she noticed with annoyance, was a smile. She fumbled the glasses; one tumbled to its side and rolled slowly towards the edge of the table. He picked it up and set it right. 'How are you?'

'Sleeping well,' she said. 'So you can cancel that follow-up.'

Between them a small man was reaching towards the Cabernet Sauvignon.

'Hold on,' Dr Rathmore said. He took the bottle and filled both Ellie's glasses to the top. The man blustered and shuffled off, muttering.

'Thanks,' she said. 'As I was saying—'

'Ellie . . . I feel I should apologise.' The tiredness that had plagued his face in the surgery had been replaced with a seriousness that was more worry and less judgement. 'When you came into the medical centre, I wasn't myself. I wasn't being reasonable.'

She couldn't remember which glass was hers, but nonetheless she took a sip that turned into a gulp. 'Were you not?'

'You know I wasn't.' He spread his hands. 'I'm sorry. I apologise.' She noticed his lack of drink. God, was she already tipsy?

'Do you now?' Yep, she thought, straight to my head. The fire in her belly was a mixture of rebellion and red wine, and she found she rather liked the burn.

'I do.'

His calmness irritated her. The flop of his hair. The concerned set of his eyebrows. The cut of his chinos. His hands, his long fingers, this new penetrating gaze. Two days ago he'd barely looked at her, and now she wished he wouldn't.

'I'm sure you've a lot going on.' She said it like she didn't mean it and immediately felt a twinge of regret. 'How's your father?'

'One of his better days today.'

'He didn't come?'

'No. He rarely leaves the house.'

They stood in silence. She recalled Dr Rathmore's reaction to Charlotte's letter, tried to read his face. Was he wondering what she'd done with it? Was he about to ask for it back? Quickly she waved to the banner that stretched above. 'Have you met Tabby?'

At this, he smiled. 'I made a house call last week. Ended up staying for dinner.'

'Really?' She tried to keep the surprise out of her voice. Dr Rathmore endearing himself to someone?

'First time I'd met her.' He poured himself a wine. 'Have you *seen* her house?'

Ellie frowned. 'Not in the last twenty years.' It was a thatched cottage on the coast. Damp and rheumatism oozed from its walls. 'She's not still there, surely?'

He nodded. Grinned. 'I'm invited back for dinner next week.'

Ellie laughed at this: Ballinn welcoming a prodigal son. Then she thought of him up there at Blackwater Hall, with the dad he referred to as *my father.* Or, even more coolly, *Albert.* She recalled what Moira had said: *His son's back for a bit. Sent away when his mother died, poor child.* She frowned. Had she failed to see things from his point of view? Had she barged into his office demanding answers to questions about his family he hadn't even thought to ask?

Before she could stop herself, she said, 'I shouldn't have gone to see your father like that. I didn't know he wasn't . . . well.'

He waved her words away. 'He told me about your visit.

Said you were the most beautiful woman he'd seen in decades.'
He laughed. For a moment she hoped he was laughing at the
audacity of it. A heartbeat later, she hoped he wasn't. 'He
was, however, under the impression you were my great-aunt
Charlotte's friend; that you had a letter for her.'

'Well,' she said, 'he's got some of the elements right.'

'He said that when he told you Charlotte had killed herself,
you became angry, thumping the table, raging then crying. He
thought you'd been drinking.'

'Killed herself? Wait, I . . .' Someone offered her a sausage
roll; she waved it away.

'He said a lock of hair fell over your blue eyes and you
pushed it back.'

'Now hang on . . .'

'I told him the Ellie I'd met had brown eyes.'

She flushed. 'I don't know what to tell you, Dr Rathmore.'

'Milo, please.'

'Milo. Obviously,' she put her glass aside, 'that's not true.
Don't you think you would've noticed if I'd been drinking? I
only saw you a few hours later.'

'I know it's unlikely you went around thumping tables. Or
raging.' He paused. 'Well, maybe the raging . . .'

She raised her eyebrows. They both smiled. She looked
away. 'We had some tea.'

'Was it an Albert special?'

'You could stand your spoon in it.' She grimaced. 'He also
set out three cups.'

Milo nodded. 'He does that sometimes. Forgets my grandmother is long gone.'

'Oh.' That made her terribly sad. 'I tried to give him the
letter. He became confused. Said first that Charlotte had
drowned. Then denied knowing anyone of that name.' This

didn't seem to surprise Milo. 'We talked a little, and he tried to sell me a painting.'

'Oh, not the painting again. He's convinced someone's about to turn up and buy it, save the estate.'

'Are they?'

'No. It's a fake. My grandparents sold the original in the late fifties. Albert's been living off it, and other paintings, ever since.'

Ellie took a sip of wine. 'But Charlotte . . .' she said. 'Albert thinks she killed herself?'

'This morning my father was slightly more compos mentis. I asked him again about your visit. His description this time was like you've told me now.' Milo paused. 'He gets confused between the past and the present.'

'I'm sorry,' she said, and she was.

'But he did remember where his memory came from.'

She leaned forward eagerly. 'Yes?' Out of the corner of her eye, she noticed Deidre O'Brien watching them intently. Ellie moved so her back blocked the incoming gaze.

'It was of his mother. Nancy. My grandma. From the night they first arrived to live at Blackwater Hall in 1958. He kept repeating the year. 1958. 1958.'

'Didn't Hugo Rathmore, the heir, die in 1957?'

'You've done your research.'

She felt a pang of guilt. 'Well, I only googled a few things.' Indicating over her shoulder, she said, 'I was put up to it.' They both turned to look. Moira and Bernie were talking animatedly with their hands, Jules nodding and scribbling frantically in his notebook, then ripping out the page and scrunching it in confusion as the women appeared to change tack. She felt sorry for Jules: local oral history was a flexible subject. Dates and places, names and events morphed so that people sat around arguing about them until a new truth was arrived upon. He looked up. Caught her eye. There was an element of pleading in his gaze.

Milo was unfazed by her admission. 'There *was* a fight that night in 1958, and Nancy had been drinking. They were all in the front room . . . I believe you've seen it?' She nodded, recalled it well. The duck-egg-blue walls. Those worn wingback chairs. That once white carpet. 'My great-grandfather, Charles, told Nancy they were sure Charlotte hadn't just disappeared. Hadn't been taken by the IRA, as some had reported. He said she'd taken her own life to escape an arranged marriage.'

Ellie's fingers tingled. *Lord Hawley?*

Before she could speak, Milo continued. 'My father said he'd never seen his mother so incensed. He and Harriet – my aunt – were afraid. He was seventeen, and before that he'd never heard a cross word from either of his parents. Hearing about Charlotte's suicide *changed* his mother.'

Ellie frowned. 'But Charlotte couldn't have—'

'According to Albert, his father said Charlotte had been headstrong. She believed women were the equal of men.' Charlotte became suddenly impossible to dislike. 'And she idolised my grandma.'

'Nancy?' Ellie nodded slowly. 'Why?'

'She'd come from nothing. An orphan. Her life was entirely built by her own endeavour.' He paused, then added, 'I admire that. Forging your own fate.'

'Why are you telling me all this?'

'Because you took the letter.'

'Ah.' She flushed. 'Yes, well—'

'And,' Milo interrupted, 'that piqued my interest. If you were game enough to steal it' – she gave him a look of alarm, but he waved it away with a laugh – 'then I could at least bend some rules and look into the medical centre's records.'

This was a surprise. 'What?'

'Yes,' he said with a slightly resigned air. 'You were right to want to check. On the twelfth of August 1939, Dr Mortimer attended Blackwater Hall. And he was a *very* thorough note-taker.'

Her heart leapt. 'And? Charlotte was being mistreated?'

Milo pressed his lips together, shook his head. Smiled a little, with . . . *pride*? 'It turns out my great-aunt was quite the rebel.'

'I don't understand.' Across the room, a commotion; whoops and cheers. Ellie turned; although she couldn't see her, she knew the birthday girl had arrived.

Milo touched her arm gently, and she looked back at him. In his hand he held a sheet of paper.

'For you.' He gave it to her.

It was a medical record from 1939. Frowning, she began to read, a drunken rendition of Happy Birthday gaining momentum around them. 'Milo, I need to tell you something about the date of the letter: it was written *after* Charlotte disappeared . . .' She faltered. Read on. And inside her, somewhere deep, something shifted, and a piece of her began to melt, thawed by the actions of a young woman eighty years ago and the sister-in-law who inspired her.

Chapter Eighteen

Blackwater Hall, County Kerry

August 1939

A photograph was taken before the guests arrived, Blackwater Hall looming behind, the party squinting southward. It was dry – a miracle – and only the spongy lawn gave away the rain that had fallen the previous day. Lady Rathmore was on edge, but the rest of the family, even Hugo, seemed to be in a fine mood and Nancy wondered what Cook had put in that morning's eggs.

'Where's Charlotte?' she asked, taking a seat at the edge of the front row.

This brought a fresh flush to Lady Rathmore's cheeks. 'For goodness' sake.'

A marquee had been erected on the lawn below, its sides hoisted to reveal a scattered collection of tables and chairs. A long trestle was piled high: sandwiches, cakes, a bain-marie waiting to be filled. But half the table was empty, and Nancy knew this was reserved for the food the staff families would insist on bringing – Teddy said it happened every year.

'Tabby! Tabby!' Lady Rathmore rushed past Nancy. The staff were trying to finish their jobs and keep one eye on the photographer, waiting for the call to take their places. 'Tabby, go and find Charlotte.'

'Yes, ma'am.' Tabby appeared from the marquee, curtsied awkwardly and started across the lawn. The crispness of her uniform sat poorly on her, as though she were the understudy for the role of maid and had been drafted in at the last minute. She waved to her brother, standing in the row behind, and gave Nancy a wink as she passed.

She returned with Charlotte, who was grinning and clutching her wrist. It was wrapped in a white bandage.

'I think I should be on the end,' Charlotte paused in front of Nancy, 'you should be beside Teddy.' She was given a look that suggested that very discussion had already been had with Lady Rathmore. 'No,' she said, 'I insist.' She wiggled onto the chair, forcing Nancy between her and Teddy. The cool of her long skirt brushed Nancy's bare ankle.

Nancy shielded her eyes from the sun. 'Your mother said you slipped in the garden last night.'

'Yes, I've asked the doctor to attend me today. Here he comes now.' She pointed across the lough; a black car crawled along its edge. 'Would you accompany me?'

Nancy turned to her. She searched the younger woman's face for signs of pain as she used her bandaged hand to smooth her skirt. Firmly she poked at Charlotte's wrist.

'Nancy!' said Charlotte. But she didn't flinch.

Nancy hissed, 'You've done this on my account?'

'All right, take your places.' The photographer moved behind the tripod. 'Here we go . . .'

The younger woman shrugged. 'While he's attending to me, you're free to talk to him. It's up to you.' They looked at one another and Charlotte was no longer mischievous.

Nancy's eyes prickled and she blinked to push the feeling away. A gentle breeze licked at her hat – a Pied Piper style that Lady Rathmore had frowned at – and she moved her hand to her head. Tilted it towards Charlotte. A staff member, Tabby perhaps, made a smart comment and the back row laughed. The photographer gave them a look – 'This is a portrait for posterity, not a pantomime' – and there was silence again. A shift in the mood.

Nancy placed a hand gently on Charlotte's wrist, the surface of the bandage rough under her fingers. Her heart felt full. 'Thank you,' she whispered, 'thank you so much.' The photographer clapped his hands for silence, and with a click of the camera captured the moment.

Chapter Nineteen

Blackwater Hall, County Kerry
March 1958

The door to the little shed at the end of the vegetable garden was ajar. Hattie sat inside with her legs stretched in front of her, an open book in her lap. Heavy rain fell outside. 'Another Kerry squelcher,' as Papa would say.

She was yet to read a page of her book. Her mind was on other things. Last night at dinner Grandmother had announced that her governess would be arriving in April. Mama had been angry at this. 'It's not 1890. Calling a tutor a governess is faintly ridiculous. And how will we afford it?' Grandmother had walked to a painting hanging behind Mama – three jugs and a handful of apples, rich strokes that made the canvas as hummocky as the lough in a storm – and straightened it with one finger. 'Some of us have made excellent investments over the years.' To this, Mama had said the local school was perfectly good and Grandmother had called Ballinn a shanty town where men had dirty shoes and beaten hats. Later, Papa told Hattie the village had a soul that no amount of boot polish or millinery could provide. He had promised to take her there next week. 'It's the St Patrick's Day parade,' he'd whispered, winking.

A crunch of gravel brought her back to the present. The

footsteps outside were purposeful, quick and direct like Grandmother's. But heavier.

The shed door opened. Through it came a man; he stooped under the low doorway, watching his feet over the threshold.

He reached across the shed for a spade. Beside it, Hattie said: 'Hello.'

'Holy Mother of God!' He jumped, scrambled backwards, fell against the door. It closed with a thump. His hand covered his face.

Hattie shrank back into the corner, silent, eyes wide.

The rain eased and the light through the single four-paned window brightened for a moment. It fell on the man folded against the door, shaking.

'I'm sorry I scared you,' she whispered, clasping her book to her chest. The shock of the intrusion was quickly replaced by the feeling that she herself was the intruder.

The man took a deep breath and his shoulders lowered. When he looked up, his forehead furrowed, eyes bright under dark brows.

Hattie recognised him; he was the man who looked just like a green-eyed Marlon Brando. But scruffier. Tomas. The gardener.

'You scared me, is all.' His voice was softer than she remembered from the day by the lake when Mama's hand held hers so tight. He was avoiding her gaze, as though she was the adult and he the child.

Hattie's book, *The Secret Seven Win Through*, felt slick in her hands. She'd read it a dozen times but really it was a little young for her and she felt embarrassed by its presence. She put it cover-down on the bench next to her. It seemed stark against the scattering of dirty tools.

Tomas took a deep breath. 'Just let me get the run of myself here.' Out of his pocket he'd produced a packet of cigarettes and a box of matches. He offered them to her.

'Oh. Well. No thank you. I don't smoke.'

He raised his eyebrows and nodded. 'Probably for the best,' he said, striking a match. The smell of sulphur followed the flicker of light.

'Mama says they help you think,' Hattie ventured as she watched the smoke roll from his mouth. There was something luxurious about it. His shoulders dropped a little more.

'Is that so?' he said. For the first time, he smiled. He leaned across his knees and folded over himself like an accordion. 'That red hair of yours . . .'

She swung her plait over her shoulder and out of sight. Ashamed.

He shook his head. ''Tis lovely.'

Hattie realised then that she'd been gripping her hands together. She looked down as she released them, the skin white and red in patches. 'Lovely?'

'That's right,' he said. They sat in silence as the rain marched around them, the pitter-patter growing louder once again. Dusk was coming; she'd been in the potting shed all afternoon.

When his cigarette was half finished, he said to her: 'What're you doing here then?' The question was without accusation.

'We moved here. When Uncle Hugo died.'

He took a drag and nodded. 'Ah yes, bad business.'

'Did you know him?' she asked. Then she blushed, said, 'Sorry.'

'Not at all.' If he thought her boldness rude, he didn't show it. 'That is, I only knew him to see him.'

'Oh,' she said, her attention on the dirt under her fingernails. She would need to scrub them before dinner or risk another of Grandmother's lectures.

'Well, anyway, I was asking why you were *here*.' He tapped

his cigarette on the dirt floor, waved his hand around the shed as though it were a grand hall. 'Here in my shed.'

'This is your shed?'

'Well . . .' He thought a moment. 'Strictly speaking, no.'

'Oh,' Hattie said. She reached up and pulled down *The Secret Seven*. 'I thought it was a good place to read.' She held it out to him.

He wiped his hands on his trousers. The creases in them were fresh. 'Ah,' he said, taking the book, 'is it an adventure?' He flicked through the pages.

'Yes, it is. And it involves a garden shed.'

'Is it as fine as this one?'

She looked at the dirt floor, which she would have to brush off her skirt before going to the house. 'No, not as fine as this one,' she said, because that was what she thought he might like to hear.

'This old place was built by my father. Bit by bit. From timber left over after we repaired the boathouse. Before it was burned to the ground.'

It was a simple structure: rough-hewn timber planked horizontally and stained in places where the rain had seeped through. It smelled of damp earth. A small stove sat at one end, the door ajar. At the other end, a dozen large sacks were laid out in rows.

'What are they?' said Hattie.

'Those sacks? Spuds.' At her frown, he said, 'They're chitting.'

'Chitting?' She weighed the unfamiliar word.

He got to his feet, took three strides to the other end of the shed and reached into one of the sacks. From it he produced a potato. It was covered in small white shoots flecked with green. They stuck out at all angles as though given a fright.

'These shoots, they let me know the potato's ready for planting. Ready for St Patrick's Day.'

'Oh?' she said.

When it was clear she didn't understand, he went on, 'We always plant them on St Patrick's Day. 'Tis lucky. These potatoes'll feed the household for a year.'

She got up then, walked over to him. He gave her the potato. A shoot broke off in her hand. 'I'm sorry.'

He laughed. 'Ah, 'tis nothing. Plenty more. We set them with the eyes up.' He indicated the shoots.

'I've never seen a potato grow before.'

'Well,' he took it from her hand, 'you come down on Paddy's Day and we'll plant 'em together.'

'I'm sorry.' She was torn. 'Papa's taking me to Ballinn for the parade.'

He said, 'No matter, we'll be well done by then. You can do both if you like.'

She did like. She said, 'What day is it . . . St Patrick's Day?'

'March seventeen. Each and every year.'

'What's it for?'

He turned the potato in his hand, lithe fingers skipping over the shoots without breaking them. 'For remembering St Patrick. He brought Christianity to Ireland.'

That sounded to Hattie like a difficult thing to travel with. 'When?' she asked.

He looked pensive. As though the question was something he himself had never thought to ask. 'Oh,' he whistled, 'an age ago. More than a thousand years. Much more perhaps. It's said he died on March seventeen. 'Tis a national holiday and,' he nodded, 'the best day to plant spuds.'

'Even for English people?'

He laughed at this and returned the potato to the sack, winding its top shut. A signal that their conversation was over. He put out his hand and she took it as an adult would. Shook it. ''Twas fine to meet you, Miss Rathmore.' When he said her name, he frowned a little, tasted the word. Then his face cleared.

She said, 'You can call me Hattie.'

He still had hold of her hand; a firm grip. 'You take care, Hattie. Up at the big house.'

'I will.' She realised she didn't know his last name, so she just said, 'I will, Tomas.'

He was at the door now and looked back. 'You come to me if you need anything. I'll do my best to put it right.'

She started to say thank you, but he'd already gone, out into the garden, out into the easing rain, out into the evening as it spilled over the dusk.

Chapter Twenty

Ballinn, County Kerry
September 2019

A hush embraced the room and Ellie turned towards the stage, where a tiny figure with a shock of white hair climbed the stairs with slow, careful steps. The hands that reached out to assist were batted away impatiently.

Bernie leaned over. 'Here she comes. The birthday girl.'

When she reached the top, Tabby turned to shine a cheeky grin upon the crowd, revealing perfect pearly teeth that Ellie was certain weren't her own.

The crowd sent up a cheer and the crow's feet at the corners of her green eyes deepened. Her skin was crinkled, like once-scrunched paper, and the tip of a birthmark crept from the collar of her crimson blouse.

'*Céad míle fáilte*. Welcome.' Even without a microphone, her voice carried, and Ellie remembered that, along with Bernie, the pharmacist and the farmers, Tabby Ryan had been a permanent fixture of the Ballinn Dramatics Secret Society. She probably still was.

'I expect you'll be wanting some advice. That's what you're all here for, aren't you?' She spread her hands in question and the crowd laughed. 'And we'll be getting to that, but first — apparently — I'm supposed to tell you a little of my life. *They* say' – she indicated a group, family members, at the base of the stage – 'that a party for a century is the time to write my own eulogy.' Another laugh. 'But I'll do that for my one hundred and tenth.' A whoop from the back. Tabby waved it away.

'In case you're no good at mathematics, I was born in 1919, into an Ireland that longed for freedom, and just like almost everyone around, our family – seven kids and all – were poor. I went to Ballinn National School before Ma sent me to work at Blackwater Hall, over there towards Kenmare.' She spoke without bitterness, although the implication was heavy. 'Da was the gardener, and I was a maid of sorts. Can't say as I was very good at it. But working there did teach me a great lesson: money might be grand, but it can't buy happiness.' She paused, grappled for words.

The crowd held a collective breath.

'Give us a proverb,' came a heckle from the back.

Tabby's face cleared. 'The impatience of youth,' she quipped. She put her hands in the pockets of her slacks, the lines down the front of her legs crisp and fresh.

'I was given a helping hand, by the lady of the house, no less, to follow my passion for teaching. I must've been the only Kerry girl in history who never wanted to emigrate, and God help me I've been happy for it. From the beginning of my training in the autumn of 1940' – here Bernie nodded to herself – 'to my last class in 1980, 'twas my life.' She stopped, looked heavenward. 'That and, of course, my fifty-three years of marriage.

'During that time, our home became the rambling house, like O'Brien's cottage was before it fell to fire. Those were the happiest days of my life.' Ellie remembered that a footprint of the latter still existed, just a tumbled section of wall tucked behind the shop. 'When the day's work was done, men and women used to crowd into our kitchen and there was talk and entertainment. Politics too. It was a cross between the Abbey Theatre and Dáil Éireann, the heart and pulse of the village.

'But times changed and so did we. People no longer cared for the rambling house. They were busy. And now every day is filled to the brim with *things*. But I'll tell you something for nothing: the secret to a good life is to learn what matters and what doesn't. And that,' Tabby said, 'is harder than it sounds.'

A shaft of sunlight peered through the high windows and cut across the hall. For just a moment, a flicker of youth rippled over the old woman, and Ellie imagined her on that stage, years before: smooth skin, a tall frame and a light and nimble stride.

'I lost my beloved Noel twenty years ago. He was my rock, my best friend. The twinkle in my eye. My parents left this world more than four decades past, God rest them. And it's been an age since my brother . . .' Tabby faltered, a tiny chink appearing in her strong and confident facade. 'Tomas, he . . . we . . .' There was a weight in the room; the crowd's silence, its bated breath. Tabby's eyes became rheumy with some long-cherished or long-forgotten memory.

Then a disturbance – a child's cry, followed by a soothing sound, quick steps and the slam of the Lobby door – brought her back from wherever she had gone.

'So . . .' she assessed the crowd again, 'some eighty years ago, I made a promise, that on my one hundredth birthday, I'd write some of our *seanfhocal*, our proverbs, in rhyme.' She looked heavenward with a roll of her eyes, as though communicating with someone above.

Moira gasped with delight, and Ellie smiled. Someone stepped onto the stage with a cup of tea. Tabby took a sip. From her pocket she drew a piece of paper. She unfolded it theatrically and waggled those wisps of eyebrows. Then, in a lilting voice overflowing with rhythm and Kerry's long-stretched vowels, she began to read.

'If you haven't any shoes,
Pull yourself up from the blues,
Because you're bound to meet a man who hasn't feet.
And no matter who your da,
You must find out who you are;
And his mistakes you'll never to repeat.

Find the path of least resistance,
Make the most of your persistence,
So the breeze may always be there at your back.
Windy days are not for thatching,
And a cold ye'll be a-catching,
If you go out when the weather's rotten craic.

Be at heaven's gates ahead,
Before the devil knows you're dead,
Because no one ever lived without a wrong.
And life is just like tea,
And I know that ye'll agree,
'Tis bitter when we make it far too strong.

For sure, the world is mighty,
From Boston through to Blighty,
But the road is always longer walked alone.
Those who travel have a story,
And tales too of glory,
But there's never been a fire like your own.'

She folded the paper away, the final sing-song of her poem coming from memory as the stanzas shortened and her voice rose:

'A hundred years
I've walked this earth
And if you cannot see:
The *seanfhocal* have led my life
And I give them now to ye.

It sends to bed
A promise made
In another time:
"If I should reach a grand old age,
I'll put my speech in rhyme."'

Chapter Twenty-One

Holborn, London

August 1940

Nancy had published fourteen articles in the last year. Although her day job was still secretarial work, at night she sat at her desk overlooking the darkness of Parker Street, pen in hand, crinkled balls of paper scattered around her feet like tumble-weed waiting for the breeze.

Teddy was gone. She heard from him weekly or less. His censored letters arrived from the front smelling of sweat. Although she knew he was stationed in France, he never revealed much. Occasionally whole sections were blacked out, or individual words, little dark marks that looked like Hitler moustaches on the page. He'd been home once on leave and they'd talked about everything but the war. And at night she'd curled herself around him until the quiet rise and fall of his breath told her that he was elsewhere. Sometimes it took until dawn. On their last night, they made love.

That was fifteen and a half weeks ago. Nancy knew this because she'd marked the date in her diary without hope or expectation, and now the small swell of her belly and the gentle nausea that followed her around like a loyal hound confirmed what she already knew.

She was pregnant again.

She'd written to Teddy on the eighth week. His reply was full of hope and joy. It filled her with happiness. And nerves. And she'd thought to herself that if the enemy could reproduce her fear and spread it amongst the British population, they would win the war tomorrow.

The street outside the flat was quiet. In the last month the Germans had carried out three raids on Cardiff. To Londoners it felt a long way away, and they went about their daily business with an air of defiance, only one ear to the sky. A Friday night eighteen months ago would have seen her going out with Teddy to the theatre or dinner or the British Museum, to wander slowly among the exhibits discussing history or life or nothing at all. But now Nancy's world had contracted to the dingy offices of the *Chronicle* and this sitting room where she sat nursing an Agatha Christie and a mug of weak tea peppered with flecks of powdered milk. Dinner had been light: a little corned beef, a potato and fresh sweetcorn, the latter given to her by her boss from his cousin's allotment. She was tired already although it wasn't yet eight o'clock.

She took a sip of her drink, the warmth soothing even if the taste was not. A fly buzzed past her ear, and for just a moment, the noise made her heart skip a beat. She put down her book, went to the window.

Outside, a boy on a bike rolled to a stop beneath her. He produced a slip of paper from his leather bag, then, glancing along the street, left his bike against the wall and disappeared out of sight. Into her building.

Nancy stepped back from the window.

Three flats were accessible from the doorway below. She and Teddy lived on the middle floor in a two-bedroom shoebox that they'd furnished bit by bit. A bed first, then a small kettle for the stovetop. A month later they had enough cash for a sofa from a friend of a friend at Teddy's work. Then a table. Some chairs. And so it went. Each item adding a little something to their lives.

Mrs McLaughlin lived below them, a round and elderly lady with a Scottish accent and poor – or selective – hearing. The perfect neighbour. She was a widow, childless as far as Nancy knew. She spent most of her evenings out playing cards with a group of women who called themselves the Dames, and each day she went for lunch at Rules, well known for serving non-rationed foods: rabbit, grouse, pheasant. Every so often, when they met by chance outside the building, she'd ask Nancy in for a cup of tea. Invariably their hot drinks would sit cooling while they talked over un-iced whisky in Mrs McLaughlin's busy front room.

The floor above Nancy and Teddy had recently been rented by a young couple and their toddler, whose name Nancy was unlikely to forget, in that they had decided to call him Winston. The father was away at war, and although Winston's mother and Nancy had class and age in common, they were ships that passed in the night.

Nancy went to the door and pressed her ear against its blue surface. She heard the entrance close – Mrs McLaughlin must have left it unlocked again. There was silence. Hesitation. Then the footsteps began, fast and light up the stairwell. Straight past her door.

The rapid beating of her heart subsided. The fear of the telegram was omnipresent on London's streets, delivery boys occasionally left standing on empty doorsteps when it was clear someone was home.

She heard a faint knock above. A muffled conversation. Then, rather quickly, returning footsteps, slower this time as they descended.

Telegrams, of course, were not always bad news. She hoped that inside the envelope pulled from the boy's pannier there was something other than death. Her upstairs neighbours had once mentioned family across the pond; perhaps they were sending good news, unaware of the fear that a telegram in wartime Britain would carry with it.

Outside her door the footsteps faltered, shuffled a little as though they and their owner were engaged in some kind of dispute, and stopped. There was a heart-pounding pause and Nancy felt the room turn on a pin. She wanted to put her hands to her ears, block out what was to come.

A sharp knock.

She jumped – from the noise, from the jolt of adrenaline that pulsed through her. From dread. Breathing slowly, she smoothed her hair and closed her eyes. She suddenly felt weak at the knees, her back aching, her body heavy. With her left hand she held together the open collar of her blouse against a chill that came from nowhere. With her right, she flicked the latch and opened the door.

The boy who stood on the other side was even more diminutive than he'd appeared from above. His smoothly parted blond hair and his tanned skin made him look like a public schoolboy. When he opened his mouth, she realised he was not.

'Missus Rafmore?' he said. His eyes were round and blue. Apologetic. They matched his voice.

At his side, pinched between his thumb and index finger, was a small piece of paper. It was thin, inconsequential almost. Nancy froze.

'Are you Nancy Rafmore?' he said again. Either his voice was becoming gentler or Nancy's hearing was failing her. He was talking through cotton wool.

She steadied herself with one hand on the door frame, cleared her throat and arranged her face into a smile. 'How rude of me,' she said. 'Please come in.'

She walked to the sofa. Sat down.

'Ma'am?' said the boy, scurrying into the room after her. 'Wait.'

He stopped in front of her. 'Can I get you a glass of wa'er?'

She must have nodded, because he disappeared. She heard the tap running in the kitchen, a shuddering that shattered the silence of the room. He returned with a glass. A Waterford crystal tumbler, the last of four.

'Teddy's glass,' she smiled.

He knelt down beside her. 'Is 'e your 'usband? Teddy?'

'Yes.' Her voice was just a breath. The water was unpleasantly warm as it slid down her throat.

She looked up at the boy. 'What's your name?'

'Jimmy.'

'Jimmy,' she said, rubbing her tummy. 'Jimmy. What a nice name.'

He tried again. 'Ma'am, is your name Nancy Rafmore?'

She paused. 'Yes,' she said, her index finger ringing the rim of Teddy's glass. 'I'm afraid it is.'

As if he was pushing it through treacle, he slowly handed her the telegram, then turned and crossed the room with slow, careful steps. She didn't look up as the door clicked closed behind him.

She fanned herself with the telegram. While it remained sealed, it was still *potential* news; something that might or might not have happened. An unopened gift, an untested theory. An unexploded bomb.

She put it on the cluttered sitting-room table. The late-summer heat was oppressive and the recent rains had turned the humidity up a notch, but now Nancy began to shiver. She went to the kitchen, flicked on the hotplate, filled the kettle.

Once she had a cup of Barry's Tea between her gently shaking hands, she returned to the table and took a seat, sipping the tannic liquid. It was Teddy's favourite brew, a taste of him. Tea, like most things, was a sensitive subject at Blackwater Hall. The family was divided, of course. Lady Rathmore drank only Lyons, but his lordship insisted on Barry's. Last summer Charlotte had made her a special brew, fifty-fifty Lyons and Barry's, winking as she added an extra teaspoon of the latter to the pot.

Reaching across the table, Nancy tidied away her notes, stacking them on the floor beside her so that alone on the table's clean surface, save her half-drunk cup of tea, was the telegram.

She picked it up with shaking hands, brought it to her nose as she often did with books. There was no scent. It was an item that smelled of exactly nothing; a void, an empty space, a hollow.

She went to the window to catch the last of the light. Any other evening she would pull her blackout curtains, switch on a lamp. Write.

But not tonight.

She opened the telegram. The text on the page was short. Square and staccato.

It wasn't from the War Office.

It was from Hugo Rathmore.

Charlotte – beautiful Charlotte – was dead.

Chapter Twenty-Two

Derrynane Beach, County Kerry
September 2019

It struck Ellie as she stepped from the car that it might well be the first time she'd been to Derrynane Beach alone. And at that time of the day. Or was it still night? A spectacular display hung overhead, the Milky Way cutting the southern sky, a billion stars flickering in the dawn. And although it wasn't yet October, the chill that nipped at her uncovered ears heralded the oncoming winter.

She started across the grass-covered dunes, one hand pulling up her hood, the other gripping a coffee.

She'd woken before 5 a.m., her mind whirling, thrown back the covers – with a sharp intake of breath at the chill air – and tiptoed down to the kitchen. Outside was only blackness, and the fluorescent light of the kitchen was so bright she felt an interrogation might be imminent. At that moment, a creak had come from upstairs. The click of the bathroom light. The running of a tap. Then slow, sleepy footsteps returning to Moira's room. Ellie had been taken with a fancy: to leave the house. To get some air. To use that quiet moment – the second morning in as many days that she'd woken with life coursing through her veins – to gather some of her thoughts and throw many others away.

The track turned to sand as her eyes adjusted to the dark. A shape passed overhead – an owl? – and the surrounding grasses waved in the wind. *The quiet chatter of a thousand ghosts.* Only this morning it wasn't quiet. It was frenzied; the grasses roaring as they were thrown in the wild air.

She reached the summit and stopped. Derrynane Beach stretched before her, a light strip in the darkness, a mile of pale sand hugging the bay, silver slivers of foam rolling landward under the twinkling sky. Dark rocky outcrops peppered its western extent, and to the east, Lamb's Head reached out into the ocean. She stood taking it in.

They'd stayed late at the party last night, Ellie hovering, hoping to get close to Tabby, hoping to ask, *Did you know Charlotte? Was she as beautiful as her portrait? I have her image with me . . .* As the crowd thinned, she had finally managed to corner the birthday girl, and Tabby had been delighted to see her.

'Ellie Fitzgerald,' she'd said by way of greeting. 'You're only a slip of a thing, but don't you look well?' Tabby was much smaller offstage, and Ellie embraced her lightly, worried at her fragility. *Ommph,* she'd said as Tabby pulled her into a firm hug. There was the scent of whiskey on her breath, but her gaze had been steady as a rock as she held Ellie at arm's length. 'I hear you're a writer these days?'

'Journalism.'

'*If you have the words there's always a chance that you'll find the way.*'

'Seamus Heaney?'

'That's him all right.' Tabby appraised her. 'You've read him?'

Ellie nodded. 'But he's nothing on *your* poetry.' She winked, and the old woman waved her hand with a *pfft.*

'A promise is a promise. And I fancy I enjoyed it in the end.

I might take it up. The hundred-year-old poet.' The notion pleased her and she laughed.

'Who was the promise to?'

'My brother, Tomas. He was a fine man. I miss him still.' She sipped from her rather full whiskey glass, and Ellie noticed several relatives hovering in the background, clearly waiting to extract it from her grasp. 'I remember the night the pact was made. Down at O'Brien's. The old rambling house. Everyone trying to impress a lady . . . that's how it came about.'

'A lady?'

'Over from London she was. Nancy Rathmore. My God. Traffic would stop for her back then.' Tabby frowned then, as though the good memory were overtaken by something less pleasant.

Ellie paused. *Nancy?* At the rambling house. Here in Ballinn? 'Nancy Rathmore? Charlotte's sister-in-law?'

At the mention of Charlotte's name, Tabby started. 'Yes,' she said cautiously. 'You've heard of her?' Her drink started to tip, the ice clinking at the glass's edge. A man stepped in, took it from her, whispered in her ear. Did Ellie imagine that he shot her a glare? Tabby batted him away.

A few eyes in the crowd had turned to them.

Ellie improvised. 'I remember the chant, about the lady of the lake. *Grab your boots and leave your drink—*'

'Yes, yes, I remember it,' Tabby interrupted. 'Made light of what happened, that ditty.'

'What did happen?'

'She drowned,' Tabby said quickly.

'You knew her from Blackwater Hall?'

'Ah, for the blink of an eye.' She smiled. 'I worked there for near-on three years. Left after she died.'

'You said Niamh Rathmore helped you in some way.' When Tabby frowned, Ellie continued, 'Your speech?'

'Did I say that?'

'Yes. *A helping hand, by the lady of the house.*'

Tabby laughed. 'No, not Niamh. Horror of a woman.' She paused, dredging her memory. For the speech or something else, Elle wasn't sure. 'No, it wasn't Niamh who helped me. It was Charlotte.'

But of course it was. 'How?'

Tabby paused and looked to the ceiling, just as she had done on stage, as though being observed from above. 'She encouraged me to apply for a scholarship. She believed – and she was quite right – that women could do anything. Ahead of her time, that one.'

Ellie wanted to reach across the years and hug Charlotte. Wanted to *know* her. Wanted to tell her: I see the things you did. Helping people. Caring. Looking through class, looking through gender.

'What was she like?'

Tabby frowned, searched Ellie's face. She looked as though she might change the subject, but then she said, 'Beautiful. Charismatic. Determined.'

'Really?' Ellie's mouth twitched.

'Oh yes, she used to sneak down to the IRA meetings. There's something I've never told anyone!' She winked. 'She despised the aristocracy. And yet she was one of them.' She shook her head. 'And due to marry one too.'

Ellie started. 'Yes, I wanted to ask you—'

'Mam?' A man appeared beside Tabby, taking her arm. 'The reporter from *The Kerryman* wants to talk to you again before he leaves. You remember him?' He spoke in that way people did; too loud, too slow. Patronising. Ellie felt a flash of anger. She gave a small grimace and turned to Tabby, intending to bid her goodnight. As she did so, the older woman took her hand. Held it firm. 'I'll see you again, Ellie Fitzgerald.' Then, with a wave, she had gone.

Ellie descended the dune, searching for the sand that lay between the tides; steady, firm, reliable. There wasn't a footprint ahead, nor any behind save her own. She paused at the water's edge, beyond the grasp of the reaching waves, and drank her now-cold coffee as the darkness lifted. Her tense shoulders dropped and she felt something she hadn't for so very long.

Calm.

'Morning!' A brisk voice was whipped away by the wind.

Ellie's bubble burst. Just like that, the world was back. She pushed aside a swell of irritation and turned to the figure who stood beside her, hood up. In his hand he held a travel mug, the top flipped open. Steam wafted from it. Strong black coffee.

She became aware of her bare face; no armour, only blood-shot eyes and pale, dry lips. 'Milo.' Her voice came in a squeak. 'Morning.' She glanced at him briefly, but he was transfixed by the rolling sea. Clouds gathered in the south, candyfloss above the ocean.

'Nice party?' he said.

'I'm a bit fragile.' She had hoped the wind would lift the fog of last night's wine. 'But yes, a nice party.'

'Tabby's a dote.' Ellie smiled; the turn of phrase was old, but it suited him well. 'Not quite as strong as she makes out, but not far off.'

'She does seem . . . vigorous. She worked at Blackwater Hall. But you know that?'

'Yes,' said Milo. 'Her and her father. She told me. He was the gardener. Hired the very day my great-grandfather, Charles, arrived in 1910.'

'Oh?' Surreptitiously she bit her bottom lip, coaxing colour into it.

'Transformed the garden, apparently. I'm afraid my hacking at the overgrowth doesn't really do it justice.'

Ellie said, 'Fancy a walk?'

They turned to track the beach, the sea lapping at their left, their slow strides matching. He said, 'I've been thinking . . .' Her heart leapt. 'Perhaps you *could* look into it?' His words were both a question and a statement. 'Because now I think about it . . .'

'Yes?'

'It would mean a lot to Albert. To know what happened to Charlotte. I believe it would help him . . .' He made a guttural sound. *Arrh.* He was, she realised, embarrassed.

'It's okay, I understand.' Although she didn't. She let the silence linger, knew he would speak again.

And he did. 'My whole life, there has been a feeling that has sat over my family. Over Blackwater Hall. It infuses everything. Even now . . . Albert hates me being there. Frets that something will happen to me.' He ran a hand through his hair. Laughed a little. 'It's the curse.'

'I'm sorry?' Ellie pulled back her hood and the cold bit her ears. 'What was that?'

'Really? You're going to make me say it again?' He rubbed his eyes. 'Albert believes Charlotte cursed the house and all that remained of her there. That's why my mother died. That's why Hugo died. So my father says.'

'Oh.' She frowned, thought back to her visit to Blackwater Hall. When Albert went to make tea. And returned, startling her. *We mustn't touch it. It's cursed.* Her heart ached for him.

'It's ridiculous, of course,' said Milo.

'No, it isn't. If it's real to Albert . . .'

'It is. Harriet told me he's always believed it. Ever since he was seventeen.' They crossed back up and over the dune. 'And if Charlotte ran away, I want him to know.'

Ellie nodded, her chest tight.

Milo shrugged, tried to lighten the mood. 'You never know, I might have cousins. Relatives.' He looked towards the sun, half lifted now from behind the eastern hills. 'That would be something.'

In that moment, he seemed so lonely that she wanted to reach out, take his hands between her own. 'I understand.' And she did. She too had no siblings. Had also lost a parent. Moira had been an orphan and Cillian an only child. They were a small rural Irish family; a rare commodity. But she'd had the village.

And Milo had not.

She paused, looked back at their trail crossing the sand. 'If Charlotte made a life elsewhere, she'll have left footprints.'

'If anyone can find them, I gather it's you?' They began to walk again.

'How so?'

'I read up on the McCarthy case.'

She froze. After it all came out – during the time Davy McCarthy was going after her, demanding apologies – people often said things like that to her: *I heard about the Stanley Street thing.* From there, the conversation could go one of two ways: a pat on the back or a diatribe about sticking her nose into other people's business.

'. . . and I can't understand why it's not being investigated,' Milo was saying. 'Have you spoken to your TD?'

His vote of confidence gave her an unexpected flush of pleasure. 'No,' she said. '*Out of sight, out of mind.*' It was what Jeremy had told her when she said she was leaving for Kerry.

'Shall we?' Milo nodded back towards the treeline, where, somewhere beyond, she'd parked the Micra. She nodded and drained her cold coffee with a grimace.

He watched her a moment, then said, 'Top-up?' His cup

was tipped toward her. It felt like a strangely intimate gesture, and she hesitated. 'I haven't touched it yet,' he said, and she realised he'd taken her silence for caution.

She looked away, smiling. Warmth crept up her face, even through the biting wind. She took the lid off her mug. 'Thank you.' She watched the hot dark liquid splash inside, then took a sip; it was as strong and bitter as it smelled.

Small dimples formed on Milo's cheeks and she realised he was chuckling.

'What?'

'That look of pleasure on your face,' he said. 'You'd think I'd offered you a mug of gold.'

They carried on, arrived at the treeline, paused by their cars.

'Thanks for the coffee,' she said.

'Thanks for the company,' he replied, then blushed, as though admitting that he'd enjoyed her company was too intimate for him, as though he felt as she did when they'd shared the coffee. He looked away, his gaze tracing the fall of a leaf dropping from a sally, landing softly on the path that led back to the beach.

Chapter Twenty-Three

Ballinn, County Kerry

September 2019

Later that morning, with a Procaffination coffee beside her, Ellie began the search for ferry passenger lists in 1940. From Dublin. From Cork. From Belfast.

I am coming on the next boat.

Departures to America were digitised and complete – a search for *Rathmore* brought up nothing – but Britain and mainland Europe were a different story. There were no emigration lists. No records. No footprints. If Charlotte had made her way across the Irish Sea – or further, to continental Europe – her departure from Ireland wasn't recorded.

She called Jules.

'At least,' he said, 'we know she didn't go to America. There was always the chance she'd crossed the pond to find her mother's relatives.'

'Speaking of relatives . . . or almost relatives . . .'

'Yes?'

'Could you look into Lord Hawley for me?' She imagined Jules scrambling to find his notebook. There was a pause. 'Hello?' she said down the silent line.

Then a muffled sound, and he was back. His voice overflowed with excitement. 'Just getting my notebook.'

'Really?' She smothered a smile.

'Leave it with me,' he said. And with a click, he was gone.

ॐ

When Dylan called, Ellie was already thinking about him. She'd got sidetracked while researching Dún Laoghaire – had Charlotte taken a boat from that harbour? – and spent an hour dragging around Google Maps looking at all the places the two of them used to go. Dublin already felt like a lifetime ago.

Her shaking finger hovered over the phone. The red cross. Then the green. Red again. While she debated, it rang out.

Coward.

She thought back to Moira, when they'd sat together in the reeds before the setting sun. *Feck him, Ellie,* she'd said, her eyes like fire. Ellie longed to be that angry at Dylan. Longed to hate him.

But she loved him still. *Didn't she?*

Beneath her fingers, the phone pinged.

I'd like to come to Kerry to see you.

Then another:

I'm so sorry x

She put down the phone and plunged her hands deep into her pockets. Trapped them where they could no longer tremble. She stood. Went to the counter. 'A turmeric latte, please, Nils. With a shot of espresso.'

As he packed the portafilter, he half turned to her, frowning. 'The work is . . . heavy?'

'No, it's okay.' She smiled reassuringly, reading Nils's latest quote written in bright blue chalk on the board behind him.

It's always darkest before the dawn.

How she hoped that was true.

He handed her the latte and leaned forward on the counter,

resting his chin in his hands. 'So, journalist Ellie, what kind of things do you write?'

She ran her finger around the rim of the double-walled glass. 'Housing, mostly.'

He made a face. 'Housing?'

'Well, the *human* side of housing.' She felt a little defensive.

'Ah, *oui*. A man's house is his castle.'

She smiled at his use of the phrase. 'I suspect Tabby Ryan would like you.'

'The one-hundred-year-old?'

She nodded. 'She's fond of proverbs. *Seanfhocal* in Irish. It means *old word*.'

'*Mais oui. Seanfhocal.* I know this.'

'Oh?'

'I am learning Irish.'

'Really?'

'I *love* languages.'

Ellie felt a stab of shame. Her own Irish was no more than phrases that lingered from her school days. It was almost as bad as her French. 'I'm terrible at them.'

He shook his head. 'Languages are like music, Ellie. Everyone has a bit of it in them, *non*?'

'Not me.' They paused. Outside, the sun broke through a cloud and hit Ballinn's green square. Several maple trees waved, the ground beneath them rich red with early fallen leaves.

'So,' he said, pouring himself a glass of milk, 'this housing . . . whose castle are you writing about?'

'Castle?'

'*Oui*, the man's house . . . his castle?'

She thought of her blog. 'I suppose I used to write about houses as . . . *more* than a place to spend the night, more than a building. Houses as . . . an anchor.' She gazed out at Ballinn's empty main street. 'Somewhere people return to when every-where else is stormy.'

'Well,' he said, wiping the already pristine countertop, 'sounds good. But . . .'

'Yes?'

'A castle is more . . . how do you say? Sexy?'

She laughed. *Castle.* She looked out of the window again. A whisper of gold lay like a blanket over the hills. And the café was empty. 'Nils,' she said before she knew it, 'want to go for a spin?'

❧

They stood with their arms draped over a farm gate and stared at the towering ruin in the field. 'Well,' said Nils, 'it is no Versailles.'

Ellie turned from him, closed her eyes. 'No . . .' Wynn's Castle was *not* as she remembered. Her mind had played a cruel trick. Her father's words had lain like a pall over her memo-ries. *Create it, Ellie: the smoke rising from the chimneys, the smell of a rose garden, the taste of bread baked on hot coals. See the soaring roof. Watch the crows circle overhead.* The castle appeared to have been abandoned for centuries. The four-storey gable – punched through with gaping holes that had once held windows – was surrounded by an impressive, imposing stone wall, but the rest of the structure was gone, scattered in the field at its feet.

On the gate was a sign.

Private. Keep Out.

'I think it is not likely, Ellie.' Nils interrupted her reverie. The day had brightened and the wind was now just a gentle breeze.

'What?'

He was looking at her, frowning. 'Your needle. Here. At this castle. In 1940.'

There were too many gaps in Charlotte's story and no threads to tie them together. That was what Ellie had told Nils as they drove west out of Ballinn. An hour and a half of winding coastal road had passed in a flash.

Why had she jumped to the conclusion that Charlotte had written the letter from Wynn's Castle? That the second word in the letterhead – obscured as it was by a smudge – was *castle* at all. It was Bernie, she realised. Bernie had echoed her own initial thoughts.

And Ellie had run with it.

Because of what it meant to her.

Nils nudged her. She followed his gaze. A huge man strode across the field towards them. He had hands the size of bowling balls and a face like thunder. Cattle scattered like pins as he passed.

''Tis a private field!'

Ellie and Nils took a step back.

As he came closer, red faced and puffing, it dawned on Ellie that she'd met him before.

'Mr O'Leary?' she said, moving forward once more to the gate. His stride faltered, his eyes narrowed. He stopped ten feet from them. Suspicious. 'Mr O'Leary, it's Ellie Fitzgerald. I came here once. With Dad.'

'*Dad?*' he looked behind her as though he expected an extra man to appear.

Ellie cleared her throat. 'Cillian. Cillian Fitzgerald. We came here when I was younger.'

The man searched her face, his brow furrowed. Then realisation dawned. Pity, sorrow crossed his features. 'Young Eleanor?'

She spread her hands. 'Not so young now. But yes.'

He removed his cap; it was stained with flecks of paint and mud. 'How are you? How's your mammy?'

'Fine, fine.' Ellie wanted to ask about his wife or children, but she knew nothing about him save his name and his face, now two decades older. She smiled. Faltered.

'And I'm Nils.'

Mr O'Leary looked up, clearly glad of the interjection. 'Neil!' He held out his hand and his meaty fingers curled around Nils's elegant digits. He turned to Ellie, beaming. 'Glad to see you're well settled.'

Nils and Ellie looked at each other, and laughed. 'Thank you,' was all they said, because the notion had clearly delighted Mr O'Leary. Her and *Neil*. Here by his field.

Ellie nodded past his shoulder at the folly towering above them. 'We thought we'd drop by to get a glimpse of the castle.'

Mr O'Leary looked around with annoyance, as though the ruin had just appeared. 'Ah yes. She's still there. Still standing. Could do with some work, o'course, but who's going to pay for it, that's what I ask.'

Ellie thought about Blackwater Hall; that mustiness, the overgrown ivy, the untended lawn that led to the lake. Wynn's Castle made it look like a new-build. 'Well . . . it's a big job,' she said inadequately.

'The place has ruined enough lives,' he said. 'Let it go to dust.'

They appraised the ruin in silence. The only sound now was the gentle grazing of cattle. The ocean, though visible in the distance, was quiet, the wind having gone to worry elsewhere. That was Kerry: four seasons in one day.

'When was it built?' asked Nils.

'Started in 1867 by a Lord Headley. Englishman, o'course.' Mr O'Leary rolled his eyes, then grimaced. 'No offence, lad.' Ellie and Nils exchanged another giggle.

Ellie said: 'Are you sure it wasn't a Lord *Hawley*?'

'No, Eleanor. Lord Headley.' He tapped his temple. '*Head*-ley. That's the one. Brought himself an architect across the Irish

Sea. But no sooner had they started work than the lord raised rents. And when people couldn't pay, they were evicted.' He seemed delighted with his audience now that they posed no threat. 'Some starved, you see? By 1886, the lord had gone. Bankrupt.'

Nils attempted an English accent without success. 'And after?'

'Abandoned,' said Mr O'Leary. 'Then used as a training centre for reservists during the First World War.'

Ellie tried to imagine it: the roof intact, the grounds a hive of activity, chimneys puffing turf smoke. 'And then?'

Mr O'Leary shrugged. 'The IRA burned it in the Civil War. Along with most everything else English. But 'tis water under the bridge nowadays. Right, Neil?' He tapped Nils's shoulder and the Frenchman nodded graciously.

Although Ellie knew the answer the moment they'd arrived, she asked, 'So no one lived here in the 1940s?'

Mr O'Leary let out a booming laugh. Leaned across the gate and looked at Nils. 'Would you listen to yer wan!' He cleared his throat. 'No chance. Sure, it's been this way since 1921.'

Ellie nodded, feeling foolish. She'd remembered Wynn's Castle from the trip with her father and seen things the way she'd wanted rather than the way things were. Was that, she thought, how she'd been with Maxwell Cray's secretary? An idea, an intimation, that she'd run away with until *it* had run away with her?

Nils was watching her as Mr O'Leary filled him in on the whereabouts of Lord Headley's descendants, and he reached across and took her hand. Squeezed it. She gave him a small smile.

'Young love,' said Mr O'Leary, stopping to appreciate them. 'Your father would have approved, I'm sure of it.' Ellie smiled; Cillian Fitzgerald would have seen the humour in the situation, that was for sure.

Mr O'Leary fished in his pocket for his phone. The jingle it made shattered the countryside peace. He held up a finger, then answered with little more than a grunt. "Tis herself above. Lunch.' He repeated his regards to 'your mammy' and started off across the field, his shoulders a little looser than when he'd barrelled towards them scattering cattle in his wake.

Ellie glared at the folly. 'A dead end.'

'No,' said Nils, letting go of her hand and leaning back on the gate. 'I don't think so.'

'Charlotte wasn't here.'

'No, but *you* were.' His voice was gentle. 'That's why you wanted to come.' It wasn't a question.

She watched a robin search Mr O'Leary's boot prints for treats. 'I was here with my dad. Once.'

'What happened to him, Ellie?'

She looked at her bitten fingernails. 'He died. When I was seventeen.'

Nils waited.

'An accident. He . . .' She glanced at the ruin. 'He was on his way here. To Wynn's Castle. I was supposed to go with him.' It was true, but not the whole truth. She pushed away the events that came after: the garda knocking at the farm's door, the incomprehensible words, the ashen face of her mum as she'd fallen to her knees. 'But I didn't.'

It could all have been different.

Nils said gently: 'And you never came back?'

'No.'

'And it is as you expected?'

She shook her head. The castle was not at all what she remembered. But when she glanced at Nils, she realised he meant something entirely different. 'He's not here, if that's what you mean. I was afraid he would be. I had this . . . this *fear* that when I looked, I'd see his face in the shadows.'

Nils took her hand once again, turned it over in his own. 'Ellie, did no one ever tell you ... the dead, they don't live in places like this.' He placed her own palm to her chest. 'It is here. That,' he said, 'is where they stay.'

When she only nodded and looked at her feet, he took his hand away and looked back to the castle. Let the silence linger. Then he cleared his throat. 'It's funny, *non*, about Charlotte ...'

She looked up, glad of the interjection. 'What about her?'

'It's funny that the paper was not from a hotel. Because she must have stayed somewhere before taking a boat.'

Ellie blinked once, twice. A hotel? She gazed back at the ruin, then dug into her satchel. Carefully she unfolded Charlotte's letter and held it to the sky.

There it was. Right in front of her. The word *Hotel*, visible through the brown stain that smeared the header.

And it was a place she knew.

'Nils, you're a genius.'

'*Mais oui*, I try.'

She took his hand and squeezed it. Pulled him away from the gate. 'I have to go.'

'But where?' He laughed at her enthusiasm.

'To Dublin.'

Chapter Twenty-Four

Holborn, London
August 1940

Nancy's birthday came and went with the flicker of a candle. Not the type that sits on a birthday cake, but one that's lit to remember those loved, and lost. It sat on her table and she stared into it as night stole the day away.

It was a tradition she'd seen practised widely on her two visits to Ireland, the lighting of candles. They shone out of windows, sat by gravesides, blinked in the wind. Tabby had told her that three burned constantly in their family home, one for each sibling lost in childbirth. And at Ballinn's village church – which Nancy had visited with Teddy – the walls were alive with a golden glow.

It was the very first day in Nancy's adult life that she'd woken on the sixth of August without a ball of excitement in her tummy. Had Teddy been there to comfort her, she might have made it through the work day, might have avoided feigning sickness and returning home by lunch. Might have put on a brave face. For his benefit. Because amongst her grief, her sorrow, the hollowness that sat where her heart should be, was worry. How would she tell him? What would she say? Could a few scrawled words on wafer-thin paper really explain that his only sister, his beloved sibling, was gone? Drowned in an accident in Lough Atoon, the midnight water that sat always watching at the base of the house.

No one knew the depth of that inky pool. At times, on a dead day, it looked almost swampy, the reeds at its edge languishing lazily in the heavy air. But when a stiff wind blew from the Atlantic, waves jumped from its surface as though driven from a thousand feet below.

But a few feet, a thousand feet, it didn't matter.

Charlotte was gone.

She fell from the punt, Hugo had written. A few words to answer none of her questions. Who saw her fall? What was she doing out there? Why didn't she swim to the lake's rocky southern shore? Drag herself up the muddy furze-rimmed waterline below the house? Or climb onto the pier on the lake's western extent? The latter was strong enough, but in a state; leaning at odd angles, heaving towards the water. Charlotte had told her that it and the adjacent boathouse had been built when Charles arrived in Ireland as temporary accommodation while the long-abandoned Blackwater Hall came back to life. 'He might still be living in it,' she had said, 'if Mother hadn't arrived with all her money.' A moment after that, she'd jumped up and run along the rickety pier, launching herself from its far end with a whoop and a splash.

Nancy felt heat on her face and pushed the candle away. But when it had no effect, she wiped her cheek. Tears coated her palm. She stood and walked through darkness to the kitchen. Felt around a cupboard until she found Teddy's glass and a half-empty bottle of cooking brandy. She took them back to the table, set them down. Contemplated them in the flickering light.

Then poured a measure.

This time last year, she'd been at Blackwater Hall. Teddy had borrowed the car for the day and invited Charlotte along for the Grand Tour, a trip around the rugged Iveragh Peninsula. On the way, they'd stopped at Derrynane Beach: walked the windswept dunes, paddled in the sea.

From there, they'd tracked north before pausing in Glenbeigh for a picnic. They ate at the base of Wynn's Castle, a towering ruin on the village boundary. It had been a perfect place for Charlotte to give a treatise on the evils of aristocracy, which Teddy and Nancy had swallowed with polite nods. 'If there's ever been an example of abuse of power, then Lord Headley is it,' she'd finished with a flourish as they'd driven away.

By the time they'd arrived at the gates of Blackwater Hall, the sun was setting over the mouth of Kenmare Bay. They'd paused, got out of the car. And as she was no longer quietly careful of her stomach, Nancy had hopped onto its bonnet, her soft plimsolls making barely a sound, to take in the view that lay beyond.

'Thank you both,' she'd said. For despite the darkness within her, there'd also been light.

Now she took a nip of the brandy and swallowed it, scrunched her eyes against the fire that slid down her throat. She shook her head, pushed back the tears. Looked into the candle.

Charlotte might be gone, but she still burned bright.

Chapter Twenty-Five

En route to Dublin
September 2019

Ellie waved at Moira, who insisted on waiting on the platform as the train pulled out of Killarney. A day trip to Dublin, Ellie had decided, was the best option for getting in and out of the city with her nerves and mind intact.

The afternoon before, she'd returned Jeremy's missed calls. He was surprised – pleased? – to finally hear from her. There was news, he said, about Davy McCarthy. She'd cut him off, said she'd come up to the city, discuss it in person. And if that was to be the case, *The Irish Times* could foot the train fare. He'd agreed – with a very suspicious 'if you'd prefer' – and she'd hung up without an iota of guilt. Well, perhaps just a little.

Her expenses taken care of, her finger had hovered over Dylan's name. She longed to press call. Longed to hear his voice, longed for him to say those words: *I'm so sorry.* But she hesitated.

If he wanted to see her, that was fine. She would travel to Dublin. But not for him.

For Charlotte.

I can see you in Dublin tomorrow. Midday, she'd messaged. His reply came back: *Yes. Lunch at the Westbury?*

Okay.

Immediately she'd turned off her phone. Didn't want to backtrack, didn't want to change her mind. But wanted to change it all the same.

To Moira, she'd said simply: 'There's something I need to check. About Charlotte.' Moira had been delighted at the news, but as she waved her away, the creases that crossed her features told Ellie her mum knew she was, once again, hiding something.

She had dressed for the city – sleek clothes and dark heels – but in her handbag she carried a pair of flats. She'd made an appointment for a blow-dry and planned to look glossy when she met Dylan, another version of the person who now sat on the train, stomach heaving with anxiety.

And now, as they paused at another tiny station, her phone rang.

'Morning.' It was Jules. 'I did a little digging into Lord Hawley.'

'Oh.' She sat up straight. Realised with a flush of guilt that she hadn't called him after her visit to Wynn's Castle.

'Big fellow.'

'I'm sorry?'

'Found a photo of him. Rotund, is what I'll say. A spiritualist, bizarrely, and more than a quarter of a century older than Charlotte.' He paused, and Ellie pulled Charlotte's photo from the back of her notebook: those doe-like eyes, that far-off look. Was she already planning her escape? A woman who hated the aristocracy destined to marry a lord.

Jules continued, 'In April 1940, he was posted to Norway, just before German occupation. He was still there when the Norwegians surrendered a couple of months later. A fascinating story, really. He hid near Bergen with a wealthy family, tucked away in a barn apparently.'

'What happened to him?'

'He escaped and took the daughter of the house with him. Married her and all her money. Their children litter Surrey.'

'So their engagement – he and Charlotte – came to nothing?'

'It appears so.'

When Jules hung up, Ellie shut her eyes. Her hands rested on her closed laptop, and despite the rocking of the train, or perhaps because of it, she fell towards sleep.

Her phone vibrated. She ignored it. Now that she'd asked for Jules's help, he would be intolerable. She twisted in her seat, laid her head against the cool of the window. He would have to wait.

Again the vibration.

She groaned and opened her eyes. The train had stopped at Mallow, the first specks of rain turning the pavement grey. Her phone sat on the tray table.

An unknown number.

She let it ring out, then tapped it into Google. Scrolled through the hits. No warnings of nuisance calls. No scam alerts. But there, on page 2, a link to a Kildare community newsletter from twelve months previously. She opened it.

The Men's Shed is now back on its winter schedule with meetings on Thursdays at 7 p.m. This week's talk: Mental Health and Divorce, From the Inside, by Dr Rathmore.

From the back of the notebook she took out a slip of paper. Albert's scrawled handwriting. And there it was, the same number, only the last digit wasn't a three as she'd thought, it was an eight. Squeezed up against the zero before it. She glanced out of the window as the near-empty train pulled away, the grey morning throwing back a shadow of her reflection.

He answered on the third ring. 'Ellie, it's Milo. Thanks for calling back.' She started to speak, but he continued. 'I heard you're on your way to Dublin?' *Christ*, thought Ellie. Her mum had clearly picked up the morning paper. 'While you're up there—' He was interrupted by a muffled voice.

'Sorry?' said Ellie.

Then he was back. 'Would you like to meet my aunt?'

'Harriet?' Her heart leapt.

'You can ask her about Charlotte. I've told her about the letter.'

Ellie opened her notebook. Slipped in the back was the letter, protected in its white envelope. 'Yes,' she said, 'actually, I'd love to.'

'Hang on . . .' chatter in the background, 'look, I've got to go. She'll be working at the Pickled Oyster around lunchtime. I'll let her know you're coming.'

She cleared her throat. 'The Pickled Oyster?'

Milo had hung up. Ellie stared at her phone for a moment before selecting 'Create New Contact' and typing *Dr Rathmore*.

Then she deleted it and wrote, simply, *Milo*.

Chapter Twenty-Six

Dublin

September 2019

If Ellie had hoped for one of those blue autumn days when Dublin's sepia tones felt historical rather than dreary, she was to be disappointed. It was raining, heavily, the wind whipping the air in such gusts that the flimsy umbrella she'd bought at Heuston station had already popped a spoke.

She took a table by a wall of glass on the first-floor lobby of the Westbury. Around her, people chatted happily, drinking coffee and cocktails, lolling on the laid-back loungers. They were wholly at odds with how she felt.

It was midday – she was exactly on time – and her gaze wandered along Harry Street and out towards Dublin's famous Grafton Street. A flower seller had set up outside; a kaleidoscope in an otherwise colourless day. Around her, people went about their business, wearing black and sporting black expressions.

Moments before, Ellie had slipped into the hotel's plush bathroom, its sleek marble surfaces in sharp contrast to her wet and wild look. The train had been late and she'd missed her blow-dry. Scowling, she'd applied her armour then reached into her bag for a comb. Nothing. Another one lost or misplaced. She'd run her fingers through her hair – making it worse in the process – then added a spray of expensive perfume and lifted her wrist to her nose. The scent had changed, the citrus overpowering, the lily-of-the-valley unnaturally sweet. She'd rubbed it off with a paper towel and shouldered her bag with a sigh.

She saw Dylan turn off Grafton Street at a half-run, his satchel tucked under his arm. The absence of an umbrella wasn't surprising, but the look on his face was. The frown he wore was new, as though in the weeks Ellie hadn't seen him he'd exchanged his expression for something a little more earnest. Watching him from the window above, she felt she was intruding on a private moment.

He was halfway down Harry Street when he stopped, turned back. Ellie felt her heart tug. It was one of the feelings she had lectured herself about. Not to feel attached. Not to feel hope. Not to feel anything.

Feck him, Ellie.

But she couldn't think like that. Wouldn't. Because to do so would be to throw away a life that sat so comfortably on her skin. Just as her perfume had once done.

She wiped her eyes, willed away her thoughts. Looked again.

And there he was: he'd stopped at the flower stall and was having a hurried conversation with the vendor. Then an exchange took place and he started once again towards the hotel, a small bunch of roses in his hand.

They were yellow.

Not a good start, she thought.

ن

When Dylan arrived at the table, he was minus his satchel and coat – both left with the porter – but he held the roses out in front of him.

Feck him, Ellie.

She pushed Moira out of her mind.

Now that he was here, Ellie felt nothing like she'd thought she would. The hurt was there, of course. As was the guilt that lingered still. But at the moment his hopeful eyes made contact with hers, she realised that in the last weeks she'd formed an extra layer over her heart, something firm and impenetrable, a sheath, and it sat between her and Dylan like a chaperone.

'Hi,' he said. 'May I?'

She nodded. His formality annoyed her. She ignored the proffered flowers, and he put them down between them as he sat. He leaned forward. 'So, how are you?'

'Fine, fine,' she said. 'You?'

He looked down at his hands, then wiped them over his eyes. 'Not great, actually.'

Her first instinct was to comfort him. To reach out a hand and take his, to tell him it was all right. Conjuring some of Moira's mentality, she pushed the impulse aside.

Coldly, she said: 'I'm sorry to hear that.'

A waiter approached and Ellie glanced at the menu, but her appetite had entirely dissipated. She ordered a Shiraz; Dylan stuck with water. A table in a far corner cheered; someone had cause for celebration.

When they were alone again, Dylan said lightly: 'How was Kerry?'

'How *is* Kerry? Fine, fine.'

'You're going back tonight?'

Ellie frowned. 'Of course.'

'Oh. I thought you'd be in Dublin for a day or two. So we could catch up. Properly.' Was he suggesting that she stay? Stay *over*?

Concerned that her face was set in an unattractive mask of confusion, she rearranged it. 'Are we not catching up *properly* now, Dylan?'

'Yes, sure. We are.' He smiled soothingly.

They sat in silence. The fire across the room cracked as a log split down the middle, releasing some long-trapped moisture.

'Ellie . . .' Dylan started.

She held up a hand as the waiter delivered their drinks. 'Let's get lunch first. I'm starving,' she lied. From the express menu she ordered the pâté, then immediately regretted it. It was the smallest option and she didn't want to be one of those girls. The type that numbed grief with hunger.

He said, 'How's your mum?'

'She's good.'

'And Ballinn? Everything good there?'

'Are we talking about the weather next?' Ellie resisted the urge to drain her glass. She took one small sip. Calmed her breath. Remembered that he too had suffered. She said, more kindly: 'Why did you want to see me?'

He watched the bubbles rise in his glass. *Perrier*. 'Ellie . . . I don't know where to start.' When he'd asked her to marry him at the outrageously priced Mulberry Garden, she'd ordered Perrier. She was already pregnant. 'It was such a confusing time. Don't you think?'

'I don't know if confusing is the right word.'

'No.' His hand reached towards her. 'No, that wasn't the right way to put it . . .' He paused, his fingers inches from her own. 'I know I said some things that were . . . harsh. Wrong.'

She looked up.

'And I'm sorry.'

She wanted to collapse, to let out a long-held breath, to feel the ground shift beneath her feet. To hear him say it. To hear those words. It meant the world. Then he continued:

'You know Mum went to school with Deborah McCarthy?'

She paused. Looked out the window. The rain was getting heavier, rolling down the glass, racing for the bottom. 'I did know that.'

'It put a lot of strain on their relationship, your investigation.'

'Right . . .'

'And I felt . . . torn. Loyalty-wise. You know what I mean?'

'No.'

A waiter passed. Ellie leaned towards him and lifted her glass. 'Another Shiraz, please.' Dylan looked at her half-empty glass. 'Is that wise?'

When the waiter was gone, Ellie sat forward. 'Dylan, what are you saying?'

'That I wasn't fair on you because my judgement was clouded.'

She frowned. 'By what?'

'My mother. She was angry at you. It was causing . . . strain.'

Strain between them? Or between Dylan and his mother? She *was* a decidedly challenging woman. Ellie knew she'd been not-so-secretly planning a Dublin society wedding. Nothing less for her son. She'd left brochures lying around their apartment. Guest lists. And Ellie had brushed her off. Or so she'd thought. Perhaps she herself had been brushed off, as soon as the scandal broke.

Her miscarriage had been days later. But now she thought about it, Dylan had been cold since she'd begun to dig.

'I took it out on you. I'm sorry.'

'You took it out on me because of . . . *your mother*?' It was every woman's nightmare.

'I was in grief. It was unfair.'

Ellie spluttered and a few people turned to look. 'I'm so sorry. You're right. I haven't been *fair* on you.'

He scrambled, tried to take her fingers, which were just out of reach. 'I mean unfair on *you*.'

She pulled her hand away. 'What do you want, Dylan?'

'I want you back.' There it was: what she'd hoped he'd say

and yet hoped he wouldn't. Before she could take in his words, he'd carried on. 'We don't need to do the big wedding thing. We can elope. The two of us. Don't worry about Mum, she'll get over it.'

She stared at him.

'And when we get back, we'll start again. It'll be as good as before. It'll be better.'

'Better?' She thought about their life in Dublin: the warm apartment, the warm embraces. A full life. A happy life? Was it? She could no longer untangle the web of what went before from what happened after. Something in her stomach shifted. She needed to leave. To be alone. To think.

Or perhaps not think at all.

She picked up her bag, stood. 'I have to go.' Her voice was hoarse. The roses she left lying on the table. 'I'm sorry.' She wasn't sure exactly what for. For everything?

Perhaps.

He got to his feet. 'Ellie, you're not staying for lunch? Please? Your wine?'

'You're right,' she said, pushing her glass to the centre of the table, 'it isn't *wise*.'

They locked eyes. A moment, a year, or three, flashed between them. She looked away. 'Wait,' he said, reaching into his pocket. 'I have something for you.' He handed her a burgundy box the length and width of her hand. A canary-yellow ribbon coiled around it like a spring. 'A gift.'

She made no move to take it.

'Please.' He slipped it in her bag and she nodded, avoiding his gaze. He took her hand, gave it a squeeze.

'I need to think,' she said.

She knew he was watching as she left, her uncomfortable shoes clicking on the polished tiles. At the top of the stairs she paused, held the handrail, descended slowly. And when she got to the bottom, she changed her heels for flats and, head high, walked out of the Westbury into the open heavens of central Dublin.

Chapter Twenty-Seven

Blackwater Hall, County Kerry
March 1958

Papa said that St Patrick's Day took winter and gave it one last loving hug before opening the door to spring. And as the morning dawned, after a week of rain, Hattie tiptoed down the quiet stairs of Blackwater Hall and out the front door into a crispness that momentarily burned her lungs. It was glorious; a rare cloudless Kerry day.

She passed Albert as she crossed the lawn, those ridiculous breeks hoisted high on his hips and the shotgun over his shoulder.

'Does Papa know you've got that?' she said. Once – when they were a team – he would have risen to the tease, but now he ignored her and carried on walking. 'Albert, you're only allowed to shoot alone *when you're good and ready.*'

He paused, turned back, held the stock end towards her so she could look along the open barrel, two discs of blue sky visible at the end. It was empty. 'Just practising my mount. Mama's going to meet me later.' He closed the gun with aplomb and lifted it to his shoulder, one green eye squinting as he sighted his imaginary target.

Hattie watched him. 'Papa says you should shoot with both eyes open.'

He lowered the gun and ruffled her hair. A little of the old Albert shone through. He was like that now: variable. It seemed the further he went from the house, the closer he came to himself.

His waxed jacket sat heavy on him, its pockets bulging. Hattie pointed to them. 'And I *can* see what's in those.'

'Well,' he said with the air of someone who had been caught out but cared nothing for it, 'it's difficult to shoot a pigeon without bullets.'

'Shells,' she corrected.

He paused. A stalemate. Then he nodded and turned, making for the edge of the woodland where the lawn was swallowed by ivy.

Hattie wondered if she'd ever eaten pigeon.

Or if, indeed, she ever would.

❧

She met Tomas in the walled garden. He stood by an overgrown arbour where small drops of dew hung like diamonds from the bare tentacles of a clematis.

She smiled uncertainly. 'Hello.'

'Happy St Patrick's Day.' He laughed; he had a lightness that had been absent the week before.

As he walked to the shed, Hattie followed two steps behind. He lifted a bag of potatoes over his shoulder, then pointed to a sack at his feet; it was a third of the size of the one he held. More sacks sat outside the shed, each small one partnered with a Tomas-sized bag. 'Make hay while the sun shines,' he said, already walking back towards the garden's archway.

Hattie shouldered her potatoes and scuttled after him. 'How are we ever going to plant all these today?'

''Tis quick work,' he said. 'And thirsty work. There'll be men all over the valley planting out this morning.'

'And girls?'

He paused, looked back at her. 'Girls too.'

From the garden they followed an overgrown gravel path through a coppice, emerging onto a field of freshly dug earth. 'Here we have the ridges. Been growing potatoes on this spot since my father started at the estate.'

Each ridge was a foot wide and as long as the field, which stretched a hundred yards down the gentle slope. There was a pleasing regularity to the rows. It looked, to Hattie, like God had raked his hand across the soil in readiness for the season ahead.

'Did you do all this?'

'I did.'

She looked up at him.

'The soil is yielding, Hattie. My father pulled the rocks out of this ground with his bare hands' – he indicated the stone wall surrounding the field – 'and still there are more each summer. Gifts from God.'

'Gifts?'

He nodded. 'They keep coming and coming. A surprise and yet . . . not surprising.'

He'd picked up his spade and was leaning on it, his eyes fixed somewhere beyond the field. In the silent blue morning there wasn't yet a breath of wind. Hattie shifted her weight from one foot to the other and dropped her sack, the thick thud drawing Tomas's attention with a sudden flinch. He took a handkerchief from his pocket and wiped his forehead.

'Everyone has their way of planting, and this is mine.' He pointed to the field's central ridge. 'We'll start here.'

'Is it normal to begin in the middle?'

He smiled, a small laugh chasing away the faraway look in his eyes. 'I got a head start.' Hattie tried not to show disappointment. 'Wouldn't want you missing the parade.'

She nodded without expectation.

Last night, Papa had announced that Hattie and Albert would join him at Ballinn's St Patrick's Day festivities. 'They most certainly will not,' Grandmother had said, her rheumy eyes narrowing. 'It's a weekday and this girl' – she'd waved a hand in no particular direction, but of course she meant Hattie – 'needs to get used to discipline.'

Tomas moved forward, indicated she should start planting next to him, that they would work together. Side by side.

Albert, as so often now, had made matters worse. He'd used his stubborn voice, learned from Mama, and said, 'Who'd want to celebrate an institution that's shackled Ireland anyway?' turning Grandmother's face so red that Hattie felt she might explode. She'd clutched her chest and heaved heavy breaths before sending both of them to bed with just a look, and without dinner.

The soil was warm at its surface, cool beneath. It crumbled in her fingers. As each potato disappeared into the ground, she felt her spirits begin to lift.

Mama wasn't at dinner either – she'd had a headache, again – and when Hattie peered into her bedroom she was fast asleep, the sheets twisted round her body like a rope.

When Hattie had dug her last potato into the ridge, she said, 'Will we get more?'

Tomas picked up the sacks, let them hang, deflated, over his arm. 'We will. We will. But first: tea.'

She followed him to the far corner of the field, where a flat stone topped the wall. Tomas reached behind it and produced a canvas backpack. Out of it he took a red-checked napkin containing two large scones, a square of butter and a jar of dark jelly.

'Bramble jam,' he said. 'Blackberries mostly, but you never know what my sister gets in there. Once she added hawthorn berries. I never forgave her.' With his penknife he spread a thick layer onto the scone and handed it to Hattie, watched with fascination as she devoured it in four bites.

'Don't they feed you in the big house?' he laughed.

She didn't want to tell him about last night's argument. Or the way she felt about Grandmother. Or how lonely she was. Instead, she said, 'Did your sister make the scones too?'

'Tabby? Yes. She takes care of me, so she does.' He said this in a way that was affectionate but also grudging. A shadow passed across his face and Hattie looked up; a skein of geese flew overhead. 'When she heard there was a little lady up at Blackwater Hall, she insisted on sending morning tea.'

'I'm not a *lady*!' Hattie laughed.

Tomas tilted his head to the side and gazed across the field. 'The daughter of Blackwater Hall is a lady,' he said. 'And one day your father will become lord.'

She'd never thought about this before. 'I'll really be a lady?'

He nodded. 'I think so. At least, 'twas like that before.'

'Before when?'

'Look! Two magpies.' Tomas's hand was outstretched, and Hattie followed his gaze. Loping along the edge of the furthest ridge were two birds, their iridescent wings glinting in the sunlight. 'That's for joy, you know?'

She'd heard the driver say the same thing during the week. 'I wish I could have some joy,' she said, her bottom lip pushing forward.

Tomas began to fold the napkin, flicking it clear of crumbs before stashing it in his bag. '*Complain not that you have no shoes, lest you meet a man who has no feet.*'

'What does that mean?'

'It means, Hattie, that it's good to be thankful for what you have: your hearth, a place to lay your head. And normally, I think, enough to fill your belly.'

'It's just that I don't like it here.' She looked down at her fingernails. They were drawing small circles on the soft sandstone. 'I wish . . . I wish I could leave.'

Sharply he said: 'You don't know what you're saying.' Then he softened, caught her eye. ''Tis not a comparison I'm making, Miss Hattie. Only something someone told me once when I too was wishing for more luck.'

'Who?'

At this question he laughed, shaking his head. 'You're a brazen one, I'll give you that.'

Although he was a man and she only a small girl, she was at ease with him. But still her cheeks flushed.

He brushed a lock of hair back from his face. ''Twas Tabby told me that. She put me on the straight and narrow, one foot at a time. She's a dote. One day, Hattie, you can visit the rambling house. It's in her front room.'

She wanted to ask him what it was, the rambling house, but he'd already stood, and she started after him as he made his way along the edge of the field. 'Would Tabby like me?'

He stopped and turned. 'Yes, Hattie. Tabby would like you very much. My sister takes care of souls, so she does.'

She continued ahead of him, puffing. 'I wish my brother would take care of me.' When they were younger Albert had been protective of her. Always by her side. Then, the six years between them wasn't a wedge but an elastic with just enough stretch to give them space but keep them together. 'But all he wants to do is go back to England. To study. But Grandmother says he has to go to university in America.'

'Does she so?'

Hattie lowered her voice. 'I don't think he likes Grandmother much.'

Tomas laughed quietly at this.

'But he likes England . . . or a girl there. He told Mama' – at this she blushed, another thing she wasn't meant to know – 'and she's going to help him get into Cambridge. He studies with her in the library almost every day. I never see him!'

They rounded the corner and walked out of the field, returning to the overgrown path that led back to the garden, back to the waiting sacks of potatoes. The crunch of the gravel was the only sound in the undergrowth.

But then, a flutter, in the trees to Hattie's left. A flurry of wings, a splash of grey in the bare branches. She turned to show Tomas, but he was already looking, already admiring the display before them. He glanced at her briefly, raised his eyebrows in the way that Albert would once have done, then turned back to the entertainment. Two pigeons. Not fighting, *wooing*, as Mama would say with a slight flush to her cheeks.

At that moment, Albert appeared through the archway of the garden, fifty feet ahead. Mama was with him, pointing to the treetops. *The most important thing about using a gun*, Papa had said as they'd crossed the heath, *is to pay attention to what's around your target, not just the target itself.* The gun was already mounted, Albert's face hidden behind the stock as it swung in an arc. *What's happening beside you, and in the distance.* He followed the noise of the courting pigeons, while Mama hung back, eyes only for her son. *Where your companions are. What they're doing.*

Hattie wanted to turn, to warn Tomas, but she couldn't look away . . . and then Albert pulled the trigger.

There was a thunderclap, an instant, and it took her breath away.

She turned back. Tomas was no longer standing; he lay on the path in a ball. His hands covered his ears and his eyes were squeezed shut. His shoulders were so rounded it looked as though they'd disappeared into themselves.

She stepped forward, put her gentle hand on him.

He struck out. Hard. Hattie tumbled backwards. Hit the ground. The *whoosh* of her breath felt like it came from another place, another body. Her shoulder wrenched painfully beneath her and she cried out, but it was garbled, deflated. She lay gasping. Felt a pressure on her shin.

A hand.

Tomas pulled himself to his knees, leaned over her. She lifted her hands protectively.

'I'm sorry,' he said. 'I'm so sorry. The gunshot. I didn't mean to ... Sometimes I ... panic ... I'm sorry.' And she knew he was.

Perhaps Hattie tried to say something, perhaps not. But no words came out as she looked towards Albert and Mama, who were searching the ground below the leafless hazel grove. For just a moment, she felt a flush of pleasure.

Albert had missed. The pigeons survived.

And then Mama, her hand on her son's shoulder, turned to them. Saw them for the first time. Took in the sight of the gardener kneeling over her daughter. Her face crumpled in confusion. Then fear. In one swift movement she pulled up the hem of her skirt and began to run towards Hattie. Crying out, pushing Tomas aside with such force that he was flung from the path.

Falling to her knees, she placed her hands either side of her daughter's stricken face.

A moment before she turned to look at Mama, Hattie locked her gaze with Tomas – his wild eyes pleading – then he melted backwards and away, into darkness and shadow.

Chapter Twenty-Eight

Dublin

September 2019

Ellie shivered. She walked in shadow along Duke Street feeling hopelessly confused and a little woozy from the glass of wine she'd dumped on her empty stomach. Sheltering in a doorway from the cold rain, she pulled out her phone to call Jeremy: no answer. Already there were three missed calls from Dylan, the last a minute ago. She sighed, flicked past them. Underneath his name was a record of that morning's call with Milo. She opened her messages. Sure enough, he'd sent a reminder:

Harriet would love to meet you, she'll be at the Pickled Oyster until 2 p.m. Xm

Ellie squinted at the last word. Was that a kiss? A mistake? She looked at her watch, then turned on her heel towards St Stephen's Green.

੭ઇ

If the Mulberry Garden was an expensive restaurant, the Pickled Oyster took fine dining to a whole new level. Reservations were near-impossible to come by and the restaurant featured the who's who of Dublin high society. Even Dylan's mother was unlikely to have eaten there, and Ellie stepped through its doors with the trepidation of one entering a world in which they surely didn't belong. She ascended the stairs to a small formal foyer. Fresh-baked bread, and perhaps something a little heartier, infused the air and from the room beyond came the sounds of dining: conversation, cutlery on crockery, a shower of laughter. A lectern sat next to the closed double doors that led from the foyer, and behind it stood a short, neat man in full formal attire.

But if Ellie expected him to speak with a plum in his mouth, she was soon put right.

'Better in here than out there, sure 'tis.' He stepped forward to take her coat and umbrella, not giving a second glance to the mutilated state of the latter. 'A fine day for fine dining.'

Ellie smiled. He was a Kerryman, o'course. And the effect of his easy manner against the formality of his suit was disarming and comforting and altogether pleasant.

'The forecast was . . . *better.*' She handed him her soggy items apologetically.

He disappeared through a door to his left – 'It'll be dry as a bone when you're done'– then stepped back behind the lectern and glanced down at a list. His body language was gently asking, *Do you have a reservation?* but his mouth was fixed in a warm smile.

'We've not seen you before, Miss . . .?'

'Oh,' she said, 'Fitzgerald. Ellie Fitzgerald.'

'Are you with the Newman party?'

She felt very out of place. 'No, no. I'm here to see Harriet Rath . . . Harriet, erm . . .' She realised, suddenly mortified, that she had no idea if Harriet used the name Rathmore or something else entirely.

'Hattie Walker?' His demeanour changed, ever so perceptibly, from friendly and accommodating to *very* friendly and accommodating.

'Yes. Her nephew told her I was coming . . .'

The man beamed. 'Milo?' He appraised her closely and smiled a little wider. 'A fine fellow.'

Ellie shifted her weight. 'We only met quite recently. Back in Ballinn.'

'North Kerry meself. But I love the south altogether.' He said this as though he were talking about another country. He paused, then came to his decision. 'This way.'

She followed him into a dining room rich with wood panelling and the most ornate ceiling she'd ever seen. Booths ran along the walls. They were upholstered with oxblood leather and full of people; the lunchtime sitting was in full swing.

The Kerryman gave her a conspiratorial wink before leaving her alone to shuffle along the bench at the end table. From her position it was almost impossible to see the faces of the other diners – the wall of the booth obscured her view. A large fireplace dominated the far wall; flames licked gently at a newly placed log.

'Ellie?'

A woman stood at the end of the table. She was striking: rich red hair that hung past her shoulders – a dash of grey at the roots – and a wholly genuine smile. Her age sat well on her. She wore very little make-up, and the green-rimmed glasses framing her face were two tones off the teal shirt that hung loosely from her slim shoulders.

'Harriet?'

'Hattie, please,' she said. 'Only my nephew and my wife refer to me as Harriet. I wish they wouldn't.' She laughed deeply and sat down to face Ellie across the booth.

She was dressed as neither waiter nor chef. Ellie ventured, 'This must be a great place to work.'

'Thank you. It's the fourth restaurant I've tried my hand at.' Ellie tried to hide her surprise. 'The first three were without Vikki. Disaster.' A speck on the white tablecloth caught Hattie's attention; she wiped it away. 'Always good to have a woman behind the woman.' She had a Dubliner's accent with notes of English.

Ellie said, 'I've heard this one's far from a disaster.'

'A different concept for me. Vikki's idea. A set menu, seasonal ingredients. Four courses. If you don't like it, go elsewhere.'

'I don't suppose many do. Go elsewhere?'

'No one yet.' A plate of food passed them, leaving a waft of cumin in its wake.

'I can come back later, after lunch?' As soon as she'd said the words, Ellie regretted them. The thought of leaving this place and stepping back out into the rain was unappealing to say the least.

'No, no.' Hattie waved a hand. 'But I've a hankering for oysters. Do you like them?'

'I've rarely had the opportunity,' Ellie admitted. She leaned back in the booth, relaxed. A tiny bit of the morning's tension left her. Her arm brushed the burgundy box that poked from her handbag; she pushed it out of sight.

Hattie caught the eye of a waiter, a man with mahogany skin and a broad smile. 'Madam?' His formality was a contrast to the Kerryman who had greeted Ellie in the foyer only moments earlier. A red carnation adorned his top pocket.

'Two Bloody Marys, Armand. And a dozen oysters, please.'

'Yes, madam.' He glided to the end of the room and pushed through a silent swinging door to the left of the fireplace.

'My best waiter. French. Fantastic. That man never forgets a face. All our regulars request him when they book.' Hattie clasped her hands and leaned forward. 'So, Ellie, Milo tells me you're unravelling a Rathmore family secret?'

It was said in a gentle way, but Ellie briefly saw this meeting from the other woman's point of view: a stranger delving into a private history, an outsider trying to get in. 'Yes.' She took out the letter, placed it on the table.

The older woman slid her thick-rimmed glasses down her nose. 'Poor Aunt Charlotte,' she said, reading. 'Worshipped by my parents, barely talked of by my grandparents. I never met her, of course – she died before I was born – but she was a constant presence at Blackwater Hall.'

'The date on the letter . . .'

'Yes,' said Hattie. 'How mysterious.'

Armand returned balancing a tray in defiance of gravity. He quickly emptied it: a plate of glistening oysters, Tabasco, lemon. As he set down two Bloody Marys, he said, 'I haven't had the pleasure.'

Hattie caught Ellie's eye.

'Oh, me?' She touched her chest and wondered if she was blushing. 'Eleanor Fitzgerald.'

'*Enchanté*, Eleanor Fitzgerald,' he said, as though verifying her name's credentials. '*Je suis* Armand.' He smiled warmly as he left.

Hattie tapped her temple. 'See? He's got you now.' She took a pinch of pepper and added it to her glass, then raised it to meet Ellie's. Both women took a sip. It was a great combination, the salty, spicy sweetness of it.

'There's a certain romance to the letter. But I don't see how it matters now. Charlotte's been gone eighty years.'

Ellie leaned forward, the vodka already a fire in her belly. 'Hattie, she could well be *alive*.' It was the first time she'd spoken the thought out loud, and the potential thrilled her.

But Hattie just raised an eyebrow, unmoved. 'She'd be, what, a hundred years old?' She washed down an oyster with a sip of her drink. Ellie thought back to Tabby Ryan's birthday party; one hundred years old didn't seem such a stretch. 'I find, Ellie, that reality can turn out to be rather dull when we look beneath the surface. My family are a funny bunch, but dull nonetheless. If it interests you, however, I'm happy to help.'

'Thank you.' Ellie eyed the oysters suspiciously.

'I can't imagine what I've got to add. But ask away.'

Ellie realised she was wholly unprepared for this. It was all so last-minute that meeting Charlotte's niece felt like an achievement in itself rather than the starting point. She reached for a shell. 'Can I ask you about a night that Albert remembers from his childhood?' She slid the oyster into her mouth. It tasted of the ocean, reminded her that she had been on the edge of the Atlantic only hours before.

'Albert is six years older than me, but I can try.'

Only six? The woman sitting in front of her looked two decades younger than her brother.

'He told me,' Ellie embellished, 'of an incident at Blackwater Hall – at dinner – when your mother became very upset because your grandfather suggested that Charlotte had taken her own life. Do you remember that?'

Hattie frowned, a faraway look in her eye. Several waiters passed, expertly balancing plates, and Ellie's stomach grumbled. She reached, with an apologetic look, for another oyster.

Beckoning a waitress, Hattie said to Ellie: 'Venison or pigeon?'

Ellie paused, looked embarrassed.

Hattie smoothed over her awkwardness effortlessly. 'We'll have two of the venison. Something already plated, it's urgent.' She turned back to Ellie with a wink. Then, 'I'm afraid I don't remember much about my time at Blackwater Hall.'

Ellie frowned. 'How old were you when you moved there?'

'Eleven.' She sipped her drink. 'But I barely spent any time in Kerry before I was sent to boarding school in Dublin.'

'That must have been hard. I'm sorry.'

'Please, don't be. It was fantastic. Life-changing. Honestly?

Before boarding school, I'd never had a friend.' She paused, then added: 'Not really.'

'What about before you lived in Ireland?'

Hattie laughed, a bitter scoff. 'I still have nightmares about primary school. Children can be so cruel. And yet my tormentors have probably turned into perfectly likeable people with children and grandchildren of their own.'

Ellie thought of Dylan. 'Do you think someone can change that much?'

'I can guarantee you that people are capable of astounding change. Both good and bad.' Hattie lifted her elbows and leaned back from the table as the waitress brought their plates. 'I must say it is wonderful to enjoy a few dishes in my own restaurant.'

Ellie looked at the Michelin-starred food art before her. 'I don't mean to pry, but . . . what is the price of the lunch menu?'

'A lot.' Hattie picked up her fork and speared a piece of venison. 'But only a portion of our revenue comes from the main restaurant. Our private rooms are the cash cow.' She indicated to where a waiter carrying champagne in a cooler was disappearing through a door to the right of the fireplace. 'We get all sorts: the great and the good. The rich and famous. Even a few politicians.' She took the celery from her Bloody Mary, placed it on her plate. 'They pay well for it.'

Returning to the topic of Blackwater Hall, Ellie said, 'Did you not spend your summers at home?'

'I only stayed at Blackwater Hall for a few months after we moved there. That place was never my home. No.' Hattie paused. 'There have been times when I've felt at home. In Ambleside, for example, before we moved to Ireland. Perhaps also with my first husband, though that didn't end well.' She sipped her drink. 'No, after Ambleside, the first real home I had – the type of home where you shut the door and inside is better than outside – was with Milo. When he came to live with me.' She took off her glasses, laid them on the table. 'He was only five years old and he completed me.'

'So young?'

'His mother had just died – breast cancer. She was young, much younger than Albert. They met here in Dublin. He'd come up for one of his extremely rare visits; he returned with a wife.' Hattie smiled. 'I'm exaggerating, of course. But it was a whirlwind romance. Majella was beautiful. She looked a great deal like a girl my brother had left behind in Ambleside.' She sipped her drink. 'When she died, I brought Milo to Dublin for the summer. To look after him. Give him somewhere . . . happier to be.' Ellie didn't know what to say. She'd thought of Milo as someone in the present, ignoring the fact that he had a past. 'My mother was already well into her seventies by then, and my father had passed away three years before. I could hardly leave him alone with Albert. It was only supposed to be for that first summer, then he'd return, start school in the village. Perhaps in your class?'

Ellie hadn't considered this. 'Yes, I suppose so . . .'

'Well, we hit it off, Milo and I.' She looked to the side, something – a cherished memory – making her smile. 'So he stayed on.'

A lump formed in Ellie's throat. 'That was kind.' She felt ignorant, ashamed that she'd asked Milo nothing about himself. That she'd blundered into his surgery demanding answers that he might not want to give.

'It wasn't all selfless. No, it was good for me too. We're peas in a pod,' she added, talking almost to herself. 'We visited Blackwater Hall every few months but Albert preferred us to stay away.'

Ellie put down her drink. *Because of the curse.* She tested Hattie. 'But . . . why?'

'Albert wanted Milo to have opportunities that weren't

available in Kerry.' Even if Ellie hadn't known the truth, she would have recognised the lie: the quick flick of the eyes, the refolding of the napkin. Hattie continued: 'As you know, Albert isn't well and we'd like him to move into a home. On his less lucid days, he's suspicious of everyone, even me. And he doesn't want to leave the house empty, because then it would need to be filled.' She gave a shrug of nonchalance. 'But, of course, he'd never want it.'

Ellie frowned. 'Who'd never want it?'

Hattie looked over her drink, surprised. 'Milo.'

'Oh?' was all Ellie could think to say, but of course it was obvious. Milo was Albert's only child.

'He has no interest. The boy's got something of a dislike for the aristocracy. A rebel at heart.'

'He won't claim the title?'

Hattie shook her head. 'He doesn't care for it. But that doesn't make any difference.'

'What do you mean?'

'It's not possible to disclaim an Irish title. *Heirs male of the body lawfully begotten.* Pure blood and all that. If Milo doesn't want it, the title goes dormant, waiting for his son.'

'And if he doesn't have a son?'

'Then the title will be no more. Plenty of females amongst the distant cousins, but no eligible males.' She shrugged. 'Milo'd love nothing better than to dissolve the whole sorry thing.'

'And the house?'

'The title and house were entailed until the seventies. Mama spent a quarter of her life in a legal battle to split the estate from the peerage. She won. The house stands alone.'

'It's a . . . beautiful setting.'

Hattie laughed. 'Very diplomatic. It's a fixer-upper. Or, as my wife would say, a money pit.'

Ellie smiled, shook her head. How the other half lived.

Hattie raised an eyebrow. 'You're just his type, you know?'

Ellie drained the last of her Bloody Mary with a cough; she wondered if the colour of the liquid matched the blush growing on her cheeks. Quickly she said, 'Can I ask . . . or perhaps it's a bit personal . . .' *Just like your last comment.*

'Ask away.'

'Why would the house hold such bad memories for you?'

Hattie put down her fork, laid it neatly across her empty plate. 'Nothing in particular,' she said, in a way that made Ellie feel that it was something very much in particular.

Resigned, Hattie leaned forward on her elbows, her chin rested on clasped hands. 'Before we moved to Ireland in 1958, only months after Uncle Hugo died – you probably know the circumstances? – we had a very happy household. My mother was warmth and love. I adored her then.' The last word hung between them. 'But moving to Blackwater Hall transformed her. It was as though she was two different people. Before Blackwater, and after.'

'Do you know why?'

Hattie's answer was a beat too quick. 'No.'

Sensing she was about to lose the conversation, Ellie changed tack. 'You said I would know the circumstance of Hugo's death. How did he die?'

'God,' said Hattie, 'I thought anyone in the village could tell you that. It was supposed to be kept within the family, of course, but you know Kerry . . .' It wasn't a question.

'I do.'

'Hugo was damaged from the war. So many were. I remember knowing someone who . . .' She paused for a moment, gone somewhere into the past. Then, as quickly as she'd left, she was back. 'Hugo was at the liberation of Bergen-Belsen, Papa believed that he never got over that. Well, how could you?

Still, apparently he wasn't a pleasant man.' She smiled sadly. 'It was believed that Charlotte committed suicide because of an arranged marriage, and it was Hugo who arranged it. In later years, I wondered if he blamed himself for her death.'

'But what happened to him?'

'He took his own life. Like Charlotte.' At this last, Ellie frowned, and Hattie added: 'So it was assumed.'

Ellie sipped her drink, added a dash of Tabasco. 'Your mother; she was British?'

'Yes. If you'd met her in her later years, you'd say she was the quintessential stiff upper lip. But before we moved to Ireland she was . . . full of life. Quite a remarkable rise. From orphan to Lady Rathmore. She and Papa met through their love of writing. They both worked at a paper in Ambleside before we left. I think she always harboured a desire to write fiction, but it wasn't to be.'

Ellie couldn't imagine swapping journalism for fiction, fact for fantasy. Even now, the two were becoming muddled in her head. She remembered the photo of Nancy and Charlotte at the garden party, how she'd decided they were leaning together conspiratorially. 'She and Charlotte got along well?'

Hattie shrugged. 'I couldn't say. Charlotte wasn't a topic that came up much. She was just always . . . there.'

'I don't understand.'

'She was everywhere on that estate and nowhere. There was no grave to mourn at – I remember my father bemoaning that. My grandmother was a very harsh woman, uncaring, and yet even she wouldn't let us play down near the lough where Charlotte drowned herself.' She corrected herself: 'Where they *thought* she drowned herself. She was beautiful, Charlotte – at least in the few photos I saw – she and my mother both. They must have made quite a pair when my parents visited Blackwater Hall in the thirties.'

'And did Charlotte ever visit your parents in Ambleside, do you think?' If Charlotte had been abroad previously, it would have given her confidence to travel in 1940.

Hattie frowned. 'I suppose there's a possibility she visited them in London.'

'Your parents lived in London?'

A clock chimed somewhere. Two thirty. 'Before the war. And during. Parker Street, I think.'

Ellie thought back to the announcement she'd found from 1936 in the *Kerry News*. 'Holborn?'

Hattie was surprised. 'Yes. I understand they saved for the deposit together. My mother was very proud of the fact that Rathmore money hadn't got them on the ladder. They did get some money a few years after they married – not much, but it would have paid off the flat – but mostly they made their own way before Papa inherited. I gather that my grandparents didn't see hacking as a very suitable profession. They thought my mother had encouraged my father, that meeting her had spelled the end of their ambitions for his political future. They didn't get along, her and my grandparents. They thought she was trouble.' Her forehead crinkled. A memory conjured. 'In fact, that was her nickname. *Trouble*. Papa often used it. Silly, really. But sweet.'

Ellie smiled.

'I, however, think it's very noble,' continued Hattie.

'The nickname?'

Hattie laughed. 'No, *hacking*. I think it's a fine profession.' She paused. 'That's what's given you the nose for this mystery, surely?'

Ellie considered. 'Yes.' *And no.* 'It interests me.' She said it apologetically, as though seeking permission. 'And at the moment, I'm at a bit of a loss.'

'Ah . . .' said Hattie. 'The little situation with the councillor.'

'I see you've done your homework.'

'He's a client of ours.'

Ellie shrank back into the booth.

'Ha, he's not here today. Good God, I couldn't have let you in otherwise.' It was almost a joke, but not quite. 'I did enjoy your article, though.'

'You read it?'

'Oh yes. The whiff of scandal is always interesting.' Hattie looked at her watch. 'Well, Ellie, I must go.' She paused. 'But I would be happy to chat again.'

'I'd like that,' said Ellie, and meant it.

Hattie stood. 'Give my love to my nephew when you see him.'

'Oh, I hadn't planned . . . I mean . . . we hadn't made plans . . .'

Giving her a knowing smile, Hattie turned to go, leaving a small white card on the tablecloth. Ellie picked it up. Heavy paper, textured, embossed in black. Just the name, *Hattie Walker*, and a number. No title, no company. It was the card of someone who was known by everyone. She slipped it into the back of her notebook, side by side with Charlotte.

Chapter Twenty-Nine

Dublin

September 2019

'Wynn's Hotel?' Jeremy said when she asked if they could walk and talk. He looked as ruffled as ever; flyaway hair and a tattered satchel slung across his shoulders.

'Yep,' said Ellie. They were standing in the busy lobby of *The Irish Times*.

'Staying the night?'

'Nope.'

They eyed each other suspiciously, then he ushered her out of the building, glancing over his shoulder. 'I need some air anyway,' he said, pulling the hood of his jacket up and ducking into a side alley. 'Coffee?' There was a hole in the wall where a group of people mingled.

'This is new,' said Ellie. It had the feel of a speakeasy.

'It's my new fave.' He often said things like that: *fave, lol, fab.* It was a technique he used to disarm people and help them to spill their secrets. It also, thought Ellie, made him appear significantly less intelligent than he was. 'The usual?' He took two reusable coffee cups from his satchel and waggled them at her. It seemed that his intention too had been to talk away from the office.

She nodded, then leaned against the alley's brick wall, crossing her arms. The rain had eased and blue sky chased away the grey. There was chatter around her, and at the end of the lane, snippets of Dublin passed by in a hurry. People, cars. Lives. Blurred into one. Already Dublin was strangely foreign to her, as though in the weeks she'd been away she had already learned to slow down.

When Jeremy returned, he passed her a coffee. Its warmth reminded her of the morning before, when she'd walked on the beach with Milo. She smiled behind her first sip.

'I don't see what you've got to be so happy about,' Jeremy said as he added several sachets of sugar to his coffee, making her wait as he stirred.

'I'm just so delighted to see you. After you fired me, you know?'

He narrowed his eyes. 'Sure.' They started towards Tara Street and stepped out into near-sunshine, leaving the gloom behind.

'So,' she said, 'you wanted to talk? Offer me my job back, perhaps?'

Jeremy cut to the chase. 'Ellie, did you know Davy McCarthy's going through a divorce?'

She didn't give two hoots for Davy McCarthy; the man had sold out Dublin and ruined her career. 'Lucky for his wife.'

They split apart to pass a pair of old ladies wandering arm in arm along the street. 'Perhaps it's lucky for you,' he said over their heads.

They came back together. 'I'm listening.' She took a sip of coffee to quell her building nerves.

Jeremy slowed his pace. 'Last week, out of the blue, I received a request for a meeting with Deborah McCarthy. She's looking for revenge.'

'Revenge sounds positive.'

They paused at the traffic lights. 'What she had to say was positive. For you, anyway.'

'But not for Davy?'

Behind them, the two old ladies caught up. They were giggling like children and Ellie longed for a moment to swap places with them. To have not a care in the world. One of them dropped her glove and Jeremy bent down to pick it up for her. They giggled some more.

He turned back to Ellie, a blush on his cheeks. 'No, not for Davy.' He fell into step with her as they crossed the road then turned to track the river. 'What she's offering isn't a smoking gun. It's anecdotal only. But it means you could have a case if you dig deeper.'

'I don't *want* to dig deeper,' she said. 'This ruined me.'

'But it could un-ruin you.' He paused at the wall that edged the river. 'Just hear what I have to say.' His forearms rested on stone and he invited her to do the same. 'From what Deborah told me, Davy's missed out big-time in the divorce. Most of the money was hers – old money, a Guinness relative of some sort. He was left with nothing.'

She weighed her coffee cup: nearly empty. 'He has his councillor's salary.'

'Less than twenty grand . . .'

'Plus expenses. And he has several non-exec board positions.' A gust of wind picked at her hair and she tucked it behind her ear. 'I know. I've profiled him, remember?' She drained her mug and Jeremy took it from her, put it upright in his satchel.

'Apparently he's driving a new Mercedes. He's living in Dublin 4. A penthouse.' He pulled at a thread on his tatty jacket. 'Valet, undercover parking. A gym.'

Ellie laughed, partly at the audacity of Davy McCarthy, partly at the idea of her boss – ex-boss – coveting a gym. 'Men like that have to keep up the illusion,' she said. 'For them, credit's easy.'

Jeremy spread his hands, his face serious. 'She assures me in no uncertain terms that he should be broke.'

Ellie stood upright, stretched her back. She was disappointed. 'What are you saying, Jeremy? That Davy McCarthy has hidden funds, siphoned off to him by Maxwell Cray? It's hardly news to me. I already broke the story.' She began to walk again. 'Is this it? This is what you wanted to talk to me about? An ex-wife's angst?'

His brows formed a hummock. 'That's not all.' He opened his satchel and took out a folder, handed her a single piece of paper.

She paused and scanned the document, tried to steady her hands. *Dear Jeremy, on behalf of my client . . . threat . . . threat . . . threat . . . Sincerely, Barton Smith, Senior Legal Counsel, Harsgrove Lawyers.* She handed it back to him and continued walking. 'They want to sue *The Irish Times*? The whole newspaper?'

'For libel.'

'But it was published on *my* blog.'

'They will argue that we – me specifically – put you up to it.'

Ellie laughed loudly. The idea of Jeremy, or anyone for that matter, putting her up to something was faintly ridiculous. 'I've taken *Dubble* down; what more do they want?' The pun didn't escape her.

'They want to change the policies.'

She frowned.

He said, 'They want to roll back the ban on public buildings being sold to private contractors. And they want to use the hysteria created by your article as an example of why the public should never be involved with the process.'

'It was hardly hysteria.'

'Heat, then. They want to use the outrage of the leftie snowflakes' – she huffed – 'to highlight the damage of public discourse on the matter.'

'I'm confused.'

'Ellie,' he said, 'haven't you been reading the news?'

'I had to give up.'

'Davy McCarthy is running in the next election.'

'For government? He wants to be a TD?'

Jeremy nodded. 'According to Deborah, that's all he's ever wanted. A seat in the Dáil.' He paused. 'Well, that and several of his assistants.'

They turned onto a bridge, began to cross the river. 'So this stunt of mine has given him a platform?'

'Crazy millennial versus stoic councillor.' She started to protest, but he continued: 'He's moving, politically speaking, looking for the centre-right vote, and if there's something that gets them going, it's public housing.'

'Everything gets them going.'

He said, 'If what Deborah told me is true – and no, she won't go on record – there'll be a paper trail.'

'And *I'm* not going to be the one to follow it.'

He spread his hands. 'With the threat of a libel case hanging over us, there's nothing we can do at the paper.'

Ellie sighed. 'McCarthy and Cray were never seen together outside their minuted meetings. I can't see where we can go with this right now.' She looked at her phone. The day was flying. 'Look,' she said, 'I'll get back to my source. You work on the ex. That's all I can offer.'

'You'd be saving my skin.'

She nodded. 'I'll try.' It wasn't just her caught up in this mess. And Jeremy had been on her side, hadn't he? He'd only been obeying orders from the top. He'd even recommended her to Vincent from that paper she'd said she'd never work for. They paused at the intersection. A matinee from the Abbey Theatre began to file out behind them.

'So . . .' she looked along the street, the flags from Wynn's Hotel flapping in the breeze, 'this is me.'

Jeremy appeared to wrestle with his curiosity, then pushed it aside. 'Keep me posted, Ellie.' He squeezed her shoulder, something he'd never done before. 'We miss you at the paper.' No jest to follow it, no cheeky smile to show that he was joking. Just a nod, a turn, and he was gone.

Chapter Thirty

Dublin

September 2019

Wynn's Hotel had existed – Ellie had read on the train – in some form or another for 175 years. The front elevation was olde-worlde grand – four floors of grey cut stone topped by a copper mansard roof – and its large French doors issued an invitation, as did the warm glow of the coach lights that flanked them.

She stepped off the street and into the lobby. Its warmth was comforting, and she removed her coat, hung it over her arm and approached the desk. A huge bouquet of lilies gave off a rich perfume and something classical played quietly in the background. Signs of fatigue – a chipped cornice, a ripple on the wallpaper, a display of taxidermy from another era – only added to the room's charm.

The expression of the woman behind the desk, however, did not.

'Hello,' said Ellie.

The woman's head, topped with short grey hair, barely nodded an acknowledgement.

'This is a bit awkward, but—'

'Do you have a reservation?'

'A reservation?' Ellie smiled. 'No. Actually—'

'I'm *sorry*,' said the woman. 'The bar's only open to residents this week.'

'Oh, I'm not here for a drink.' Ellie laughed, tried to defuse the tension.

Behind her, there was a commotion. A group of people spilled noisily through the front doors. One of the men came straight to the desk, using his elbow to dislodge Ellie from her position. 'Hey there,' he said in a drawl as he pushed a flop of hair from his face. 'Where's the bar?'

'The *bar*' – the woman repeated the line she'd delivered moments before – 'is only open to residents this week. Do you have a reservation?'

'Reservation? Oh no. We don't want to stay here.' He laughed lightly.

'I'll have to ask you to leave.' The woman fixed him with a stare that could freeze the Liffey.

'We only want to—'

'No,' she said flatly.

The man stared at her, then turned to his friends. 'We'll come back later,' he said, inclining his head: *Would you look at this one?*

As they left, the woman muttered, 'I'd say by next week you'll have forgotten all about us. There'll be a new Instaphoto bar in town. Ah, Terrance,' she said as a large man appeared from the door behind her, 'this lady was just leaving.'

Terrance, his head sitting squarely on the countertop of his shoulders, held out a sizeable arm towards the hotel's entrance. 'This way, miss.'

'Look,' said Ellie, standing her ground, 'do you keep records for the hotel?'

Terrance's arm stayed steady, a tree trunk hovering in mid-air.

'Records?' parroted the woman.

'Yes, records. Of hotel guests.'

'You're not here to photograph the bar?'

Ellie adopted a confused look, hoping that it was somehow endearing to this viperous woman. 'No.'

A small nod to Terrance, who moved to stand at the lobby's entrance, and the woman turned her entirely changed face back to Ellie. Her eyebrows, which were thinly drawn and which Ellie had taken for acerbic, now moved away from each other as if they'd been caught snuggling at an improper moment.

'We've had a time of it. One of these influencies sent a picture of our bar to Instawhatsit last week. There's been a constant stream of *young people* ever since.' This woman, Ellie could see, rivalled her mum when it came to tech knowledge. 'They take photos, ask for a glass of water, then stay for hours getting shelfies all over the bar. Even with some of the guests. Can you imagine?'

'Savage,' said Ellie. She paused. 'Perhaps we could start again?'

'Will we?'

'Yes.' Ellie smiled, pushing her advantage. 'I'd like to confirm the details of a guest.'

The woman's eyebrows inched together again. 'We can't release guest details. GPRD. Or GDRP? You know. EU regulations. Brussels . . .'

'From 1940.'

'Ah. Well, I don't—'

'It's my grandmother. I'm trying to trace her.' *Where did that come from?* Ellie reached into her bag. 'She wrote a note from this hotel in 1940. Or at least it was on paper from this hotel.' She put the letter carefully on the desk, treating it like a family heirloom – and somehow it was starting to feel like one. 'This is the last we heard from her.'

'Can I?' When Ellie nodded, the woman took a pair of red-rimmed glasses from behind the desk, perched them on her nose and began to read. 'She ran away?'

'And never came back.' Beside the letter she now placed Charlotte's portrait; that porcelain skin, the blonde hair swept up into rolls, pinned with the jewelled comb. 'This is her.'

The woman touched the letter. 'Who was it written to?'

'Oh. My mother,' Ellie blurted. 'She died last year . . . and I found this in her things.' Oh God, she thought, I'm a terrible, terrible person.

The receptionist's face softened and she picked up Charlotte's photo. 'Your grandmother was beautiful.' She looked at her watch. 'I would need to ask my manager . . .'

'I've come all the way from Kerry.'

The woman appraised her. 'Perhaps,' she said, 'considering my poor manner towards you, and, well . . . there've been a few complaints about me on Tripadvisor . . .'

'I could leave a good review, make mention of the Instagram situation.'

'That might be helpful.' She busied her hands with something on the desk. 'I could always have a quick look in the archives. We've guest books dating from 1927, but I'll warn you, there are a few gaps.'

Ellie nodded. She hoped the look on her face was grateful enough without being desperate. 'Thank you.'

'What's your name?' The woman took out a notepad.

'Ellie.'

'And your grandmother?'

'Sorry?'

'Your grandmother. What was her name?'

'Oh, Rathmore. Charlotte Rathmore.' Ellie nodded. 'Early August 1940.'

The woman smiled kindly at her. 'Come back in an hour. I'll see what we've got.'

&⁊

When Ellie returned, a different woman stood behind the front desk. Younger, blonde. Smiling. There was now a line of people waiting. And no one taking selfies. It appeared that Terrance was doing his job.

Ellie paused. Where was her ally from earlier?

She returned to the doorway, asked Terrance. 'I'm just a temp,' he shrugged, 'because of the Instagram situation.'

'So sorry for the waiting,' said the woman when Ellie finally got to the front of the queue. Her Eastern European accent rolled the *r*'s and her hands worked quickly on the keyboard. 'What name is reservation?'

'Oh, I don't have a reservation.'

'I'm sorry, we are fully booked tonight.' Already she was looking behind her to the next person in the queue.

'Actually, I was speaking to your colleague. About an hour ago. She was going to leave me some . . . documentation.'

Her face brightened. 'Ellie?'

'Yes.'

'Sinéad had to leave. Busy woman. Always busy.' She said this in a way that suggested she didn't understand such busyness. 'I have book for you.' She took a large leather-bound tome from the top of a filing cabinet and placed it on the far end of the reception counter. 'Okay?'

Ellie nodded. 'Thank you.'

It was a guest book, almost identical to the one that sat on a small table at the far end of the lobby. But this one was faded, the once-rich red of the leather now pale at its edges. *Wynn's Hotel* was embossed on the front in gold. She opened the cover. It made a delicious creak and she resisted the urge, in a room full of people, to smell it.

April 1940–October 1940 was written on the title page. She flicked to the back. It had been filled to the very last line. Carefully she travelled back in time. October. September. August. The fifth, fourth, third of the month.

The surnames were a mix of Irish and English. O'Sullivan, Byrne, Kelly. Smith, Reynolds, Jones. Each entry noted a date, a name and a forwarding address. There was a space for comments. It was a wonderful snapshot in time. And yet Charlotte's name was absent.

Ellie rubbed her eyes; the day was getting the better of her.

'Excuse me,' she said to the blonde woman, who was busy tapping away at the keyboard, her backlog of guests cleared. 'Do you need ID to check into the hotel?'

'Yes. Passport preferable. EU driving licence okay.'

She knew it was silly to ask, because there was no way this girl could know, but . . . 'Back in 1940. Would you have needed ID?'

'Identification? In 1940?' She didn't appear confused by the question but instead looked at Ellie as though she might be slow. 'During Emergency?'

'Yes.'

'I think very likely. Yes.'

'Do you?'

'In 1940, you don't travel without identification and permit. Very difficult.'

Ellie appraised her. 'Really?'

'I do master's in history at UCD. A profile of de Valera.' The girl shrugged. A noisy young family entered the lobby and she turned to beam at them. Ellie had been dismissed.

She sighed. Wynn's Hotel was another dead end. The paper from Charlotte's letter could have come from anywhere: a relative, perhaps, who had stayed here before journeying to Kerry?

She turned back another page to the second of August. Doherty, Doyle. Walsh. Three Quinns, one after another. A note from a Marianne Moore thanking Wynn's for a memorable stay. She ran her finger down the page, her heart dropping with each line. Nothing. Nothing. Nothing.

But wait . . . a name. Right there. Not Charlotte Rathmore but another name. A name Ellie recognised. And not *just* a name, an address.

She stood back from the page, her hands resting either side of the book. The chatter of the family next to her dropped to a hum as her mind whirled.

'Thank you,' she said to the girl, who threw back a small smile. Ellie took a photo of the open page of the guest book, donned her coat. If she hurried, she could make the five o'clock train. She felt the urge to get back to Kerry. To chase this new lead.

To chase these new *leads*.

෪

She made the train with minutes to spare, and as it pulled away, she called Milo. He answered on the first ring and she cut to the chase.

Asked for his help.

He agreed immediately. That very night, he promised, he would make enquiries. Help find answers to the questions that she'd posed. She could almost see the cogs turning in his mind, almost imagine the conversation. And she wondered if he thought it would change things.

If it could erase the past.

Chapter Thirty-One

Holborn, London

August 1940

Her doctor had said, after checking her vitals and taking in her pale appearance, that Nancy should be eating more protein.

'And how,' she said, 'am I supposed to do that?' Her green ration book – issued to pregnant women – already allowed her extra milk and eggs.

Without looking up from his notes, he slid a tiny, almost transparent piece of paper across the desk. On it was a name and address. 'Mr Hodges owns the bookshop in High Holborn.' He referred to his notes. 'Just around the corner from where you live.'

She knew the one. Imaginatively named after the man himself.

The doctor continued, 'He has an addiction to sweet tea.'

'Sweet tea?'

'Yes. Not that you heard that from me. He also has a nephew, a prolific little hunter. If you were in the market for extra protein, you might start there.'

She said, carefully, 'I don't have sugar and tea to swap.'

The latter was a lie. Teddy's love of Barry's Tea meant that they had brought back a dozen boxes from Ireland last year, ordered from the company's shop in Cork. Tea rationing had begun only a month ago, and Nancy had hidden the stash under the wardrobe.

'Protein is necessary for the baby. Sugar and tea . . . are not.'

Wartime London was changing. Rapidly. Those like Nancy who would once never have considered breaking the law were now dabbling in the black market. Rationed goods were useful barter and scarce items even better. A little luxury – chocolate, a fine brandy, a particular brand of cigarette – could go a long way to lifting one's mood and ever so slightly bolstering the British spirit.

Now, as she arrived back in Parker Street, she carried a bag containing two sausages, some sad-looking vegetables, her rationed supply of butter, bacon, sugar and tea and, nestled at the bottom, a whole jointed rabbit ready for the pot.

Mrs McLaughlin, her ample frame taking up half of the narrow hallway, was locking the door to her flat as Nancy entered the building. Darkness was falling and the bare bulb did little to illuminate the staircase beyond. She quickly closed the front door, trapping the light inside.

'Off to the club?' she said.

The large woman jumped with a cry of surprise. She put her hand to her breast. 'Lord. What a fright you gave me.'

Nancy apologised as she put her shopping down and rubbed the base of her aching spine.

Mrs McLaughlin laid a hand on her arm. 'How are you, pet?'

'Fine, fine.' She knew there were shadows under her eyes. Charlotte's ghost had kept her awake these last nights.

The older woman acknowledged her reluctance to be drawn. 'How's the wee one?'

Relieved, Nancy smiled. 'That's why I'm late.' She laid a hand on the bump under her loose-fitting swing coat. 'Doctor's appointment.'

'A general practitioner working late? We must be at war.'

Mrs McLaughlin had an overt dislike of the medical profession and had proudly announced to Nancy, over a dram of whisky, that she'd not visited a surgery in twenty years. 'A tot of the good stuff and plenty of blood pudding. That's all you need.' She'd taken to giving Nancy – after she'd disclosed her pregnancy – a weekly supply of rich, salty black sausage sourced from somewhere near the border, which arrived well wrapped on her doorstep each Wednesday morning. It had crossed Nancy's mind to enquire as to its origin, but she didn't want to push her luck and instead gratefully accepted the gift.

Mrs McLaughlin looked down at the carrot tops spilling vividly over the edge of Nancy's tote bag. 'Hope you've some meat in there?'

'A few sausages. Some bacon.'

The old woman made a pained face. 'Last time' – by this, Nancy understood Mrs McLaughlin to mean the Great War, or World War One as people had started to call it – 'sausages became a depository for rusk and water.' She rolled the *r* with a flourish.

Nancy had to admit the sausages she'd been handed did look suspicious. She raised her eyebrows and turned to the mailbox. A solitary letter sat at an angle inside. She took it out, frowning. Her name and address were written in small, neat handwriting.

'That's why we called them bangers. Burst like water mains when you fried them up.'

Nancy grimaced. Something to look forward to.

'So then, that'll never do.' Mrs McLaughlin replaced her key in the lock. 'I've a piece of lamb in here, would only go to waste.'

'Actually,' Nancy picked up her bag and shifted the contents, 'I also have . . . this.' She pushed the carrots aside. The pale flesh of the rabbit was just visible in the dimness.

Mrs McLaughlin nodded her approval. 'You're full of surprises. Can I ask . . .'

Handing over the piece of paper with Mr Hodges' details, Nancy winked. 'He's keen on sugar and tea. But I doubt he'd say no to a dram or two.'

Before the war Nancy would have soaked the rabbit meat in buttermilk, to draw out any last gaminess, and cooked it for hours in a low oven with plenty of wine and butter. Now when she returned to the flat she made a quick stew, sealing the flesh before adding diced carrots – and their tops – and small pieces of turnip and potato. She mixed a beef Oxo cube with hot water and poured it into the pot, threw in a couple of bay leaves and then, as her stomach grumbled, leaned back on the countertop and picked up the letter from her bag. She turned it in her hand. Examined it.

The writing didn't belong to Teddy, but it *was* familiar. There were no return details. A pink notice – *OPENED BY CENSOR/AN SCRÚDÓIR D'OSCAIL* – covered one side of the envelope and a green stamp had been haphazardly affixed on its top right-hand corner. It was postmarked *Baile Átha Cliath*.

Dublin.

She opened the envelope and withdrew a single piece of paper. It was a letter, written in a neat hand on headed paper. *Wynn's Hotel*. Its date was a week old, 3rd August 1940.

My dearest T,
Whatever you hear, do not believe it for a moment. Life twists and turns, as you well know and my situation is this – I can no longer remain at Ink House. The place is as dark as midnight . . .

Nancy steadied herself against the kitchen countertop. The rabbit stew had begun to bubble, its rich aroma filling the small kitchen. She didn't know whether to laugh or cry or do both at once.

Charlotte was alive.

Chapter Thirty-Two

Ballinn, County Kerry

September 2019

The alarm clock on Ellie's bedside table read 9.30 a.m. She groaned and swung her legs out of bed, her toes curling as they hit the cold laminate floor.

Last night the train from Dublin had paused at Limerick Junction for what felt like days before rolling into Killarney two hours late. Moira had met her at the station, taken her bag and bundled her into the car, where she'd slept for the hour of winding road back to the hill farm. She'd mumbled snippets – *I found something, someone you wouldn't expect* – before waving off her mum's questions and tumbling into bed towards a dreamless sleep.

The smell of bacon greeted her as she opened the kitchen door.

'Here she is!' said Moira, waving the warped metal tongs that had been in their household since the turn of the century. Ellie knew that voice. It was the tone her mother used when she wasn't alone. When there was a guest in the house.

A figure wearing a grey-and-green argyle jumper turned to her. 'Ah, Ellie. Jolly good work yesterday. Wynn's Hotel: very clever!' His eyebrows, as always, had a life of their own.

He tapped the table next to him. It was neatly laid with

Moira's best napkins, folded into triangles and tucked under themselves so they resembled three white crowns. It was a streak of formality in an otherwise informal kitchen.

Ellie sat cautiously. 'Jules. What a surprise.'

'I wanted to be here to celebrate the returning conqueror.' She looked at Moira. 'Mum . . . invited you?'

'*Mammy*,' muttered Moira, still hovering over the cooker.

'She did,' said Jules, pouring her a Moira-strength cup of tea from the hideously ugly teapot.

'When?'

'Last night. She called me to tell me you'd made a new discovery.'

Discoveries, Ellie wanted to say. But she savoured the moment, which was too delicious to break. They were both looking at her intently; Moira holding the tongs at half-mast in front of crackling bacon that was starting to smell on the other side of well done, and Jules with his wiry eyebrows lifted by curiosity.

'Coffee,' was all she said in reply, standing and patting Jules's shoulder before pointing out the burning frying pan to her mum. She flicked on the kettle and left the room as Moira and Jules danced around the kitchen attempting to save breakfast from its carbony demise.

She returned brandishing a plunger and a pack of ground coffee, bought in Bewley's the day before. 'Anyone?' She held the treasures aloft for all to see.

Moira politely declined, overtly topping up her tea cup to the brim. Jules gave a small nod when Moira wasn't looking, subtly pushing his cup of watery tea to one side.

Ellie scooped coffee into the plunger. The smell of the steam as the hot water hit the grounds reminded her instantly of her apartment – her and Dylan's apartment. The morning ritual that had let her take a breath before the day began. She pushed the thought aside.

'So, we're all ears.' Jules had a piece of toast halfway to his mouth, a dollop of marmalade hanging precariously from its edge.

'Wynn's Hotel,' Ellie said, carrying the plunger to the table, 'is a nice place. Timber panelling. A chandelier. A big jar of free sweets on the front desk.'

'And?' said Jules, taking a bite. 'Good record-keeping?'

'Well . . .' she poured the coffee, 'they do keep records. Of a sort. Guest books.'

'And?' He nodded in encouragement.

'And,' she said, 'unfortunately I didn't find Charlotte's name in the book.' The two faces before her fell.

'But I thought . . .' Moira placed a dish of white pudding on the crowded table. She looked at Jules. 'I'm sorry, Jules, I thought she said she'd found Charlotte.'

Jules patted her hand. 'Not to worry.' He gave Ellie a look that appeared to say, *That's disappointing, but let's not give up.* Then he turned his attention to the spread before him. 'But we'll still have the breakfast, won't we?' He had the decency to look abashed as he picked a crumb off the grey arm of his jumper.

Ellie shook her head. *The way to a man's heart . . .* 'But although I didn't find *Charlotte*'s name,' she continued, placing a fried egg on her plate, 'I did find another one.'

Jules's hand paused over the bacon. 'Another name?' If his eyebrows shot any higher, they'd be on the ceiling.

'Yes. One that we all recognise.' Ellie let it hang, watched her audience hover with anticipation. She sipped her coffee, savouring both the taste and the moment.

'Well?' Moira said with exasperation. 'Who? Who was it?'

'I'll give you a clue.' Ellie waggled her eyebrows. '*A hundred years I've walked this earth . . .*'

'Oh my,' said Jules, just as Moira said:

'Get away with you.'

Ellie nodded. 'Tabby Deenihan. Or, as we know her, Tabby Ryan.'

Moira frowned. 'They stayed together? Her and Charlotte? At the hotel?'

Ellie shook her head. 'No, the handwriting in the guest book matched Charlotte's. I think she travelled under Tabby's name.'

'She *stole* Tabby's identity?' Moira looked stricken.

Ellie sipped her coffee. It was heaven. The cogs of her mind began to turn. 'Perhaps.' But she doubted it. She thought back to Tabby's speech: *I was given a helping hand, by the lady of the house, no less.* Tabby had paused, searched the sky for an answer when Ellie asked her about it. Said that Charlotte had helped her apply for a scholarship.

And Ellie had known, even then, that she was holding something back.

Jules set his fork beside his abandoned breakfast. 'It must have taken some nerve to travel on someone else's papers in 1940.'

Ellie nodded proudly, taking ownership of Charlotte's daring. 'Via hackney to Kenmare probably, then by train onward to Dublin.' She'd researched the route the night before, as her own train had rolled through the darkness.

Moira said, 'And the boat?'

Jules scratched his chin, spoke before Ellie could. 'From Dún Laoghaire? To Liverpool, perhaps?'

'Probably.' Ellie paused theatrically. 'And on to . . . London.'

'London? How can you know that?' He leaned forward, his elbows hovering dangerously close to the bowl of baked beans.

Ellie took her phone from her pocket and opened her album. Chose the photo of the guest book, spun the image to face them. 'There was a forwarding address.'

Jules read: '28b Parker Street, Holborn, London.' He put

a finger to his chin. 'Now,' he said, 'there was, of course, no census during the war. Only National Registration Day in 1939. I have a friend at the archives at Kew. I'll give him a call.' He nodded to both of them, clearly delighted that Charlotte's trail had moved to more familiar territory.

Ellie raised an eyebrow. 'We don't need the records at Kew.'

'Why not?' asked Moira.

'Because,' said Ellie, 'I *know* who lived at 28b Parker Street in 1940.'

A gasp.

'But how . . .'

'I met Harriet Walker in town.'

'Albert's sister?' said Jules, his eyes on Ellie.

Ellie buttered a thick slice of soda bread. Took a bite. Appraised her audience. 'And Hattie – as she prefers to be called – told me a little of her family's history. Nancy, Teddy, Albert and Hattie moved to Blackwater Hall from Ambleside in 1958. But before that, her parents lived elsewhere.'

'Parker Street?'

'Yes.'

They all paused, considered the consequences.

Jules said: 'The letter was to Teddy Rathmore, then.'

Ellie ran her finger over the table's surface, imagining Charlotte's words beneath her print. 'I don't think this letter was written to Teddy.'

'But *My dearest T . . .*'

'Someone else supported Charlotte. As she had supported them.' She pictured two women, their heads together in cahoots, a photo taken. A summer's day.

A favour given.

And a year later, a favour returned.

Moira's face crumpled. 'The letter was to . . . Tabby?' She looked between Jules and her daughter, confused.

Ellie shook her head, closed her eyes. Conjured Charlotte's words, so deeply etched in her mind: *You encouraged me to seek out my own destiny, and so I will.*

'It wasn't Teddy or Tabby. Or any other T's we know.'

'Who then?' This was Jules.

'Trouble.'

'Trouble?' Moira and Jules said in unison.

'The orphan. The friend. The woman who made her own way. Trouble, so called by her husband and family. The one that Charlotte trusted the most.' Ellie paused. 'Nancy Rathmore.'

Chapter Thirty-Three

Holborn, London

August 1940

The day after Nancy received Charlotte's letter, there was a knock at the door. It was a Sunday afternoon and the heat had drawn people out into London's parks and streets. Hitler might be winning the war, but when it came to the British spirit, he was losing the battle.

Mr Hodges' nephew had come up trumps during the week, with Nancy swapping half a bottle of Irish whiskey for a whole hare. It was a ten-year-old Jameson, and didn't seem like anything special to her, but she could tell that Mr Hodges was trying to hide his delight at the prospect of the proposed exchange. She'd haggled and he'd thrown in a couple of pigeons, which Nancy dropped off at Mrs McLaughlin's, her new partner-in-barter.

If Teddy were here, she thought it unlikely that he'd partake in the hare stew she'd cooked. Many people in Kerry believed that hares housed the souls of their grandmothers, and he had picked up on this folklore as a child. Nancy had never known her own grandmother, of course. Or her mother, for that matter. But she thought of them now, wondered how it was when her mother was in her grandmother's belly, just as her own daughter or son grew in her belly now.

She cast the thoughts aside as she gave the pot one last stir, then turned off the gas and started for the door, wiping her hands on her apron. Pushing aside the fear that a telegram might be waiting on the other side, she tentatively inched the door open and peered into the dim hallway beyond.

'My God.' She gasped.

Charlotte.

As real and as alive as Nancy herself.

She was standing there on the scuffed mat, a neat suitcase on the ground beside her, her hair swept back into a loose French bun, dressed as Nancy had never seen her before. Not working class perhaps, but very near to it. Her brown coat was too big, her shoes scuffed and low heeled. Two things, though, gave her away as upper class: her pale hands – unlined and unmarked – and the look in her eye, one of confidence, an unwavering gaze in a wavering situation.

The two women embraced. 'Here I am.' Charlotte did a slow turn, her arms flared from her sides. A demonstration of her existence.

'Charlotte, I . . .' Nancy felt hot tears on her cheeks. There was a part of her that hadn't believed the letter. She'd pulled it out each night and reread the text. Compared the handwriting to previous letters. She'd wanted to ask someone . . . anyone . . . if it was just a dream. But Charlotte had begged her not to, had trusted her to keep the secret.

Downstairs the front door slammed shut. Nancy took a step back and Charlotte picked up her case and entered the flat, closing the door behind her.

'Where to begin?' She laughed, and a sprinkle of her old self scattered around the room. She went to the sofa, rubbing her lower back. 'I'm exhausted. Can I sit?'

'Of course. Of course.' Nancy's mouth was dry.

'What is that *delicious* smell? And you! You look fantastic. Your complexion. Beautiful ... flawless.' Charlotte's eyes dropped to her sister-in-law's stomach. 'When you wrote to me with your news, I was *so* delighted!'

'Charlotte ...'

'And what a place! It's just as you described. Only better, I think. So cosy! Well done you!'

Her enthusiasm was bringing on a headache. Charlotte breezing in, waving her hands, making small talk. It was like meeting a ghost and discussing the weather.

And yet Nancy played the game. 'You're just in time for tea. It's rabbit,' she said. Like Teddy, Charlotte was unlikely to eat hare, and Nancy had very little else to offer. A tiny lie, she consoled herself, in comparison to Charlotte's.

'It smells amazing.'

If Nancy had expected Charlotte to be apologetic, bashful, upset about her disappearance and subsequent reappearance, she was to be surprised. The younger woman's eyes were underlined with a light shadow, but on the whole, she was glowing.

'Drink?' asked Nancy. 'Not much to offer, I'm afraid. Tea?'

'No coffee?' Charlotte said with a wink.

Despite herself, Nancy laughed. 'No. No coffee.'

Making a slight pout, Charlotte said tea would be lovely, and Nancy disappeared to the kitchen. She took the opportunity to splash her face with cold water, and while the kettle boiled, she watched the slow and steady trek of a solitary cloud across an otherwise immaculate sky.

Passing a weak black tea to Charlotte with a look of apology, she pulled a chair from behind the dining table and faced it towards her sister-in-law. It had the look of an impending inquisition about it, and Charlotte eyed her suspiciously over the top of her cup.

'I received a telegram nine days ago. It was from your

brother.' Charlotte rolled her eyes. A childlike gesture. 'In it, he told me you were dead. Drowned in the lough.'

It wasn't clear if this news came as a surprise to Charlotte. Putting her tea to one side, she said, 'Well, that's that, I guess.'

Nancy raised her eyebrows. 'That's what?'

'No one will be looking for me. So that's positive.'

'Is it?'

'Yes, of course.' This was said as though it were self-evident.

'Charlotte. Your family think you're *dead*. And then a week later I receive a letter from you telling me you're arriving shortly and will I just keep this *teeny-tiny*' – she held her thumb and index finger millimetres apart – 'little secret to myself?'

'And you did?'

'Yes.'

Charlotte smiled. 'I *knew* I could trust you.' This she said with triumph.

'I should have told someone.' Nancy looked at her hands. 'But I wanted to see you first.'

Charlotte ignored the probe. 'Who would you tell?

'Your parents for one!'

'And Teddy?'

'Teddy doesn't yet know that you're . . . dead.'

Charlotte raised an eyebrow.

'I wanted to wait. Until I heard from him again.'

She frowned. 'You've not heard from him?'

A sigh. 'It's only been a couple of weeks. That's not uncommon.' But it was. Nancy dug her nails into her palms and smiled calmly. 'If I'm not concerned,' she lied, 'you shouldn't be either.'

Charlotte nodded, smoothed her skirt. It was brown like the coat she'd removed. On her top half she wore a hideous blouse, a sickly shade of pink with puffed sleeves. A caricature of a normal everyday kind of girl.

'You're looking at my clothes.'

Nancy smiled; it was nearly a laugh. 'Were you trying to fit in?'

Charlotte looked down. 'Don't I?'

'No,' Nancy said, 'you look like a swan who's donned a pair of curtains.' She went to the window, slid it open and sat on the sill. Dusk crept along the streets. New air entered the flat, heavy with humidity. From a silver tin she took two cigarettes. She held one out, but Charlotte shook her head.

'When did you start?'

Nancy flicked the lighter and let the flame hover. 'After Teddy left. It felt like something to do.' She realised how stupid that sounded. But it was true. Her hands had been restless and her mind had been numb. Smoking helped her think. 'The doctor recommended it. For my nerves, he said. Four a day.' She took a drag. 'I've heard it also stops you putting on weight.' She pointed to her stomach, patted it protectively.

Charlotte nodded. 'I'd love to try but I can't stand the smell. Reminds me of Father.'

Nancy leaned out of the window, blew the smoke away. It dissipated easily into the still London night. A small piece of tobacco was stuck to her lip and she removed it with thumb and index finger, dropping it into the ashtray. 'So,' she said, 'what happened?'

'Can we not eat first?'

'No.'

Charlotte leaned back on the sofa, her legs stretched out. 'It's complicated.'

'I'd hope so. Faking your own death and disappearing abroad would have been a pretty drastic act for something uncomplicated.'

Charlotte sipped her tea, her eyes all the while on Nancy. She appeared determined to stretch the moment, to encourage her sister-in-law to fill the gaps with chatter as she once had. But Nancy blew a long stream of smoke from her lips. Lit another cigarette. Held the silence.

In the last ten months – living alone, writing, thinking – she'd changed. Her tendency to waffle had gone, along with the need to wear the right thing, speak at the correct moment. They were at war. And women were also fighting. Fighting back against inequality, against oppression. They were capable, resourceful. Strong. A change was washing over Britain, and Nancy had been swept up in it.

She tapped out her cigarette and closed the window. Darkness was falling and she flicked on a standing lamp. Its bulb cast a dim yellow light. She pulled down the blind and took a piece of black fabric from behind the bookshelf, hanging it over the rail, fastening it to the buttons she'd glued to the side of the window frame. Over her shoulder she said, 'Blackout rules.'

She went to the kitchen and bedrooms – one of which was Teddy's makeshift study, his papers still scattered across the desk – and repeated the process. When she returned, she said, 'Well?'

'No blackout yet in Dublin,' said Charlotte. 'I was so taken by the city. It was fascinating. I walked the streets at night, just looking. So much light.'

'You walked the streets of Dublin alone? At night?'

'It's perfectly safe.'

Nancy took her inquisitor's chair once more. 'Just because nothing happened doesn't mean it was safe.'

The wistful look slipped from Charlotte's face.

Nancy sighed. 'Well,' she said, 'at least tell me how you got here. Or, never mind here, how did you get to Dublin?'

'First I walked to Waterville . . .'

She frowned. 'That must be at least fifteen miles?'

Charlotte shrugged. 'It was, I admit, farther than I'd

imagined. But I'd been walking, in the weeks prior. A little more each day. Before I left home, I could walk up Cottah Mountain and back in a little over three hours.'

'I'm impressed.'

'When I arrived, I took a hackney to Kenmare. Then a train to Dublin. I stayed at Wynn's Hotel.'

'You didn't fill in the guest book, did you?'

Charlotte nodded, and Nancy's heart dropped. Footprints to her front door. 'It's a requirement these days. I *had* to show identification.'

'And the address?'

Charlotte nodded again. 'But don't worry, they'll never know it was me. I've covered my tracks.' She winked, and Nancy suppressed the urge to hang her head in her hands.

'And no one recognised you?'

'In that coat?' She gestured to the brown trench perched on the edge of the sofa. 'No. I had an even *more* hideous blouse than this one. And a hat.' She paused. 'It was also brown.'

'Oh dear.'

'Yes, I know. Anyway, no one was looking for me. Why would they be? I left my pearls scattered by the lough. And the rowboat adrift. With an oar and a bit of blood.' She rolled her skirt up. A thin red mark ran down her thigh. A cut that was healing nicely.

'Suggesting what?'

'A struggle.'

'Oh God.' Nancy's forehead felt clammy.

Charlotte shrugged. 'What?'

'This is fraud. It's . . . *wrong*.' Nancy hardly knew which was worse.

'Don't worry,' Charlotte said with a nonchalance that Nancy found unsettling. 'No one will be blamed.'

'But they will be. You're . . . you're . . .'

'What?'

'A Rathmore. In Kerry. They'll start with ex-IRA and move out from there.'

'They wouldn't. Everyone in Ballinn knows I'm sympathetic. Anyway, they'll all have alibis, all for each other. That's the way it works, even if someone *had* taken me.' She laughed at the irony.

'Charlotte!'

'I'm simply saying it will be fine. I'm sure of it.'

'The telegram didn't suggest that everything was fine.'

Charlotte shrugged. 'We fought. Terribly.'

'I see.'

'I threatened to run away and kill myself.'

Nancy flinched. 'What?'

Charlotte looked to her hands.

'Was it about Lord Hawley?'

'That was . . . I suppose . . . part of it.'

'Surely it was to be delayed? Was he not posted to Norway in April?' Although where he was now, Charlotte had never said. Norway had surrendered to the Germans in June.

'Yes to both your questions. His next leave wasn't to be until Christmas, but no one's heard from him for six weeks.' She looked up at Nancy. 'I'm sorry. It was such a summer. I . . . I couldn't write to tell you everything.'

Nancy pulled her chair forward, smoothed her skirt. 'Please. Don't worry about that.'

For the first time, Charlotte's eyes welled. A tear spilled from one corner, running a path down the centre of her cheek. It dropped onto the back of her hand. She smeared it distractedly with her finger.

'And,' said Nancy gently, 'you refused to go ahead with the marriage?'

Charlotte sniffed, dropped her head. 'Well, I . . . gave a reason. Why it couldn't happen.'

'What kind of reason?'

She gave a wet laugh, wiped her eyes roughly. 'A very . . . *thorough* reason.'

Nancy leaned in and hugged her, the pink blouse rough under her skin. 'Everything will turn out for the best.'

There was a pause, then, 'Nancy?'

'Yes?'

'Oh, Nancy. I'm pregnant.'

Chapter Thirty-Four

Blackwater Hall, County Kerry
March 1958

The fallout from the misunderstanding in the garden was inevitable.

If Albert's aim had been true, Mama would never have been searching the ground for pigeons that weren't there. Would never have looked left and seen Tomas leaning over Hattie, supine on the path, the wind knocked from her. None of that would have happened. Instead, Tomas would have helped her to her feet. Apologised. Said he was jumpy. Bad with loud noises. Bad with surprises.

She would have hugged him and it would have been all right.

But it didn't work out that way.

Grandmother had looked at her with mild disdain when Mama carried her back to the house. 'What's this?' Her voice was low and calm, in stark contrast to Mama's high-pitched hysterics.

'The gardener. He attacked her. Thank God . . . oh thank God I was there.' Mama's hands were shaking, bird like. She'd lost weight since they'd arrived at Blackwater Hall.

Grandmother merely raised a thinly drawn eyebrow. 'The gardener? Tomas?'

'Yes, Tomas! Of course. Did I not warn you about him?'

The older woman put one hand out towards Hattie. She, not having been approached by Grandmother before, looked nervously at Mama, who was now so white that her complexion matched the crisp shirt she wore under her tartan jacket.

At Mama's nod, she stepped forward, lifting her gaze as the old woman knelt in front of her, one hand leaning heavily on her cane. Her breathing was laboured, as though the act of showing interest in her grandchild exhausted her. They had never been so close before. Grandmother's rheumy eyes were surrounded by sparse eyelashes dabbed with mascara, giving the effect of a poorly made pinwheel. Her look was searching. Not kind. And yet not cruel.

'Are you hurt?'

Hattie became aware of a firm, warm hand on her upper arm. She looked down and was surprised to see it belonged to the woman in front of her. Mama was now sitting in a chair by the fire; she'd removed her shoes and pulled her knees to her chest like a coiled spring.

'What happened?'

'I fell over.' She looked at Mama as she spoke. 'The shot, it scared me. I tripped.'

'And?'

'Tomas helped me.'

'What were you doing out there? This time of morning?'

'Setting potatoes. It's lucky: St Patrick's Day.' At the pursed lips, Hattie began to waffle. 'He gave me scones and jam for breakfast . . .'

Grandmother nodded and dropped her hands and gave the slightest flick of her head to indicate that the interview was over. Uncertainly, Hattie backed out of the room. Not quite closing the heavy wooden door behind her, she crouched in the dark hallway, ear to the crack.

'Nancy,' said Grandmother.

Mama murmured.

The older woman spoke again. The volume of her voice indicated that neither had crossed the floor towards the other. 'This is the fourth time you've asked me to remove the gardener. The first time you suggested that he was poor at his job. Then you said he was lazy. The third time . . . well, I can no longer remember your argument . . . I will ask you once more not to interfere with my staff. Tomas Deenihan worked here with his father, who pulled this garden back from the brink.' She coughed heavily.

There was silence after that. A rustling kind of noise. The clang of metal. Mama had stoked the fire.

'I beg your pardon?'

'I said' – Mama's voice was closer – 'he's *damaged*.'

'Weren't they all, Nancy? Weren't you?'

'Not like that.'

Grandmother said, 'You must have seen . . . things during the war. You're certainly not the girl who visited here before.'

'Well,' Mama laughed cruelly, 'you didn't like *her* either.'

Footsteps. Not from the room. From down the hall. Hattie pushed into the hollow of the doorway. A door opened. Someone, Cook perhaps, hummed as they crossed the far end of the hallway. The music drifted towards Hattie, fogging the murmurs on the other side of the door.

Grandmother cleared her throat. Her voice was hoarse when she spoke again. 'Things have been difficult. But we must all learn to live together. If Teddy is to take the reins . . .'

'If?'

'. . . then you must learn how to run certain parts of the estate. Firing staff because you have taken against them is simply not done.'

'The man is dangerous.'

'We've established that Hattie fell of her own accord, and Tomas was merely assisting her.'

'I don't trust him. He . . . he looks at me in a strange way.'

Grandmother sighed.

'And at Hattie,' said Mama. 'Also at Albert. He stares.'

'I hardly think that's fair.' Grandmother's voice moved away, towards the window. 'The man is never near the house and you spend all your time in the library. With Albert.'

'You know, Niamh . . . he isn't *right*.' Hattie had never heard Mama use that name before. Niamh. *Nee-ve*.

Grandmother sniffed. She took two slow steps towards the door, then turned back. Hattie held her ground. Held her breath.

'Look to yourself, Nancy. Seeing ghosts where there are none. Hiding in the dark. I may not have much liked you before the war, but I did at least envy you. All that potential. All that passion. Charlotte and you . . . peas in a pod.'

A sharp intake of breath. 'Don't talk of Charlotte . . .'

Grandmother ignored her. 'But look at you now.'

Mama's voice was quiet again. 'It's this place. I don't feel comfortable.'

'The house is two centuries old. It's damp. What more do you want me to say? We remain here because the estate is something for local people to look up to.'

Mama laughed cruelly. 'People don't look up to this house. They look *down* on it. Perhaps there's something in those rumours about the ringfort . . . the luck that's plagued this family . . .'

'Families around here are no strangers to grief.'

'No. But they work through it. They talk about it. You won't.'

'I have my own ways of coping.'

Silence. Perhaps Mama was shaking her head. Perhaps she'd

wrapped her arms around her body, thinner every day. Perhaps she was doing nothing. 'Charlotte is everywhere in this house,' she said quietly, 'but not in our conversations.'

'Charlotte is dead. Nothing more.'

'Yes.' Quick footsteps towards the door. 'I know.'

Hattie fell away and scampered under the hall table. It was poor cover, but it didn't matter; when Mama came through the door, she wasn't looking for her daughter. She paused and appraised her own reflection in the oval mirror opposite. She frowned at herself sadly; then, a moment later, the look was gone.

Chapter Thirty-Five

Holborn, London

August 1940

Charlotte, who had professed to want *only a little dinner*, finished her plate of stew almost before Nancy had started.

'Delicious.' She smiled apologetically. 'I've never had rabbit before.'

Nancy cleared her throat and pushed the pot towards her. 'There's more. Go on. Didn't you know that food waste is a punishable offence nowadays?'

Since her revelation, Charlotte had cried fitfully on the sofa and Nancy had taken a spot next to her, comforting her gently, her mind whirling with questions. Now, as they sat at the small table, the wireless quietly playing inappropriately jolly Ella Fitzgerald in the background, she wanted to ask: *What will you do now?*

Instead she said, 'In the morning, I normally leave for work before eight. You don't need to get up early. Get a good sleep and we'll talk properly tomorrow night.'

Charlotte nodded. 'Thank you.' She laid down her fork, her plate once again clean. 'I know I've put you in an impossible position. But I didn't have anywhere else—'

Nancy held up her hand. 'Say no more about it. We're family.'

'Don't use that word.' Charlotte smiled sadly. 'My family – I mean, not *Teddy*, of course – they never cared for me. They only care for themselves. For the Rathmore name.'

'Charlotte, your parents must be distraught.'

She bit back a sob. 'Mother said it would be better if I was dead rather than pregnant. At least that way the cancelled marriage could have been explained away.'

Nancy put a hand to her mouth, covering a sharp intake of breath.

'They threatened to send me to a laundry. Do you know how they treat girls in those places? What they do to them?'

Nancy lowered her eyes. 'You want to keep the baby?'

'Of course.'

'Who's the father?'

Charlotte hesitated. She wiped her brow. 'Well, what does it matter now?' she said. 'It was Tomas.'

Tomas Deenihan. The boy about whom Nancy had joked with Charlotte. Had she *encouraged* this?

'Do you love him?'

'Yes.'

'Well, that's something.' She instantly regretted her insufficient response. 'What I mean to say is . . . that's wonderful.'

'But?'

'But . . . could he not have come with you?'

Charlotte gave a bitter laugh. 'He's gone away.'

Abandoned. Nancy felt her heart reach out to the girl. 'Oh, Charlotte, I'm so sorry.'

'Father made it happen.' The dark look in her eye, Nancy now saw, wasn't caused by thoughts of Tomas. 'How I *hate* him.'

'I don't understand.'

'When I found out about this' – she touched her stomach – 'I told Mother. I had no one else. I thought we would find a way.' Nancy was surprised at Charlotte's naivety after the resourcefulness she had shown in getting to London. 'She went straight to Father. He threatened to fire Tomas, his father and Tabby. The family live on their wages. All nine of them.'

Nancy took a sip of water. She felt hot and cold all at once. 'And Tomas left? You couldn't go with him?' Nancy knew what she was suggesting would have been scandalous and near-impossible. They would have had to go to a city, find jobs, blend in. Get married immediately, certainly.

'Father stipulated he must join up. Join the army.'

'Oh God.' Nancy knew that thousands of Irish had joined to fight with the British, despite their country's neutrality. Many back home considered them traitors.

'From the moment I told Mother, I never saw him again. But I went to the village to visit *his* mother.' Charlotte picked at a piece of fluff on her skirt. 'She wouldn't let me through the door. I learned that scandal is not just for the aristocracy.'

'Did the whole village know?'

'No one knew, and she wanted to keep it that way.'

'Where is he now?'

'I don't know. But he'll wait for me. I'm sure of it. I wrote to him. Let him know where I am. That I'm . . . alive.' At this last word, she almost laughed.

Nancy reached across the table, took Charlotte's hand. It was cold. 'You've been through so much.'

Charlotte's chin wobbled. 'I won't be a burden to you. I promise.'

'Charlotte, I'll help you. Of course I will. But your family . . . I know they were angry, but they think you're dead! This . . . this is' – Nancy spread her hands – 'crazy.'

'When Tomas returns to Ireland, I'll go back. We'll move to Cork, or Dublin. No scandal necessary.'

'I need to think . . .'

Quickly Charlotte said, 'I have a work permit.'

'You don't need one. You've got British papers.'

'I didn't travel under my own name.' She looked at Nancy as though her sister-in-law had taken leave of her senses. 'That would have been madness.'

'Please don't tell me you have forged papers?'

Charlotte laughed. 'No. Of course not.'

'Then how . . .'

She stood and lifted a finger. 'Wait.' She left for the spare room. Nancy heard the click of a case.

When she returned, she took Nancy's plate and replaced it with an identity card and a letter. It was a work permit for the Royal Arsenal, Woolwich. A filling factory. Both were issued in the same name. Tabby Deenihan.

'Tomas's sister?'

A photo of Tabby was affixed to the travel permit. She looked almost entirely *unlike* Charlotte. A dark-haired girl with a round face. The tip of a birthmark visible above the collar of her blouse.

Nancy raised her eyebrows. 'You crossed a border with this?'

'There might have been bribery involved.'

'Charlotte . . .'

'There's a war on. Everyone has a price.'

Nancy shook her head. Almost laughed. It was like a thriller novel. She paused, said: 'Charlotte, filling factories are . . . dangerous.'

The younger girl shrugged.

'I can help you. We'll find you work elsewhere.' As Nancy said this, she wondered how that would be possible; altering a work permit for an Irishwoman was unlikely to be easy.

As if reading her mind, Charlotte said, 'That will be difficult.' She tapped Tabby's documents. 'This is me now. I'm Irish. An immigrant.'

Last month *The Times* had run a piece on the rise of Irish

immigration; a huge influx had forced the Department of External Affairs to impose requirements for new workers. A British liaison office had been set up in Dublin to facilitate the new arrangements, and it was no longer possible for the Irish to travel to the UK for work without pre-approval, although Nancy had heard that in reality it still happened.

Charlotte said, 'Tabby offered it to me. Willingly.'

'That's a terrible risk for her.'

'She was already sympathetic to our relationship. She covered for me countless times so Tomas and I could meet. Telling Mother I was visiting people in the village, undertaking charitable work.'

'Does she know you've come here?'

Charlotte shook her head. 'It was too risky.'

'And what did she get out of it?'

'You're very suspicious.' Charlotte folded away the documents. She shrugged. 'The equivalent of two years' munitions wages. Enough to qualify as a teacher and more.'

Nancy had heard that munitions wages were good. Very good. Particularly for a working-class Irish girl. But not so good for an aristocrat. She looked at Charlotte's soft hands.

'It's hard work, Charlotte. And very . . . dirty. You'll be covered in sulphur. They're not called canary girls for nothing.'

'So I've heard.'

'And you're pregnant.'

'As are you.'

'Yes. And I work at a desk.'

'I'm decided on the matter,' said Charlotte. 'I'm here now. I've made my bed and now I'll lie in it. As Mother would say.'

Nancy said, 'You don't have to work. I can look after you.' Although she didn't think she could. She struggled to make ends meet as it was.

Charlotte stared at her hands. She traced the life line on the

left, then checked the right. 'Do you remember what you said
when you visited Blackwater Hall last summer?'

Nancy frowned.

'You said – or rather, *implied* – that I wasn't used to getting
my hands dirty.'

She thought back to their conversation, in the walled garden
a year before. She and Charlotte, under the clematis.

'I'm not sure I implied anything of the sort.'

'But you were thinking it.'

'Oh, so now you're a mind reader?'

Charlotte laughed. 'Have I surprised you?'

'Yes.' There was no hesitation in Nancy's reply.

'Well then, give me the benefit of the doubt. I'm determined
to step into this new life. To have Tomas's baby. To marry and
make our own way, not shackled by my family, or his. Like
you and Teddy.'

It was a fantasy. Fraught with so many potential complica-
tions that Nancy couldn't bear to consider them all. But she
would help Charlotte face them, one by one. She kept her face
impassive, said, 'There's a major problem we need to tackle.
And you're not going to like it.'

'What is it?'

She looked down at Tabby Deenihan's photograph, then
reached out to tuck a loose strand of Charlotte's hair behind
her ear. It was a motherly gesture. From a woman who had
never had a mother, or been one.

'Your hair.' She held up the identification. 'I'm afraid the
blonde will have to go.'

Charlotte looked miserable.

'And,' Nancy said, 'after that, *Tabby*, we'll talk.'

Chapter Thirty-Six

Ballinn, County Kerry
September 2019

Buoyed by her discovery at Wynn's Hotel, Ellie had called Sergeant Beddy Cullen on the train from Dublin. The local garda station was only manned every second Tuesday, but she knew that Beddy could be found in the nearby towns of Waterville or Kenmare during the rest of the week. She tried Ballinn without expectation, then both other stations. Each said that he was at the other, but the latter connected her to his mobile and eventually she caught him at home. A TV blared in the background. And . . . was that the sound of a child's tantrum? Or more than one child? Beddy as a father. Now she'd heard it all.

He hadn't exactly promised to dig out any records about the Rathmore tragedy, but he had used the phrase *look into it*, which in Ellie's experience implied *I'll pretend to help out to get you off my back*. To this, she'd said, 'I look forward to *collecting* them from you. This mystery is such a *basket* case.' She wondered whether the subtlety would be lost on him two decades after his childish theft from the church collection basket.

The conversation had been, if not friendly, congenial and Ellie had planned to chase him up – via text message – today. Jules had put a spanner in the works, appearing at her mum's breakfast table. But, she had to admit, it had been a nice morning.

On her urgent list was to see if Milo had visited Tabby as promised on the phone the evening before. If he hadn't, she would make a visit herself to ask questions that must be answered. Jules had offered to go with her. 'I'm grand, I think,' she'd smiled, then felt guilty at his crestfallen face. 'But I'll let you know how it goes.' Before he had been able to argue, Moira had offered to drive him, and his bike, back to the village.

Now that the house was empty, Ellie lit a fire in the chilly sitting room and piled it high with peat and sally, which crackled stubbornly before settling into a roaring blaze. She'd watched from the window the comedy unfolding on the driveway. Jules attempting to remove the wheels from his bike. Scratching his head. Then, Laurel-and-Hardy-like – finger to the air – shuffling off to the shed. When he was out of sight, Moira had whipped off the two wheels, thrown the bike in the back of the car and folded herself into the driver's seat. Jules returned with a spanner held proudly aloft, the momentary look of triumph erased by confusion when he saw that the job had already been done. He threw his hands in the air, jumped into the passenger seat and, without hesitation, burst into laughter.

She fetched her coat and handbag, both still damp from yesterday's soggy Dublin streets, and brought them to hang in the sitting room, then opened her notebook and took out Charlotte's portrait once again. Appraised the young woman. 'What were you running from?' she asked softly.

Within minutes, steam began to rise from her handbag and she leaned forward to move it away from the fire. As she fumbled with the handle, something fell out. It was a burgundy box, the yellow ribbon coiled like a spring.

She frowned.

When she'd walked out of the Westbury with her head

held high, she'd had no idea what she'd really meant by *I need to think*. It was non-committal and at the time it was all she could manage. But *should* she think about it? His offer. Such as it was. *We can elope. The two of us.* Was that how they would repair their damaged relationship, with a quick and solitary marriage? Cover the cracks with a layer of plaster so that on the outside everything looked smooth and strong?

She had expected to feel a surge of adrenaline when she'd seen him. She had expected to *know*. Had expected to want him back. But it hadn't been like that. *It's all your fault.*

She pulled at the yellow ribbon and opened the box. A silver comb lay inside, nestled in a pool of blue velvet. She tipped it into her hand. It was heavy, and so cool it felt wet in the warm room. Turning it over, she saw three hallmarks. She knew enough to recognise the middle symbol – the shape of a Monopoly house. The comb was platinum.

Underneath was a note. It said, simply:

Don't lose this one. Dylan xx

It was a reference to her habit of losing combs. Here and there. Everywhere.

Of course it was.

But it was a terrible, terrible choice of words. And they cut like a knife.

The comb tumbled to the ground with a dull thud. *Don't lose this one.* She let out a cry – half sob, half scream – then, taking a breath, she clenched her jaw and ripped the note to shreds. When she threw the pieces into the waiting flames, they ignited as they fell, burning to ash in front of her eyes.

Chapter Thirty-Seven

Blackwater Hall, County Kerry
April 1958

Lady Niamh Rathmore was buried in the family cemetery near an old chapel that had long since decayed to three walls of rubble stone and mortar. The graveyard stood above the rolling hills that fell away towards Kenmare Bay. It was as fine a place as any to be put to rest, but Mama said that even in death, Grandmother would find fault with the view.

Hattie had listened at the door as the doctor told Papa that Grandmother's heart had simply given out in the night and she wouldn't have known a thing. She wondered what sort of thing it was that she was supposed to know.

It was the first funeral she'd ever been to. The wake took place at Blackwater Hall, the front room full of the people – Ballinn residents – that Hattie had, only two months ago, so desired to meet. But now they were there, she wanted nothing more than to run and hide in the labyrinth of rooms that she'd previously sought to avoid. She wasn't sad that Grandmother was gone. Not that she would ever admit that to anyone. The old woman had frightened her and, aside from St Patrick's Day, they had barely exchanged a word. But for the first time Hattie contemplated what it would be like to lose someone she truly loved. To never see them again. Papa. Mama. Albert. Even

Tomas, who had become her only companion on the estate and whom she snuck out to meet whenever Mama was in bed with a headache – now a regular occurrence.

He was there, at the funeral. Grandmother, whom Hattie had never heard speak well of anybody, had insisted on his continued employment at Blackwater Hall after the 'incident'. She said his father had transformed the estate's gardens from a heathen jungle into something cultured and refined.

Since St Patrick's Day, Mama had forbidden Hattie and Albert from seeing Tomas. At this news, Albert had frowned momentarily then agreed to abide by the new rule. He had taken to obeying Mama's every command and Hattie knew it was so she would help him return to England and the girl he'd left behind.

The congregation was made up of Blackwater Hall estate workers, who numbered only a few, and their families, who numbered many. Hattie sat in the front row between Mama and Albert. Her dark blue dress, which hung just below the knee, covered itchy woollen stockings, and she wedged her hands between her legs. She sat still like Mama and her brother, while Papa leaned forward, a red cushion beneath his knees. When it was time to take Communion, Mama shook her head and said, 'That's not for us,' as the village filed silently past.

&

In the aftermath of the church, the wake and the burial, Blackwater Hall was quiet, and Hattie was alone in the front room, the fire crackling at one end, the gentle heave of floor-boards upstairs above as someone paced back and forth. Papa perhaps. She had made a space for herself under the dining table, a book before her, her legs seesawing as she lay on her front, displaying a lack of propriety that Grandmother would have chided her for.

The door next to the fireplace opened and Grandfather stepped through. He took a seat by the fire, then lit a cigarette and inhaled deeply. The footsteps upstairs had stopped, and the house was still once again.

But now Mama entered the room.

'Charles.' She acknowledged Grandfather and gestured to the chair next to him. The fire popped. 'May I?'

Hattie couldn't hear a response, but Mama took a seat, sweeping her feet at an angle underneath her. 'It was well done,' she said. 'As well done as these things can be.'

A nod, perhaps.

'She would have been pleased.'

'Pleased?' said Grandfather.

'Well, perhaps *pleased* isn't quite the right word.'

Grandfather lowered his feet from the footstool and stood slowly. He shook his head and walked to the sideboard. 'What a preposterous thing to say, Nancy.'

'I'm sorry . . . My choice of words . . .' She rubbed her temple. 'It's been a long day.'

'My wife was pleased with nothing in life. She'd have been distinctly *displeased* with her send-off, no doubt. But,' he said, pouring himself a generous measure of whiskey, 'we'll never know.' He lifted an empty glass towards Mama, his eyebrows raised in question.

She nodded.

His socked feet were silent as he moved slowly back to the fire and handed her a drink, amber liquid honey like behind the cut glass. 'Things will change around here.'

What he said was true. Grandmother had loomed over the house, omnipresent. It had been a constant effort to avoid her. The only peace Hattie found was in the kitchen, where Grandmother would never venture, and the walled garden, which was muddy from the ceaseless Kerry rains.

Mama sniffed at her drink. 'I'm happy to take on Niamh's role in the house, if that's helpful to you. Oversee the purchasing. Assist with the accounts.' She paused, stared down at the carpet as though already planning what rugs to buy. Hattie knew she hated that white carpet, hated tiptoeing across it for fear of leaving prints. 'I can manage the staffing too, if you like. That kind of thing.'

Grandfather nodded. 'I wondered when you might say that.'

Mama looked at him sharply, her neck a pale slip above her high collar. The dress was an elegant cut but her figure had diminished so much in the past months that it bunched at her waist. She rubbed her bare arms, the faintest goosebumps appearing, picked out by the firelight. 'What do you mean?'

'Niamh told me you'd been pushing to remove the gardener.'

Mama shook her head, pursed her lips. 'I'm quite sure she is mistaken.' She corrected herself. '*Was* mistaken.'

Grandfather swirled his whiskey.

Mama continued, 'I merely expressed concern after the incident with Hattie.' At the mention of her name, Hattie shrank further back under the table. 'Having a man like that around children is stressful for . . . a mother.'

Grandfather took a deep breath. 'Yes, the events of St Patrick's Day. A shame. The man's troubled, you know?'

'Yes, I know.'

More rapid footsteps upstairs, a creak. Grandfather lowered his voice, a habit that would take years to break. 'As Hugo was.'

In profile, the rise of Mama's cheekbones was stark. 'But Hugo never became violent? Surely?'

'These things manifest in many ways.' Grandfather touched the medals pinned to his front of his blazer and drained the last of his whiskey. Stood. 'I would be glad of assistance with the more . . . womanly duties on the estate. I'm sure you'll handle the finances and staff with due care.'

'I will,' said Nancy, standing to watch him go. She put her untouched glass to the side and walked to the mantelpiece, running a hand across its green marble surface, inspecting for dust that surely wasn't there.

Chapter Thirty-Eight

Cahercillin Farm, County Kerry
September 2019

'Ellie?' Moira's voice was loud. She leaned out of the car window. 'Ellie! Where're you going?'

'For a walk!' Ellie stomped along the boreen that wound down the hill towards the sea. The Micra was in reverse, tracking her progress. It wobbled dangerously close to the drain that rimmed the lane.

'Lovely weather for a walk,' Moira said.

Ellie was soaked. Drenched. The cold rain had matted her hair. Three sheep watched her progress with moderate disinterest as they chewed their cud.

Moira stopped the car. Pulled on the handbrake and got out. Stood in front of her daughter. 'What is it?' She took Ellie's face in her hands. 'What. Is. It?'

'Nothing. I . . .' Ellie felt tears hot on her face. 'I just . . . He gave me a . . . I saw Dylan in . . .'

Moira let go of her daughter, went to the passenger-side door. Its usual creak of defiance was absent as she pulled it open with force, as though it understood resistance was useless. The shoulders of her blue sweater were already soaked, dark patches spreading down her front. 'Get in the car.'

Ellie trudged round, winced as the door slammed behind her. Chewed at her nails as Moira pulled away.

They followed the boreen back up the mountain, winding through the rain as it tap-tap-tapped on the windscreen, trying to get in.

ஃ

The comb lay on the table in front of them and the fire had burned to ash in the too-hot room.

'*Don't lose this one,*' Ellie repeated, sipping her tea. It was remarkably strong, Moira having concocted one of her special brews, the kind made for shock. Milk, sugar, a good long stew. 'It was just unfortunate wording.'

'Ellie, you know I don't like to interfere . . .'

'Do you not?' Ellie almost smiled. Her eyes were red raw with tears.

'. . . but I did assume you would see him.'

She nodded, remembering the worried expression on her mum's face as the train pulled away from the station the previous morning. 'I'm sorry. I should have—'

Moira held up a hand. 'And I'm proud of you.'

Ellie put down her tea. This was not what she'd expected when Moira had bustled the two of them into the house, sent Ellie to change while she herself had turned left to flick on the kettle. 'Proud?'

'Yes. For two reasons. I'm proud you faced Dylan. Even if you didn't tell me. I understand that you love him. That you can't just turn that off.'

Ellie dropped her gaze to the comb.

'But more so, I'm proud I've raised the kind of daughter who gives people the benefit of the doubt. Who looks for good in others. Because if you lose that, then every step forward in life is a step backwards.'

Ellie sipped her tea, hiding a sob.

'But . . .'

'But?'

'Hindsight is the best insight to foresight.'

'Did you get that from Tabby?' But she was right, and deep down Ellie knew it.

'Mum?'

'Yes?'

'Thank you. For everything.'

'No need, love.'

They embraced, and Ellie leaned her cheekbone on Moira's shoulder, realised that although she herself was now dry and warm, her mum was still soaking wet.

Moira started. 'Oh!' She held her daughter at arm's length. 'I saw Beddy in O'Brien's.'

'Just now?' Ellie frowned, rubbing her eyes, rubbing away her thoughts. 'I thought the station wasn't manned till next Tuesday?'

'Well he's here today. Renewing a shotgun licence, so Deidre said. For a blow-in.' She leaned forward, whispered, 'A hunter. Apparently the man goes around in khaki.'

Ellie gave her a look.

Moira raised her hands. ''Tis only what Deidre said. Anyway, on my way out of the shop, Beddy told me he wants to see you.' She paused. 'Deidre's ears were practically flapping.'

'I've only asked him to dig out some files on Charlotte.' This was good news. Ellie put the comb back in its box and shut it away in the coffee-table drawer. Out of sight.

'Files?' whispered Moira.

'They're not contraband, Mum.' She put her notebook in her satchel. Procaffination called and hopefully soon so would Milo. She needed coffee and phone reception, in that order.

Moira stood, poked at the fire. A hopeful flame flickered

and died. She added three pieces of turf and the two women watched the smoke curl up and away. 'He said he'd be in at the station until one o'clock.'

'It's already after half twelve!'

'Is it?' Moira looked down at the faded tan line on her wrist where a watch might once have been. 'I thought it was morning still.'

Ellie grabbed her coat from beside the fire; it was dry now, slightly stiff. Throwing it and her satchel over her arm, she paused at the hallway mirror. Applied her armour: lipstick, red as blood. Then gave her mum a flurried wave as she took the keys for the Micra and strode out the door.

ᴣ๑

The Ballinn garda station, a rough stone building, sat on the western edge of the village. A traditional garda lamp-post stood sentry outside, a lonely indication of the building's official status.

Ellie pushed open the peeling door and stepped into a hallway with a noticeboard on one side and a long line of coat hooks on another. A single fluoro jacket hung alone, the word *GARDA* emblazoned on its back.

'Hello?'

A voice echoed from afar: 'In here.'

She followed the call into an office on her right. Inside was a large laminate desk, topped with a monitor and a spread of papers. A cup of coffee stood steaming, a hand wrapped around it. That hand, Ellie noted, belonged to Beddy Cullen, though a much larger version of the Beddy Cullen she'd once known.

'Ellie.' He got to his feet. His frame was substantial and his cheeks had the rosy glow of someone momentarily too hot or commonly quite tipsy. 'What's it been? Sixteen, seventeen years?'

Ellie took his outstretched hand; it was warm, his grip firm. It felt, surprisingly, like the handshake of someone reliable. 'Beddy. Great to see you!' she said with exaggerated brightness. 'You look . . .' She searched for the word.

'Fat?' He belly-laughed.

She felt her face flush. 'I was going to say . . . happy.'

He grinned, patted his stomach. 'Family life,' he said, 'it suits me.'

She eased into the plastic chair opposite him. A small fan heater aimed under the desk was belting out warm air and a radio played in the background.

She said, 'I know you have to leave shortly' – he looked at his watch and his brow wrinkled, as if time was an annoyance better left alone – 'but the files on Charlotte Rathmore . . .'

'It's not really my area, Ellie.' He pointed to the corner of the room, where a collection of stained cups huddled next to a jar of Nescafé.

She suppressed a shudder and shook her head. *No thanks.* 'But you mentioned to Mum that you wanted to see me?'

He rummaged in the desk drawer. 'I got you these forms. Document release applications.' He looked apologetic. Almost. 'Got to follow the rules these days.'

Ellie was surprised. And disappointed. This was the guy who had found a copy of a mid-year paper three days before the exam and sent it to the entire class. The teacher thought she'd transformed her teenagers into aspiring physicists. The illusion didn't last long, but it had earned Beddy a certain notoriety.

But now, it seemed, he'd gone soft. In more ways than one.

She glanced at the forms. 'This'll take forever.'

'You've got plenty of time, so I hear.' This too was surprising. That he'd checked up on her showed more nous than she'd given him credit for. The look he gave her was mildly challenging, but she was more than up to the task of wiping it from his face. She'd done some homework of her own.

She pushed the forms aside and smiled sweetly. 'Bernie mentioned she saw you in church last week. Still devout, are you?'

He'd lifted his cup halfway to his mouth, where it now hovered. 'Yes, I'd say I am. These days.'

'And your wife. She's very religious, isn't she? On the church committee and the like.' A reluctant affirmative. Ellie broke eye contact and placed her hands on the desk. She traced the pale moon of a cup ring with one finger. 'I hear she's from an old Galway family. Did someone mention . . . well, isn't her uncle a *priest*?'

Beddy shifted in his seat.

'No . . .' continued Ellie, 'not a priest. A bishop, no less! Bishop of Galway and Kilmacduagh.' When he didn't reply, she began to shoulder her satchel. 'Will I come back next week?'

He put down his cup and held up a hand. From his desk drawer, he took two folders. Theatrically he licked one chubby finger and opened the first. 'The disappearance of Lady Charlotte Rathmore,' he said. 'Quite an event in the parish.'

Ellie's tongue lingered at the roof of her mouth as she considered her next comment. 'You eejit.' She dropped her satchel to the ground, wincing at its heavy thud, and sat back down.

Beddy shrugged. 'You were always so straight-laced at school. Wanted to see if you'd changed.' His grin returned.

She reached across the table. 'I have.'

'So I see.' He pulled the folders back and flicked through the papers as though they were a deck of cards. 'There was a substantial search for this Charlotte character. Five days. Then a group of locals continued to look, for more than a month.' He raised an eyebrow. 'What's your interest in the case?'

She paused then. Considered her next words. *I can't get*

Charlotte out of my mind. She ran, just like me. She shouldn't be forgotten. 'A passing one,' was all she said. It was hardly an explanation.

'I suppose you want to write about it?'

The thought had certainly crossed her mind. 'It's a possibility.' Beddy Cullen, too, had changed. He had become a man who saw things instead of only wanting to be seen.

He leaned forward. 'That wasn't much of an answer.'

If she showed fear now, she knew, she'd lose him. 'It wasn't much of a question.'

He sighed. 'I don't know what you're up to, but I don't want to be implicated in it. I don't want anything like your Stanley Street scandal following me around.' He pushed the files towards her. 'I'm only doing this because you think there is some kind of secret here, worth investigating.' He flipped over the cover of the top one, and placed his hand on the front page. 'And while some secrets from the past are fine to see the light of day, others are best kept hidden. If you get my meaning . . .'

'I do.'

They paused. A truce declared.

He took his hand away. 'The file contains details from the scene. Observations. There are some interviews. Not many. The family wanted to announce her death a couple of days after her disappearance. Pretty quick work, if you ask me.'

She raised an eyebrow.

'The IRA was blamed initially, but there was no evidence and every suspect had an alibi – pretty common in a village like this.'

'I can imagine.'

'A few things were missing. A pearl necklace, which was found by the lough. A ruby ring. A brooch that looked like a butterfly. Apparently quite distinctive.'

'A butterfly *brooch*?'

He took the top folder back, started flicking through. The pages were yellow and dog eared, the scrawled handwriting faded. 'No. Sorry. A *comb*.'

A butterfly comb. 'Can I see that?' Ellie reached across. 'Are there any photos?'

The phone rang. Beddy gave her the page with one hand and picked up the handset with the other.

The text was an interview with Lady Niamh Rathmore, almost illegible apart from three bullet points: *pearl string, ruby ring, sapphire and ruby butterfly comb.*

Beddy hung up the phone. 'I've got to go.' He stood, pushed the folders towards her. He'd already started out the door, his implication that she should follow him. 'I'll need those back, Ellie.' He was pulling on his fluoro jacket, its padded weight further broadening his frame. Opening the door inwards, he stepped back, motioning her out. 'Really got to go.'

'Erm . . . thank you,' she said.

'Drop them back next week, and for feck's sake, don't tell anyone I gave them to you. I had to go into the restricted archives for the 1958 file.'

Ellie stopped short. 'What? What 1958 file?' Her scalp was tingling.

'You asked for everything on the Rathmores.'

Had she? She'd forgotten that.

He was in the car now. 'The murder in 1958?' he said, frowning at her. 'I thought you were interested in that.'

He started the engine, put the siren on and pulled out of the driveway, turning left towards Kenmare.

Chapter Thirty-Nine

Holborn, London

October 1940

For a month and ten days the Germans had battered London, the nightly raids incessant. The city, at first in a state of shock, now went about its daily business as one would drive onward in a storm – steady, watchful but determined to reach the destination.

Most nights, Charlotte and Nancy retreated into the bowels of Holborn station, where makeshift bunks had been erected. They huddled with neighbours and workers, none of whom they got to know well in the darkness.

The day after Charlotte arrived, the two women sat down to concoct their cover story. 'We need to explain your Irish papers. And also that accent. Posh English with a smattering of Kerry. It's an odd mix,' said Nancy as she got out a notebook.

They were to be cousins; their estranged mothers, once loving sisters, had fallen for the same man, Charlotte's (Tabby's) mother capturing his heart and running away to Oxford. The lovers spurned both their families. Which, Nancy said as she penned their fictional family tree, was a shame because his family money could have saved Tabby's mother from the ravages of tuberculosis. Tabby and her father moved to Kerry to live on his English family's estate, where she met her soon-to-be husband, Seamus. And now Seamus was at war, fighting with the British, of course.

Charlotte had winced, rubbed her tummy.

'Are you okay?' said Nancy.

'It's a little . . . complicated. Don't you think?'

Nancy said, 'Families *are* complicated.'

But with nightly bombings and the feeling that Britain's grip on the war was sliding, Charlotte's sudden appearance was never questioned. London was like a lake in springtime, the heat of the war turning society upside down so the stratifications became muddled and new. Charlotte was simply introduced as Cousin Tabby, and that was that. Nancy's neighbours trusted her and, by extension, accepted that she could vouch for the heritage of her new roommate.

Charlotte found her job at the Royal Arsenal difficult. It was repetitive, monotonous work, and there was an ever-constant fear of what might go wrong. One spark and . . . well, Nancy dared not think about the results. She would, she knew, find it very hard to put so much trust in the other girls. Careful hands were not all they needed. One metallic hairpin and the whole place might go up.

Regardless, Charlotte insisted that she loved it. She said, more than once, 'It's the first real work I've ever done. In my whole life. I've time to make up for.'

A few weeks after she arrived, a package appeared on the doorstep. 'Ah,' she said, as she nearly tripped over it as they left for the shelter. '*This* is the reason I wrote your address in the Wynn's Hotel guest book.'

Inside the parcel were five packs of Barry's Tea. 'There's talk of rationing it, even in Ireland. I'd planned to buy some in Bewley's, but they were out. But the bell boy at Wynn's . . . I left him quite a tidy sum and he promised to forward a supply.'

As with everything tea related, it felt like they were talking about contraband, which in a way they were. The package lacked the censor's stamp that had crossed the front of Charlotte's letter. 'Did you know that Ireland has fewer than two hundred censors? I checked,' she said when she noticed Nancy inspecting the wrapping. 'If they'd seen this, they'd have taken it for themselves.' She laughed and Nancy shook her head – was there nothing the girl hadn't thought of?

In the two months Charlotte had been in London, both women had begun to show. Nancy was small for her six months and Charlotte's five-month belly was as big as her sister-in-law's. Neither woman had been to the doctor since Charlotte's arrival. Charlotte had refused; she was nervous that she'd be forced to give up her munitions work. And Nancy was reluctant to jinx her own pregnancy. She felt good. Strong even. The baby had given her little discomfort. The soreness in her breasts had eased off to nothing in the last week and she had been sleeping better. The remaining three months would fly by, she knew, and January – finally – would bring her the child she needed, the child she wanted. The child who would complete her marriage, her family, her life. And the chance to be the mother she'd never had.

She had given Charlotte the spare key to the post box, and each evening the girl rushed into the hallway, unlocked the box and searched inside for the missing element of her life.

'Nothing,' she said today, as she returned to the flat. 'Nothing again.' Although she didn't know where Tomas had been posted, she'd written dozens of letters to Kerry for him to read on his leave. She'd been met with silence.

'It's war, Charlotte,' Nancy soothed. 'It's not easy for the men to write. I haven't heard from Teddy for weeks and I'm not worried.' She was, of course, but she'd put on her calm face. It was wholly in contrast to the dread that grew within her. And if she'd once had a niggling suspicion that Tomas's intentions weren't honest, she now believed that to be the case. As far as she was concerned, the handsome boy with the voice of a nightingale appeared to have discarded Charlotte to her fate.

She changed the subject. 'How's the factory?'

'Next week,' Charlotte said, 'I'm being photographed for a new poster. Pregnant canaries, that kind of thing.'

The news alarmed Nancy. 'Is that wise?'

Charlotte flicked her now-brunette hair. It dropped forward over her shoulder. A few millimetres of blonde were starting to show at the roots. 'I hardly think munitions factory propaganda is going to make its way to Ballinn, do you?'

De Valera, determined to hold on to Ireland's neutrality, was tightly controlling the national news. *The Irish Press* blatantly refused to report on the happenings on the continent, even though the war of words over British access to the country's ports continued.

'You know how these posters go. It'll be like a cartoon. *These women are doing their bit.* Something defiant. That kind of thing.'

Charlotte was taken with London and its resilience. She marvelled constantly. At the invincibility of St Paul's Cathedral. At the bus network that ran through the ever-changing streets. At the barrage balloons that pockmarked the sky. When the Palace of Westminster had been hit three weeks previously, she insisted that they take a walk to see the statue of Richard the Lionheart and his sword, which had been bent but not broken during the attack.

And Nancy had to admit that London life – even war-time London life – suited the girl. Although Charlotte was exhausted, she rose very early each morning, bringing a cup of tea and a smile to Nancy's bedside before departing on her commute. And each evening, she returned, drained but happy, to regale her with stories of the factory girls, fascinated by their ordinary lives. Everything, it seemed, was new to her.

Dusk fell over the city. The smell of dinner filled the flat. They always ate before dark, ever ready to retreat to the shelters below the city streets. Tonight was pheasant cassoulet – courtesy of Mr Hodges' nephew – made to a recipe that Charlotte had learned at Blackwater Hall.

'I didn't know you could cook,' said Nancy, the first night Charlotte had offered.

'A little. Mother didn't approve, of course.'

There was little of which Lady Rathmore *had* approved. The more Charlotte had told of her home life, the more Nancy understood her motivation to leave. There had been moments when she'd thought Charlotte heartless, but it seemed now that the accusation was better laid at the feet of the Rathmore family.

Hugo had been at Blackwater Hall, on leave, when Charlotte told her mother about the pregnancy. He had already made plans for Lord Hawley, his future brother-in-law, to facilitate a promotion to put him behind a desk hundreds of miles from action. *He* had also told Charlotte it would be better if she were dead than disgrace the family in this way. And, she said, he meant it.

They sat down to eat, Charlotte in Teddy's seat, Nancy opposite her across the small table. They laid out formal place settings and had taken to using the best cutlery and two crystal wine glasses, which they ceremoniously filled from the water jug. They figured they might as well. War could steal such things at any time.

There was a rap at the door.

'That'll be Mrs McLaughlin,' said Nancy, leaving her place. 'I promised to loan her *The Murder of Roger Ackroyd*. She's never read an Agatha Christie.' She threw her eyebrows up in a way that said, *Can you imagine?*

Charlotte indicated her food. Hunger gave her an almost wild look.

Nancy picked up the book from the coffee table. 'You start.' She looked at her watch. It was almost 6 p.m. The habitual nervousness that accompanied nightfall in London took seed in her stomach. She opened the door.

A boy stood on the welcome mat. He was familiar. Blond hair neatly parted at the side. Smooth tanned skin. Blue eyes. A boy who looked public school but wasn't.

'Jimmy.'

He nodded slowly, but his eyes registered surprise. Or perhaps fear. His anonymity was a cloak that Nancy had just removed.

'Nancy Rafmore.' This time it was a statement.

She nodded and he handed her the telegram. 'Thank you,' she said, but of course she didn't mean it. 'Thank you, Jimmy.'

He took two steps in retreat. Nancy closed the door. Then, without looking back to Charlotte, whose eyes she could feel boring into her back, she turned the envelope over in her hands.

It was labelled *Post Office Telegram*. She opened it.

And dropped to her knees. Behind her, the clatter of falling cutlery. Before her, the end of her future. Her tears dropped onto its surface like raindrops on the autumn's fallen leaves.

Chapter Forty

Ballinn, County Kerry
April 1958

The very moment Tomas said goodbye to Hattie, the sun peeked from behind a cloud for the last time that day.

'I don't understand.'

He had been cleaning a spade, pushing it in and out of a bucket of sand and vegetable oil. It scraped away the rust and made the battered tool shine, so he'd told her days before. Putting a light hand on her shoulder he said, 'I need to find a new job. Somewhere else to work.'

'But you work here,' she announced with that kind of certainty only a child can muster. The confidence of someone who sees a situation one way and has never thought to consider it another. 'Just like your father did.'

''Tis true, he did work here. But life moves on. *You've got to do your own growing, no matter how tall your father was*, so Tabby says. We can't all be our parents.' He turned, his head dropped.

Hattie didn't want to be her parents. She wanted to be herself. 'But who will look after the garden?'

Tomas shrugged. 'There'll be plenty of lads lining up for the job. The missus will put out a note, I expect.'

The missus was Mama now.

'But we've just planted the peas. And the spuds are sprouting.'

Tomas wiped off the spade with a rag and took it into the shed. On the other side of the dim interior Hattie saw an apple crate loaded with items. Personal things. Books, a Thermos, some folded woollen clothing.

She wiped her eyes. 'What does Tabby say?' Lately she had taken to asking about the inner workings of the mind of Tomas's sister. Though she had never met the woman, she felt she knew her. Tabby never ceased to ply Tomas with wisdom, who passed it on in turn.

He appeared from the shed's interior. 'She says we'll make do – 'tis a new beginning. *A windy day is not for thatching.*'

'What does that mean?'

'It means,' said Tomas, 'that now's not the time to plan for the future. For the moment it's best to just . . . not resist.'

'What do you mean, not resist?'

He turned the pitchfork and the spade to face her. 'If the wind hits these, which will fall first?'

She shrugged, then pointed to the fork. 'You haven't stuck that in properly.'

He made a small sound, almost a fast sigh, but his eyes crinkled at the edges. 'You're a divil.'

'The spade then,' said Hattie. 'Because there's more surface for the wind to hit.'

'You're not just a pretty face.'

She blushed. When she looked in the mirror, she didn't *see* a pretty face, but she liked it when he said so.

'I'll have my reference,' he said. 'I'll get a new job.'

'Where?'

'Something'll come up, and I have a little put away.'

It surprised her how much adults lied. 'I'll talk to Mama.'

'No!' His voice rang out, harsh. He let the spade fall to the ground. The *thwack* made Hattie jump. 'No.'

She lifted her chin. Stood tall. 'I will.'

He grabbed her arm and pulled her close. His eyes were glazed when he released her.

Hattie turned to go, not afraid for herself, only that someone might have seen them. She glanced back at him there, his faded blue shirt neatly pressed but threadbare, his shoulders broad but rounded. His face in his hands.

Suddenly she knew what to do.

Chapter Forty-One

Holborn, London

October 1940

The miscarriage came two days after the telegram. The doctor said there was nothing to be done. That the shock of Teddy's disappearance could not have caused the stillness of the baby's beating heart. That he must have passed from this world some weeks ago, in the cocoon of his mother's tummy.

But Nancy blamed herself. She blamed the Germans. She blamed the blond-haired boy who delivered the telegram. The man who wrote the words. The person who transcribed them.

She took time off work. Her boss was sympathetic, to an extent. Teddy was only missing and, no doubt, to him, the death of a child yet to live was much less distressing than the stories of destruction he published each and every day. He had also lost a child — a son — to the bullets of the enemy. He said she could take a week.

At night she stared blankly at the walls that surrounded her. Charlotte tiptoed around the flat. Nancy could see the girl change her way of dressing, her way of moving; always trying to hide her bump with loose coats or objects held just so. Once, she would have appreciated the gestures for what they were, but now her mind felt heavy with the dark fog that had descended and she turned her face away to look at some unknown thing in the distance. Some forgotten future.

A letter followed the telegram a few days later. On the first reading, the words had blurred into a muddled mess. It told her nothing new: Teddy's whereabouts were unknown. She held it in her hand and sat on the windowsill watching Holborn go by. There was activity, much of it. People with places to be, things to do. Family to love. She thought she'd seen Jimmy cycling down the footpath, his leather bag full of ill tidings. But it was just a blond-haired boy with a coat that didn't fit him and a sack strapped over his back.

Nancy was bereft of ambition. She'd packed away her notebooks, her typewriter. Tucked them under Teddy's desk, which was now strewn with female things: a hairbrush, a pot of cold cream, a powder puff that left a pale coating on its veneer surface. The scent of Yardley lavender water lingered in the room. In a drawer, she'd found a tiny pair of sheepskin booties, tucked under a pile of papers. Whether they had been hidden there by Teddy or, more recently, Charlotte, she didn't know. She stashed them back in their hiding spot and wiped away a tear.

Under her bed was a small box; her own collection of things for the baby. A pair of booties similar to those she'd just found. A tiny sweater. And a knitted woollen rug she'd bought in Dublin when she and Teddy had been on their way to Blackwater Hall the previous year, when she was, once again, pregnant.

She'd shown the letter to Charlotte, who had put her hand to her mouth and flung her arms around Nancy, sobbing and heavy. Nancy cooed and soothed her. Stroked her hair. Told her everything would be all right. But in her heart, she felt a drop, a fall, as all her aspirations and hopes tumbled out of her, scattering to the far corners of the flat and beyond.

Charlotte's bulging belly had pushed against her, and she, God help her, had for that moment wished that their places were reversed.

After that they'd barely spoken of Teddy. Nancy told Charlotte it was preferable to be a prisoner of war – because surely that was what he was – than being thrown into battle day after day. Occasionally Charlotte would bring up a tale about him: the time he put a frog down Hugo's back; the birthday he'd made her a slingshot, the wrath of her mother when she'd found out. And Nancy would nod, pretending to be entertained, until Charlotte gave up and switched on the wireless, someone else's voice filling the air.

The night before she was due to return to work, Nancy made an announcement. 'I'm coming to the factory,' she said, 'to work with you.'

Charlotte put down her fork. The blackout blinds were already closed, and they had the wireless on low, one ear always open for the sound of sirens. 'Pardon?'

'I don't want to work at the paper any longer.' Nancy took a spoonful of Colman's and dabbed it on her plate. They were having a ploughman's for dinner. Bits of everything: cheese and pickles, a little cold cooked cabbage, some leftover rabbit that stuck between her teeth.

Charlotte was quiet. When she started to say, 'No, you can't—' Nancy held up her hand.

'It isn't right. Me working in a comfortable office. You in a factory, surrounded by danger . . .' Her lips cracked with the effort of smiling.

'We're all very careful.'

'You need to be looking after yourself.' Nancy gestured to the belly Charlotte was hiding under a double layer of napkin. It was the first time her pregnancy had been referred to since the miscarriage.

'I *am* looking after myself,' she said, placing a small square of cheese in her mouth and closing her eyes, savouring it.

'I want to keep an eye on you.'

Charlotte's face was soft, unreadable.

'Will you make enquiries for me tomorrow?'

'Aren't you over qualified?'

Nancy scoffed. It felt like a slight, although she knew it wasn't. 'Over qualified? Hardly. I've seen the posters. The advertisements are . . . well, everywhere. I want to *do my bit.*' She repeated the government slogan again, as she had done to herself countless times over the previous days. *Do my bit. Do my bit. If I can't make a family . . . I should do my bit.*

Charlotte reached across the table, took Nancy's hand in her own. 'Take a few weeks to think it over. After everything . . .'

Nancy drew her hand away under the guise of scratching her arm. 'If you could at least enquire . . .?'

'Yes, yes. Of course.'

'Thank you.' Reluctantly she reached across to take the hand that Charlotte still proffered. It was warm against her cool skin. 'Thank you,' she said again. With effort, she turned her concentration back to dinner and away from the swell of Charlotte's stomach, which sat between them like a third person, waiting to be heard.

Chapter Forty-Two

Blackwater Hall, County Kerry
April 1958

Even though she knew it was wrong, Hattie dragged a chair over to the painting in Mama's room. It was a picture of sweet peas, white and purple, cascading over a trellis somewhere sunnier than south-west Ireland. A gilt frame trimmed its edges.

She lifted it off the wall.

Hattie had been in the room with Mama when Grandmother had shown her the safe, given her the code. She'd also been there when Mama changed the combination and placed the item inside. It must be valuable and would make the world of difference to Tomas and his family, but it meant very little to Mama, who, as far as Hattie was aware, had rehung the painting haphazardly and not touched it since.

She opened the safe and took out its contents, replacing the painting in its skew-whiff position, a thin wedge of bright wallpaper visible on either side of the frame.

On her way back to the garden she passed Albert. The gun was cocked open over his forearm and he took confident strides towards the house. 'Forgot my knife,' he said, indicating his belt, which hung unadorned on his hips. 'A quick patrol for hares is in order. Don't want your spuds getting munched, squirt.' At any other time Hattie would have told him hares didn't eat the poisonous potato leaf. Albert frowned as she hid her hand behind her back. 'What've you got there?'

She paused, considering her answer. 'A gift,' she lied, 'for you.' This last she added as a warning: *Don't make me show you.*

He grinned, feigned disinterest, then made a grab for her. She turned and ran from the house and left him laughing in the doorway.

One day, years later, Hattie would reflect that it was the last time she ever saw Albert that way.

She returned to the shed just as Tomas closed the door and bent down to pick up the apple crate at his feet. Straightening, he slowly cast his eye over the walled garden, its neat beds raised in lines, the occasional row of vivid green poking from the dark earth.

The air was heavy with the scent of damp; a thunderstorm was brewing over the Atlantic and headed their way. It was nearly five o'clock, the end of Tomas's last day. The first heavy drops of rain plopped on the path, turning the pale gravel grey. More droplets followed – *splat splat splat* – until they rolled together into a shower and Hattie squealed and ran the last fifty yards, skipping over freshly tilled earth.

It was pointless to seek shelter. She was soaked already. 'I have something for you.'

Tomas raised his eyebrows. A drip of water fell from his nose. 'It had better not be pity,' he laughed, as though he were suddenly a man without a care in the world.

Hattie held out her hand. 'You can sell this. I think it's worth a lot of money.'

Tomas frowned and looked down at the item in her hand. Its stones were dull in the greying sky, but there was no doubt they were real. Tarnished silver held them together. It looked like it hadn't been polished in an age.

His brows set in a frown, as though he were searching for something in a forgotten past. Hattie stepped back.

'Where did you get that?'

'It's mine,' she lied.

His eyes never wavered from the comb. 'You've never worn it before.'

'Mama . . . she wouldn't let me. It's for special occasions.'

Water pooled around the joins that held the rubies and sapphires together. They were surrounded by dark stones. Obsidian. 'When did she give it to you?'

Hattie paused. 'For my birthday.'

He put out his hand, palm hovering over the jewels as though he were dowsing for something within. Something secret. Something hidden.

When he snatched it from her, she didn't flinch. He held it at eye level, examined its butterfly shape. Breathing heavily, he dropped the apple crate from where it rested against his hip.

She looked at the ground. 'It's for you. So that you can start thatching. Even though it's . . . windy.' She grappled for Tabby's words, which before had given him so much comfort.

From the closed fist that held the comb, thick blood mixed with rain, dripped to the ground and soaked into the gravel by Tomas's feet. He looked towards the house. Then he brushed past her and was gone.

Chapter Forty-Three

Ballinn, County Kerry

September 2019

Ellie stood outside the garda station and watched the squad car disappear into the distance. She looked at the files in her hand, holding them out in front of her as one would someone else's newborn – with interest and trepidation.

Behind her right temple: a throbbing. She needed caffeine. And quickly.

She stashed the two folders into her satchel. The rain had started again, and she flicked up her collar and walked across the village square towards Procaffination.

A voice: 'Ellie! Ellie!'

Jules hurried towards her, the hood of his waxed jacket over his head, a small backpack with a helmet hooked to it slung over his shoulder. There was no sign of the bike.

She used the tail of her coat to cover the satchel. 'Two doses of you in one day?' But she couldn't help but smile, remembering that morning's pantomime between him and her mum.

'Moira said you were at the station.'

'When?' She tried to keep the exasperation out of her voice. And failed.

'Just now. She called me.'

Ellie narrowed her eyes. 'I see.'

'And . . . I wanted to talk to you about the Royal Arsenal.'

Ellie's mind was stuck in 1958. 'The what?'

'The Royal Arsenal.'

She wiped her eyes with her hand. 'Can we get out of the rain?'

She continued her direct route to Procaffination, Jules walking beside her, matching her strides, his canvas shoes woefully inappropriate for late autumn in Kerry as he splashed down the path where holes were becoming puddles.

'You'll bring the whole pond with you,' she said, smug in her leather boots.

'Where are we going?' he asked.

'Caffeine.'

❧

Nils was behind the counter at Procaffination and looked unsurprised to see her again. 'How was Dublin? Did you find your needle?'

She nodded, and he grinned as he turned to fill the portafilter, already anticipating their orders. They took a table beside the window as more customers filed in behind them. In the corner, four men in rough clothes and muddy wellingtons sat with their heads close together in conversation, each with a plate of beetroot chocolate cake before him. Two of them, Ellie realised, were the farmers Nils had offered a tea on the house only a few days before. She felt a warm swell of pride for her new friend.

Once Nils had set down their drinks and returned to a group waiting at the counter, Jules dunked his almond biscotti into the thick froth of his coffee.

'Well?' Ellie said. 'What's all this about Arsenal? I'm not much of a football fan, just so you know.' She handed him her sweet freebie: a small choc-chip cookie.

Jules frowned, then his face cleared. 'Not *Arsenal*. The *Royal Arsenal*. Woolwich. London.' The last word he imparted with meaning, but Ellie still stared blankly.

'Have you been on Nils's turmeric lattes?' she asked, concerned.

Jules sipped his cappuccino. It left a frothy moustache on his clean-shaven face. His eyes twinkled, and Ellie sensed she was about to learn something about Charlotte that he'd assumed she already knew. 'Well?'

'No turmeric lattes, no,' he said jovially.

'Jules!'

He put down his coffee. 'You haven't talked to Milo yet?'

Ellie frowned, and took out her phone. Two missed calls. And two messages. The first:

Talked to Tabby, she had a LOT to say. Call me?

No kiss to sign off as there had been the day before, mistake or otherwise.

The second:

Don't worry, I've given Jules the info. But also, I want to show you something: will you call to Blackwater Hall? I'm here all day.

She read the last message twice. 'Jules?'

'I was on my cycle this morning and ran into Milo on his bike . . .'

The rain was audible on the windows, and they turned to watch it roll down the glass. 'You two are mad.'

Jules took the comment as a compliment. 'We were both on our way home and we got to chatting.'

'He saw Tabby last night?'

'Ellie, she *sold* her work and travel permits to Charlotte Rathmore, a couple of weeks before the girl disappeared.'

Ellie slapped the table. 'I *knew* it.' A couple of heads turned towards them and she waved an apology to Nils, trying to wipe the smile of triumph from her face. There had been something about Tabby that night at the party. A flicker that had crossed her face. The way she'd looked to the ceiling as though searching for an answer, rather than simply remembering. *She encouraged me to apply for a scholarship.* 'And Tabby was able to fund her way through teaching college?'

Jules nodded. 'Her original plan was to work at a munitions factory. By August 1940, she'd already applied for, and been granted, a permit. She was due to leave Ireland any day.'

'For the Royal Arsenal?'

'The very one. Charlotte gave her the equivalent of two years' munitions wages. Just like that. And I should imagine that wasn't too shabby for a village girl.'

'Can we get the records from the factory?'

He looked surprised. 'You think Charlotte took the job? A girl who'd never worked a day in her life?'

Charlotte Rathmore, Ellie knew, was full of surprises. She'd defied her upbringing and wanted nothing more than to shake off the cloak of privilege and see the world for what it was. In sheltering her from real life and squashing her desire for independence, her parents had locked the door. But Charlotte had found the key.

Ellie glanced across the village square. 'I'll bet you a couple of rounds at Sheehan's.' It was the only decent pub in Ballinn, if a bit dingy. The Southern Green served tasty food, but its floor was so sticky that Ellie would be inclined to leave a coin exactly where it dropped.

Jules held out his hand across the table. She shook it.

'Did Tabby tell Milo anything else?'

Jules shook his head. 'Not that he mentioned.'

Ellie pulled out her phone and tapped the screen. 'I'm calling him,' she mouthed. Wedging the phone between her jaw and shoulder, she took the two folders from her satchel and placed them on the table, one next to the other.

The phone rang out.

Jules frowned. 'Are those . . .?'

Ellie held up a hand. 'You didn't get them from me.'

His eyebrows leapt, then he glanced furtively around the near-full café.

Ellie sighed. 'This is the file on Charlotte's disappearance. Gardaí notes, interviews. A list of things that went missing with her.'

'What did she take?'

She handed him the list of items, then ran her fingers through her wet, tangled hair. 'The string of pearls, of course,' she said, reaching into her satchel for a comb. 'A ruby ring. Pretty sizeable, apparently.' She came up empty handed. 'And a . . .'

Jules waited. 'A what?'

Ellie closed her eyes. Tried to recall. She pulled out her notebook, slipped Charlotte's portrait from the back cover. Those doe eyes. That faraway look. And . . . yes, there! The comb that pinned her hair. In black and white. Three hues of darkness.

Sapphire.

Obsidian.

Ruby.

'A comb. *This* comb. I saw it at Blackwater Hall.' The dusty cabinet; she'd wiped its surface. Tried to peer to the tarnished item beyond. But the dirt had coated the underside of the glass.

'It says here' – Jules indicated the file in front of her – 'that the piece was a gift from Charlotte's mother for her sixteenth birthday. And Niamh Rathmore, apparently, was given it for *her* sixteenth birthday. Handed from mother to daughter.' He looked at her. 'And that it was never recovered.'

'That's not possible.' *Don't touch that! It's cursed.* 'If it disap-peared with Charlotte, how can it be at Blackwater Hall?' Ellie flicked through the remaining pages, some urgency now. Page after page. Until she reached the end of the folder from 1939. And the beginning of the folder from 1958.

Curious, she opened the first page. A clip held together a thin stack of paper. Mostly printed sheets with handwritten notes. The typeset was large and blocky. She turned it over.

Glued to the top of the second piece of paper was a photo of a woman. Dark hair, and a beautiful face marred by tiredness.

Ellie looked closer. A sharp intake of breath. She glanced around at the other customers, then snapped the folder shut. Leaning forward, she hid it with her arms. They needed somewhere dim and empty to read it.

'Jules,' she said, 'we'll be wanting another drink.'

He nodded, pushed his seat back. The chair's legs screeched on the tiles.

'No' – she looked at her watch – 'a proper one.' Her palms sweated as she quickly gathered her things, clutching the folder to her chest. She gave Nils a wave, mouthed, *See you soon.*

As they crossed the square to Sheehan's, the rain came down harder and, for the first time, Ellie's boots began to leak.

Chapter Forty-Four

Holborn, London

February 1941

There had been no news of Teddy for three months, and adrenaline shot through Nancy each time footsteps passed the flat door.

Mrs McLaughlin had acknowledged the miscarriage without a word. She'd taken Nancy into her front room soon after and given her a large whisky, and together they'd sat and listened to the soothing rhythm of the mantel clock. When it had chimed on the hour, Nancy handed her the empty tumbler and attempted a smile. 'Don't bother with that smiling business,' Mrs McLaughlin had said, her own glass still half full. 'I don't need any of that.' Nancy had nodded and shown herself out, a little lighter, a little better.

She had become fiercely protective of Charlotte over the following months. They worked together at Woolwich, Nancy taking up the slack when Charlotte was unable to carry on. The hours at the factory were long – seven until five – but Sundays were a half-day, and they lived for them.

The work was hard, more so even than Nancy had expected. That, with the added tension – the fear of bombs from outside and inside – put her on constant alert. But Charlotte, however unlikely, seemed to be made for it. She'd put her feet up at night and say, 'God, don't you love that throb, right at the back of your heel? The standing's horrible but it's worth it just for this small pleasure.' Her unwavering enthusiasm kept Nancy from the brink.

Christmas had been a quiet affair. They dined on wild goose, courtesy of Mr Hodges' nephew, and Nancy concocted a Christmas pudding – bulked out with breadcrumbs and grated carrot – and topped it with holly dipped in snowy Epsom salts. They'd kept aside the last of the brandy and tipped it on the cake in a moment of decadence, striking a match and watching the blue light flicker over the gently crisping greenery until it began to smoke and they flung open the windows to cold air, and even Nancy let out a burst of laughter.

After lunch, Charlotte became a *seanchaí* and held a rambling house for two in their Holborn sitting room. She told Irish folklore, recounted tales of Tír na nÓg and sang the same haunting tune Tomas had performed at the Ballinn Dramatics Secret Society the year before.

'How *is* the rambling house?' Nancy had asked.

'Gone. Burned to the ground,' said Charlotte. At Nancy's look of horror, she added, 'An accident. A dry spring, a thatched roof, a wayward spark. The O'Briens have moved above the shop. And Tabby has a mind to start a new rambling house.'

Charlotte had finished at Woolwich three days before New Year. On her last day, a photo was taken with a small group of friends for the factory's newsletter. Five girls gathered around her, and in one hand she clutched a small cake, baked from donated rations. With the other, she held Nancy's hand. The camera's shutter had clicked moments before a cold downpour drenched the girls.

Although they could get by on Nancy's wage – which was higher than her job at the newspaper – Charlotte had taken her ruby ring to Hatton Garden and received a sum of money for it. Nothing like its worth, but a substantial windfall none-theless. When she presented the funds to Nancy, she'd waved them away. 'Keep them safe – you'll need them when you get home.' At that, Charlotte had nodded, though not necessarily in agreement. It was the first time either of them had talked about her future and the possibility of a return to Ireland.

After her miscarriage, Nancy had half-heartedly tried to convince Charlotte to evacuate to the countryside, where, on the outbreak of war, maternity hospitals had been provided by the Ministry of Health. Following the birth, mother and child stayed at their countryside billet awaiting the end of the war or a reason to return home, whichever came first. But Charlotte's factory colleagues had recounted tales about the initial evacuation.

'It was shambolic,' she repeated to Nancy, 'completely sham-bolic. Mabel's sister ended up at the wrong hospital – if hospital is the correct word: a converted school with walls so damp that water ran down them. She took a train straight back to London, gave birth at home.'

Nancy had heard the rumours, of course: tales of over-crowding and gastroenteritis. She'd offered to write a story on it, but her then boss had said there were more pressing issues at hand than the 'clucking of women who put themselves in that inconvenient state at such a time'. But still, the result of the decentralisation of maternity services was that London was left with a scarcity of midwives. Nancy had been told to wait until her seventh month before contacting the overstretched service, and all discussions with her doctor were held in the chaste kind of manner that made her wish she hadn't bothered with the time and expense. Charlotte had been visited at the flat by a dour midwife three weeks previously. She prodded the girl as though she were bread dough on its second rise. 'Maybe,' Charlotte had said as they watched the fat woman waddle away along an almost empty street, 'all the good ones were sent to the country.'

Now, as the two women sat on the sofa under a pile of blankets, Nancy was filled with worry. In the last week, the glow had dimmed from Charlotte's cheeks. It was clear that the pregnancy was taking its toll.

When Charlotte saw Nancy observing her, she made a show of brightening. 'I'm fine. It's close now.' Cracked lips rimmed her tight smile. Her hair, now showing a wide blonde streak down its parting, was dishevelled. She looked half the girl who had turned up on Nancy's doorstep nearly six months ago, and yet underneath the blanket she was twice the size. 'I'm ready,' she said in a way that suggested she wasn't.

'You need another visit from the midwife.'

'Big Bertha? I don't think so. I'd rather be seen by a veterinarian.'

Nancy laughed. 'Well, I'll call the Royal Mews in the morning,' she said, 'and if I can't get through, I'll see if someone other than Bertha can be found.'

Charlotte nodded and closed her eyes, a quick shiver crossing her shoulders. Nancy took this as consent.

'It'll be all right, you know.' It was a statement.

Charlotte nodded. Her hands were resting gently on her belly, her swollen feet propped on a kitchen chair. 'I'm just so tired.'

Nancy nodded. 'It's normal.' She'd picked up two books on midwifery at Mr Hodges' bookshop and studied them at night. They were dry reading. And overwhelming.

'Tea?' She put her hand on Charlotte's; it was noticeably cold.

'Mmm, thank you.'

February had started with a cold snap, the frosty mornings scattered with snow, the mercury barely rising during the day.

Nancy went to the blackout curtain, pulled a corner aside. The darkness was flecked with falling flakes of snow. She bent down and looked at the sill. An inch of white powder had settled against the glass.

There had been no postal delivery for two days and the streets were eerily quiet. Nancy hated to think that there was news of Teddy and the cold, of all things, was keeping it from her. Charlotte had heard nothing from Tomas – though Nancy could hardly blame the snow for that – and no longer checked the post box with anticipation; or if she did, she didn't show it. When she thought of the man who had altered Charlotte's future so dramatically, Nancy boiled with rage. How he must have enjoyed his conquest.

To push aside her thoughts, she went to the wireless, switched it on. Mussolini, it seemed, had declared southern Italy a war zone, enacted martial law. *Just another day.* She glanced at Charlotte, to see what she had to say on the matter, but the girl had closed her eyes, leaned her head back, her breath a fog in the room. Nancy felt guilty for the chill in the flat, but what could they do? She stepped into the kitchen, lit the gas, leaned back on the counter and watched the blue flame flicker. Before she and Teddy were married, they'd joked – or half joked – about eloping to Italy for their nuptials and simply forgetting to return. They'd buy a small farm, keep chickens, eat sun-warmed tomatoes fresh from the vine. She'd whispered that languages weren't her forte and he'd insisted it didn't matter because she would just be at home, baking and having children. But he'd said it with a wink. Then, more seriously, 'We could start the first English-language Italian newspaper.' She asked, 'There're none?' He'd shrugged and said, 'The *best* one then.'

Her grasp on the course of the war had lessened since she'd left the newspaper. Back then, she could have waxed lyrical about current events. Now she felt like she needed a map table to keep track of who was where. The battles in North Africa were moving at pace; more than a hundred thousand Italian soldiers had already been taken prisoner. Ireland continued to grip on to neutrality despite last month's bombing near the Curragh.

And the Luftwaffe's nightly raids on London continued.

She swirled hot water around the pot and made a weak brew — they'd grown used to it — with the last of their ration. Her surplus had been exchanged for increasingly meagre cuts of meat over the last two months. And the cold winter had been hard on the fresh vegetable supply. Already she was dreaming of spring and the first crisp greens, the splash of colour from the city's now-brown allotments.

When she returned, Charlotte had moved from her position on the sofa, the wireless's murmur the only noise to fill the empty sitting room.

From the spare room: a crooning.

'Charlotte?' Nancy set the tea on the table, hot liquid splashing her hand. She swore softly and put her palm to her mouth.

The girl was sitting in the dark, the door cracked open, a weak slice of light illuminating her figure, hunched on the bed. She put up a hand. 'I'm fine, I'm fine.' A veil of sweat had formed on her brow.

Nancy knelt in front of her, placed her hands on her sister-in-law's knees, her head angled to catch Charlotte's line of sight. 'You don't look fine.'

Charlotte gave a small smile, the effort to form it evident. 'I'm fine. She's just moving around.'

Nancy frowned. 'You're in pain. We need to get help.' Her insides were tightening. She started to stand.

'No!' Charlotte grabbed her hand. The force of her grip was electrifying. 'Just wait. Wait, a moment.'

Nancy let the iron grip subside before peeling away the burning fingers. Her heart was beating hard in her chest and she took a deep breath. Despite the cold room, her armpits felt damp. Charlotte leaned forward and, with another gasp, gripped her hands around her knees.

Nancy reached out and gently stroked her hair. It was soft, messy. 'Will you try lying down? I'm going to get some blankets and water then go—'

'No! Please . . . God, please don't leave me.'

One moment they'd been talking quietly on the sofa, cocooned in warm blankets, joking about Big Bertha, and now suddenly everything was wrong.

Nancy ran her hand down Charlotte's arm and let it fall to the bed, intending to push herself to her feet. The blanket was wet. Very wet.

'Is that . . . Has it . . . broken?'

Charlotte began to cry, hugging her arms tightly around herself.

'I need you to breathe slowly. Like this.' Concentration began to clear Nancy's mind. 'Listen to me, Charlotte. The baby's coming. Tonight. I need to get help.' She stood quickly, stepped back from the girl before she could protest.

Still counting to herself, she left the room. She thought there was little chance of an ambulance navigating the snow. The flat could be made warm – there was a gas heater that they had until now used sparingly. It was as safe an environment as any. If only Jerry would stay away.

She took a woollen coat from the hat stand and the electric torch that hung next to it. When she opened the front door, cold air hit her like a wall. Quickly she descended to the ground floor, paused beside the telephone.

The line was poor. In this weather, and considering the last week's heavy bombing, she wasn't surprised. She replaced the receiver, tried again. The ghost of a voice tried to reach her. Loudly she repeated, 'Can you hear me? Please. Can you hear me?'

The creak of hinges. Behind her, Mrs McLaughlin's large head poked through her doorway, a look of mild concern plastered on her face. It was the most impressive display of anxiety that Nancy had ever seen her show.

'Problems, dear?'

Warmth was radiating from her flat and the old woman had a flush to her cheeks. She looked toasty and, as she stepped out of the door, she pulled her tartan shawl a little tighter. 'What a night to be out.'

Nancy fumbled with the receiver and dropped it. It clanged against the wall and then swung silently. She picked it up. Replaced it.

'We need a midwife. Upstairs. Now.'

Mrs McLaughlin had accepted Nancy's story about Charlotte's heritage without question. She had swallowed the complicated tale of feuding sisters and Kerry relations with silence and a look that said *I wish I hadn't asked.* 'Is it time?'

'Yes,' said Nancy. She tried to gather her thoughts, but it felt like chasing a dropped bucket of marbles down a staircase.

'It's too early, surely?'

'A week or two, I suppose.'

Mrs McLaughlin nodded and disappeared into her flat. Over her shoulder she called, 'I'll get to Great Ormond Street. Bring someone back.'

'The raids could start any minute.'

'Then I'll find a shelter on the way.'

Nancy followed her. 'It's snowing.'

'Is it?'

'You know it is.'

'I'm tougher than I look.' She was speaking from the

bedroom, her voice muffled. When she emerged, she appeared to be ready for a polar expedition. 'Forty years in the Highlands. This is nothing.'

She breezed past Nancy with an air of purpose. Paused at the door to select a walking stick. Her boots were huge clumps of leather and Nancy's eyes lingered on them.

'They were my husband's, God rest him.'

'Thank you,' Nancy said as she followed Mrs McLaughlin out of the flat. 'Thank you.'

'Nothing like a bit of excitement to keep the old ticker going.'

Nancy suddenly felt a shiver of fear. 'I don't know if you should . . .'

Mrs McLaughlin stopped, put her hands on Nancy's shoulders. 'Keep her calm, keep her warm. Focus on ambulation.'

'Ambulation?'

'Yes, keep her walking.' She retrieved her hands and fastened her top button. 'And talking.' Wound her scarf a second time around her neck. 'And a tot of whisky for the pain.' She opened the front door. Snow danced in the darkness. 'Get some water boiling. A big pot. And gather some clean towels.'

The instructions performed magic – Nancy's breathing slowed, her mind cleared. 'I'll get them ready.'

'Good. Your *cousin*' – Mrs McLaughlin raised a scant eyebrow – 'will be just fine. Women give birth every day. Early, late. On the street. At home or in a field.' She paused, stepped back inside, squeezed Nancy's arm. 'With and without help.'

Nancy felt a prickle behind her eyes. Blinked once . . . twice . . . three times. She nodded. 'Thank you,' was all she could think to say as Mrs McLaughlin walked out into the night.

Chapter Forty-Five

Ballinn, County Kerry

September 2019

Sheehan's was almost empty; just a couple of locals perched on stools, nursing pints and passing the time of day. They took a table by a smouldering fire. The liquorice smell of burning turf was almost overwhelming, and a thin layer of smoke clung to the ceiling like candyfloss.

'Wine?' Jules said, making for the bar.

Ellie nodded. 'Red, please.'

The pub was quiet and its walls were so lined with things – Irish paraphernalia, old Guinness bottles, green rugby shirts – that the voices from the bar didn't carry. Ellie gazed across the square; the rain had finally stopped, but beads of water clung stubbornly to the glass of the warped sash windows.

When he returned, she took out the second folder and laid it open in front of him. He leaned in, squinted. Appraised the black-and-white photo: a woman, dark hair messy around her face, eyes that might have been blue. 'Who *is* that?'

Ellie flicked the photo over.

His eyes went wide. 'Is this . . .' he turned to the second page, 'is this a *murder* case?'

Ellie nodded. She took a sip of her red. It was full of all the wrong kinds of tannin and had a peaty aftertaste – and not in a good way – but she felt immediately warmed.

'Nancy Rathmore was *murdered*?' Jules was shaking his head. He took a long draw of his Guinness. 'Milo would have mentioned this. Bernie would have said. Someone surely . . .'

'No,' said Ellie, turning the page back, tapping it. 'Nancy Rathmore wasn't the victim.' She fanned the papers across the table.

'What?'

'She was the perpetrator.' *Moving to Blackwater Hall transformed her. It was as though she was two different people. Before Blackwater, and after.* Ellie took another gulp of her drink as she recalled Hattie's words. 'How could we not have known about this?' she whispered, looking down at Nancy. Those eyes; so haunted, so hollow. What had possessed her? What had happened on that day in 1958?

'The lips of Ballinn aren't as loose as we thought,' Jules said.

Ellie turned the page. Then put her hand to her mouth. 'Jules. The victim.'

'Someone we've heard of?'

'Oh yes.' She handed him the report.

His eyebrows leapt to the ceiling. 'My God.'

She leaned forward for her wine, thinking it might be a two-glass day. 'Tomas Deenihan, Tabby Ryan's brother. She mentioned him at the party.'

'Nancy Rathmore *killed* him?'

Ellie was poring over another piece of paper. 'It says here she pleaded self-defence.' Her finger raced down the page, following the scrawled handwriting. 'Tomas threatened her . . . He'd been fired for . . . theft.'

'What'd he steal?'

She flicked through the pages. Paused. And then . . . 'Jules, you're not going to believe this. Tomas stole the butterfly comb.'

⁊▲

While Jules pored over the manslaughter file, Ellie began a Google search for Tabby Deenihan. At the top of the results was a short article from *The Kerryman* about Tabby's one hundredth birthday, which referenced her maiden name. In the feature photo Ellie and Milo hovered in the background next to a table loaded with wine. They were deep in conversation. Shortly after that, he'd given her the surgery records that had changed everything. That had changed the way she felt about Charlotte. About Nancy. And a few days later, Hattie had confirmed that her mother had once been love and kindness.

Ellie thought back to that meeting at the Pickled Oyster. The warm restaurant. The intimacy of the setting. The revelations about Milo's past. Hattie had been forthcoming, and yet, at the time, Ellie had felt she was hiding something. The events of 1958 put a new slant on that.

She glanced at Jules. The expression on his face told her that he too was finding it difficult to imagine a woman like Nancy being implicated in manslaughter. Ellie was sure they were missing a vital piece of the puzzle, and her gut was telling her it wasn't there in that folder.

She turned back to her computer. Back to Tabby Deenihan and her search results.

There were a couple of historical hits mentioning Tabby at the local St Patrick's Day parade, where she was shown with a group of teenagers in costume, part of the Ballinn Dramatics Secret Society. Each photo, each instance, it was *this* Tabby who appeared, the Tabby who had lived in Kerry her whole life, who had worked at Blackwater Hall, who had sold her identification to an aristocrat so that she might follow her dreams. The Tabby Deenihan who later became Tabby Ryan.

But nothing about *that* Tabby. Ellie added 'England' to the search, then 'London'. Neither option returned anything of interest.

Jules glanced up from the file. 'Looks like Teddy Rathmore was out for the day in Tralee when it happened.'

'Nancy was alone?'

He shrugged. 'How many staff would they have had at that time?'

'Apart from Tomas? A housekeeper? A cook?'

'*I saw him with the comb and confronted him* – this is Nancy's interview – *and he went wild. He threw the comb. There was blood on it, I don't know why. Then he attacked me. I was frightened. His hands were around my neck and I pushed him back . . .*' Jules squinted. 'The writing's scrawled . . . *against the mantelpiece?*'

'The mantelpiece? In the front room?'

'No. In the library.' He turned the page. 'Hattie was there.'

'What?' Ellie put her drink aside and took off her jacket. The warmth of the room had become stifling. 'Poor Hattie.'

'Poor Tomas. Apparently he was killed instantly.'

Ellie rubbed her temple. It was beginning to throb. 'And Albert? He was there?'

'No . . . it says he was out by the lake. Hunting hare.'

Ellie made a face. No Kerryman would hunt hare. And yet Albert wasn't a Kerryman, not then at least. He had spent his first seventeen years in England before moving with his family to a house on the edge of the Atlantic that he'd never left.

She looked up. 'Do you think Milo knows?' She thought of him banished as a toddler, not for Albert's lack of heart, but for his excess of it. Because Albert believed in the curse. First Hugo's death, then Tomas's. Then Milo's mother. He couldn't bear to have his child close. And the only way to keep him was to send him away.

Jules appraised her. 'I think if Milo knew, he would have said.' He cleared his throat and shuffled the papers. 'Any luck with the Royal Arsenal?'

'I . . . I haven't looked yet.' She turned back to her computer and began a new search. This time the results were endless. The Royal Arsenal had been a major munitions factory on the shores of the Thames since the seventeenth centaury. During World War Two it had employed thousands of people.

Tens of thousands.

Ellie's heart dropped. Another haystack. The same needle.

Images littered her search: canary girls stacking cartridge cases, a royal visit in 1917, aerial photos of more than five hundred hectares of factory and office. She noted that although Greenwich Heritage Centre had acquired its archives, they weren't yet all digitised. She sent an enquiry to the email address provided.

Jules tapped the page in front of him. 'They interviewed Tabby, you know? She'd been worried about Tomas working at the estate. Said that when he returned from the war, he was a changed man. But she denied he was a thief.'

'Why?'

'Because he loved his job, apparently. She doubted he would do anything to jeopardise it.'

'It was hard times. Ireland in 1958. Rural Kerry. That comb would have been quite a prize.'

'The interview is very explicit. She said he was . . . damaged, but that he knew right from wrong.'

Ellie nodded. So many losses, so much grief. She thought of Albert up there over the hill, hidden on the plateau. Holding on to the horrors of his past. What must it be like for him to live alone at Blackwater Hall, where secrets soaked like water into the walls? Where ghosts lingered in empty corners. Disappointment. Disappearance. Death. And to believe, to *truly* believe, that all those tragedies, those past and those yet to come, were inevitable.

'Another drink?' said Jules, watching her.

She glanced in surprise at her empty glass. When had that happened? 'I—'

Her phone vibrated. She look down. *Milo.*

'Hello?'

'You'll call up to the hall?' His voice was bright.

She smiled at their new-found intimacy. 'Now?'

'Okay.'

When she hung up, she said to Jules: 'Do you want to come with me? To Blackwater Hall?'

He shook his head, smiled. 'You go, Ellie. I'm here if you need me.'

Outside, the sky had turned to blue, the clouds tracking east and inland, towards the ivy-covered house with the French doors on the edge of the parish.

Chapter Forty-Six

Blackwater Hall, County Kerry
April 1958

Tomas pushed open the French doors and stepped inside. Hattie was two strides behind him.

'Stop!' Her heart pounded so hard in her chest that it hurt.

The room was empty and his boots left muddy footprints as he crossed. A single candle cast a feeble yellow light.

'Tomas,' she said, 'wait.'

He spun around. 'Where is your mother?'

'I . . . I don't know.' She reached out to grab his arm, then stopped herself.

For the first time, she was afraid of him.

He turned into the hallway. It was dark, as always. To the left, a sliver of light shone from under a doorway. It was coming from the library.

He strode towards it, flung open the door. Stepped inside.

'How dare you!' Mama's voice, angry, tumbled over itself from the room.

Hattie rounded the corner to see her standing, an open book upturned at her feet.

'How dare you,' she said, this time quieter. She was taking in the sight of Tomas. His muddy boots. The drip of water off his dark hair. His hand, bloody, holding a jewel.

He held the comb aloft. 'Where did you get this?' There was a quiver in his voice, a thrumming menace.

Mama's mouth opened and closed. Then, as though remembering something, she straightened, set her shoulders. 'I might,' she said, her voice suddenly full of authority, 'ask *you* the same thing.'

'*Where* did you get this?' This time he rotated the comb in his fingers, holding it by the prongs.

'It was here in the house when I arrived.'

'It wasn't.'

A harsh laugh escaped Mama's mouth. 'I beg your pardon?'

'I said: it wasn't. It disappeared with Charlotte.'

Mama stepped back as if struck. *Charlotte.* The aunt that no one talked of. The shadow in the corners. Her hand went to her mouth and she sat. Quietly said, 'I don't know anything about that.'

He acted as though she hadn't spoken. 'How did you get it?'

Mama closed her eyes.

A bolt of lightning lit his face. Lit the sky. 'How?'

'It was,' she said tiredly, 'a gift.'

He stopped then. Took two breaths. 'A gift?'

'Yes.'

'From who?'

'It doesn't matter any more.'

His laugh was cruel. 'Oh, Nancy. It does.' The use of her first name was an intimate threat. 'Who?'

Mama's hands shook; she steadied them on her knees. 'Charlotte gave it to me.'

He laughed. 'Liar.' A deep rumbling of thunder rolled around the room, and Tomas stepped back, next to Hattie.

Mama frowned. She seemed only now to notice her daughter standing frozen in the doorway. Her voice was hard. 'Harriet,' she said, 'please leave us.'

Hattie started to argue, but at the look on Mama's face, she quickly turned, slipped out of the room. Paused behind the door, an eye to the wide crack left by ill-fitting hinges.

'Liar,' he repeated. He'd stepped forward again.

Mama nodded, the flush from her cheeks gone. She took a deep breath. 'Sit down, Tomas.'

He remained standing.

'Charlotte . . .'

Tomas's shoulders tensed. 'What of her?'

'She didn't kill herself,' said Mama.

'I knew it.'

'And she wasn't taken.'

At this, he paused. Frowned.

'She left,' said Mama.

In the silence that followed, Hattie held her breath and listened to the tick-tock of the mantel clock, the crackle of fire.

'What you're saying is impossible.'

'No,' she said, 'it isn't. She . . . she had to. Leave.'

He cried out. A whimper. 'No . . . no.' Finally he sank into the sofa behind him. Hunched over. One hand on his head, the other holding the comb weakly, until it tumbled from his grip to fall on the carpet.

Mama bent to pick it up. From her sleeve she pulled a white handkerchief and wiped the comb. Scarlet stained the linen.

'I don't understand.'

She put the comb on the table beside her and clasped her hands, her elbows on her thighs. 'She . . . she came to me. In London. Her plan, such that it was, was to return. Not here, to Blackwater. But to Ballinn.' With coolness, she said: 'To you.'

Still he did not move. 'She didn't. Return.'

'No.' She looked away from him, towards the fire, watching as a half-burned log sighed and settled into the silence. 'She died.'

Tomas sat like a statue.

A flicker of frustration crossed Mama's face. 'It was during the Blitz.'

'The Blitz.' He repeated the word as though he'd never heard it before.

Mama sighed and stood. She went to the mantel, took a log from the basket and threw it on the fire. Hattie moved her position. Improved her view. Mama was using the poker now to coax the flames to life.

Tomas raised his head. 'Was it sudden?'

'Yes.'

'I don't believe you.'

Mama turned to him. 'What?'

'That she came to you. In London. Why would she do that?'

She gave him her handkerchief, already stained with blood, and he took it with a confused look. Then, lifting a key from around her neck, she went to her desk and unlocked the bottom drawer. She took out an envelope.

She waited for Tomas to clean his hands, then she handed it to him.

He opened it, pulled out a letter. The new blood from his cut smeared the header and he shifted his grip, his finger slowly following the words as though dragging a plough through unyielding soil.

'She ...' Mama searched for words, 'she was running from . . . her family.'

'It doesn't make any sense.'

'Doesn't it?' said Mama. A rumble of thunder, louder now, cut through her words. 'An affair with Lord Rathmore's daughter? What did you think would happen? You'd walk off into the sunset, start a family, live happily ever after?'

Tomas shook like a leaf.

Mama went to the sideboard, turned two glasses upright

and poured a generous measure of whiskey into each. She brought them to the sofa, handed one to Tomas. He made no move to take it.

'Why didn't she tell me?'

'She wrote to you. Many times.'

Tomas shook his head. 'I never received any letters.'

Mama set the glass beside him.

Loudly, he repeated, 'There weren't any letters.'

'How was I to know you didn't receive them?'

Hattie watched Tomas turn this over in his mind. He was stroking the letter, dragging his hand down and over the page as though he could wipe away the words.

'The day after she disappeared,' said Mama, 'I received a telegram. From the family. It said only that she had drowned in the lough, nothing more.' She took a sip of her whiskey and coughed. Put it aside. 'Then that letter arrived.'

He turned the page over, as though some trace of Charlotte might remain on the other side.

'Three days later, she turned up on the doorstep. She told me, of course, of your affair.' Mama tucked a strand of dark hair behind her ear. Lately, it had become unruly. 'Tomas, she intended to return.'

He put a hand to each of his ears and rubbed them as though he could erase her words. Then he dragged them down over his face and formed a steeple at his mouth. 'And you never thought to tell me she was dead?'

Standing there gazing into the fire, she looked so small. So delicate. Her blouse was loose on her, her cheekbones hollow.

'I . . .' She placed a hand on her hip. 'I'm sorry. I didn't think . . . It was wartime. Everything was . . . muddled.'

Tomas closed his eyes. Behind his hands, his lips were moving silently.

'Surely you can understand that?'

He shook his head slowly. 'And you return to Blackwater . . . and you say nothing?'

'You clearly didn't know that Charlotte had only run away,' she replied rapidly.

'Only? Only?' His voice was rising again.

'You thought she was dead already!' Mama said, the tone of her voice matching his. 'What was the point?'

'The point was' – Tomas swore – 'the point was, I would have known, all these years. I thought . . . I looked at everyone in Ballinn as though they could have been responsible for her disappearance.'

Mama's voice was soothing. 'I'm sorry. I thought it was best.'

'And you think firing me is also best?' He flinched as lightning lit the room.

'I'm worried about you . . . around my children.'

'Are you?'

She turned to face him. 'A mother will do anything for her children.'

'Even destroy an already broken man?'

'Yes,' she said, without hesitation.

And in the same quick heartbeat: 'When did she give it to you?'

'I'm sorry?'

A clap of thunder broke the air, rattled the windows. Tomas dropped the letter. When he spoke again, his voice was louder. It vibrated like the panes of glass had done only moments before. 'The comb. When did she give it to you?'

Mama whispered, 'Just before she died.'

Tomas shook his head. 'Just before she died? In a bomb blast?'

'Please' – she put her hand to her chest – 'I don't want to go over all this. It was . . . terrible.'

'How long was she in London with you?'

Mama looked into the distance. 'Not long. A few months.'

Tomas stood. 'Because the scandal, as I'm sure you know, was not just that we fell in love' – Mama began to shake her head – 'but that there'd been consequences to what we'd done.'

'Yes, there were *consequences*. She left. And then she died.'

Tomas stood, knocking over the small table. His untouched whiskey spilled across the carpet. 'You're blaming me for Charlotte's death?'

'Surely you already blamed yourself?'

He stepped towards her. One step, then two. 'Tell me what I need to know.'

Hattie opened the door a little, breathing heavily. The tension in the room both repelled and attracted her.

'You don't need to know anything. If it weren't for you, Charlotte would still be alive.'

'That's not true!'

Mama stepped back until she was against the wall. 'It is true! It's true. A beautiful life snuffed out because of you!'

He grabbed her by the shoulders, shaking her. 'Tell me!' he yelled. 'Tell me!' She began to cry, his face an inch from hers. 'Tell me now!' he hissed. 'Did she have my baby?'

And quietly Mama answered him.

Chapter Forty-Seven

Blackwater Hall

September 2019

As Ellie stepped up to the ivy-rimmed doorway, it struck her just how much had happened since she'd knocked on this very door only a week before. Then, she'd come here unwillingly, unenthusiastically, the words of an unknown woman in her pocket and the urge to pass them on in her mind. She felt, still, a touch of apprehension now as she rapped on the door, but this time it was not for herself, but for Charlotte. For Nancy. Their memories. And for those left behind.

Albert.

Hattie.

Milo.

In her bag she carried the two folders. But she would leave them there. Concealed. Until she knew the truth. Until she had all the answers. Or at least until she had the answers that could be found.

Above her, the clouds were moving off, leaving bright blue where before there had been only grey. The lough, a mirror on her previous visit, now rippled with gentle movement as it filled from the streams rolling off Cottah Mountain, white rivulets swollen with the morning's heavy rain.

She knocked, then stood back. Brushed her fringe from her face.

A moment later, footsteps. The turning of a handle.

And Albert was there. 'Hello.' That accent, trapped somewhere on the Irish Sea.

'Albert.' She was pleased to see him. And looking so well. His cheeks were flushed and he wore a dark blue knitted jumper that hugged his slim frame, the crisp line down each elbow a telltale sign of newness.

He smiled. 'Ellie.' She swallowed her surprise at his recognition. 'Milo's in the library.' He motioned for her to step inside.

The hallway was dark, as it had been before, but its smell was different. Then, it had been musty, but now fresh pine clung to the air, mingling with a tang of chalkiness. A pile of tins and discarded brushes stood by the wall. 'Redecorating?'

Albert patted the door frame. 'This place is held up with limewash and now it has a new coat. Milo's been busy. Even mopped the floor.' This he said with pride, as though it might be a once-in-a-decade event. Ellie looked down at her feet. The black-and-red quarry tiles shone. Albert watched her with a steady gaze. Did he remember her visit or had Milo told him an Ellie was due to call? He cleared his throat, prompted: 'Third door on the right.'

Ellie turned; a strip of light cut into the gloom. She looked back. 'Will you join us?'

'In the library?' The look on his face changed. 'No. But we'll have tea after.' He motioned again for her to lead on, and by the time she reached the door, he was gone.

❧

Milo sat at a small bureau, a large pile of books towering next to him. He wore rough trousers and a tartan shirt, the sleeves rolled to his elbows. A golden leaf was stuck in his flaxen hair.

'Been gardening?' she said by way of greeting.

He looked down at his trousers; green stains covered his knees. He spread his hands. 'How can you tell?'

'Just a hunch.'

He stood. 'You saw Jules?' He gave her a guilty look.

Ellie stepped forward. Appraised the room. It was lined floor-to-ceiling with books. 'I saw him. And he told me about Tabby.' To ease his guilt, she added, 'Jules can be very persuasive.' A fire flickered under the green marble mantelpiece on the far wall, but the room was icy cold.

'You did say he was starting a historical society . . .'

She had said that, hadn't she? That day at the surgery. It felt like a lifetime ago.

Behind the bureau, a large sash window framed the woodland that sat at the base of the mountain. The slope was bathed in sunshine and a new scour of purple, a recent rock fall, cut its face. It was bright out there now, the clouds off to bother another place, somewhere inland.

Milo went to the fire. 'No matter what I do, this room's always Baltic.' He threw a large log on the flames. 'Albert never comes in here. I'm surprised the books have survived.'

'Speaking of books . . . the ones you dropped at Threadbare . . .'

'Yes?'

'Why those?'

He shrugged. 'A random assortment of classics. I wanted an excuse to meet Bernie. She'd been bringing Albert Meals on Wheels.' He turned his back to her, poked the fire. 'I just wanted to check she was grand.'

Not a gold digger? 'And how did you find her?'

'Colourful.' He teased: 'I hope you paid handsomely for the books?'

'An outrageous price.' Outside, a group of starlings rose from the woodland. She watched them wheel westward and out of sight. 'So,' she continued, 'you wanted to show me something?'

He nodded. 'In the garden.'

She stepped forward and reached towards his face. He looked alarmed, surprised. Pleased? She plucked the leaf from his hair. Held it up. Then dropped it into the fire to curl into ash. 'The garden?' She looked to the woodland beyond.

'Down by the lake, through the trees, there's a walled garden.'

'A secret garden?' She felt her fingers tingle. Hidden doors. Rusty keys. Long-forgotten treasures waiting to be found.

He laughed then. Started for the door. 'No, Ellie. This isn't a Gothic children's novel.'

Before she followed him, she turned, stepped up to the fire, the words from the file burning a hole in her bag. *And I pushed him back against the mantelpiece.* She ran her hand across the dusty stone.

It was as smooth and flat as the day it was made.

❧

They passed through the blue room towards the French doors. Albert was there, folded into his wingback chair. 'Where're you off to then?'

'The garden, Albert.' Did Ellie only imagine the shadow that passed across Albert's face? When Milo said *Albert* rather than *Dad*?

He cleared his throat. 'I thought we'd have tea.' Beside him, on the table, were three cups and the tarnished silver teapot, steam rising from its spout.

Milo went to the fire, worried at the flames. 'In a bit, will we?'

But Albert was getting to his feet. Leaning down for the tray. 'I'll bring it out. You've cleared the arbour. The perfect

spot.' He glanced out of the window. 'And the rain has cleared.'
Ellie watched the two men lock eyes; they matched, green as
the hills beyond.

'Well . . .' Milo's gaze flicked to the teapot. Ellie could
almost see his thoughts. *Could you stand your teaspoon in it?*

Albert picked up the tray. 'Jolly good then.'

'All right,' said Milo, taking it from him. 'I'll just go and
make a new pot. Nice and hot.' He winked at Ellie as he went.
Whispered, 'He's having one of his good days.' He tried to say
this with exasperation, but she could see that he was pleased.
Very pleased. She watched him leave the room. Noticed, as he
passed the sideboard, that the O'Conor – its copy, at least – had
been replaced on the wall above.

Albert watched her appraise his son, appraise the painting.
He smiled. 'What's it like out there, Ellie?'

'Chilly.'

He turned from her. Went to the sideboard. From it, he took
three thick woolly blankets. He put one in her arms. 'Shall
we?' He opened the French doors and stepped out into the day.

As she followed, Ellie glanced to the far end of the room,
towards the cabinet. Someone had cleaned the glass. And the
item inside. It sat proud of the navy velvet that pooled underneath, the rubies two red drops of blood on its wings. And the
sapphires, previously so dull and lifeless, reflected the sunlight
that streamed through the window so that it spread across the
ceiling, speckled like stars on a clear Kerry night.

Newly cut grass stuck to their feet as they crossed the lawn.
A dozen sparrows pecked in the debris, searching for grubby
treats beneath. Albert's step was surprisingly quick, and Ellie
walked close beside him, their elbows touching as they went.

They entered the woods and followed a path through the

trees. It was covered in leaves and humus but firm underfoot, as though it had once been gravel or stone. Fat drops dripped from leaves overhead, reminders of the recent rain, and Ellie peered through the foliage looking for a wall.

And there it was, not far into the woods.

'They chose this spot to shelter from the wind, I imagine,' said Albert. 'When they built the house.'

An archway led them into the garden.

It was, in a neglected way, beautiful. A rough stone wall, head height, with once-espaliered fruit trees sprawled across its surface. She turned, trying to orientate herself. The western wall was lined with a messy proliferation of raspberry plants. Knobbly berries dripped from them; dark red, well past their best. The garden was alive with birds, noisy and fat with the fermented fruits of September.

Albert followed her gaze. 'We've had our fill of berries this year. And Milo's started on the vegetable patch.'

A little digging had been done. Rich earth recently turned. But there was serious ground left to cover. Some sort of machine might be in order, Ellie thought. She pushed the idea aside. That wasn't, Moira had always lectured, what gardening was about. It was the wonder of pulling something from the soil one minute, only for it to end up on your plate the next. Ellie had always been uncertain about her mum's garden; windswept and barren on the mountain's edge, it wasn't exactly a haven of tranquillity. And its produce – floury potatoes, slug-eaten cabbage, the odd forked carrot – had always been . . . entertaining. Nonetheless, she had to admit that there was nothing like a spud pulled from the ground – boiled and smothered in butter – to make her feel at home.

As though reading her mind, Albert said, 'The potato ridges are in the field behind the woods. They haven't been set for years.'

On the southern wall, in shade, sat a square rubble-stone ruin. Rotting timber was piled inside. An old stove, rusted so that its top had fallen in on itself, sat at one end. Albert stared at it, frowning. As though he'd forgotten it was there.

'This is the arbour?' said Ellie, pointing to the eastern wall, where a wooden frame was hugged by woven sally and bathed in afternoon light. A wild and unruly climbing plant weighted down the archway, a single blue flower hanging amongst the wilted summer blooms. A huge pile of matching foliage sat beside it.

The arbour had indeed been recently uncovered.

'Clematis,' said Albert, stepping forward to pluck the last brave flower. He gave it to Ellie, who took it, appraised its star shape, the sapphire hue of its petals. She didn't need to hold it to her nose to smell the almond fragrance.

She tucked it behind her ear, and raised an eyebrow.

Albert nodded, his gaze moving far away. He was going somewhere, she knew then. Going away. Like he had done the week before.

The arbour looked rickety, but there was a wrought-iron chair and round table on the far side of the garden. 'Wait here a minute, Albert.' She carried the setting over, put it next to the arbour. 'Take a seat.'

'My mother's eyes,' he said as he watched her. She placed a blanket across his knees, not wanting to acknowledge his changing state. Carefully then – testing its robustness – she took a seat in the arbour.

A robin, small and wiry, had followed her across the garden. Ellie leaned down, flipped a muddy stone near her feet. 'Try under here,' she said to the tiny bird, willing him closer.

When she looked up again, Albert was back, his eyes clear. He ran a finger across the table, let the water drip from his fingertip. 'How is your mother, Ellie?'

Ellie frowned. 'I didn't realise you knew my mother?'

'You said you were back for her health?'

'Oh. Yes. That's right. She's much better, thank you.'

'We need to look after our parents,' he said. The robin hopped quickly forward to pull a worm from the earth, then flew off and paused on the foundations of the tumbled shed. 'And your father?'

Ellie looked to her hands. A ball of mud from the rock sat in her palm. 'He's . . . not with us any more.'

'I'm sorry.'

'It was a long time ago.'

'What happened?'

'A car accident.'

'What a terrible thing.' He reached across, patted her hand. 'Thank goodness you weren't with him.' He said it kindly, something to fill the space.

Ellie spoke before she could think. 'I *should* have been with him. I . . .' she touched the mud in her palm, swirled it into an earthy stigmata, 'I was supposed to join him that day. He was going on a trip.' She squinted, conjuring the memory. 'He loved history. Every weekend we went sightseeing. And he had such a collection of books.' Albert was watching her intently, lucidly. 'We were supposed to visit a ruined castle, but I was out with friends the night before, and I got home the next morning later than I'd promised.' She looked at Albert. 'I had the car.'

The robin was back for second helpings, he paused to look up at them, cocked his head to the side. Ellie would never forget that image of her father slipping out of the front door without a backwards glance. In her memory, in her dreams, she always tried to turn his head, to see his face. But it was never there.

'He took the keys from my hand and left without me. And never came back.'

She turned away, wiped hard at her eyes. Never before had she told anyone what she'd just told Albert. Not even Dylan. And certainly not Moira, who had been out at work that morning and missed the whole confrontation. Or lack thereof: her father had always shown anger through silence.

She hadn't mentioned it to Nils either, that day they'd hung their arms over a gate and peered at the ruin on the edge of the sea.

There was warmth on her fingers and she turned back to Albert. His hand was there on hers. 'If you continue to hold on to this, it will destroy you,' he said. He reached forward and took the flower from behind her ear. Twirled it in his fingers. 'My mother's eyes were as blue as this clematis. Bluer, if you can imagine it.' He brushed a petal. 'Bad things happen to good people, Ellie.' He placed the flower back behind her ear, then frowned, peering in the direction of the potato field, somewhere in the distance.

Ellie took a breath. This was her chance to ask him about Tomas.

'Albert, I wonder—'

He flinched and looked around, dropping her hand. As though just noticing she were there. 'Hello,' he said, appraising her.

'Albert, I wanted to ask . . .' She stopped. He was dredging his mind, just as he had done days before. A slight tremor in his hands. 'Albert, I'm Milo's friend Ellie. We're having tea in the garden.'

He glanced at the table, suspicious. Then: 'Tea? Would you like some?' The plum, the pluck, was back in his voice. 'Let me . . .' He began to stand, pushed away the blanket from his knee. 'Are you here to see Mama?'

'No, no,' she soothed, alarmed at the sudden change.

'Sorry for the wait.' Milo was there, a tray full of crockery and a face full of reassurance. 'Albert, we're having tea.' He placed a hand on the old man's shoulder, nodded carefully.

Albert sat.

'The place needs rewiring,' said Milo. 'Fuse went. Had to boil the kettle on the range.'

Ellie raised an eyebrow. 'That's very Robinson Crusoe of you.'

'This is your new wife?' said Albert, looking at Ellie with his head tilted to the side.

'No, Albert, Ellie's just a friend.'

Albert looked between them and laughed, shaking his head. He muttered, 'A friend.' He pointed at the tray. 'You've forgotten the fourth cup.' Then he stood and batted away his son's hand. 'But don't worry about me, I'm off to find your *friend* some flowers to go with that one behind her ear.' He wandered to the far end of the garden, laughing to himself.

'I'm sorry,' said Milo. He poured the tea – it was beautifully brewed – then took a seat next to Ellie in the arbour. 'Normally he's back for a few hours once he's had a good morning. Did something set him off?'

She took the flower from behind her ear. 'His mother,' she said. 'It was the same when I was here before.'

'They were very close.'

Ellie looked back towards the house; just a collection of chimneys above the treeline. One puffed brightly. 'The tea's better for being made over the fire,' she said as she took a sip.

They watched Albert talking to himself as he gathered a jolly orange posy of nasturtiums.

'Hattie said he's refusing to go into a home,' said Ellie.

'He's stubborn.'

'Why won't he go?'

Milo considered his answer. 'Pride, firstly. But I think

it's . . .' He hesitated. 'You remember when we met on the beach that morning?'

'Of course.'

'And what I told you.'

The curse. 'You don't believe it, do you?'

'No, it's not that. If Albert goes, he's worried I'll stay here alone. He's worried about what will happen.'

'To you?'

'Yes.'

'Does he believe it's the house or the comb that's cursed?'

Milo flinched at the word. 'They seem to be one and the same in his mind. He told me once that both of them changed his life.'

Ellie frowned. Now was the time. 'Did you know Tabby had a brother?'

He looked up, surprised. 'Yes. Of course. That's why I asked you here. I wanted to tell you something about Tomas.'

Did he did know? 'Yes?'

But Milo said something she didn't expect. 'They were in love.'

'What? Nancy and Tomas?'

He laughed. 'No, not Nancy.'

'What do you mean?'

He reached across her. For a moment – a terrible moment? A wonderful moment? – she thought he was about to embrace her. But he brushed the edge of the arbour, pushing aside the curtain of clematis to reveal the etching beneath.

Chapter Forty-Eight

Ballinn, County Kerry

September 2019

The white thatched cottage hung on the edge of the ocean. Below it, foam-tipped waves licked at the rocky coastline and a hundred gulls wheeled offshore, diving for a hidden shoal. And surrounding it: green. Endless green. Fields that ran to the sea.

Ellie stepped up to the worn doormat, *Fáilte* – 'Welcome' – woven into its surface, and rapped on the door. Took a step back. Wondered at the right thing to do. Traditionally, neighbours in Kerry did very little waiting at doors; they walked right in, the unspoken rule being that one's kitchen was always open. Abiding by this rule, a voice called from inside.

'Come in.' It was Tabby. 'The tea's wet.'

The interior of Tabby's house was not what Ellie had expected. Firstly, it was open plan; its western half an oak-trimmed kitchen, the eastern half a sitting room with a huge corner sofa and an oversized coffee table. Secondly, it was cosy warm. And thirdly (Ellie couldn't believe what she was seeing), the entire southern wall – which had been hidden on the drive down the hill, its aspect facing only the sea – was made entirely of glass. The view beyond was breathtaking. As though someone had taken a picture of Kenmare Bay in perfect light, at the perfect moment, and even then ramped up the colours.

Ellie realised her mouth was hanging open. She closed it, but continued to gaze around the bright interior with its white-washed stone walls, its indoor plants and its grey slate floors. It made her Dublin apartment look old fashioned, and it was a thousand miles from the worn, dim interior she'd expected. There were only two things that didn't surprise her about the house: Tabby Ryan, who stood at its centre, one hand holding a pot of tea; and the reassuring smell of baking.

'Like it?' Tabby said, though it wasn't really a question, because no one could walk in and *not* like it.

'It's . . . wow.'

The large open fireplace was set but unlit. Tabby followed Ellie's gaze.

'Underfloor heating.' She indicated the dark stone tiles.

'It's stunning,' Ellie said. The house. The underfloor heating. The view.

Tabby winked. 'Better to spend money like there's no tomorrow than to spend today like there's no money.' She turned and went slowly to the oven – a black range set into a second fireplace – and withdrew a tray of scones. Ellie wanted to ask *Can I help?* But she felt that Tabby was the sort of woman who might take that as a slight. She took a seat at the concrete countertop and pulled her eyes away from the view beyond.

'My grandson's an architect. It started with a plan to convert the range to oil.' Tabby swept her hand behind her. 'Then things . . . escalated.'

They sure had. A door at the far end of the room lay ajar; Ellie caught a glimpse of the corner of a bed.

'Just one bedroom,' said Tabby. 'The road may be longer walked alone, but I'm partial to an expedition.' She laughed and set down the tray, pushing aside a pile of papers, indicating them with a nod. 'Been at the poetry. Turns out I quite like ballads.'

Ellie considered her next move and decided to step right in. 'Tabby, I've just been up at Blackwater Hall.'

'Oh yes?' The old woman walked around the counter and took a seat, easing herself into it with a small wince. 'How are they up there? How's Milo?' She said his name with such affection that Ellie smiled.

'They're grand. I had tea with them both in the walled garden.'

'The garden? Really?' Tabby pushed the tray of scones forward. 'I've forgotten the jam . . .'

'Please, let me.'

Tabby nodded. 'It's in the fridge. Behind that cupboard.' She pointed. 'No . . . that one to the left.' The fridge was outrageously large. Ellie sorted through a shelf of jars. *Raspberry and Hawthorn Conserve. Elderberry and Whitethorn Jelly. Blackberry Jam.* She picked the latter, brought it back to her seat. Began to butter a scone.

'You mentioned at your party that your father was the gardener at Blackwater Hall?'

'He was, o'course. He had a knack for it. One that I didn't inherit.' She waved to the lack of garden out the window. 'I prefer to forage.' The contents of her fridge were certainly testament to that.

'I saw a photo of you both,' Ellie continue, 'from Blackwater Hall in 1939. The summer party.'

The old woman nodded. 'An annual event. It stopped after Charlotte disappeared.' This time she said Charlotte's name easily, as though she'd been practising it in the days since her birthday. Which, given her conversation with Milo, she had.

'Milo tells me you sold your identification to Charlotte in 1940?'

'Yes. She wanted to leave and I didn't.' Tabby said this

simply, as though it were the end of the story. But Ellie knew it wasn't.

'Why did you tell me she helped you get a scholarship?'

Tabby reached across to pour the tea. 'Because it was true.'

'What do you mean?'

'She *did* help me apply. Charlotte had as good a way with words as she had with people. She was a talent. And a fine actress.' Tabby smiled a secret smile. 'She *loved* the stage. I don't know where she got it from. Both her parents were deadpan. But' – she pushed a cup towards Ellie, indicated the milk and sugar – 'we wouldn't have the Ballinn Dramatics Secret Society without her.'

Ellie's hand hovered over the milk. 'What?'

'Charlotte started it. The society. When she was fifteen years old. Her family thought she was teaching literature to local girls.'

Ellie laughed. 'You're kidding?'

Tabby raised a thinly drawn eyebrow. '*In every land, hardness is in the north of it, softness in the south, industry in the east, and fire and inspiration in the west.* 'Tis what we say, is it not?'

Ellie smiled. Her father had once told her that, when she'd announced her interest in journalism. 'It is.'

They sat in silence. Out in the bay, a yacht rounded Dinish Island, its sails white against the dark folded cliffs.

After a moment, Tabby looked at her watch. 'My grand-daughter will be here soon. She's very protective of me. Wouldn't like to think that someone was digging into my family's past. So,' her voice softened, 'you'd better get to asking whatever it is you've come here to ask.'

My family's past.

Ellie put her cup aside. Swept the crumbs from the counter and brushed them onto her plate. She appreciated Tabby's bluntness. It reminded her of Hattie. 'Your brother was also in the summer party photo. He worked in the gardens too, didn't he?'

In lieu of an answer, Tabby said, 'May I see this letter Milo told me about? This charity shop find?'

Surprised, Ellie nodded. She took it from her satchel, where it nestled next to the folder from 1940.

Next to the folder from 1958.

Tabby took a thick pair of glasses from the counter and read the letter. When she had finished, she looked up. Ellie felt she was being assessed. For her nerve? For her boldness? Her inability to tread lightly around someone nearly seven decades older than herself? 'The spit of the mother,' Tabby said.

Ellie smoothed her hair with her hand, sat a little taller. She thought she had some way to go until she developed Moira's charming yet undeniably matronly features.

'But that's where the similarities ended. Charlotte had spirit. Passion. She was interested in other people's lives. In their plight. And I can tell you, in those times life was full of plight.' Tabby reminisced as though no one else was in the room. 'A girl like that – high-born yet so . . . lovable – was bound to get into trouble.' She gazed into her cup. The tea steamed gentle wisps.

Ellie prompted, 'What kind of trouble?'

Tabby stood. She steadied herself on the counter, then went to the window, where the sun shone a halo around her white hair.

'Tabby, I found something in the garden. Two names. Intertwined. Charlotte and—'

'Don't.'

'And Tomas.'

Tabby spoke without turning. 'You always had an inquisitive mind.'

Ellie took a sip of tea, burned her tongue. Added some milk.

'Charlotte was pregnant, wasn't she?' She said this as casually as she could. Because it was obvious, wasn't it? She had known it when she'd seen those names etched into the wood in the arbour. Charlotte and Tomas. Written so that they shared the O. Tomas's name vertical across Charlotte's. And the date, 1940.

Tabby's shoulders dropped. She pressed her hand against the glass, then let it fall. 'Yes,' was all she said. She went to the sofa, sank into it. Closed her eyes. 'No one knew. Only Ma and Charlotte's parents. Her father arranged for Tomas to go to war and Charlotte was to be sent to the sisters.'

'Did they love each other?'

'I think so. At least, in the way the young love.' She considered for a moment. 'I suppose, in the end, he was more taken with her.'

'Why do you say that?'

'Because she never returned.'

'What happened to her?'

'I don't know.' And Ellie could see that the woman was telling the truth. She knew, because she'd already seen her lie.

'Did she write?'

'Ah, she did. Dozens of letters. At first. Ma burned every one of 'em. Never even opened them. They kept coming and coming. Then, one day, they just . . . stopped.'

'God,' said Ellie, her brow furrowed in sadness. 'Who else knew that Charlotte didn't drown in the lough?'

Tabby took a deep breath. She shook her head. 'It must have been the only time my mother ever kept a secret. *He who keeps his tongue keeps his friends.* Even my father didn't know.'

'And Tomas, when he returned?'

'That,' said Tabby, 'is the saddest part. My . . . greatest regret.' She looked down at her hands, examined her gnarled knuckles, as though they were that way for gripping such a secret for so long a time.

'You never told him?'

'No.' She closed her eyes. 'Will you fetch me a glass of water, Ellie?'

When Ellie returned, Tabby had resettled herself, her legs now propped on the sofa, a blanket across her lap. One arm lay over the backrest, so that she could watch the sea. Ellie handed her the water and she took a sip, nodded. *'Hindsight is the best insight to foresight.'*

Ellie sat on the far end of the couch. 'Isn't that the truth.' But she wasn't sure which part of her own life she was referring to. Of all the loss – she pressed her hand to her stomach – how much had been avoidable in the end?

'Tomas shouldn't have gone back to work at Blackwater Hall when he returned in 1944. But he did. He was changed, Ellie. *Much* changed. He became . . .' Tabby paused. 'Unpredictable. It wasn't something anyone talked about then, o'course. Shell shock. All the lads had it, in one form or another. And when he returned, he mourned Charlotte so deeply and . . . violently that Ma warned me never to tell him about the letters. He believed that she drowned and that was it. And once that first moment to tell him passed . . .' She looked at Ellie, her eyes rheumy. 'How do you go back on something like that? Desperate, it was. The guilt overcame me at times.'

Another Tabby sat before Ellie now. Tired and serious. A woman who'd carried with her a great secret and had kept it from someone dearly loved.

'I don't understand . . . Why would Tomas have been given work at Blackwater Hall? Niamh and Charles Rathmore knew about the pregnancy. As far as they were concerned, Charlotte drowned herself *because* of it. Did they not blame him?'

Tabby ran her fingers across her forehead. 'That was Ma's handiwork. She was a hard woman. A match for Niamh Rathmore. Our home needed income – Tomas was expected to work, but he couldn't get a job. Who was going to employ an Irishman who'd fought for the English? Ma went to the big house, told them in no uncertain terms that she'd reveal Charlotte's secret – the pregnancy – if Tomas wasn't given his old job back working with my father in the gardens.'

'Quite a gamble,' Ellie said.

'And didn't it pay off? I s'pose Niamh Rathmore's concern about losing face outweighed what Tomas had done. That's saying something. But she never spoke to him again. Tomas worked there for fourteen years without so much as a word passing between them.' Ellie wondered whether now was the moment to mention the case file in her satchel, but Tabby carried on. ''Twas difficult to know what would happen when Ma died. Would I need to carry on the blackmail? It kept me awake.'

'But Tomas died first,' said Ellie.

'Yes.'

Ellie hesitated. 'Tabby, I know what happened. In 1958. And I'm sorry.'

Tabby looked surprised. She linked her hands together, set them in her lap. The two women stared at each other. Ellie looked away.

'Sean Reilly always said you were the brightest in his class.'

Ellie almost laughed. 'There were only twelve students,' she said, repeating what she'd said to Bernie the week before.

But Tabby was serious. With one hand she rubbed the gnarled knuckle of the other. 'Arthritis.' She looked up. 'I'm like this house, Ellie. Young on the inside. Old on the outside.' She laughed. 'My thatch could do with replacing.'

'*Windy days are not for thatching.*'

She smiled. 'I'm glad my poem left its mark.'

'It did.' Ellie had thought of it a dozen times since.

'Can you imagine burying a scandal like that in Ballinn?' Tabby was back in the past. Back in 1958.

'No,' said Ellie. 'How *did* you bury it?'

'There's only one thing worse than being talked about, and that's *not* being talked about,' Tabby said. 'Tomas had become an outcast. Very few people cared what happened to the boys who fought in *that* war. They were sometimes cruel, the villagers, back then.' She nodded. 'They've improved.'

'But why did Nancy Rathmore *kill* your brother?' Ellie wanted to hear it for herself.

'It was self-defence. Manslaughter,' said Tabby. Her voice was devoid of blame or bitterness.

'And you believe that?'

She frowned. 'Of course. Tomas had become unstable . . . he'd let his temper get the better of him.' She sighed. 'And yet deep down, he was good.' Now she was lost in thought. 'He was once a very good man.'

Ellie said, 'I'm sorry.'

'Me too. Every day. But what's done is done. A misunderstanding.' Tabby began to fold the blanket from her lap. 'For every mile of road there are two miles of ditches, Ellie. Two sides. Two stories.' The colour had returned to her cheeks. 'Tomas was no thief,' she said. 'My brother was a complicated man . . . no . . . he *became* a complicated man. Before that, he was full of light and joy. He loved Charlotte with a fierce passion. I can only imagine what it was like returning home; her missing, his future gone. His life was over.' She looked at Ellie. 'Have you ever felt that? Like life was over?'

Ellie lowered her eyes. 'Yes,' she said.

Tabby nodded, leaned forward, took her hand. Patted it. Examined the smooth skin under her own. 'Then you'll understand. Tomas thought naught for that comb. All he cared about was Charlotte, and what could've been. Material possessions meant nothing to him. He was broken by life and loss. And broken by . . . love.'

Chapter Forty-Nine

Holborn, London
February 1941

Charlotte was lying very still on the bed when Nancy rushed through the bedroom door. She felt the girl's forehead. The heat of it surprised her, and she pulled her hand away. She listened for breath; a shattered whisper.

'Charlotte,' she said loudly, shaking her shoulders. 'Charlotte!'

A moan in reply.

'Mrs McLaughlin's gone to find help. She'll be back any minute now.' She nodded, mostly to herself – Charlotte had not yet opened her eyes. 'It's snowing outside and your little girl will be born into a winter wonderland; how about that?' She cleared her throat, feeling suddenly patronising. 'I'll get some water boiling.'

She filled a large pot and set it on the gas, turning the weak flame up as high as it would go. Gathering towels and the dregs of a bottle of whiskey, she returned to Charlotte's room.

'Come now, let's get you up.' *Ambulation*, Mrs McLaughlin had said. She had also read advice to that effect in her books on midwifery, both of which sat unfinished, hidden away in the top drawer of her bedside table.

Charlotte shook her head in reply but started to roll on her side nonetheless. Nancy helped her to sit, swinging her feet to the floor, one arm around her shoulder. The movement brought a cry of pain. 'Walking will move the baby along,' she said, all encouragement, though she had no idea if it was true. 'It gets the little one in the right position. Head first.' She cringed. *Head first?* It sounded like she was giving a diving lesson.

She tried to imagine Mrs McLaughlin's ample frame moving through streets filled with debris and snow, resisted the urge to go to the sitting-room window, pull aside the blinds and look for the footsteps of her neighbour. Suddenly she felt that it should have been her that went and Mrs McLaughlin, with her cool head and her calm instructions, who stayed.

ều

Two hours later, when the baby came, it wasn't as described in Nancy's books. No crowning head, no practised breathing, no pause at the shoulders with the body a slippery trail behind. Instead it was blood and limbs. Tangy metallic smells. Ragged breaths.

And fear.

The feet appeared first. Or rather, a single foot. Charlotte lay back on the bed, a towel covering her legs, Nancy kneeling between them. The embarrassment she'd felt about the position evaporated when the younger woman paid her no attention but instead began to murmur to her mother, a rolling barrage of excuses and apologies.

Nancy told her to push, although whether that was the right thing, she had no idea. Her hands, covered with blood, gently tugged on the baby's leg, willing another to appear. All the while she cooed at Charlotte, telling her how well she was doing, how soon it would be over.

And it was.

She pulled the second leg free and the baby slid out, quiet

and lifeless. She rubbed the chest with two fingers, coaxing
life, while Charlotte tried to pull herself upright.

'Lie down,' Nancy said, placing a hand on her shoulder.

'Is she . . .?' she murmured.

Nancy turned the baby upside down. It was something
she'd seen a foster mother do to the runt of a litter of puppies.
Gently, she shook.

Charlotte cried out. Pain and horror mingled. 'What are
you doing?'

'It's okay.' Nancy turned her back on the girl, hiding her
tears. The words caught in her throat, pushed away the truth.

Suddenly Mrs McLaughlin was there, her face drained, her
lips blue. She took in the sight before her with a quick sweep
of her eyes, then put her arms out. Without a word, Nancy
handed her the baby, slippery with blood.

'Bring me a pot of warm water. And some towels for Tabby.'
With one swift movement the woman turned the child on its
stomach, tiny limbs hanging like a rag doll's.

Nancy hesitated. *Who?*

'Your cousin,' Mrs McLaughlin prompted. 'We need to
keep her warm.'

Nancy nodded and left the room. She went to the trunk
at the end of her bed and flung it open. No towels. It was
full of bedding, brand-new white sheets she'd bought in a fit
of domesticity before the war. They lay waiting for a special
occasion.

Frantic, she pulled them out one by one, their neat folds a
reminder of their newness. They were silky smooth. Egyptian
cotton, high thread count. Unabsorbent; useless. She flung
one across the bed in frustration; it opened and floated down,
catching the room's cool air beneath it.

And then, so close, the sound of a siren. A long single
wail. As always, it sent a shiver down her spine, a zing of

adrenaline through her veins. With shaking hands she stripped the blanket from her own bed, pulling the scratchy wool into her arms so it didn't drag on the floor. As though it mattered if it did.

When she returned to the bedroom, Charlotte was propped up, a mountain of pillows behind her. Her eyes half open, her pale face crossed with a slight smile that was framed by lips of faintest blue. A stain of red crept across the bed.

With apprehension, Nancy stepped into the room and laid the blanket across Charlotte's legs, willing her heart rate to slow, willing the Luftwaffe to slow. Then sat gingerly on the bedside. It creaked in protest. And there, under her sister-in-law's chin – a tiny head, pointed almost. Pink skin.

'The air-raid sirens . . .' Nancy looked from Charlotte to Mrs McLaughlin. 'We should go.'

A frown of confusion crossed the older woman's face. 'Sirens?'

'I thought I heard . . .' Suddenly the silence outside struck her. Realisation dawned. There were no sirens. No deep collective grumble of a hundred engines. No bombs.

She looked again at the bundle in Charlotte's arms. There. The tiny mouth, moving. Opening, closing, tasting life outside for the first time.

The noise, the siren, had been a cry.

The baby was alive.

She reached her hand out and touched Charlotte's cheek. It was as cold as her hands had been only a few hours before. 'You're freezing.'

Mrs McLaughlin cleared her throat, came forward. Laid a hand on Nancy's shoulder. 'A word?'

Nancy followed the older woman to the living room, risking a glance back at Charlotte, whose eyes had closed, the up-and-down of her chest slow and arrhythmical.

Mrs McLaughlin took her hand. 'She's bleeding heavily. I've seen it before . . .'

Nancy frowned. 'But there's help coming? The hospital are sending a midwife?'

'As soon as they can.'

'Which is when?'

The silence gave her an answer: *I don't know.*

The wireless was still on. A murmur of voices cut through static.

'The hospital was entirely overrun when I arrived. The weather. It's caused havoc, people are freezing, sick. They only have three midwives; one they couldn't reach, the other two were on home calls. I left an address, it's all I could do.'

'You said you've seen this before.' Nancy suddenly noticed her blood-encrusted nails. 'When?'

Mrs McLaughlin hesitated before answering. Her voice was uncharacteristically quiet. 'My daughter. Just the same.'

Nancy looked up. 'Your daughter? I never knew . . .'

'The baby, my granddaughter, also died.'

'I'm so sorry.' Nancy couldn't place this conversation in context with what had just happened, what was happening, here in her home. And yet, she could.

'It was a matter of hours. For the baby, at least.'

Nancy nodded. 'We need to get both of them to hospital.'

Mrs McLaughlin gripped her hand a little tighter. 'Nancy, I think the best thing is for you to take the baby to find help.'

'And Charlotte?'

Confusion ran across the old woman's face like a ripple on water.

'Charlotte. That's her name,' said Nancy. 'She's my sister-in-law . . .' Her voice became pleading. 'Teddy doesn't know . . . no one knows. She begged me.'

'You need explain nothing to me.' Mrs McLaughlin picked

up a blanket from the sofa, the one that had lain over Charlotte's knees only hours before. Held it out. 'You're quicker than me. Take the baby and go to Great Ormond Street. That's the most important thing to Charlotte . . .' she paused, as though tasting the name, approving, 'now.'

Nancy looked at the blanket; its jolly blue was jarring. 'I'd rather stay.'

'And I'd rather be a twenty-two-year-old burlesque dancer. You have to go.'

She knew what Mrs McLaughlin was trying to do. Bring her back to reality. In a roundabout way. 'I . . .'

She was given no time to reply. 'You can return with a doctor.' The woman reached out to tuck a strand of Nancy's hair behind her ear; said softly, 'You must do it.'

Nancy watched Mrs McLaughlin go to the kitchen, a limp hampering her gait. She swallowed, trying to push down the fear that gripped her. If she left Charlotte, she couldn't help her. But if she didn't leave, she might die. The baby might die.

When she returned to the bedroom, the air felt cool once again and the light was dim. She knelt next to the bed, her knees cracking. Charlotte's head was tilted back, lit now only by the bedside lamp, which cast a shadow over one side of her face. On the other side her skin was almost translucent, and she appeared even younger than her already too few years. When Nancy and Teddy had visited Ireland only eighteen months before, his sister had been on the cusp of womanhood. Teetering on the edge of a new life. Grown. Blossomed. But now she looked like a child again. And all Nancy wanted to do was fold her arms around her, hold her tight. Instead she said, 'I need to take the baby. Get to a doctor. I'll be back before you know it. With help.'

Charlotte nodded, eyes almost opening. She smiled slightly, her pale lips thin, then murmured something inaudible.

'I'm sorry?' Nancy leaned closer. She brushed a damp strand of hair off Charlotte's sticky brow. It was half brunette, half blonde.

Charlotte cleared her throat; something rattled deep in her chest. 'Not . . .' a shadow of a smile graced her lips, 'Big Bertha.'

The pressure building in Nancy's chest came as a sob, caught between a laugh and something dark. Then a prickle of heat behind her eyes. A wetness, a cool line running down her cheek. She turned away to brush the tear aside, to pretend – to herself – that she didn't know why she was crying.

'Not Big Bertha, I promise,' she said. Her voice sounded strange. Not just strange. A stranger's voice.

With her eyes closed once more, Charlotte said, 'The wardrobe . . . go to it.'

Nancy did. Opened it.

'No . . . no . . . underneath. Reach underneath.'

Awkwardly, Nancy knelt down, felt under the wardrobe. The wooden floor was coated with dust. At the back she found a small fabric bag. She pulled it out.

'Nancy?' Charlotte's voice was so quiet it was almost already a memory. 'You must protect this child . . .'

'Of course, of course I will.'

'. . . when I'm gone.'

Nancy stared at her friend. The baby was still, too still. 'Don't talk like that.'

'Take it,' said Charlotte. 'If you need to bribe someone. Buy something. Take it.'

Despite herself, Nancy almost laughed. It released a little of the pressure in her chest. She thought of this girl – so high born, so innocent – bribing her way onto a ship to Liverpool. Travelling on someone else's identification. *Working* on someone else's identification. During her six months in London, Charlotte had been nothing if not surprising. Her resilience, her aptitude for hard work with those soft, soft hands, her enthusiasm for the war-torn city. The way she'd marvelled at Big Ben and wondered out loud if there were teams of little men up there turning the hands. The time Nancy had roasted an over-hung pheasant so unpleasantly gamey that she couldn't stomach it — and watched Charlotte eat every last bitter bite. 'Waste not, want not,' she'd said, patting her stomach. And of course, the time she'd turned up on Nancy's doorstep, very much alive, with a cheeky grin and a growing belly, and implanted herself into her life.

Nancy opened the bag. Even in the dim light, its contents glittered.

'If anything should happen to me . . .'

'Nothing's going to happen to you.'

'But if it should.'

She took the item out. Sapphires, obsidian and rubies. It sparkled in the room's pale light. She shook her head; her voice caught in her throat. 'Nothing . . . nothing will happen to you.'

'Take it.' Charlotte took a ragged breath. 'Be prepared.'

She'd worn it, of course — this butterfly comb — the first time Nancy had met her. And the second. And countless times after that. Though never in London, where she had become someone else as easily as one might change one's clothes.

Nancy arranged her face into a reassuring smile. Nodded. 'You're being silly, you know that?' Her grip on the bag tightened. 'But just to humour you . . .' She slipped it into her skirt pocket, then went back to the bedside, took Charlotte's cold hand in her own, wrapping her fingers around it like a binding. An image came to mind, and she tried to push it away. It was too much. Too much to take in. Because they both knew what was happening.

Charlotte was dying.

Nancy's mind was full. Full of grief. Full of horror. Full of a memory that she would never forget, as long as she lived . . .

Charlotte walking casually towards her across the sloping green lawn of Blackwater Hall . . .

'And the baby?'

'Of course.'

With a grin on her face, her hand in a bandage and a plan up her sleeve . . .

'You'll keep my baby safe?'

'Yes.'

Holding on to Nancy's secret – another miscarriage, another piece of her gone, another forgotten future . . .

'Please?'

Implanting herself into Nancy's heart.

'I will.' And now she was crying, and when the clock behind her chimed, she realised that her tears fell in perfect time . . . *one, two, three.* She counted them, hoping that the very act might calm her in the way that it had calmed Charlotte only hours before. But it didn't. It couldn't. The bells went on and on. Until she realised it was midnight, and a new day was coming. She squeezed her friend's hand. 'Charlotte, I *will* keep your baby safe,' she said.

Charlotte gave her a small smile – as though she thought the world had been put to right and that was the end of the matter – and before Nancy could say any more, before she could shake the girl awake or say *I love you* or scream *Don't go*, she slowly closed her eyes. Dark lashes on pale cheeks. Lips a little parted, as if about to whisper a secret to someone fortunate enough to be party to it. And then she breathed her last breath, long and easy, a final whisper goodbye to a world she'd hardly known.

Behind her, Nancy heard a howl of anguish; a deep and

primal sound that shook her to her bones. She looked towards the doorway, searching for Mrs McLaughlin; angry, mad, boiling to her core that someone Charlotte barely knew would steal this moment. Intrude. Take her death for their own. But as she turned, she caught sight of a wild reflection in the half-open wardrobe door, and she saw that it wasn't Mrs McLaughlin who had howled at all.

It was her.

She closed her mouth and the cry stopped. And when she put her forehead to rest on Charlotte's chest, nestled next to the bundle of new life, she turned her head to the side, her ear pressed against damp cotton, listening for a thumping that was no longer there.

Chapter Fifty

Ballinn, County Kerry

September 2019

Ellie slept fitfully, and each time she woke – either too hot or too cold – Tabby's words whirled in her mind like a pinwheel. If Charlotte had disappeared, pregnant, surely there would be a trace of her – births were recorded, deaths were recorded. She couldn't just be a ghost, a shadow; she must have left an imprint.

By six, she had given up on sleep. She pulled on a thick woollen jumper and equally chunky socks and padded out into the kitchen. As the kettle boiled, she stood by the window and hugged her arms around her body. Just enough darkness lingered to throw back a hint of her reflection. She looked as half awake as the morning outside, where a golden blanket was chasing away the edges of darkness. The sky was almost clear, puffs of cloud suspended in mid-air like the breath at the end of a question. They moved slowly eastward, pushed by a gentle Atlantic wind.

Her phone had chimed twice on the drive up the hill from Tabby's, and she'd pulled the car to the side of the road before she passed the point of reliable reception and disappeared into the wonderful technological black hole of the hills ahead. A message each from Dylan and Jeremy.

Jeremy had asked if she'd done any work on the McCarthy–
Cray case. She grimaced at the way he put it – *Any joy from
your source?* – when she thought of all the trouble that had come
after the tip-off.

She simply replied, *No, no joy.* In truth, she hadn't con-
tacted Maxwell Cray's former secretary – the woman had
disconnected her phone after the *Dubble* blog post went viral
and ignored Ellie's efforts to get in touch. She added, *I'll keep
trying.* And she would. Later.

Her own life had taken a back seat to the welcome distraction of finding Charlotte. Her story was heart-wrenching and
compelling; it would make for a fascinating read, a beautiful
tale. Even without all the answers. A book, perhaps?

But did Charlotte's truth really belong to Ellie?

A click brought her back to the present. The kettle had
boiled and her first hit of caffeine was only minutes away. She
turned to the job in hand: three scoops of coffee in the plunger,
and her favourite mug, large and blue.

The message from Dylan had been a long text apologising
for bringing his mother up at lunch – Ellie almost laughed
at the turn of phrase: *bringing up Mum*, as though she were
the result of an upset tummy – and saying that he was sorry
but that everything had been confused back then, when he'd
blamed her for the miscarriage. That word, as always, sent a jolt
through her veins, flipped the pit of emptiness in her stomach.

It was just so difficult after everything we went through . . .

I felt that you'd retreated . . .

If you had talked more about your grief . . .

Was she was taking some time to think, as she'd said she
would? And would she get back to him, say, within the week
with an answer? At the deadline, she'd shaken her head, cast
the phone aside.

The smell of coffee filled the kitchen and she poured

herself a cup and cradled its warmth. Upstairs the creak of a floorboard told her that Moira was awake. She took out the teapot and refilled the kettle. Waited as slow steps descended the stairs.

'Morning.' Moira looked almost as bad as Ellie felt. Her hair was a tangle, her dressing gown tied skew-whiff, and her slippers – although the same style – were different colours.

'Don't we make a pair?' Ellie said, pulling out a chair, which Moira sank into gratefully. 'Late night?'

'You didn't hear me come in?' Ellie shook her head and put the teapot on the table. Moira smiled. 'You're an angel.'

'I'm not sure about that.'

They sat in companionable silence as the day began to grow. Outside, a robin hopped along the windowsill and paused, looking in at the two women as though he considered them entertainment. When they only stared at him, he moved on.

'Even a bird finds us unappealing this morning,' said Moira, but the smile that flickered across her face gave Ellie a rush of warmth in the cold room.

The previous evening, after taking a moment in the Micra to reread Dylan's message, Ellie had turned off her phone, stepped out of the car and started towards the house. Moira had met her at the door, smelling of perfume and wearing her 'for best' coat.

'I'm off to dinner,' she said as they'd passed like ships in the night. 'I've left you a casserole. And the fire's roaring. There's a bottle of wine in the fridge.'

Ellie was unused to her mum having evening plans. And the barrage of comforts that Moira had listed were highly suspicious. She wore, too, a smear of lipstick – strikingly similarly to Ellie's armour – and a rose of colour on her cheeks. 'Where are you going?'

'Oh . . . out for dinner.'

'So you said.' Ellie had paused on the threshold, blocking
the door.

'Just off to Kenmare for a bite to eat.'

'With?'

'Bernie,' Moira said quickly – too quickly – as she opened
her handbag to look for something that wasn't there.

'Is there an occasion?'

Moira held her hand out for the car keys. 'Sorry, love?'

'Is there an occasion?'

'Oh,' she said, turning sideways to get past her daughter.
'Bernie's been . . . promoted.'

'At the charity shop?'

'Yes,' said Moira carefully. 'She doesn't want anyone to
know. But I thought it might be nice to celebrate.'

Ellie grinned. Stepped aside. 'Have a *lovely* time.'

She thought back to her visit to the charity shop, the afternoon she'd been given the box of books. Bernie had been visibly
horrified by the thought of a promotion. She'd implied that man-
aging Threadbare was about as appealing to her as turned milk.

And Kenmare? A forty-five-minute drive for dinner. A town
full of fine restaurants. No, this was not a date with Bernie.

Now Ellie took a sip of coffee and peered over her cup,
appraising her mum. 'Nice evening?'

Moira flushed. 'Very nice, thank you.'

Ellie waited, but Moira left it at that. 'What did you eat?'

Moira feigned interest in the back of the milk carton. 'Fish.'

'Fish? What kind?'

'Monkfish. It was delicious.' Before Ellie could ask more
questions, Moira said, 'Would you like some eggs?'

Ellie smiled. 'Lovely.' She reflected as she poured her coffee
just how many secrets families held, and that no matter the
intent, they could not stay buried for ever.

❧

Ellie settled down into the comfy sofa at Procaffination. It had appeared since yesterday and was tucked into the back corner of the café, nestled between two towering indoor plants. 'Delivered last night,' said Nils. 'The driver, he turned up late. *Très* late.'

Ellie laughed. Down here on the edge of the ocean, Kerry was often forgotten about. By Dubliners, by politicians, by delivery drivers. It could take a week to receive a parcel from the next county. Nils patted the sofa and waved to – Ellie assumed – the glorious autumn day beyond.

She turned.

And saw a familiar face.

The bell chimed as Milo pushed through the door; hurried steps, a creased brow. His mind in another place. Or time. And Ellie was hit with a sudden realisation that she desired to know where. Or when.

'Oh, hi,' he said, surprise chased away by the ghost of a smile. Nils's eyes flicked between them and he left quickly to busy himself elsewhere.

'Hi.' Ellie was annoyed at the flush that crept up her neck. She was nervous, she reasoned, about telling Milo what she'd discovered.

He pointed to the sofa. 'May I?'

She nodded.

As he sank down next to her, the give of the plump cushions leaned them together. Casually she pushed her unopened laptop to the side, using it as an excuse to reposition herself, legs crossed, elbow piercing the armrest. Friendly but aloof. Two new acquaintances passing the time of day.

'How was Tabby?' said Milo.

'She was . . . formidable.' *Your great-aunt was pregnant.* She wanted to say it but didn't know how.

'And her house?'

She shook her head. 'Unexpected.'

'Old on the outside, young on the inside.'

'Like Tabby.'

He laughed. 'Just like Tabby.'

Nils arrived with coffees, set them down with two macaroons, on the house.

Milo picked up his cup, cradled it for warmth. Or comfort.

'They were lovers, of course,' Ellie said. 'Charlotte and Tomas.'

Was that satisfaction that crossed his face? Pleasure at having played a part in unravelling the mystery? 'It's a nice thought, isn't it? Love crossing boundaries?'

'Yes, I suppose it is.' She hesitated. 'But their love had consequences . . .'

He frowned, and it twisted her stomach in a knot. In her excitement at the afternoon's discoveries, she'd tried to assume ownership over Charlotte's memory, as though she alone had an interest in finding her. When in fact Charlotte wasn't a possession to be found. Kept. She belonged to no one.

Milo put aside his glass, the coffee half gone. 'She was pregnant, wasn't she?'

Ellie nodded, pleased that the words had been taken from her. Pleased that he'd come to the same conclusion as she. 'I'm sorry I didn't call straight away. When I found out.'

He laughed, and Ellie felt the knot in her stomach unravel as though someone had tugged one end of it and, like a shoelace, it had fallen loose. 'I don't need daily reports, El. Don't worry.'

She took a quick breath. Very few people called her that. *El.* It was intimate. But not unwelcome. She took a quick sip of her coffee to hide her confusion and . . . something else? Pleasure? 'So we now know that Charlotte went to London, stayed with your grandmother. Then what?'

His eyes on his coffee, he said, 'What did Tabby think?'

'She didn't know.' Lulled by the warmth of the café and the sweet smell of baking bread, they settled back into the sofa to go over Charlotte's story again. She was an aristocratic rebel who'd fallen in love with the gardener's son. When she found out she was pregnant in 1940, her mother threatened to send her to a Magdalene Laundry. She was certain to lose her child. Tomas went to war, not by his own choice. And Charlotte saw her chance – a new identity, a new life, a child, and the intention to reunite with him once the war was over. She went to London. Sent letters back to Kerry. And then, one day, those letters simply stopped.

'And,' Ellie said, 'there's this.' She took a photo from the back of her notebook. 'The comb. She took it with her when she disappeared. But now it's at Blackwater Hall. She must have returned it at some point.'

Milo frowned. 'How do you know she took it?'

'It was in the garda file.'

'You've got the file?'

She was almost there, almost at the point when she would tell him about 1958. About the manslaughter. Ask him what he thought it meant. But she stopped herself. Thought back to Hattie. The woman knew what had happened; she'd been there and yet she'd said nothing.

'I borrowed it,' she said. 'Charlotte also took a ruby ring and a necklace of pearls, found scattered near the lough.'

He almost smiled. 'I know about those pearls.' He nodded. 'Grandma sold them to pay for Albert's wedding. Hattie told me never to tell him. The horror he would have felt, money from one of Charlotte's possessions . . .'

Ellie raised an eyebrow. 'How much were they worth?'

'A lot.'

Charlotte had sealed the deal by casting aside such a treasure; no one would guess that she would run away and leave behind an item that could set her up for a new life. 'An expensive red herring.'

'And not very subtle.'

'No,' said Ellie, 'but then no one was looking for subtlety. A pregnant Charlotte – a great scandal if it had got out – was gone. And that was all that mattered.'

Milo looked into the middle distance. 'You make my family sound rather cold.' He cleared his throat, his eyes flicking to the clock on the far wall. 'I have to go. House call. Tabby, would you believe?' Ellie wondered whether it was social or professional; the two seemed as thick as thieves. When he stood, she felt an unexpected jolt of disappointment. 'But I'd love to hear more,' he added.

'I'll let you know when—'

'Are you free tonight?'

She paused. She definitely was. But the thought of spending the evening with Milo – the thought of blurring boundaries – made her nervous. She laid her hand on her stomach, as she'd taken to doing. Let her mind linger. 'No,' she lied. 'I'm sorry. I can't tonight. It's . . .' she grappled for a reason, 'Mum's birthday.' *I'm a terrible person.*

'Right,' he said.

She flushed for the second time that day. 'Erm . . .'

'Not a problem.' He smiled professionally. 'Just an idea.'

She ventured, 'Next time?'

'Sure,' he said in a way that made her wonder if there would be. But he added, 'Say happy birthday to your mum for me.'

Moira had only met Milo once before, in passing, in the village. 'I will,' Ellie said with a little too much enthusiasm.

He started to go, then turned back. 'I'm glad it's you looking into the family history. Keep me posted.'

Guilt lay heavy in her stomach. 'Of course.'

Then he said, so casually, so comfortably, 'Thanks, El.' And her heart leapt.

જી

Ellie planned to search the UK parish databases for evidence of Tabby Deenihan. Deaths. Births. Marriages. *Details.* A woman couldn't vanish into thin air; she had to leave a trace.

Caffeine was threading through her veins, focusing her mind. But her thoughts were also being pulled in other directions – how to reply to Dylan, what to do about Jeremy and Davy McCarthy – and, more surprisingly, the regret over declining a date with Milo. Or had it been a date? No. Just a catch-up between friends. Surely?

She opened her email. It was full of the usual junk, which she quickly selected, one after another, and mass-deleted. There were three messages left: one from Dylan, checking in; one from Jeremy, repeating his question (*Any joy with the source?*); and a third from a man called Les Mills, the head archivist at Greenwich Heritage Centre.

Ellie,

Thank you for your question regarding Tabby Deenihan. A bit of background for you:

Explosive munitions factories were split into those that made the material (manufacturing factories) and those that put the manufactured material into shell cases (filling factories). The filling factories tended to take a higher proportion of female workers, hence the large number of photographs of women in places such as the Royal Arsenal standing next to long lines of shell cases stretching far into the distance.

I can't say for sure whether Tabby Deenihan worked there in 1940/41 without visiting the archives, but we are at present digitising thousands of images and I have run a search through the incomplete database. I hope you find the attached files useful.

She clicked on the first attachment. It was a black-and-white photo of six women standing outside a huge brick building. The vintage was immediately apparent by their Mary Jane shoes, their swing coats, the curl of their hair.

The woman at the centre of the picture held a cake with one hand, the other five gathered around her. One girl stood closer than the others. They were smiling and yet the sky behind them was grey and ominous and the ground beneath their feet dark speckled as though it had just begun to rain.

Ellie squinted and zoomed in on the image.

Behind the cake, the unmistakable swell of heavy pregnancy. And that face ... so familiar. The high cheekbones, the tidy nose, that cheeky grin. And yes ... there they were: dimples.

She felt a surge of adrenaline. *Found you.*

Although her hair was dark, the face was unmistakably that of Charlotte Rathmore.

And next to her, another familiar face.

Ellie opened the second file. It was a scan of the back of the photo.

Farewell party for Tabby Deenihan,
attended by colleagues, 29th December 1940

Back L–R: Mabel Hughes, Ivy Alexander, Jennifer Stary, Meredith McCarthy

Front L–R: Tabby Deenihan, Nancy Rathmore

She flicked back to the photo; there they were in black and white. A heavily pregnant Charlotte, and right beside her, the woman who had hidden her, the woman who'd helped her.

Her sister-in-law, Nancy Rathmore.

Chapter Fifty-One

Holborn, London

February 1941

As Nancy stepped out into the street, she didn't know if the haze was inside or outside her head. Her mind was woolly, as if she had just woken. Or perhaps not woken at all.

Mrs McLaughlin had given her no time to understand as she'd pushed her out the door. 'Time is of the essence, Nancy. You *can* save this baby. Don't make the same mistake I did.'

Charlotte is dead.

Charlotte is dead.

Charlotte is dead.

The words echoed in Nancy's head. They were written across her vision and she couldn't blink them away. Couldn't think them away.

The baby was motionless in her arms. She pulled the blanket tighter as she walked the streets, her torch off, her eyes adjusting to the dark. The ground was uneven, strewn with obstacles, and she tripped – tired and confused – through the night.

In the back of her throat, a sob caught. There was a pain deep in her chest, but she knew for certain that if she yielded to the grief, she would never make it to the hospital. She would lie down here on the cold street and the baby – this piece of Charlotte, this treasure – would simply slip away.

She focused on her feet. One in front of the other, her breathing laboured in the icy air. And then a familiar sound, high pitched. Immediately she paused, willed it away, *wished* it away, but it not only remained but grew louder, stronger.

She paused in the shelter of a doorway, switched on her torch and set it lamp-first in the snow. Kneeling down, she pulled the blanket back, gazed at the pale face. She removed a glove, brushed a tiny cheek. It was cold.

'No. No. No,' she cried quietly. 'No, no, no.' She bounced the bundle gently, mimicking Mrs McLaughlin's movements. The baby's eyes opened and she laughed out loud, a sudden rush of adrenaline coursing through her veins. On the other side of the street, a shadow flickered. Someone disappearing in the opposite direction.

It was too cold, far too cold, to carry a newborn like this outside in the snow. She looked at her watch. It would take twenty minutes, if not more, to reach Great Ormond Street Hospital. Did they have that long before the bombs fell?

She turned and focused her attention eastward. No low hum, nothing on the horizon but inky blackness. Pressing back into the doorway, she opened her coat, reached beneath her sweater. The cold air hit her skin like the slap of a thousand rubber bands. She unwrapped the still bundle and placed the naked baby under her blouse. She was fire against the cool body. She pulled her sweater back down, thinking how scratchy it was compared to the place from which the newborn had just come.

She took a deep breath, buttoned up her coat and stepped back out onto the street. She looked heavenward, flakes of snow landing on her eyelashes. 'I'll protect the child,' she whispered, as she moved now with new purpose, her arm around the precious bundle.

She was only five streets from the hospital when it began.

A sound. Growing from a hum to a drone to a roar. A swarm

of bees with a single purpose. After five months, Nancy knew it well. The Luftwaffe was coming. And the bombs would too. She quickened her pace, slipped once, twice, falling to her knees.

Four streets.

But then ahead of her a familiar orange glow, a halo that spread from the skyline to blend with the grey haze of the night.

Three streets.

And the thunderous sound of a hundred bombs. A thousand, perhaps. The ground trembled beneath her feet. And above her, darkness.

Nancy stopped and looked up.

Then saw no more.

Chapter Fifty-Two

Blackwater Hall, County Kerry
April 1958

Tomas recoiled as if struck. His voice was loud, broken. 'She had my baby?'

Mama sidestepped along the wall, moving behind the sofa. She rested her hands on its back. 'Yes, but she died. In childbirth.'

Covering his face with his hands, he gave a cry like a wounded animal. He turned his back to Mama, and Hattie shrank back from her position at the door. 'I don't believe you.'

'I was there.'

The energy in the room changed, from a wildness to a calm stillness, only the roar of heavy rain to fill the silence. He dropped his hands by his sides and took a deep breath. 'You were there?'

Mama's voice was small. 'Yes.'

Down the corridor a door slammed, footsteps stopped in the hallway. Hattie heard the rustling of clothes. Someone removing a coat, most likely sodden from the deluge outside.

'When she came to me in London, she was so afraid. She begged me to keep it a secret. Tomas' – Mama's voice was full of comfort, but her body was rigid and alert – 'she was planning to return to you, when the war was over. But when she didn't hear from you, I assumed you had abandoned her. Had your fun . . .'

'My fun?'

'When we came here, though, when I saw you by the lake . . . I hadn't understood that you cared for her.'

'*Cared* for her?'

'And now I see that it was a mistake not to tell you. But it felt . . . too late. It was the past. Over. Finished.' She spoke in a soft voice as she moved from behind the sofa to stand in front of him.

Hattie dared not move. An angry gust of wind licked down the chimney, sparks flying from the fire. Tomas's left hand flexed and opened, his right brushed the back of his neck, massaging the muscles beneath his shirt collar.

'And our baby? Was it a girl?' He said this with near-forgotten longing.

Mama shook her head.

'She died?'

One tear after another began to drop on Mama's white blouse, large grey marks blossoming where they fell. 'No. It was a boy.'

'A boy?' His right hand dropped heavily by his side.

'He was early, tiny. I'm sorry, but he didn't—'

The room flashed white, then the air cracked, split by the sound of thunder that shook the house to its bones. Tomas moved quickly then. He grabbed Mama by the throat, swung her towards the wall. Hattie screamed. There was a thump from the other end of the corridor. Someone had dropped something. Footsteps followed.

Hattie pushed open the door, ran towards Mama.

'Did he survive?' Tomas demanded as Mama batted at his hands. 'My boy?'

Hattie grabbed him by the shirt. 'Stop!' she screamed. 'Stop!'

He released one hand from Mama's neck and pushed Hattie away without looking. She stumbled. Fell backwards, the wind knocked from her lungs. She rolled to one side, gasping.

The footsteps were close now. From where she lay on the floor, Hattie saw feet. Large feet, loose socks. She would always recall them as red, but in fact they were blue.

'Where. Is. He?' Tomas had lifted Mama from her feet.

Hattie began to push herself up.

Mama's eyes fluttered and focused momentarily. They looked behind Tomas, to the figure beyond. They opened wide with surprise. With relief.

With love.

'Where. Is. My. Son?'

'He's here,' she whispered, and closed her eyes.

Chapter Fifty-Three

Ballinn, County Kerry
September 2019

Ellie's finger hovered over her phone. She should call Jules, and yet the discovery that Charlotte was still in London by the end of December 1940 wasn't so much as a revelation as a confirmation of her suspicion. But he did owe her a round at Sheehan's, and breakfast already felt like yesterday.

He picked up on the fourth ring, the sound of wind roaring in her ear.

'Ellie,' he said brightly. 'What news?'

She paused and looked outside. The day remained beautiful – a spattering of cloud, breathless air, a gasp of sunshine that had escaped the summer. 'Where are you?'

'Riding to the village.'

She imagined him pedalling the fixed-gear, some sort of inappropriately light-coloured attire flapping in the breeze. 'I'm at Procaffination – meet me here when you arrive?' Waiting only for a noise of affirmation, she hung up.

She turned back to the laptop and looked once again at the photo before her. It both answered questions and raised them, but she didn't know which was more important.

Charlotte had taken the job at the factory and Nancy had joined her. It seemed almost infeasible that Nancy – who had risen from foster care to marry well and, according to Hattie, begin her own career – would take on a role as a canary girl. And yet Charlotte had. But the latter was out of desperation, or obligation. What were Nancy's reasons?

The body language between the two women was warm. Certainly, the photo from the summer party of 1939 gave the impression that they were . . . sharing a secret? Planning a subterfuge? In cahoots? And in fact – Ellie thought of the bandage on Charlotte's hand – they were. This photo at the factory, too, showed them to be very close. Nancy holding Charlotte's hand. The younger woman's head turned slightly towards her sister-in-law, smiling through the shadows of fatigue that lay under her eyes. She looked heavily pregnant and must have been close to her time. Ellie counted on her fingers. How far gone could she have been when she ran from Ireland? Two and a half or three months? That seemed plausible. Not much less – she would have had no way of being sure – and yet much more than that and she would have begun to show.

So she was due in February. Late January at a push.

At the sound of a clunk, Ellie looked up. Jules had leaned his bike against the window and now blustered through the café door, letting in a breath of cool air, a healthy flush to his cheeks. 'You were quick,' she said.

He slapped his leg. 'Thighs like steel.'

She raised her eyebrows. 'Cappuccino?'

'No, the good stuff, I think.' He waved a tea pantomime to Nils, then pulled off his jacket to reveal yet another argyle jumper, this time with diamonds of purple and black. She had to admire his persistence.

'You owe me lunch.'

Jules sat heavily. 'That's good news – the Heritage Centre got back?'

Ellie nodded and turned her laptop to face him.

He squinted. 'Who *is* that?'

'Charlotte.'

Jules put his hand to his mouth. 'But . . . but . . .'

'She's pregnant. Yes.' Ellie told him what she'd learned from Tabby the day before. Told him about the etching on the arbour.

They sat in silence as Jules considered the news. Then, 'But her *hair* . . . Tabby had dark hair as a girl?'

She recalled the summer party photo: Tabby standing in the back row, dark hair just visible under her cap. 'It's a disguise of sorts.'

He frowned. 'That woman holding her hand . . .'

'Nancy Rathmore. It appears they worked together.' Ellie pointed to the image of the photo's description: *Farewell party for Tabby Deenihan, attended by colleagues.*

Nils arrived with coffee and a teapot. He placed the latter down in front of Jules, and added a strainer, a pot of steaming milk and a saucer of sliced lemon.

Jules rubbed his hands – slightly pink from the fresh air – and peered into the pot. A lively, sweet scent emanated from it. He added lemon and offered Ellie his milk. She waved it away. 'So,' he said, 'the question is, where did Charlotte have the baby?'

'London, presumably.'

He looked thoughtful. 'During the war, pregnant women were evacuated out of the cities into makeshift maternity hospitals in the countryside.'

'Sounds stressful.'

'I think,' he said, 'in some instances it was.' Ellie tried to imagine being away from family and friends for the birth of a child. Being in a place you didn't know, with people you'd never met. It sounded unsettling, uncomfortable. Terrifying. 'Many women didn't go. It was their choice, after all. But,' he said, taking a sip of his tea, 'it was a risk to stay.'

'Why?'

'The German bombs for one thing.' He leaned forward to check the image of the photo's reverse. 'Charlotte's baby was born sometime after December 1940: January, February? Bang in the middle of the Blitz. Pardon my choice of words.'

'Yes, I see.'

'And the crowding for another – plenty of casualties, not enough doctors, very few midwives.'

'How do you know all this?'

'My grandmother lived in London during the war. My father would have been nine or ten when he was evacuated to Devon. Didn't see his parents for years. It had a significant effect on their relationship. But Grandma liked to regale us kids with tales of hardship. Mostly when we wouldn't finish our dinner. She was fanatical about waste.'

'And your grandfather?'

'Fought and never returned.'

Ellie was filled with sadness. So many lives taken by war, their loss rippling through the generations. And even those who returned had been taken in their own way. *Damaged*, as Hattie had said.

'But,' Jules continued, 'now it's simple. Now we find the birth of a Deenihan child in the United Kingdom in 1941.'

Blow away the hay. 'Okay.' Ellie picked up her laptop and placed it on her knees. She opened a search engine and typed in *birth records UK*.

'I have a friend at the General Records Office,' said Jules. 'He's very high up. I once took a case for him – messy divorce – and if I do say so myself, it came out rather in his favour . . .'

Ellie scrolled down to a genealogy website. Clicked on it, then typed *Deenihan 1941* into the search bar. 'Ouch,' she said under her breath. 1,402 results. *Not great.*

'. . . a situation with a wandering wife, I'm afraid. The chap was very upset. Never recovered . . .'

She scrolled down the page, then frowned and clicked *Advanced Search*. The default time frame was set to plus-or-minus ten years. She changed this to zero and hit *Search* once again. This time 153 results were returned. All displaying the date 1941. Better.

'. . . I kept in touch with him all these years – we meet annually at the Caledonian – and the long and short of it is . . .'

Ellie flicked through the results, page after page. Deaths were listed, as well as births, baptisms and burials. To the left of the screen she found a filter. She clicked *Births & Baptisms*. Pressed enter. 52 results. Much better.

'. . . I think I hold enough sway to have him look into birth records during the war.'

She scrolled down the first page of results. Skipped to page two. There were no Deenihans, only Dinihans, Denihams and Deenihams. The results encompassed surnames *like* Deenihan, but not *only* Deenihan.

Jules had paused, and when Ellie paid him no attention, he said, 'What're you doing?'

'Looking for the birth of Charlotte's child.'

A blank stare.

She put the computer on the table. 'I'm on a genealogy site . . . I'm searching for Deenihan births in 1941.' She let Jules blink twice, then continued. 'There were fifty-two births in 1941 for the surnames Deenihan, Dinihan, Deniham and Deeniham.'

'There were?'

'Yes,' she said. 'I'll see if I can narrow it down.'

She opened the search box once again and sandwiched the surname between quotation marks, then hit enter.

A pink bar appeared across the screen.

Sorry, we could not find any results matching your search criteria within Births & Baptisms. Please try modifying them or try selecting a different event.

'Perhaps she was nearer to her time than we thought?' said Jules, still looking with awe at the web page in front of them.

She changed the search date to 1940.

No results.

'Aargh,' she growled, pulling her hands through her hair. The coffee was making her agitated. Or perhaps it wasn't just the coffee. 'This friend of yours at the records office . . .'

'Yes?'

'Do you have his number?'

'I'll call him tonight.'

Ellie felt the fire in her belly splutter and fizz. Such progress, and now a dead end. Charlotte, right there in 1940, heavily pregnant, close to her time. Within reach. And now she'd disappeared once again, washed down a whirlpool of time. A shadow, and yet so very real.

She put her head in her hands. Her right temple was beginning to throb. She'd come so far, felt so close. And yet when it came down to it, Charlotte had been determined to disappear. From her life, from her fears, from her family.

Her family.

A jolt ran through her. She leaned over the laptop and typed a new surname: *Rathmore.* Then hit enter.

She frowned, squinted. She couldn't believe what she was seeing. But then of course she *could* believe it.

It was obvious.

Your search has returned 1 result.

She turned the screen to Jules. He started to say something. Stopped. Started again.

Then, as though someone had removed the speck of grit that clogged the cogs of his mind, he said, 'My God.'

'Yes,' said Ellie, 'my God indeed.'

Chapter Fifty-Four

St Thomas' Hospital, London

February 1941

Heaven smelled like toast. That cocooning aroma of bread browned to perfection, slathered in butter and covered with a thick layer of jam. Strawberry perhaps, or raspberry. It was a smell to live with forever. Warm, homely, a simple pleasure.

And the afterlife was full of sounds. Unexpected noises. The gentle murmur of voices. Whispers. The clang of metal on metal, followed by an almost apologetic shuffling. The quiet sound of busyness.

She moved her toes a little. They were there, she could feel them, wiggling in the softness that one would expect of heaven. She was perfectly warm, perfectly comfortable. But wait, no, what was that? A new sound . . . or feeling? The pulse of a steam train, perhaps. A rhythmic drumming. Footsteps, getting closer. Louder now. Stronger.

She groaned, then there was a pressure on her arm. The throb was *inside* her head. It began to clear, like fog in sunshine.

'You're safe. Shh . . .' a voice said. It was gentle, female, young. 'You're safe.'

It murmured once again and the throb – the train, the drumming, the footsteps that had entered her head – turned away and disappeared. Into the distance. Into the darkness. Into warm and welcome oblivion.

ह

When Nancy opened her eyes, Heaven was bathed in low light. She blinked once. Twice. Three times. She held her hand up in front of her face. It was there, for sure. But it was just a shadow, or rather, the opposite of a shadow, its pale form standing proud in the dim around it.

Footsteps to her right.

'You're awake, that's wonderful.' It was the voice again. She looked towards the sound; there was a shape in front of her.

Nancy tried to say, 'I can't see.' But her voice cracked.

'You're in St Thomas' Hospital, you're underground. You're just fine. A bang to the head, a shock,' said the voice, and Nancy felt pressure on her hand. She almost pulled away, a reflex. Fingers slid around hers. 'You're fine,' the voice repeated.

Nancy blinked again. Began to see. Two eyes, dark brown. A smile. A hat, white. She tried to pull herself into a sitting position and the hand let go, came behind her, propped her up. 'That's it.'

'Thank you,' said Nancy in a half-whisper. There was a ward around her now, a dozen other beds. People in bandages. People asleep. People eating.

She frowned, as though making such a face might chase away the remaining fog. Might bring back a memory of why she was here.

'You were lucky,' said the nurse. She was beautiful. Early twenties at most. And hands as soft as silk. As soft as Charlotte's. 'Both of you.'

Nancy tilted her head to the side. *Both of you.* She looked at the nurse, and her gaze rested on the small bed beside her. A cot. A bundle there within.

A memory shifted. Charlotte surrounded by blood. Her cold hands reaching out. *You must protect this child.* The walk in the snow. The sound of the sirens. The murmuration overhead. The darkness. The nothing.

'He was hungry,' said the nurse. 'He's slept all morning.'

Nancy nodded, the small movement enough to send a throb to her temple. She couldn't take her eyes away from the bundle beside her, the rise and fall, the tiny nose protruding between hat and blanket. Charlotte's baby boy . . . alive.

Protect this child. 'Can I?' She looked at the nurse. 'Can I hold him?'

The nurse nodded, turning to pick up the bundle.

He was warmer than she expected. And somehow heavier, as though he'd drunk his weight in milk. She peered down at his face, searching for signs of Charlotte.

'He's an orphan now,' she said. The heavy feeling in her eyes threatened to overflow and, when it did, two tears dropped from her chin onto the sleeping child's cheek. Spring rain on a peach. 'My sister-in-law . . . Charlotte. So young. The blood . . .' She lifted one hand and wiped her face, tried to speak more slowly, but the heaving of her chest threatened to escape. 'I wanted to save her . . . Charlotte . . . I was all she had.'

The nurse sat gently on the bed beside her and leaned in to look at the boy. 'It is a difficult time to be born,' she said. 'He's a miracle. A miracle boy.' She smiled, a shimmer in her eyes.

'A miracle,' Nancy repeated, gazing at him. She tucked a wayward hair behind her ears. Considered what a fright she must look. 'What will happen to him?'

'His birth needs to be registered.'

Nancy nodded. 'And then?' His little arm pushed its way out of the blanket. She took his hand; his grip was strong.

'He'll be sent to the country.'

'I can take him.'

'I'm sorry, that wouldn't be allowed.' The nurse continued after a beat too long, 'But I promise you he'll be safe.'

Nancy thought about her own childhood: the orphanage, the rotating foster families. Safe but alone. She traced a finger over the curve of his forehead. 'Don't worry, little one,' she said, her voice cracked from the pain of it, from the memory of it. She looked at the woman in front of her. 'I was an orphan too.'

There was a call from across the room. A groan of pain, of urgency. The nurse squeezed Nancy's shoulder. 'When the doctor arrives, I'll have to report this.'

Nancy touched the baby's cheek. His tiny lips pulled apart and he yawned, wide enough to reveal a pale pink teardrop dangling at the back of his throat. His hat was too big for him, sliding down over his eyes, and she removed it to reveal a shock of dark hair.

At that moment, he squirmed and leaned into her, his cheek pressed to her breast. He opened his eyes. And Nancy fell in love.

❧

Hours later, she walked quickly through the streets. Resisted the temptation to glance over her shoulder. It wasn't quite mid-afternoon and yet she felt that she had been gone for an age.

Around her vehicles moved slowly through the debris: makeshift ambulances, army trucks, the occasional ambitious bus picking its way along altered routes from one end of the city to another. She felt eyes on her, and yet no one was looking.

The snow had almost melted and a weak sun shone down from a clear blue sky. The biting chill had been replaced by the kind of wet cold that seeped into bones. Last night's raids had been incessant, and those being carted away weren't just injured; many were hypothermic from waiting as the rescue crews worked to shift the surrounding debris.

'Normally,' the nurse had said, 'we'd try to keep you in for a few days, but as you can see . . .' She waved a hand around the ward. The floor space was filled with camp beds.

Behind a curtain around her bed, Nancy was getting dressed. 'I understand.'

Her coat had a streak of dried blood down the front – hers, she supposed, from the cut in her hairline – and it was rough against her hand as she ran it across her body, checking she was all still there. There was something hard in the pocket of her skirt. She slipped her hand inside, felt the cool surface of Charlotte's butterfly comb.

'There's also a shift change shortly,' said the nurse, 'and that can be the best time to get moving.'

Nancy nodded again. The nurse had been nice to her. Kind. She had been subtle in taking away the boy, putting him with the other babies in the nursery.

She smoothed the coat tightly around her, then pulled the curtain aside. 'I suppose . . . I suppose I'll need to sign something?'

The nurse nodded. From her pocket she withdrew a yellow piece of paper. It was thin, one side jagged as though ripped from a raffle book.

Nancy held out her hand and took it.

Across the hallway there was a cry. She looked up. A woman walked towards them, a bundle in her hands. She smiled when she saw Nancy. 'This is her?' She had a look of expectation about her, as though Nancy might perform some miracle. 'What a night you've had. We'd keep you in, only . . .' She too waved her hand around the ward. 'Abby will sort you out. Put you on the register. Are you sure you're fine to leave?'

Nancy looked at her with confusion.

'She's just fine, aren't you, Nancy?' said the nurse – Abby – with tenderness.

Nancy nodded, looked down at her hands.

Abby took the baby from the woman and waved her away.

Now Nancy was almost at Parker Street. She was tiring. Perhaps it had been a mistake to leave the hospital so soon. And yet it had seemed like the best thing. To avoid delays. To avoid questions. She stopped for a breather. A man paused to ask if she was well. She pulled back from him a little and said she was, thank you. He moved on, shaking his head.

In the hospital, Abby had handed her a pen, and Nancy had looked at the paper in her hand.

Register of birth.

A date had been filled in: *5th February 1941.* And the place: *St Thomas' Hospital.* It shook in her hand, that piece of paper, suddenly heavy, as though it were made of gold.

'I just need you to fill in the rest,' Abby said efficiently, betrayed only by her nervous smile.

A sheen had formed on Nancy's brow, and under the coat she felt her stomach quicken, a little tic where once her own baby would have been. She placed her hand on it softly, as though willing what was once there to return.

'How is this possible?' she asked.

A doctor was moving down the ward, checking patients, exhaustion plastered on his face. Abby smiled in a small way, said quickly, 'All I need is for you to fill in the names.'

Nancy laid the paper on the bedside table and gazed at the empty boxes, outlined in red, waiting to be filled.

The boy in the nurse's arms squirmed a little, cooed. He was so tiny, so alone. He was a miracle, wasn't he? A Rathmore. He might even grow to look like Teddy. And yet he was a piece of Charlotte. *Protect this child.*

Abby had said, 'Quickly.'

The breath Nancy had taken was so deep it hurt, her lungs expanding to fill the empty hollow in her chest, a cavity that had been worn away by grief and sorrow. She began to write. Mother's name. Father's name. Father's occupation. She paused, looked up. 'Abby . . . that's short for?'

'Alberta.' The doctor was moving closer. 'My mother was Italian, God rest her.' She said, 'I need you to give me the form. Go now. I'll handle this.'

Nancy nodded, took the boy with her left hand and with her right scrawled a name on the paper. Handed it over. 'Thank you.' She struggled to say the words, to make them real. 'I'll cherish him for ever. I'll do anything for him. I'll do everything for him.'

Abby leaned in and stroked the boy's cheek. The whites of her eyes shimmered, though she appeared determined to will her emotions away. She looked down at the paper in her hands, at the name Nancy had scrawled there in haste. She closed her eyes, smiled. When she opened them, a tear dropped to her cheek.

Nancy turned into High Holborn. Or was it? She retraced her steps. Turned once more. Confused, she looked around for a familiar feature. There: Hodges' Bookshop, its front window smashed, a handwritten sign, *Open as usual*. She turned the corner and stopped.

Number 28b Parker Street had been replaced with a hole the size of a house. But even as she stood there, her world gone, she didn't feel alone. She hugged Albert tighter and walked towards the rubble.

Chapter Fifty-Five

Blackwater Hall, County Kerry

April 1958

'He's here,' Mama repeated, looking over Tomas's shoulder.

Albert. She meant Albert. Albert was here.

He stepped forward, picked up the poker. And this scene, this moment, would never leave Hattie; it would stay with her for the rest of her life, replayed in slow motion, over and over. In her head. In her heart. Albert's face, a mixture of fear and determination. His momentary pause, indecision.

Mama's arms dropped loosely to her sides, her head rolled forward. And Albert decided. He moved swiftly, swinging the poker like a cricket bat. Whether he was aiming for Tomas's head, Hattie would never know. There was a sharp crack, the sound of breaking bone. Like the sacks of potatoes he had once heaved over his shoulder, Tomas fell to the ground.

Released, Mama slid down the wall, her hands clasped at her neck, gasping for air. A fish out of water.

'Mama,' Albert said, dropping the poker with a dull thud. As he knelt next to her and took her in his arms, his gaze hovered somewhere across the room until, perhaps for the first time, he noticed Hattie. He locked eyes with her, his forehead furrowed, his eyes green under dark brows. And in the cushioned light of the grey day, she remembered something. That morning by the lake; the burned pier, the gunshot. The gorse sprig, and the man who'd held it. When Tomas had first turned to her, he'd looked like a green-eyed Marlon Brando. But scruffier. Handsome under his weathered face. She'd thought she recognised him.

And now she knew why.

⁊❧

When the gardaí arrived, the poker was gone, thrown in the same lough where Charlotte was supposed to be. Mama said that Tomas had stolen from her. Had become angry when she confronted him. That he'd attacked her.

She'd pushed him, she said, hard away from her, and he'd hit his head on the green marble mantelpiece and fallen to the ground like a sack of potatoes. She used those words, *a sack of potatoes.* Just like Hattie had imagined it.

'My daughter was the only witness.'

When the gardaí had talked to Hattie – in the blue room, away from the blood-splashed carpet of the library – she could see Albert outside, sitting on the edge of the woodland. The thunderstorm had rolled on and the lake's surface shimmered with movement as the mountain streams poured in. Hattie repeated what she'd been told to say, Mama hovering behind the garda as he gently asked her questions.

'Was Tomas angry?'

'Yes.'

'Did Tomas hold your mammy around the neck?'

'Yes.'

They looked to Mama, who had set her face in a grim expression, her lips pursed together as though she was worried that something might escape from between them. The red marks on her neck were turning purple, the outline of fingers just visible at the edges.

'Do you think your mammy was frightened?'

Hattie had nodded. Really, she wanted to scream, but nothing would come out. She looked at her hands, and although they were clean, she wiped at her palms with fury.

When the garda asked if anyone else was in the house when it happened, Mama said, 'My daughter's had quite a shock; is this really necessary?' and at that moment Papa had arrived and taken charge and Hattie was bundled away to the kitchen, where Cook had sat her down with a hot milk that was so sweet it tasted like syrup.

And now, as she sipped her drink, a shiver rippled through her body. She thought back to the frantic aftermath, to the whispered discussion between Albert and Mama. His despair. Her determination. She'd taken his face in her hands and said, 'You are my son, I'd do anything for you. No one will take you away from me.'

Albert had paused, his face blank, all the colour gone from his cheeks. His eyebrows had drawn together, compressing the skin between them in light furrows; an expression that Hattie found, over the years, never left him. He was gripping his hands as though he was worried about what they might do next. When she tried to lay a hand on his arm, he backed off as if struck, then his face softened, only a little, and he nodded at her. 'I'm sorry.'

As Albert left the room, Mama had picked up the comb and set it beside Tomas. She closed her eyes, and two tears spilled from their edges. Never – not then, not ever – did she ask Hattie who had given it to him. But Hattie would know, would remember for the rest of her life. Would carry the knowledge for ever.

And the guilt.

Mama took a deep breath, walked back to the sofa and picked up a piece of paper. The letter.

'Is Albert my brother?' said Hattie, who had stood unmoving as Mama moved around her.

Without meeting her gaze, Mama said, 'Yes, he's your brother.' She tucked the letter into her novel, then, walking slowly to the middle of the bookcase, slid it into a gap on the very top shelf. 'You must never tell him otherwise.' She held out her hand. 'Come here.'

As they left the library, left Tomas, left a piece of her behind, Hattie glanced up at the place where the book had been put.

The ABC Murders by Agatha Christie.

At the kitchen table, Cook wept silently beside her. Tomas was gone, and Hattie's life would never be the same again.

Chapter Fifty-Six

Holborn, London

February 1941

Nancy walked slowly to where her front door had once been. Three men in blue uniforms were clearing debris. She asked, 'Are there any survivors?' but from their unhurried movements she already knew the response.

They shook their heads. 'We found a lady and child, probably from the top floor.' The man who replied looked exhausted, his face covered in dust and grime. He coughed, then apologised, and they looked at each other for a moment, surely – Nancy thought – thinking how ridiculous it was to apologise for a cough in the middle of a war.

She sat by the side of the road and waited. For what, she didn't know. Shortly, there was a call from the men. Two bodies had been uncovered. She didn't need to look, but she wanted to. And there they were. Charlotte, wrapped in a woollen blanket, her face unmarked and peaceful. And the shape of Mrs McLaughlin, carefully covered.

When the men asked for their names, Nancy said it was Mrs McLaughlin from the ground floor and her niece who had been visiting from Edinburgh. Tabatha Deenihan. Only nineteen years old. She wept as she said it, her tears taken for sadness rather than deep, soul-piercing grief.

৯৯

Later, as she was sifting through the debris, Nancy picked up Teddy's favourite glass; unbroken, unchipped, pristine. She found Charlotte's money, hidden in a biscuit tin. She discovered the charred remains of her own bed and the smashed wooden box she had only last night opened to search for blankets as Charlotte bled to death giving birth to her son. Some items were completely destroyed, others almost untouched, as though they'd been placed there and sprinkled with a thick layer of dust. From underneath a fragment of their kitchen table she pulled out her box of letters. From Teddy. From Charlotte. She opened it, took out the top one and for the first time in almost six months began to read: *My dearest T* . . .

A single tear rolled down her cold cheek and she nestled Albert closer. It was afternoon already; she needed to find somewhere to stay, get some help, feed the boy. She gathered the belongings in the suitcase she found under Charlotte's bed, and marvelled at how little she cared for all the inanimate things she'd lost. Things that she'd once thought made a home.

She picked up the suitcase and ran her eye over the chaos left behind. Less than twenty-four hours before, she and Charlotte had been sitting on the sofa – which she'd found half flattened under the bath – huddled together, laughing about Big Bertha the midwife.

She stumbled back onto the street. Light-headedness overtook her and she suddenly realised how hungry she was. Despite the pervasive smell of food at the hospital, she'd not eaten since last night. And Albert needed milk.

She could retreat to Holborn station, but she might be recognised. The February sun was sinking low in the western sky, and she turned that way, towards the city centre. There was a shelter not half a mile away. They'd be safe there.

She squinted into the glare, one hand clutching Albert, the other holding tightly on to everything she owned in the world. It wasn't much, but it was more than enough.

Figures walked back and forth across the street. Mr Hodges came out and removed his shop sign; another day over, even though the debris of last night's bombs still smoked in the street.

Footsteps behind her. Three women passed, asked if she was all right. She said *yes, thank you* in the way they all did these days, with a thin veil of mistruth. The women carried on, arm in arm, their eyes drawn by a soldier walking down the street. They giggled at him, but his head didn't turn. He was looking ahead. Only ahead.

His face was obscured by the glare, but Nancy felt his eyes on her. Staring. Her heart had stopped, she was sure of it. It had ceased beating in her chest. Then, with a thump, it started again, so loudly that she dropped the suitcase on the ground in surprise. Something inside it shattered. The glass, she realised. The glass that she'd kept safe all this time. Teddy's glass.

She recognised his gait now: strong, purposeful. It quickened. Then he was running. Running towards her with a desperate need.

Her vision blurred, and for just a moment she thought the effects of the bang to her head were back. But no. It wasn't that. Something hot ran down her face. Tears. So many tears.

Only when he was right there – one step away – did she see his face. Those dark eyes, that blond hair licking out from beneath a hat that was, just now, being thrown from his head and away from them towards the debris of their home on the fringe of the shattered street.

He called her name and took her in his arms. His familiar face was warm as it nestled into her neck. She wailed, her legs buckling beneath her, his arms catching her. Albert cocooned

between them. And as Teddy held them close, one hand on
her, one on his son, he murmured, 'We'll always be together.
From now. For always.'

And she knew it was true.

Chapter Fifty-Seven

Dublin

September 2019

Ellie paused outside the Pickled Oyster. It was a mizzly Monday morning in Dublin and the city swirled around her like the edges of a maelstrom; she at its centre, idle, still. It struck her that the last time she'd entered this building, her mind had been full of Dylan and her crumbling life; now, only a week later, she was back with a new focus, a new confidence and, for the first time in as long as she could remember, a flicker of hope in her heart.

Over the weekend, she had called Hattie to tell her that progress had been made in the Charlotte case. She'd almost laughed at her own description, *the Charlotte case*, as though she were heading up an investigation. Hattie had first sounded taken aback, then asked if they could discuss it over the phone. Ellie had said she'd prefer to meet.

There was no one to greet her in the foyer. But when she looked into the restaurant, it was a hive of activity: tables being laid, a crackling fire, the lingering scent of furniture polish mixed with rich roasting aromas. The room was bathed in light, the atmosphere completely different from the intimacy and calm of her previous visit.

Ellie had hidden away at the farm for four days. She hadn't

ventured into Ballinn for fear of running into Milo. She'd thought he should be the first to know, but Jules had convinced her otherwise. Hattie should be told, and *she* would tell Milo. That was the right thing to do.

But Ellie had a secondary motivation for meeting Harriet face to face. A pregnant aristocrat in 1940s Ireland, her desire to disappear, the implications of her actions. A treatise on Irish society's treatment of women and the lengths to which women went to escape it. She wanted permission to write Charlotte's story.

She caught the attention of a waiter as he bustled past, a tray of gleaming cutlery balanced expertly on his palm. 'Is Harriet in?'

He paused, looked at her. That bright white smile such a contrast to his dark skin. His hair immaculately combed. A red carnation in his top pocket. 'Eleanor,' he said, '*bienvenue*. Welcome back.'

Hattie had been right: the man had a memory for faces. And, it seemed, names. She paused momentarily.

'Armand,' he prompted.

'Armand,' she said, trying to lock his name away. 'It's busy in here; sorry to interrupt.'

He looked about him as if in surprise. 'Just another sitting,' he said. He swung the tray in a swooping arc and placed it on the table beside them. 'I'll let Ms Walker know you're here.'

'Thank you.'

She leaned awkwardly against a booth. A dozen staff flitted here and there and she marvelled at how, in a couple of hours, the whole place would settle into calm clockwork, the rushed preparation just the faint flicker of a memory.

Hattie appeared from the swing doors looking relaxed. She smiled to the staff as she passed, reassuring them with a wave of her hand that she wasn't there to inspect, only to breeze through.

'Ellie.' Today her hair was piled on her head. It was a youthful do that somehow suited her. They embraced. The scent of warm bread lingered on her skin.

Before Ellie could say anything, Hattie said, 'I need coffee. But somewhere else.' She started towards the door. 'Shall we?'

❧

'So,' said Hattie, an espresso untouched in front of her, 'I take it you've dug up the great family secret?'

Ellie put her coffee down. She hadn't expected this. For four nights she'd considered how she might tell Hattie, explain to her what she'd found.

'You're adopted, aren't you?'

Hattie smiled, touched her hair. 'The first redhead in the family.'

'Nancy – your mother – couldn't have children.' Ellie said this quietly, softly. Afraid to offend the woman sitting before her. But she needn't have worried. Hattie shook her head and sighed. It was an exhale of air that threw with it a thousand emotions, but none of them were sadness.

'Being adopted didn't make any difference to me,' she said. 'I knew I wasn't my parents' biological daughter even before we went to Blackwater Hall. It wasn't a family secret. Mama always insisted that they were my true parents, that Albert was my true brother. To her, blood and love were the same thing.'

Ellie's heart tugged. For Hattie, for Albert. And for Nancy, who had held on to her children with everything she had.

'Hattie . . .'

'Ask what you're going to ask.' Her directness made Ellie think of Tabby; the secret she'd kept all those years. The two were similar, which was ironic really, considering what she'd discovered.

Ellie put down her coffee, used her spoon to stir it, although she hadn't added sugar. She thought back to that moment in Procaffination when she'd typed the name *Rathmore* into the search bar.

Your search has returned 1 result

Albert Rathmore

Born 5th February 1941

She had known immediately what it meant, because in the photo from the Royal Arsenal taken only six weeks earlier, Charlotte was heavily pregnant.

And Nancy Rathmore was not.

She leaned forward, said gently, 'Albert was Charlotte's son, wasn't he?'

'Yes.'

'And Charlotte died in childbirth?'

Hattie looked surprised. 'How did you know?'

After finding Albert's birth record, Ellie had searched for Deenihan *deaths*. And now that she had a date, everything was clear. She'd narrowed it down to Albert's birth date. Fifth of February 1941: the death of one Tabatha Deenihan. In a few succinct sentences, she told Hattie what she'd found. As she spoke, a heavy rain thrummed on the café windows, washing down in willowy streams and distorting the people outside into a kaleidoscope of figures.

When she'd discovered that Charlotte had died that night in February nearly eighty years before, Ellie had felt such an unexpected sense of overwhelming loss, she couldn't speak. She'd put her hand to her mouth and shaken her head, tried to imagine what had happened. Jules had watched her with concern, let the silence linger between them. Put a hand on her own. 'Oh, Ellie,' he'd said, as though Charlotte had just faded away right there in her arms. At that very moment. Closed those dark doe-like eyes and never again reopened them. 'It doesn't seem fair,' she'd said, putting her free hand to her chest and letting out a sob. Then Nils was there, turmeric latte in hand. 'For the stress?' she'd said with a half-smile. But he'd shaken his head. 'No, Ellie. Just for you.'

'I see,' said Hattie, when Ellie had explained the online records.

'Tomas – the estate gardener – he found out, didn't he?'

A ripple of worry crossed Hattie's features. 'What do you mean?' she said sharply.

'The confrontation with your mum. In the library at Blackwater Hall.' Ellie reached into her bag. 'I have the file.'

'Don't.' Hattie put her hand up, palm outward. 'Please, leave it there.'

Ellie nodded, slid the folder back into the safety of her satchel. 'You were there, weren't you?'

For a moment Hattie didn't answer. Absent-mindedly she ran her finger around the rim of her espresso cup, then, as though she'd just returned to the present and realised she was being observed, she quickly withdrew it. 'Yes,' she said. 'It was' – her gaze was somewhere in the distance – 'an extremely difficult thing for a child to witness.'

'I'm sorry.'

She took a deep breath, making eye contact now with Ellie. 'After that, of course, they shipped me off to boarding school.' She smiled, although the joy didn't reach her eyes.

Ellie was reminded of their previous meeting, when Hattie had mentioned knowing someone who'd been damaged by the war, just like her uncle Hugo. 'How well did you know Tomas?'

Hattie smiled in a small way. 'Tomas and I . . . we became friends, as unlikely as that sounds. A man near to his forties, a girl not yet a teenager. He was a gentle soul. But even when we first met, I could see there was a darkness in him. Not a natural malevolence, but something that had been left by war.

And it was triggered whenever he considered the things he'd lost.'

'You mean Charlotte?'

'What?'

'He lost Charlotte. They were lovers.'

'Who told you that?'

'Tabby Ryan. His sister. He was the father of Charlotte's child, wasn't he? Albert's biological father.'

Hattie looked torn. She began to say something, then stopped. 'Before I answer,' she said, 'can I ask what you're going to do with this information?'

Ellie smiled in a way that she hoped was open, friendly. The kind of expression that instilled confidence. Trust. 'This story . . . it captures the imagination.' Hattie tilted her head, her eyes on the younger woman. It was a calculating look. Ellie didn't like it. 'Particularly after the referendum on the Eighth Amendment. The Tusla scandals. Women went to great lengths to protect themselves. Back then,' she placed her hand on her stomach, 'and now. Nancy's lost babies, and what she was willing to do to be a mother. The guilt she must have felt, the anguish. About keeping Albert, but also the miscarriages. Unfounded guilt, but nonetheless real to her.' The reasons rolled off her tongue.

Hattie said nothing.

'I would very much like to record the story.'

The older woman took a deep breath.

'To write a book.'

Hattie leaned forward. 'No, Ellie, I'm afraid I can't allow that.'

Ellie willed herself not to flush. She bit her tongue.

'I'm sorry. But no.' Hattie placed her hand on her breastbone. 'I'm not thinking of myself – it means very little to me – but I worry what it would do to Albert. You know, I assume, about his superstitions?' Ellie wanted to say *and this would change everything for him*, but Hattie continued, 'And there are implications for Milo's future.'

Ellie frowned. 'Milo?'

'*Heirs male of the body lawfully begotten*. Albert was illegitimate.' This next she said with consideration: 'My father was the last legitimate heir in the whole family tree. The information gives Milo a chance to dissolve the peerage. And yet . . .'

'And yet?'

'There's a certain irony, isn't there? If Milo claims the title, it will have arrived with him via the female line. Not only that, via Irish blood. Mama always thought that Charlotte would have seen the humour in that.' At Ellie's look of surprise, she said: 'We discussed it before she died. When to tell Milo. When to give him the choice.'

'And what did you decide?'

'We didn't. Milo wasn't even ten years old when my mother died.'

'Your father, Teddy, never knew about Albert's parentage?'

Hattie shook her head. 'That was one of the reasons I was sent to boarding school, after Mama being so adamant that I would attend Ballinn National School. Can you imagine asking an eleven-year-old to keep a secret like that?' Ellie saw in her expression a deep, deep hurt.

'And what about Albert?'

'This information would come as a total shock. He and my mother were extremely close. Right to the end. To have been kept in the dark like that, well, I can't imagine how it would make him feel.' And Ellie could see it then, that very same expression that had passed over Tabby's face. Another woman who had kept a secret from a good man and in doing so had left a deep groove in her soul.

She said gently, 'You don't think Albert has the right to

know that Charlotte was his mother? That Tomas was his father?' *While it's still possible.* She tried to imagine the implications: eighty years of never knowing you were adopted, learning that your adoptive mother killed your biological father. And that your biological mother hadn't died cursing those who came after.

On the contrary: she had given them everything.

Hattie considered the question, then folded her hands in her lap. 'Ellie, Albert's health is failing. And as you saw, it isn't just physical. After the situation with Tomas . . . he was never the same. Never. There was no one for him to talk to, only Mama. He migrated inward and, I'm afraid to say, he rarely comes out.' Ellie thought of the two Alberts she'd seen: one wary and confused; the other hospitable, kind and full of life.

'According to the gardaí report, Albert wasn't there when Tomas was killed.'

Hattie rearranged the cutlery beside her, moving the small spoon to the outside of the knife. She muttered to the table setting, 'I hate it when they do that,' then began to say something else. Stopped. 'Albert did see . . . some of it . . . the aftermath, perhaps,' she said, flicking her eyes just over Ellie's shoulder, then refolding her napkin. 'But at the time, Mama thought it simpler if it was just one witness. To make things more streamlined.'

'Streamlined?'

Hattie rubbed her face, left a small smear of mascara. 'I'm sorry, it was such a terrible memory. I can't recall the specifics.'

Ellie said, 'I understand,' but really, she didn't. Had Albert seen his own father killed or not? She supposed, in the end, if he never found out about his parentage, it mattered just a little less. The dregs of her coffee were cold, but she drained them with a small grimace. 'Hattie . . . this story . . .'

'I'd really rather you didn't,' said Hattie, in the kind of voice one might use towards a petulant teenager after the first wave of the row is over.

Ellie sat back in exasperation. She was overwhelmed by the need to be heard once again instead of being buried beneath a scandal too deep to crawl out from. She wanted to say, *I'm afraid I have the right to tell this story*, but her mouth wouldn't form the words. Hesitating, she reached forward to pluck the solitary flower that sat in the middle of their table. It was the exact hue of the one she'd tucked behind her ear only days before. The blue of Nancy Rathmore's eyes, according to Albert. He'd said that just after he'd listened intently to Ellie's outpouring of guilt, to the feelings of blame that still lingered so many years after the death of her own father. He'd taken her hand, held it tight, just as she had done to him on the day they'd met. 'Bad things happen to good people, Ellie,' was what he'd said. Had he been thinking of his mother, of Nancy, and what she'd done when confronted by Tomas?

She appraised the woman opposite her. Thought about the list of publishers she would approach and the proposal she would put to them. It consisted of a one-thousand-word outline. A dozen people she would interview. An introduction. Twenty chapter headings.

And a tag line.

What would you do to protect the ones you love?

Her time was up. She hesitated.

What would Charlotte do?

But that was clear, wasn't it?

'I understand, Hattie.' And she watched the book, the story, her new focus, float away.

But Hattie was already lifting her handbag onto the table, taking out an envelope.

She slid it across the table. It was blank, unaddressed.

This was a first for Ellie. Suddenly she felt that she'd

stepped into a world from which she quickly wanted to retreat. She looked at Hattie's impassive face, trying to read her intention. 'I don't want your money. I said I understand. And I really do.' She spread her hands. 'I found Charlotte. That's enough for me.'

And, she realised with a glow, it was.

Hattie laughed, warmth returning to her features. 'Ellie, if I had any spare money, it wouldn't be sitting in an envelope for you.' She touched her roots, a finger dragging along her scalp. 'I'd get my hair done, for starters.'

'I've just accused you of bribery, haven't I?'

She raised an eyebrow. 'At least I can see you're an honest kind of hack.'

Running her fingers lightly over the envelope, Ellie said, 'So what is it?'

'It *was* supposed to be a deal.'

'What kind of deal?'

Hattie appraised her appreciatively. 'I wasn't sure what you'd tell me today, and I wanted to come prepared. I *was* going to give you what's in that envelope if you promised not to write Charlotte's story. Not to look into Albert's past. To leave Milo to me. To leave the Rathmore family where it belongs . . . in the recesses of history.'

'And now?'

'And now' – Hattie nodded – 'you've sufficiently impressed me. So I'm giving it to you freely.'

Ellie thought back to their earlier meeting. She'd mentioned nothing about writing Charlotte's story then; the idea hadn't even occurred to her. It was only in the last days, as the secrets had been stripped away, layer by layer, that she'd considered it. 'How did you know I'd want to write it?'

'I could see your hunger.'

Ellie rubbed her tummy. 'Hardly.' She said the word now

with a soft County Kerry *a*, instead of the Dublin *hoardly* that only two weeks before would have been her retort.

'I can recognise it in you,' Hattie said. 'Ambition. It's like looking in a mirror.'

Ellie spread her hands. 'I needed something new, a project. A way to make ends meet, not just financially but . . . something fulfilling. But Charlotte's history belongs to the Rathmores. I'll find a way.' She was jobless and rudderless, but she would pick herself up. 'I'll find my own path out. Rectify my mistake.'

'Your path is clearer than you think,' said Hattie with a smile – warm, almost motherly. Full of . . . pride? She reached across and lifted Ellie's chin. Then tapped the envelope. 'Perhaps you didn't make a mistake after all.'

Chapter Fifty-Eight

Blackwater Hall, County Kerry
November 2019

How rare it was, a crisp, dry November dawn in County Kerry. And yet as Ellie, Milo and Jules gathered by Lough Atoon, not a lick of cloud sullied the hue that lit the sky. The blackened remains of a long-forgotten pier stretched out into the water.

Beside them, a spade lay against a knee-high pile of rocks; purple sandstone like the hills beyond.

The air was as still as anticipation, the lough's surface a mirror perfectly reflecting the ivy-clad facade of Blackwater Hall as it sat proud at the top of the sloping lawn. A murmuration of starlings throbbed and morphed over the valley beyond, a strange creature painting the sky.

The envelope had contained a smoking gun. When Ellie saw the contents, she had looked at Hattie in amazement and said, 'He'll stand by this?' and the older woman had nodded, already gathering her bag. 'He will.' Ellie had felt a heaviness lift from the pit of her stomach. From her shoulders. She'd stood and embraced Hattie, held her longer than was polite.

She went on, then, to *The Irish Times* offices and presented the envelope to Jeremy. He'd hugged her in a rare display of openness and she'd shrugged as if to say, *You doubted me?*

Armand, a man who never forgot a face, agreed to testify

that Davy McCarthy had conducted three dinner meetings in the private rooms of the Pickled Oyster – where he was a regular – in July. Himself and another man, no scribe present. The table, Armand said – and the reservations record confirmed – was booked under the name Mr Smith, but the bill was settled on a credit card issued to Maxibuild. The company owned by Maxwell Cray.

The case against *The Irish Times* had been dropped, and in the furore that followed, an independent committee was rapidly formed to investigate the dealings between McCarthy and Cray.

The Stanley Street site had been returned to state ownership and a new tender was issued for the building of one hundred and twenty new flats for public housing.

For Ellie it had been not only vindication but the possibility of a return to a life that had, until only a month before, been everything she'd ever wanted. She had been offered her job back – with improvements: a promotion to property editor, the youngest in the publication's history. When Jeremy had told her – over the phone while she sat in Procaffination, her copy of *The ABC Murders* open in her lap – he'd taken her silence for delight.

'I'll think about it,' she'd said, gazing out onto Ballinn's quiet square, where now-familiar faces went about their daily lives.

Milo had told his father that Ellie and a friend might come to fish the lough one day when the weather was nice. Not to worry if he woke to find an extra car at the house. When Ellie and Jules had driven up to the estate early that morning, the dawn was just a promise. But Albert had been there, watching the Micra pull up to the house, wincing as Ellie crunched into second gear. He was silhouetted in the open side door of Blackwater Hall, now completely free of ivy and painted a beautiful clematis blue. The smell of woodsmoke sat in the cool air and Albert held a tray of tea. Three cups. One each for Ellie, Jules and his son, who had just appeared from the warm interior of the house. 'You're not joining us, Albert?' Ellie had said.

'Not this morning, my dear, but you'll be glad to know that Milo's made the tea.'

They'd stood near the door, cradling their drinks and watching a heavy mist roll down Cottah Mountain. It clung to the sides of the fell as though for dear life, and as it reached the bottom, it dissipated like magic. Changed form until it could no longer be seen. As though, at that very moment, it decided it could simply . . . disappear.

Around them, piles of building materials covered the driveway. Scaffold boards, poles, stacks of purple Valentia slate. Bags of sharp sand and lime. Soon the work would begin. Blackwater Hall would come to life once again.

'But how will you pay for it?' Ellie had asked Milo when she'd visited them the week before. She'd taken on Bernie's Meals on Wheels route; it took her around the parish, and its boundaries, as far as Blackwater Hall. With Milo moved in full time, Albert no longer needed the meals, but Ellie always put three aside and visited in the evening, so they could sit together and eat. Some days Albert knew who she was, and others they met as though for the first time.

'I sold something,' Milo had told her. 'With Albert's permission.'

The butterfly comb.

'He knows about Charlotte. About who she was to him and how she died. Harriet and I decided; I told him.'

Ellie had gasped; she hadn't expected it. 'And?'

'And the change in him has been remarkable. He'll never be the man he might have been, so Harriet says, but on his good days he's . . . better.'

'And Tomas?'

Milo had shaken his head. 'Harriet insists that he must never know that Tomas was his father.'

When they'd finished their tea, Albert had taken their cups. 'Happy fishing, you youngsters!' Ellie had noticed Jules's delight at being included in the term, and as the three of them left for the lakeside, Milo had said, as natural as anything, 'Thanks, Dad.' Ellie's heart had warmed at the look on Albert's face.

'Ready?' said Jules now, his voice a whisper in the quiet morning.

Milo lifted the shovel and began to dig.

When Ellie had hung up the phone on a gobsmacked Jeremy – promising to get back to him by the end of the week – she'd taken a small box from her bag. Inside was the platinum comb that Dylan had given her; his olive branch. She ran her finger over its teeth, their ridges cool to the touch. It was a thing of beauty.

She'd closed the box, and left a note for Nils – John had arrived the week before and they were busy serving tea to a local book group, all smiles and cakes *on the house* – then walked up Ballinn's main street to the post office. Three minutes later, she'd dropped a heavy padded envelope into the post box. She hadn't bothered to add a note. The return of the comb would tell Dylan everything he needed to know.

The hole Milo had dug was now knee deep and two foot square. He put the spade aside. 'That'll do.'

Jules nodded. 'Shall we?'

The three of them walked through the sparse undergrowth of the woods at the end of the lough. A wheelbarrow waited for them where the trees met the edge of the lawn.

It had been a week since Moira had sat Ellie down to reveal what she thought was a bombshell. She'd been nervous, her hands gripping a tea as weak as dishwater, her brow knitted in a knot that Ellie thought might be an attempt to look imploring.

'The thing is, Ellie,' she had said, 'for so many years after your father died, I had you to think of. To care for. To put my energy into. But now you've flown the nest . . .'

Seventeen years ago. Ellie scratched her nose. Wondered whether to interrupt. She knew what was coming and felt a swell of happiness now that Moira was ready to admit it. But she understood – she had *learned* – that in order to speak the truth, we need the space to do it.

'I must admit I've been—'

'Delighted I was gone?' Ellie had joked, trying to relax her mum. It had the opposite effect; Moira put her head in her hands. Ellie leaned over. 'Oh, Mammy,' she'd said, with warmth and comfort. 'I'm sorry, I didn't mean . . .'

'I've been lonely.' Moira began to cry, a soft sound. A gentle, slow sob.

Ellie felt that her heart might burst. Moira suddenly looked smaller. Delicate. A woman with needs. Desires. Someone with a life outside the four walls of her home, outside of her daughter. Outside of their shared – and cherished – history. She'd leaned in and put her arms around her mum's shoulders.

Moira wiped her eyes. 'Silly old Mammy,' she said, 'blubbing like this.'

'No, not silly.'

Moira took a deep breath. 'There's something I want to tell you.'

'Is there?' Ellie smiled conspiratorially.

'What's that grin for?'

'Nothing . . . nothing . . .' Ellie leaned back in her chair. 'You know, Mammy, it's been nearly twenty years since Dad died. And there isn't a day when I don't think about him. God, barely an hour . . .'

Moira nodded, her eyes welling once more.

Ellie reached out a hand, laid her fingers lightly on her

mum's. 'What I mean is, he's still here.' She touched her heart, thought of the moment with Nils at Wynn's Castle. 'But you' – she took Moira's hand and squeezed it – 'you're *here*.'

'So you know?'

'I know nothing,' said Ellie, 'but I suspect everything.' She grinned. 'I'm kind of a detective now.'

'He's a good man.'

Ellie nodded, her heart full. Happy for her mum, sitting there in that small kitchen, her life expanding around her once again. She took both Moira's hands into her own. 'And I couldn't be more pleased. For both of you.'

Now she looked across the wheelbarrow at Jules. 'Ellie, you be careful. Of your back.' Over his argyle jumper – this one had shades of blue – he was wearing a thick Puffa jacket. It was unzipped, ready for the exertion ahead. His eyes were bright in the morning light. He was shorter than Moira by half a head, and when they held hands, Ellie noticed, their fingers inter- twined like the ivy that covered the walls of Blackwater Hall.

She made a strong-man gesture. 'Let's do it.'

They carried the stone between them, Jules and Ellie shoulder to shoulder at one end, Milo at the other, walking forwards, his arms behind him, gripping the rounded edges with hands that were larger than Ellie had previously noticed.

Jules held the stone upright in the hole while Ellie and Milo filled the base with rocks and topped it with soil so that it stood proud of the mound.

When Milo touched her shoulder and said, 'Do you want to say something?' – to which she'd shaken her head – a zing rang through her veins. A butterfly stomach; something she'd not felt for years.

Last week he'd asked her out for dinner. He didn't call it a *date* specifically, but the nervousness in his voice suggested that it might be just that. It had been two days before she posted the comb to Dublin and she'd said she couldn't, that she and Moira were taking a little trip. It was a throwaway comment, tossed out in the heat of the moment to give herself time. For what? *To think?* When she'd arrived back at Cahercillín Farm, she'd put the idea to her mum – who was equal parts delighted and confused – and they'd packed the car for a weekend in Clifden, where they'd spent two nights in a hotel she could ill afford. It was there that she told Moira about the fight with her father, that day when he'd walked out the door without looking back, and never returned. And Moira said all that mattered was that he'd loved Ellie more than life itself. That he would be *so* proud of her. Of everything she'd achieved. Of the woman she'd become.

Ellie reached into her jacket pocket, pulled out a sprig of gorse, brave yellow flowers hidden amongst spines. She'd plucked it from a bush at the edge of the woodland. She felt that Charlotte would like its simplicity. Its perseverance in the face of an approaching winter. Its courage at flowering when everything else had given up. Bending down, she placed it next to the stone.

When she'd returned from Galway, she had asked Milo to meet her in Procaffination. Over a slice of carrot cake – and pointed eyebrow waggles from Nils – she'd told him about her miscarriage, about Dylan. And he had told her about his divorce, his broken heart that was only now mending. She'd touched his hand and marvelled at its warmth. Hattie had invited him to Dublin to reassure him that the revelation about his biological grandparents – about Charlotte and Tomas – needn't change anything. 'But it does,' he'd said. 'Now I can choose whether the barony lives or dies.' *And?* 'And . . . I haven't decided.' But he'd smiled. 'I think Charlotte would find a certain justice in it. Her grandson, Tomas's grandson, inheriting down the female line. But she'd also relish the moment the peerage disappeared, just like that, confined to the recesses of history, where these things belong.' He'd sighed then. 'It's ironic, isn't it?'

'What is?'

'Either way, Charlotte wins.'

She'd smiled at that. 'Yes,' she'd said. 'Charlotte wins.' She thought of the girl, just nineteen when she'd left her life behind, embarked on a journey into the unknown so that she would never need to be separated from her child. She looked at Milo, felt a sense of calm, because although Charlotte was gone, a piece of her remained. Two pieces actually: Milo and Albert. One so damaged, the other in the image of his grandmother: stubborn, caring. Strong.

'Milo?' she'd said.

'Yes?'

'One day soon, in a month or two . . . will you ask me again? To dinner, I mean.'

Now, by the lake, she looked up from the stone and caught his eye as he kneeled beside her. Jules nodded. 'Good job, Ellie,' he said, patting her shoulder. 'Very good job.' He left them then, in the growing light.

Milo put out his hand and she took it. Still so warm despite the morning's chill. He moved his fingers a little, and now they plaited together. Ellie ran her gaze over the text, white indentations on the rounded purple stone. It looked nothing like a grave, but already a piece of nature nestled into the side of the lake.

In memory of Charlotte Rathmore

1921–1941

They stayed a while, hand in hand, to watch Blackwater Hall emerge from darkness as the sun rose over the eastern reaches of Cottah Mountain. Before long, the house's windows – peering from that ivy-clad exterior – began to twinkle and the blue slates that lay like scales on its roof turned to magenta in the golden morning light. Then, for a moment, a shadow crossed the lawn. The outline of a gentle curve. Reaching around the house. Gripping it in a hug.

A perfect circle.

Epilogue

Dún Laoghaire port, Dublin
August 1940

Charlotte's hand rested on her stomach. What future lay in there? When she returned, after this war was over, she and Tomas would find a place to live, somewhere they could be themselves. Shake off their class, start again.

As the boat pulled away from Dún Laoghaire, she fancied that the wind on her face felt fresher than anything she'd ever known before. Her small leather suitcase sat at her feet – everything she owned in the world inside – and one hand gripped the cool railing. The ocean ahead was aquamarine, and in the distance, there was only horizon.

Wind whipped a piece of her hair free, and she pulled out the butterfly comb, secured the wayward strands. The ruby ring on her finger had deterred questions, and already the name Tabby Deenihan rolled off her tongue with ease. She looked back at the harbour. A hundred yards now separated her from Ireland. Never before had she been so far from home, and the thought – rather than jolting her with fear – brought a smile to her face. It was quickly followed by a spontaneous laugh.

A man next to her turned, tossing the butt of his cigarette overboard. 'First time I've heard a laugh like that in near twelve months,' he said in a soft Liverpudlian accent. Charlotte suddenly felt a small measure of guilt. Europe was at war. People were dying. Lives scattering like leaves in the wind. He put a hand to the brim of his cap, tipped it. 'Thank you,' he said, 'for brightening my day.'

She turned back to the sea. There was something in her heart that had never been there before. A warmth. A glow. A lightness.

She was happier at this moment than she had ever been before.

And now, she was free.

Author's Note

People joke about characters living in a writer's head rent free, but the heroine of *The Midnight House*, Charlotte Rathmore, appeared one day out of the blue, moved in uninvited and made herself comfortable. It was while I was working overseas as a geologist, a modern nomad, never long enough in one place to hang my hat. But she always came with me: the young woman standing by a lake, her long skirt waving in a gentle breeze (was there a tang of salt in the air?), a battered suitcase in her hand. I wondered who she was. Where she was going. The landscape was hazy, just that lake, inky blackness, and a sense that the coat she wore – too big – wasn't her own. It seemed she planned to run away, but from what or to where I did not know.

Some years later, I moved to south-west Ireland. It was an accident really, a visit that turned into an idea to renovate an old house that hung on the edge of the sea. Behind that house was a mountain. And on that mountain was a lake. It perched on a plateau just out of sight of the ocean. The first time I hiked to its gorse-rimmed shore (the tang of salt in the air) I saw a ripple, as though two feet had stood at the water's edge. There I placed the ivy-clad house where I just *knew* that Charlotte had lived. When I sat down to write, she turned towards me, smiled, and began to walk away.

Finally, I could follow.

Here on the westernmost fringe of Europe, where jagged

fingers of purple sandstone plunge dramatically into the angry froth of sea, both my story and I found a home. I can understand how the Irish diaspora – flung far across the globe – always long to return. The pull is inescapable. Mesmerising. Mysterious. In Ireland, truth is hidden beneath many layers: history piled onto folklore, intertwined with landscape. I would clear my head with icy dips in the sea under the shadows of an abbey, then walk home past standing stones that stood like sentries in the fields. My new neighbours were layered in the same way too. They went to Mass but would never look at a new moon through glass. Even our young friends said they'd heard the banshee wail: at first I thought they were teasing, but a few whiskeys later I realised they were not. And this wild landscape, part tamed by generations of rough hands, is the perfect mirror in which communities like this can view themselves: vast histories stretching back generations, their imprints left on the land.

As I was writing *The Midnight House*, I'd often stand in the garden and look to the hill beyond. In the distance, nestled in the heather-clad slopes at the head of the valley, is a ring fort. It's been there for millennia, and our house was built of the same purple sandstone as its perfect curved walls. Sheep graze at its base, and a new holiday home stands nearby. A famine cottage sits in the field opposite, where cultivated farmland runs to the coast.

Layers, everywhere I look.

Under the roof of our house we found a piece of timber signed by a long-dead carpenter. *When this comes down, pray for me. Tim O'Shea, 1911.* We located Tim's family: they live nearby and there were tears all round. The thrill of delivering a message from the past was intoxicating. And so Ellie Fitzgerald was born. I saw her discover a mysterious letter from a girl – enter Charlotte – who'd disappeared long ago.

It was then that I knew that *The Midnight House* would be told over several generations. And how could it not? I couldn't separate the layers of Ireland, past and present, old and new, rumour and truth. And weaving the Irish landscape into the story was as simple as stepping outside my front door. I held young Hattie's hand as she met Tomas by the still waters of the lake where he'd left a thousand posies for his love. I stood beside Ellie as the wind whipped across Derrynane Beach, worrying at her doubts and grief, before Milo came to stand by her side. And I walked with Charlotte, step by step, as she turned and started over the mountain and away.

I went with them – and I am so very grateful that you came too – to south-west Ireland, and beyond.

Acknowledgements

I started writing the novel you hold in your hands in 2019 with just the sniff of an idea (Charlotte disappearing over the mountain behind Blackwater Hall, small suitcase in hand) and many drafts later I sent the manuscript to a shortlist of three agents. Only one of those had a #1 next to her name (and I still have the notebook to prove it!). She works with some of my favourite authors, and I already thought of her as The Perfect Fit for *The Midnight House*. Thank you, Becky Ritchie, (and the entire AM Heath team) for your vision, kindness and hard work: you've always been Number 1!

A huge thanks to my editors, Sherise Hobbs and Bea Grabowska. You're the dream team. Full of patience and kindness, you gifted me exceptionally skilled and insightful editorial input, and saw the potential in *The Midnight House*, never wavering in your belief. Siobhan Hooper designed the cover, and I think we can all agree it's a stunner. I loved it from the moment it hit my inbox. Lucy Hall and Emily Patience are the superstars in marketing and PR, two completely foreign languages to me, and I'm so grateful to all the team at Headline Review who have worked tirelessly to make this book a reality.

I was fortunate to have a few early readers. Mum — to whom the book is dedicated (surprise!) — was so positive, sending all her thoughts from 10,000km away. Lorraine Mace read an early draft of the first few chapters and her encouragement was a catalyst for the next 100,000 words. Long-time family friend, Kaye Matthews, gave me a big thumbs up and a great confidence boost. And Jess McCarthy was a knightess in shining armour when I was thinking about bailing on the whole thing. I urge anyone who finds themselves in Midleton, Cork, to please drop into the fabulous *Midleton Books* and say a big thank you to Jess (and Bones) from me!

Clement McGann helped me get Charlotte's documentation in order before I sent her across the Irish Sea. Over many months, he also generously shared fascinating tales of life in Ireland during that time, some of which were precious family memories, and many of which made their way into the book. Thank you also to Les Tucker from the Archive Department at the Royal Gunpowder Mills for your valuable input into life in the munitions factories.

Thank you to the Stoffell clan for your constant encouragement – I love you all. And to Nicole and Ray, whose humour and insight into Kerry's rich traditions and Ireland's unique vernacular weave their way into every nook and cranny of the book.

Go raibh maith agat to Ireland's great beauty, County Kerry. You're not just for the summer.

Penultimate thanks to Harry and Bertie. Although you aren't able to read this (on account of being dogs), I think you'd like it. And finally, to my husband, Barry, because – apart from reading and helping me shape, trim and modify many endless drafts late into the night – you have, over many years, helped me understand what life's all about. I love you more than I can ever say.